FLYING THE LIFELINE:

VOLUME 2 SCENE CALL

PATRICK R SHAUB

Eagle Training Solutions, LLC
1111 Highland Hills Drive
Marble Falls, Texas 78654
Orders: www.amazon.com

Printed in the United States of America
ISBN 13: 9781523340149
ISBN-10:1523340142
Library of Congress Control Number: 2016900486
CreateSpace Independent Publishing Platform
North Charleston, South Carolina

For Dad. My hero.

ACKNOWLEDGEMENTS

I thank God, whose benevolence kept me alive to fly the lifeline and then write this book from about the lessons I learned. I hope my efforts praise and please you. Thanks to my wife Linda who always backs me and encourages me to follow my dreams. Her character appears in this book, but she's a better person than that. Thanks to the members of America's military who served before me and are my example. Thanks to the ones with whom I served who helped make me who I am. And thanks especially to those who serve now. I never go to bed at night without a prayer for your safety knowing that you men and women are on watch all over the world risking your lives and leaving your families behind in our service.

Likewise, a smart salute is rendered to my friends and colleagues in the emergency services: fire fighters, police and emergency medical service providers. This includes those talented and able people who work in America's hospitals and emergency rooms. Your sacrifices and love for others will be rewarded.

And to the many friends who helped me and encouraged me to publish my work thank you, also. Wayne Phillips offered me the use of this book's title from an article he wrote after an interview with a helicopter pilot we both know. Other friends and professionals who offered advice, encouragement and assistance in the production of this book are Cary Camden, Shawn Coyle, Dylan Foley, Stan Gove, Raven Herron, Jamie Greening, Rod Machado, Keith Miller, Ed Oshinski, Diane Titterington, Max Trescott, Eileen Winston and Chip Wright. I know I have forgotten people I hope will forgive me. That mistake and any other errors in the text or production thereof are all mine.

PROLOGUE

"For thou *art* my rock and my fortress; therefore for
thy name's sake lead me, and guide me"

Psalms 31:3.

He was drifting off to sleep late on a summer afternoon. A little boy lay with his head on a pillow at the foot of his bed. He looked back toward its head and a picture that hung above the headboard. An angel stood unseen above and behind two children crossing a rickety bridge over a flooded stream. The lacy curtains in the little boy's window moved gently in a breeze that whispered across the bedroom. It was to him as though an angel was passing by and he uttered a prayer just before his eyes closed. The last thing he saw was the angel's wings. "God, please make me an angel.

1 FLYING TO THE ISLAND

I didn't like it but I was out of the Marine Corps. I had no ideas and no prospects for work. All I had ever wanted was to become a Marine pilot and fly helicopters. I did that and then they threw me out. The only positive thing I could see about my situation was that I had nowhere to go but up. That's when I counted my blessings. I started with Linda, my brilliant and supportive wife who thought the Marine Corps was stupid but who knew I wasn't. She knew that despite this setback I'd blossom even when I wasn't at all sure of that. We had three sweet little boys, twins five and our "spare" who was two. We were all healthy. We had food in our bellies and a roof over our heads. That made us better off than most of the population of the world. We also had some cash. Although at the moment I was unemployed we had saved some money while my Marine Corps career was in full swing. Linda had a job teaching high school. That money equated to time that I could use to search for something profitable to do with my life. I just hoped I wouldn't use up all that time before I found a job I wanted outside of flying Marine helicopters.

When I had to move out of base housing we rented a little house in Irvine, California, the town between the two Marine Corps Air Stations on which I had served. Since I had no plans for my future I didn't know where else to go. I should have moved farther away from the bases. It was hard on me to hear the thunder of the big helicopters passing, to look up and see my shipmates flying overhead. As I watched them I knew that, like it or not, I had to move on. When my Marine Corps career was clearly heading for the rocks I signed up for more education. I figured if I was going to job interviews I didn't want to trust that a potential employer would see a former Marine captain and say, "I think I'll make this guy a manager." So I took courses at night school that led to a Master's degree in Management. I wasn't attending an Ivy League school. It was instead a satellite campus of a business school in San Diego. The mother school had a good reputation. In looking into it the syllabus appeared to offer instruction in what I considered practical knowledge for a guy in my situation. I figured the degree in management would help my future employers see me as someone ready to run the show on some level, rather as I had as a Marine captain. So weekday nights during my last few months as a Marine I left the base and went to school. And after I hung up my uniform for the last time I kept going to school. It was the transition I needed to keep me moving forward those times when I wanted to sit down and feel sorry for myself.

It became increasingly gratifying for me to go to school again after so many years as a Marine. I quickly made friends there with people who had no connection to the military. Even though most of my classmates were not veterans they let me know they respected what I had done during my career to date. I had much to learn about my classmates and about being a civilian. From the day I graduated from college I had always served as a Marine. I had a lot to learn. My classmates helped me with that. They became for me a valuable network of contact with the civilian world of work. One night during a class break one of my fellow students gave me a lead on a job he thought might fit me. He said that the McDonnell-Douglas airplane factory in Long Beach was looking for a flight line safety manager. It sounded like work I had done as a Marine

Corps squadron safety officer. So I applied. It wasn't long before I got a phone call from Douglas. When the phone call ended I had a date and time for an interview.

I realized it would be the first time I interviewed for a job since I worked waiting tables at a steak house back in my college days. I made a couple of copies of the resume' my classmates had helped me write. I put them and a notepad in a leather valise. I got both my suits cleaned. When the day came for the interview I took out my "wedding and funeral" suit. It said "serious," which is what I would expect to see from a person applying for this job. In dressing I felt like a gladiator preparing for combat, a knight donning his armor. "I looked at my semi-dressed self and spoke out loud, "Where is my squire?" But I dressed alone in the little rented house in Irvine. My wife and kids at school would not bring me my sword and shield today.

When all that remained was to don my jacket I examined the nearly finished product in the full length mirror. My shoes shone like black mirrors. Sharply creased navy colored trousers broke neatly at the shoe tops. My crisp, starched white shirt was tucked in Marine Corps style, bloused at the back and without a wrinkle. Like my shoes my belt shone like patent leather. I placed a single Cross pen in the shirt pocket. I moved the knot a hint to the left to straighten the brand new silk tie I bought just for this event. I had spent more money on it than I had paid for my last six military haircuts. And I noted that the tie cost about the same as my first civilian haircut. Pulling a twenty out of my wallet at a civilian barber shop helped me understand why civilians have longer hair than Marines. I put on the jacket, turned this way and that examining the image in the mirror. Examination complete I leaned up close to the mirror and said to the guy looking back at me, "*You look like a Marine officer in an interview suit.*" I hoped that was okay.

It turned out that it was. The executive doing the interview was a former Navy pilot about my age. He was shaggy in the hair department in my estimation. Otherwise he looked like me in many regards. He was even wearing a suit not dissimilar to my own. In passing through the cubicle farm toward his office I noted that the other guys we passed in the office wore suits like mine as well. I guessed I had unconsciously chosen to interview wearing the McDonnell-Douglas uniform of the day. I supposed that if I got a job here I'd have to get used to wearing that uniform.

I didn't like the clothes I was wearing but I immediately liked the former sailor who was interviewing me. It appeared he felt the same way about me. He had read my resume, but re-read it and hit the highlights out loud for me. He hit the highlights that paralleled the job description.

"Yep, you've got all the qualifications. Since you were an aviation safety officer in the Marines you know the drill." As a Naval aviator himself, he knew what a military safety officer did for a living.

"You know how to keep pilots alive and keep them from bending any metal. The challenge here will come from working with the best guys in the business. Many are former military, but they have gone way beyond what they were back in those days. They are a level of test pilot the military never sees. Many are old enough to be our fathers. Most have lost more logbooks than we have in our file drawer at home. And that level of experience doesn't just describe the pilots. It pegs the engineers, too. And they know it. You already know that pilots all believe they're good. Test pilots see themselves less like the common good pilots. They see themselves as..." He looked at the ceiling. "What's the word?"

"Gods." I said. ""Maybe demigods, but gods nonetheless."

He pointed at me as though I had just stated the case perfectly. "Right! And then there are the engineers. In case you haven't worked with engineers before let me sum up the attitudes of the ones here at Douglas. They believe in their designs as highly as the test pilots believe in their flying skills. They believe their designs can do anything. But problems arise when an engineer who believes his design is fool proof gives it to a test pilot who believes himself bulletproof. For example: when the engineer says offhandedly that his four engine jet will fly on one engine you can bet a test pilot is going to try it out and see if it's true. If he gets away with it he'll try it again…inverted. You can't stop the engineers from bragging. But you can sure as heck see that the test pilots don't take the engineers braggadocio as a dare."

It would be a new environment for me working here. But I knew I could handle the job. I had a skill at shepherding Marine pilots into adult behavior. I had gained a good deal of experience at it over the past few years.

"I'm used to keeping a close eye on pilots and their egos," I replied. "Some of my squadron mates took to calling me, 'Mom.' Others called me 'the safety Nazi.'"

"And you were okay with that?" he asked.

I waved as though brushing a fly away from my face. "It was good natured. Sure, I was okay with that moniker. I liked the ribbing I got. It meant they liked me. They did, too. They knew I cared for them, even while I was taking away some of the fun they planned to have killing themselves. I got the squadron safety job because I liked who I worked with. I told them I liked them so much I wanted them to stay alive to enjoy their company. One of my buddies called me a sissy. He meant it, too. I told him that I probably was a sissy because I have always planned to grow old flying aircraft. I also told him that he was going to have to be a sissy too because I planned to keep some friends like him around to tell stories with in my later years."

The Navy guy smiled. "I like your approach. It is not exactly what I expected when I saw your Marine Corps background. You're not very *autocratic*, shall I say?"

"You mean I'm not a pushy, loudmouth jarhead," I stated unequivocally.

"Not that I can detect," he replied. "And for this job that is a good way to remain. That background of yours may cause you to face a challenge here. Convincing those test pilots, especially the former military guys that you aren't a "pushy jarhead" will take some skill, lots of diplomacy, and probably some time."

He looked at me and laid a finger across his cheek contemplating that part of the job. He scowled a little. "You're still a Marine," he said, and then he smiled. "Sorry, you can't help that. But you seem like a nice guy and someone who can get along with people. That's what we need running our safety program, not a bossy drill sergeant. The people designing, building and flying our airplanes here won't accept that. They want a peer, a colleague and a professional. They want to work with a team player who knows how to keep us all doing what we already know is right safety-wise. But at the same time I want someone who has some backbone. We all need a watchdog, someone who won't let us cut corners to get a job done if cutting that corner could get someone hurt."

I realized as he talked that he wasn't interviewing me anymore. He was training me for the job. I think at that point he and I both knew he had the right man for the job. An interview would probably have ended right there. He already seemed to know as much about me as he wanted to know to make a decision about my employment there. But the Navy guy went on about the details of the job. They were exciting.

He said that I'd be helping design test programs for aircraft prototypes. I'd be working right alongside the company engineers and test pilots looking at the plans from the safety aspect. I'd also spend a lot of time on the flight test line looking at operations from a pilot's perspective. The flight test line was in Yuma, Arizona. Since half of the Yuma airport was a Marine Corps Air Station, I'd been there plenty while flying Marine helicopters. If I got the job, working there for me would be like going home.

When he had covered the information about the tasks I would perform as part of the design team he stood up. "I suppose you'd like to see the factory, huh?" I nodded like a kid who'd been offered a banana split. I had visited the Bell Helicopter factory once. I was impressed. I could only imagine what it would be like to see the projects in a plant that built airliners.

He stepped around his desk, took off his jacket and reached behind the office door. He grabbed a couple hangers and offered one to me. "I don't suspect we'll need these where we're going." I took off my jacket, and put it on the hanger. He hung it with his on a hook behind the door. Then we spent the rest of the morning getting to know each other while he gave me a tour of the factory. I couldn't have been happier at Disneyland. The main factory building was immense. It extended for probably fifty acres behind the office building. I expected to see a couple airliners inside. I was surprised to find that the building contained the operation building the newest Navy trainers. The hangar next door was equally large. In it were a dozen of the latest four-engine Air Force transport planes in various stages of construction. There was room around each with more room to spare. Looking out across the assembly floors I was impressed. It reminded me of old World War II films of bomber plants with people all very busy and directed in what they were doing. Those black and white films of bare aluminum airplanes being built made an impression. But this factory was building airplanes that people of those former days could not have imagined. And this experience in aircraft manufacture for me was in color, full of sound and smells both familiar and unfamiliar.

I would have paid money for that tour but I got to see the whole place for free. Although I knew they were busy, my host encouraged me to talk to the people who were building these amazing airplanes. I took full advantage of the invitation. I got to talk with the people who did the work while they accomplished their tasks. I asked questions about what they were doing. But I also asked them about themselves and their backgrounds. I came away overwhelmed with the longevity of many of those people with McDonnell-Douglas. They had been building airplanes for Douglas all their working lives. Some had been with the company longer than I had been alive. Many had actually been in those black and white films I remembered seeing as a kid.

I walked up the ramp of an Air Force C-17 transport plane that was near completion. The engines cowlings were missing but it appeared that otherwise it was ready to push out the door. I noticed that people walking by nodded or smiled at me. They could see I was enjoying myself being immersed in what they did for a living. They must have sensed my wonder and respect. Seeing them smiling and working together toward making this airplane fly, I thought, "This would really be a good place to work. " As my host stood outside and engaged in conversation with the airplane's builders, I walked through the cavernous fuselage. I naturally gravitated toward the cockpit. For me, that had always been the business end. Bundles of cables hung out of parts of the instrument panel. But where they were installed, the instruments were just black glass screens. There were only a few round dials I recognized. I felt uncomfortable there. This airplane was already a generation younger than those I had flown in the Marines. I didn't understand it. Because it was alien to me I didn't feel the need to fly it.

That surprised me. I had always ached to fly a new aircraft. But flying was still very new to me back then. Those first airplanes I flew had always been the contents of my pleasant dreams. They had carried me like a flying carpet. These behemoth transport plans would require systems managers to build, and more systems managers to fly.

I knew standing full up in this vast cockpit that this job would be another fork in the road of my professional career. This would be the direction that would take me out of the pilot's seat for good. Since I was a young child, inside the cockpit was the only place I longed to be. It had been my work, my recreation, my passion. I had always believed that it was the only place I would ever work. This flight test safety job represented the end of one dream and the beginning of a new one. Building airplanes would be exciting and interesting. Still, looking at the flight controls of that C-17 I wondered if I was ready to take that fork lying before me.

I knew I would become engrossed in doing this new occupation. I would have it possibly for the balance of my life. I wondered if building airplanes would become the passion that flying them had always been. I came to the conclusion that even if it didn't, this job would probably at least suit me for a while. I walked out of the cockpit, across the vast cargo bay and down the loading ramp. It led to the fork that would take me away from flying helicopters, from flying anything. I just kept walking.

The next stop was the company cafeteria. It was big enough to feed a thousand people at a sitting, although at the moment is was mostly unoccupied. The food was industrial. There was plenty of it and it was cheap. The Navy guy and I gathered what we wanted on a fiberglass tray. The sailor picked up the tab. We talked some more over lunch about our time flying Navy aircraft. Then we headed back to his office. Once we got there it was pretty clear the interview and the chatting was over. I expected to pick up my jacket and valise and be shown the door with a hearty handshake. After that I expected to be sent down the road with the standard post-interview greeting. "We'll be in touch." Instead, just before we got back to his office the sailor stopped short in the wide hallway running alongside the cubicle farm. People passed us coming and going. I looked across the wide room holding dozens of eight by eight foot workspaces. Heads bobbed briefly above the walls of the cubicles here and there and then disappeared. I looked back at the sailor who was holding his chin as though thinking some deep thought.

He didn't ask me what I thought about the tour, as I suspected he might. He didn't ask me if I had questions, another likely possibility. He just said, "Well, do you want the job?"

That came as a surprise to me. I kept my mouth shut and let my brain take over for a minute. It was something I had resolved to do more often in my new post-Marine Corps life. I thought perhaps that this was a test of my resolve. The 'how to' books on interviewing I had been reading told me to play it coy at this point. Maybe it was because the offer came before the "We'll be in touch" part that I was unprepared to answer by the book. Being frank turned out to be a hard habit for me to break. I was just inclined to do what I always did: answer honestly. So instead of keeping my own counsel as I had promised I would, I just said, "Sure." I didn't think about it much. "Sure," I said again. "I think I'd like this job."

That was a good enough answer from the sailor's perspective. He smiled widely and clapped me on the shoulder. Then he shook my hand. He looked relieved. I thought maybe I'd feel that way too. I didn't. I didn't feel anything at all. I tried to recall the guidance I'd read in the interview books. I was supposed to have said, "Well, I'd like to consider that." Followed by that came the recommended, "Can I get an offer in writing?" Later perhaps I should have considered asking, "What can I expect from the compensation package?" I didn't say any of that. In the truest sense, it wasn't a formal job offer. It just got us past the interview stage and down to the business of passing the first mile marker on my new path away from being a pilot. Then a very important person in my life came to mind.

"Hey, I just want to say here at the outset that my wife will want to know what I'm getting us into."

The sailor looked puzzled.

"How about I call you tomorrow and let you know for sure after I talk about it with her?"

I could see that he was still taken aback. Certainly he must have seen me as a truly typical former Naval aviator. Being one himself he knew the rules. And he knew that I knew them also. He was unaccustomed to a reply that inferred a Navy wife had anything to say at all about a Navy trained pilot's career. During my assignment as a flight instructor in the Naval Air Training Command I was told by my nautical brethren that when a Navy pilot makes a career decision, Navy wives were not consulted; they were merely 'informed.' In the past I too had informed Linda, but only about military deployments. When I had a choice of duty stations, she always had a full say, and a veto vote if she wanted to use it. That was an odd thing in itself in my Navy pilot circles. But Linda was practical. When I got sent somewhere unexpected she had no more choice about accepting it than I did. Deployments, especially long ones, were like that. They always came hard to us. All I could do when I got one was shrug my shoulders and tell her, "I've got no choice in this one."

The circumstances of the deployment were not something I liked telling her about, either. I always felt like I was lying. There was no use speculating about a deployment's length and location. The length was always longer than I was told it would be. Three day deployments were sometimes weeks long. Months long deployments started early and ran late. Often the location I was told only included that spot as part of the deployment. I might be going to MCAS Yuma. It was as likely that I'd end up on a Navy ship far out at sea. Although it was unspoken, I could just as easily be killed flying into a dusty desert landing zone as I could flying off a ship at sea. I lost friends to aircraft accidents in both places.

I wasn't in the Marines anymore, though. My future and her future would be a matter of discussion and agreement between us from here on out. I owed her a debt. After twelve years of following me and my assignments, I was going to pay her back, starting today. While I was deployed she had gotten the car oil changes done, mowed the lawn and taken care of the host of chores that should have fallen upon me. She even had our last baby while I was on the far side of the planet being a Marine. If there was ever a time I was going to ask her what she thought I should do with our future it was going to be now.

The sailor paused for just a moment. A realization came to him slowly and with it a lopsided grin. I think he realized that I was a little less a Marine than he had originally thought. I think he liked me all the more for it. In the end he nodded.

"Well, okay then. Let me know what you work out with the wife."

I could tell he wasn't worried about how things would turn out, though. In fact, I'm sure he was certain I would take the job. He turned confidently back on his course to his office as though a deal had just been struck. As I remained in trail behind him he said over his shoulder, "When you're ready we'll talk compensation and so on. I'll tell Human resources to send you the package and offer letter."

As I walked on I didn't even notice that mile post in my new life go by. I was as good as a former pilot as well as a former Marine. And in my new bosses opinion at least I was already McDonnell-Douglas Company's newest employee.

Inside my new bosses office I put on my jacket and grabbed my valise. We shook hands again. Everything that he had needed to say had been said before we reached his office. The ball was now in my court. It would probably appear to an observer that I would certainly call him tomorrow to accept the job. The offer letter which would already be on his desk would be in the out basket before he hung up the phone.

He did what was right company security-wise and led me back through the cubical farm. I figured I would soon be planted there. I tried to speculate where exactly I would sit as we passed quickly through it. He led the way out into a main hallway that went left to the manufacturing floor and right toward the entrance lobby. Large, detailed models of current and historical M-D aircraft stood everywhere in glass cases lit from below. The place had dawn of aviation, art deco look about it. We passed quickly through this cool space, through a double set of heavy glass doors and into the heat of the Southern California sunshine. There we parted.

I looked at my watch. In an hour the Interstate heading toward Irvine would be locked up with rush hour traffic. It made no difference. I was in no hurry. A slower trip would give me time to think. I wanted to be on firm ground with this when it came time to present the day's events to Linda. I walked alone into the sea of cars that was the factory parking lot. The cars here would soon be forming the rush hour glut I knew was coming.

Overall, I felt pretty good. I had my first interview since college and came away from it with a job offer. I was batting a thousand. More important to my devastated ego, I had someone say they thought my experience in the Marines was valuable. Today I was appreciated for who I was. What I had done as a Marine was respected enough to pay what I expected would be a handsome wage. I began looking down the timeline figuring out where this job would take my family and me. Certainly we'd stay in Southern California. We'd probably make enough for a mortgage on a little house in a big neighborhood. We would blend into the sea of people in the Los Angeles area like an ink drop in the ocean. I would step out of one uniform and into another. I would work with people just like the ones I had worked with on the inside of the fence at the Marine Corps Air Station. I might even be the boss for some old squadron mates one day when their time in service ended.

I was lost in such thoughts as I navigated the parking lot to my little gold sports car. I set the valise on the roof and took off my jacket again, opened the car door and tossed it and the valise into the passenger seat. Then I dropped down into the driver's seat. I loved that car like the girl who bought it for me. A month or two after my last long deployment to Okinawa I came home from work and found it parked in the driveway. It was a classic sports car, a pampered and brightly waxed, gold Datsun 280ZX. It had a sporty black vinyl cover across the nose. I was wondering which of my friends had bought the cool sports car when the front door opened and Linda stepped out wearing a bright smile.

"Who is here, and whose car is that?" I asked.

"Me and yours, in that order," she answered.

She had seen the car for sale in a driveway as she headed home from work through the Marine Corps base housing area. She stopped immediately and walked up the driveway to look at it. It was the model of car I most admired at the time. The front door of the little base house opened and she met its owner. He was another Marine who was about to change duty stations. As moving military people always do he was parting with things that couldn't go with him. He was practically giving the car away. Linda bought it from him on the spot. She wrote a post-dated check she'd have to move savings to cover. The Marine was good with that and handed her the keys. When I got home later in the day, there it sat in our driveway. She said I needed it. Maybe she meant to say that my ego needed it. I had just brought home the letter announcing the unexpected and undesired end of my Marine Corps career not a week before. It made me sad. She gave me the sports car. Now I was happy. Who was I to argue?

As always happened as I settled into the driver's seat my concerns evaporated for the moment. Looking out at the Long Beach airport I felt like I was in the cockpit of a racing plane. I fired up the engine and listened to it purr for a moment. I dropped the windows and let in the cool Southern California sea breeze. Slipping the car into reverse, let out the clutch and backed out of this one of thousands of McDonnell-Douglas employee parking places for the first time. I suspected there would be many more of these events in my future. Then I dropped the transmission into first gear and let my foot off the gas as I started the slow roll past the long lines of lesser cars. I was pointed toward Lakewood Boulevard which along with my current route paralleled the Long Beach airport fence. A runway hugged the other side of it.

No pilot can pass an airport and keep his eyes on the road. I might be something else soon, but today I was still a pilot. I scanned the runway as the car coasted slowly along the airport fence line. I looked across the runway pavement at another parking lot where aircraft were parked. They were small civilian models, mostly airplanes. They were single and twin engine varieties with propellers and a couple light business jets. I knew the names of every model. Nearer Lakewood Boulevard there were a couple helicopters tied down near the distant fence.

I glanced back in the direction I was driving. That led me to look down the runway. In the distance airplanes were lining up on final approach to land. Their landing lights were on, making a sparkling line of diamond lights for miles out into the distance. I was going slowly enough to keep from wrecking my car while watching each plane's approach.

I watched two of them touchdown. I graded each landing, of course. In the distance a third airplane came into silhouette and then focus out of its brilliant landing lights. As I got to the McDonnell-Douglas gate at Lakewood I came to a stop. I looked away from the airport for the first time in several minutes. It was just a glance to the left down Lakewood to clear traffic. Before I could determine what I was seeing, the car grew dark as an aircraft, its shadow and the roaring beat of rotors passed obliquely and immediately over my head. I ducked, jammed on the brakes and whirled my head back to the right to see a helicopter whiz across the runway. Flying not much higher than the surrounding airport fence it darted toward the helicopter parking area on the other side of the runway. The pilot deftly raised the nose, rolled the machine on its right side and swung the nose back in the direction from whence he came. The rotors formed a cone as the pilot pulled up on his collective lever to add a large dose of power. With it he stopped his steed from flying, brought the helicopter to a smooth stop exactly over the only open spot in the helicopter parking area and landed. The aircraft settled lightly on its skids like ballerina taking a bow.

The helicopter was a Bell LongRanger. It was the stretched version of the military Bell Jet Ranger I had flown as a Marine Corps flight student in the Naval Air Training Command in Milton, Florida. Later I flew the Jetranger again as an instructor. This LongRanger at the Long Beach airport however, was completely civilian. It was hot looking, prettily tricked out compared to the orange and white military trainer I had flown. It reminded me of my sports car. It had a metallic paint job, mostly blue but with a starburst of metallic gold stripes starting at the nose. The gold spread back over the fuselage toward the tail. Unlike the military variant I flew, this civilian job had wire strike protection probes sticking out above and below the cockpit. They were as the name implies, devices for protecting the aircraft from striking wires by cutting them. They looked and functioned like long bayonets. More martial looking than safety related, I chuckled a little and wondered why Marine Corps aircraft didn't all have a set. The windows of this LongRanger were lightly tinted blue. Unlike the squatty military version this aircraft sat up proudly on high skids. There were little pop-out float bags mounted to the skids. They looked too small to support the aircraft upright during a water landing. They were another option civilian helicopters had that Navy helicopters lacked. I flew often over water in those single engine Navy birds training fledgling pilots to land on ships. I knew I was flying an anchor if the engine quit. Without floats those helicopters would float just long enough for me to catch my last breath before they rolled over and sank.

More than anything, those floats on that LongRanger told me what that pilot did for a living. He flew over water. I wondered where. The sun shining through the overhead window of his helicopter allowed me to see the pilot clearly. He wore a ball cap, sunglasses and a headset. That was novel. I had always wore a flight helmet since I started flying in the Marines. The civilian pilot also wore a short sleeved t-shirt, not a flight suit. I saw him raise one hand and adjust something on the instrument panel. I knew he had just started the stop watch feature of his clock to time his two minute engine cool down period before shutting down the engine. I involuntarily took a deep breath and relaxed. I had done the same thing at the end of each training flight I flew in Florida.

Mentally at least I was in the cockpit with him. The flight was over. Tension was off. I could smell the sweet aroma of burning kerosene from the exhaust. I loved that smell as much as Linda's perfume. It often gave me a similar rush. I heard the sound of rotors swishing rhythmically as the helicopter idled. In my dreamy reverie I ignored the building stream of cars that swung past me out of the parking lot. A popping sound brought me out of my daydream. The helicopter's engine made that sound as the pilot closed the throttle to shut off the fuel.

I looked around and noted that at that moment there was no traffic on Lakewood Boulevard and no one behind me either. I thought myself a little silly. Instead of watching that helicopter as I had been doing the past couple minutes, I could have been heading home on Interstate 5, the iconic "I-5" that runs the length of the left coast of America. But then I gave into another impulse as I dropped the car into gear and rocketed under the flight path of an approaching airplane. I kept one eye on the helicopter. Its blades were now winding slowly to a stop. Up ahead I saw an opportunity to turn off the road. I took it and swung into another parking lot. This lot was at the airport fence next to the parked helicopter. I wound up the windows and shutoff the engine.

By the time I got out of the car the pilot was tying down the blades of the LongRanger. I leaned on the car roof for a moment and watched the pilot finish his business and walk into the hangar. The hangar doors stood open. Inside I could see a number of helicopters that were parked close together, side by side. One of the parked birds was a Huey. It appeared to be the Navy model I had flown. I flew it as a student as well as the Jet Ranger. I flew it again as an instructor before the Navy traded the Hueys for new Jet Rangers.

Continuing to follow the second impulse that pulled me away from my trip home I reached back into the car. I left the valise and grabbed my jacket. I shook it out, put it on and headed across the little parking lot to the front door of the hangar office. A sign over the door announced the obvious. It was the headquarters of a helicopter service. Why was I doing this? I didn't really know. When I pulled the door open I saw a lady sitting at a counter. She was on the phone. She looked up, gave me a friendly smile and waved a few fingers at me like she knew me. She covered the mouthpiece.

"Be right with you!" she silently mouthed.

I looked for a chair and found a cheap and well-worn vinyl couch instead. It looked like quite a few pairs of dirty blue jeans and probably oily tennis shoes and work boots had rested on it over the years. There was a coffee table in front of it with a scattered batch of helicopter trade magazines on it. Like the couch they too looked well used. I took a seat and picked up one of the magazines with a picture of a little training helicopter on the cover. I noted that I had never seen either the magazine or the helicopter it depicted before. I got the immediate impression that I knew very little about civil helicopters. I didn't know that I was about to find out just how little I knew.

The lady ended her phone call and greeted me from across her desk. I flopped the magazine back on the table and stood to meet her at the counter.

"How may I help you?" she said as she flashed me another bright smile.

I thought that perhaps my intentions weren't obvious. Perhaps I didn't look like a Marine in an interview suit to her. Maybe instead I looked like a client. Maybe I looked like somebody who had an American Express platinum card in his pocket -- somebody who wanted to buy some helicopter time. Maybe she was just a nice lady. I smiled back winningly.

"Hi! My name is Paul Stone. I'd like to talk to your chief pilot if he's available."

Did that come out of me? I thought. I wondered what the heck I was going to say if she said 'yes.' Instead she said, "Why sure! Hold on a minute and I'll go get him!"

As she turned and headed down a hallway to do so I wondered if all her responses to questions sparkled like that. Then I speculated that she was probably thinking about that American Express platinum card I looked like I might be carrying. I returned to the couch and the trade magazine. I didn't get much farther into it than I had a moment before when the brilliant lady reappeared. This time she had a man in tow that I had to assume was the chief pilot. He looked like the famous rock star of the era, Frank Zappa. His curly mane was Zappa black and shoulder length, shot here and there with strands of gray. So too were his bushy eyebrows and a much bushier mustache. It hung down over his lower lip, trimmed more-or-less to follow its curve. It made him look more like a smiling walrus than any helicopter pilot I had ever met. His face was deeply tanned. He had laugh wrinkles in the corners of his eyes. He was dressed in a Hawaiian print shirt with the top two buttons open. They emitted a cloud of hair. He stuck one of his hairy arms out and walked through an opening in the counter past the brilliant lady.

"'Name's Mike," he said. I introduced myself by my first name and met his firm handshake. It occurred to me that I had no idea what I was doing here or what I was going to say. For some reason I felt perfectly at ease. That might have changed if we had made small talk. Instead he released my hand and said, "C'mon back to the office." Then he turned to head back from where he had come. He led the way down a short and narrow corridor bordered by several small and unoccupied glass offices. Each office had in it a battered wooden desk, a couple of cheap office chairs and lots of clutter. A dirty window looked out of each office into the hangar. Each office had a view of the helicopters parked there. The Huey caught my eye. Even through the dirty windows I could see that the paint job on it was awful. It was the antithesis of the sparkling LongRanger that I had watched land a few minutes earlier. The Huey was painted a milk chocolate brown. The paint appeared to have been applied with a broad brush, not with a spray gun. Along its length several narrow stripes of dark chocolate brown reached from nose to tail. I wondered who would do that to a fine old bird like the Huey.

At the end of the hall we stepped into Mike's slightly larger but equally cluttered office. The place smelled mildly of petroleum products and old coffee. He pointed to the chair near the door and asked me to take a seat. Then he walked around his desk and turned toward a coffee machine on the credenza behind it. He picked up a used Styrofoam cup and filled if from a half pot that was probably several hours old. He pointed at a short stack of fresh cups and offered me one.

"No, thanks." I replied. "I'm wired enough at the moment."

I wasn't lying. I felt like I had taken amphetamines. I didn't know why I had asked to meet this man, why I had asked to take his time or what I was going to say next. I sat down and looked past him and out his office window. From my seated position I could only see the rotors and the tops of the several helicopters behind him. The Huey's was the biggest one of the lot. I remembered standing on top of a helicopter like that. I admired the engineering of that rotor head. Even now I knew the workings and function of each of the control levers on that rotor system like I knew the pattern of veins in the back of my own hand. I had examined every bolt and cotter pin on Huey rotor systems before each of the many flights I flew in them as a Marine flight instructor.

Mike sat down with his coffee and drew a loud slurp of it through his mustache. He eyed me while he did so. I could feel him waiting for me to say something. When I didn't, he initiated the conversation. I could tell he had no idea why I was there when he said, "What can I do for you?" I shifted my focus from the Huey to him. I looked directly into his eyes and paused. His eyes were the darker chocolate color of the Huey's stripes. His black pupils appeared to bore into me. He squinted slightly. I took a breath, wet my lips and said as sincerely as if I had rehearsed it, "I want to fly for you."

The comment was full of an absolute sincerity. It felt visceral. It felt as though I was witnessing the beginning of a private conversation between two people I did not know. I knew that the guy I was watching actually meant every word he said. It just didn't seem like the guy was actually me.

Mike and his smile seemed to deflate. His shoulders and the ends of his mustache both fell. I knew now that he had thought I was a potential client. He was clearly disappointed in himself. He must have felt fooled. Now he had admitted this job hunter into his inner sanctum. Had he known I was looking for a job when he first met me he would have turned me away in the front office. I could see I was in trouble.

"I'm a pilot," I offered. I thought I sounded confident.

Mike was unimpressed. So I tried, "I just got out of the Marines." Mike's face brightened a little. One corner of his moustache rose a scintilla.

"Semper Fi," he replied.

If my confidence had flagged at all it returned with that fraternal greeting Marines share. 'Semper Fi,' short for Semper Fidelis means "always faithful." It's the Marines' motto. It meant that despite the situation in which we now found ourselves we were fellow Marines. I knew that it was only that common association that would keep me attached to the gossamer thread of his attention. It wouldn't last long. So while I had his attention I told him about my background and my flight experience. I was frank. I wasn't cocky. And I was respectful of the time he at first unwillingly gave me. I kept my outline general. I noted that as I spoke he grew more interested. I was encouraged when he put his elbow on his desk, his chin in his hand and began to stroke one side of his mustache with his fingers. I assumed the body language meant he was going to shut up and listen for a while.

I held nothing back. I even told him I had just interviewed with McDonnell-Douglas, that I had a job offer in my pocket. I told him that I didn't want to move from a Marine uniform into a business suit. I wanted to keep flying. It didn't seem to make a difference. He was already ahead of me. Mike squinted a little. "Did you say you flew '53s in the Marines?"

I nodded. The Sikorsky CH-53 was at the time the largest helicopter in the western world, let alone the United States Marine Corps.

"I flew 46s," Mike said as a matter of fact. The CH-46 was the next largest helicopter in the Marine Corps fleet. I thought it a good thing that his experience was in flying big Marine helicopters as I had. Then he caught me off guard. "That's not good. I can't use a pilot who flew big ships."

"You flew 46s. You made the break into small civilian helicopters."

"Yeah," he responded. I saw his eyes shift away from me and toward the door. I knew that I was suddenly losing his attention. I saw him shift his weight. He was getting ready to dismiss me. As he shifted a bit he went on. "I got a break and flew a lot of small stuff when I got out. What you flew doesn't fly like anything we have."

I pointed over his shoulder toward the hangar. "I flew Hueys, too."

He didn't even turn around. "So did I. Everybody our age did. There's a million Huey pilots came out of Vietnam and half of them have approached me about flying that one. That's the Navy model out there." He threw a thumb over his shoulder. "That's one of 'em we probably both flew," he said. "At least I did when I was a new lieutenant working to get Navy wings. Its serial number is in my logbook. The Navy's selling them off. We bought that one at a government auction."

"Yeah," I replied. "I heard that they were going to be sold out the gate when we got rid of them. I might have flown that one to the bone yard."

In making that comment I felt as though I had made a wrong turn. We were both missing something. Thankfully while I was thinking about that he went on.

"Currently I fly that Huey out there in the hangar. So does my partner. I don't need to hire a Huey pilot. Until recently nobody else working for us was permitted to fly it."

Okay, I thought. *He has a partner in this business. He's not just the chief pilot. He's an owner. He is going to be interested first hand in how I can make him some money.*

"We use that Huey for heavy lift work," Mike continued. "We just got a seismic contract in Wyoming. That's where that Huey is going next week. When we got the contract we realized we'd need to let someone else fly it. We have to stay here and run the business. The person who will be flying that job will be gone for six months at least. That means he'll be flying six months times seven days a week. I've got pilots lined up with probably lots more Huey time than you have who want the job."

That's when I suddenly saw what we had both missed. His hangar was full of the Bell 206 model, The Jet Ranger and LongRanger. "'How about 206s? I asked. "Can you use a Jet Ranger pilot?" As he drew breath I knew what he was going to say. I was prepared for it.

"We both got Jet Ranger time before we got into Hueys for our wings, didn't we? Is that what you mean?"

I smiled. I had just realized he didn't know how things had changed at flight school since he got his wings. "No." I replied. "I've got eleven hundred hours in Jet Rangers besides the basics we both got in flight school."

That got his attention. He squinted again. Both his hands dropped to the desk and his weight shifted back in his seat. He leaned toward me. "How'd you get that?"

I looked past him and nodded at the Huey. "Like I said, I probably flew that Huey out there to the bone yard. Then I picked up the Navy's new Jet Rangers from the Bell Helicopter factory in Fort Worth. That's what we're training in nowadays. They call it the TH-57 'Sea Ranger.' And I've flown a lot of instructor time in them."

His face brightened. "I didn't know that," he said. "The Navy's flying all Jet Rangers in their helicopter training pipeline now?"

I nodded once. "Yep, they're doing things a little differently in the Naval Air Training Command since we went through. No more Huey time for student Naval Aviators. The brand new Jet Ranger is the only training helicopter in the Navy. The new one is the TH-57 Charlie model. You and I flew the real basic and battered Alpha model to get our wings."

Over the years at this flying service Mike had encountered a hundred people like me, all looking for flying jobs. Some had been grossly unqualified. Even those who met all the qualifications rarely got as far as I had. He always shook off the job hunters by saying he didn't have any jobs to offer. So he surprised himself when he stood up and looked back over his shoulder. His gaze shifted across the livery he and his partner had in the hangar. He looked out the hangar doors. His focus came to rest on the helicopter that had zipped so recently over my head on the McDonnell-Douglas parking lot.

I noticed that he began stroking his mustache. He was thinking again. He lowered his gaze and slowly turned back toward me. I could tell that a plan was developing. He raised his eyes and looked at me. A question was forming in his mind. His black pupils focused on me through his bushy eyebrows. One eyebrow rose up. The corners of his mustache lifted slightly into what might have been interpreted as a smile. "'You ever fly a LongRanger?" he asked.

I came home in my interview suit that afternoon with not one, but two job offers. Linda knew which one I wanted, and that was all she needed to know. She said that if I took a job at a factory she'd kill me if I didn't kill myself first. "Besides," she said, "you need to break the mold you've fallen from. I've seen you unhappy since before you left for Okinawa with that infantry battalion." She scowled remembering how tough it had been for me working for a lieutenant colonel who didn't like pilots. He'd made it clear that he didn't like me in particular.

"I'm tired of watching you getting beat up. You were doing something you didn't like for somebody who didn't appreciate your hard work. It's a new day for you, Paul. I want you to do what makes you happy. Flying makes you happy."

And that is what cinched my civilian career choice. Early the next morning I called the executive and former Navy man at McDonnell-Douglas and thanked him for his consideration. The conversation was brief. He seemed to understand immediately why I would take a flying job over the desk job he had offered to me. That closed the door to the job in a suit at McDonnell-Douglas. I never looked back.

My first flight in a civilian helicopter took place later that week. Pay sucked. Linda didn't care. Helping us out in the money department was the "stupidmarinecorps." It had become a single word for Linda, Oddly, I thought later, they had paid me a thirty thousand dollar bonus to remain in the Marines for five years. The Navy and Marines were short of pilots at the time and tried to bribe us so we wouldn't leave for the airlines. Most of my buddies shunned the bonus. They had no intention of extending their enlistments. Those guys called the Naval Air Training Command where we served as instructors, "the airline training command." They got their turbine airplane time there. And when their end of active service date came up they headed out the door to be airline pilots.

I never wanted to fly an airliner. Besides, I was a dedicated Marine and a helicopter pilot. I had no intentions of leaving the Marine Corps for the next couple decades. I'd sure sign on for the bonus. As I saw it, thirty grand to stay in the Marines was just a pile of free money. I signed on for the maximum commitment and took the whole thirty thousand. Then the next year they passed me over for promotion: twice. When that happens your time as a Marine officer is through. And so I got out of the Marines against my will after less than two years into the five year contract. Surprisingly, on my way out they paid me the balance of the bonus as though I had stayed for a five year commitment. Instead of paying to keep an experienced aviator in the Marines, the bonus money supplemented my low civilian wages and allowed me to learn to fly LongRangers as a civilian pilot. Thank you, stupidmarinecorps.

I missed the fact that the money was a blessing. It was only one of the countless number of them that unknown to me then were raining down on me. I thought I had failed. Instead, a complex and wonderful plan was falling into place. A prayer was being answered I no longer remembered praying. One day I'd realize just how many times my failures and unexpected forks in the road had led me to an affirmative answer to that prayer. At the moment I was still bruised and bleeding from the beating I had received from the Marine Corps promotion board. The healing began in earnest the day I reported to work flying to the island.

I found out quickly that Chief Pilot Mike and his partner were sharp business men. They worked their aircraft in every facet of the helicopter business. One source of their revenue was made by supporting the oil rigs off the coast of California as well as the industry's seismic business elsewhere onshore. Through those connections they garnered the contract in Wyoming that was the reason they had bought the brown Huey.

One day while walking past the Huey I could make out a six digit number on the tail showing in outline through the brown paint. The light was just right. I copied it down. That evening I checked my Marine Corps logbook. I had indeed flown it as an instructor in the Training Command only three years before. At the time I saw the Huey and I crossing paths as civilians an act of irony or serendipity. I would learn much later in life that such things were anything but accidental.

Being accustomed to the regimentation of the Marine Corps I found it refreshing working for Mike. The business was as un-military as I could imagine. I never knew what the company was going to be doing day-to-day. While waiting to go to Wyoming, the Huey worked odd jobs in the LA Basin. It lifted air conditioners to the tops of sky scrapers. The old brown bird even lifted stranded four wheel drive vehicles on occasion. Los

Angelinos liked to drive their Jeeps and Land Rovers up dry washes and into the deep ravines in the mountains and deserts that surround their city. There they would bottom out or flatten all four tires, often far from where conventional tow trucks could reach them. The Huey snatched quite a few out of the mountains while I was working for Mike.

One day after I started working for the Long Beach helicopter service I looked out on the ramp to see what looked like the chocolate Huey. It was certainly a Navy model. But it was sporting the olive drab paint job of an Army helicopter. It even had "United States Army" painted in black letters on the tail boom. It also had machine gun mounts in the doors, less the machine guns. It turned out that Mike was flying it on the set of a Hollywood movie studio. They were using it in a movie about the Vietnam War. Mike may have told me which movie it was, but I forgot it as soon as he told me. I do recall how much money he told me he was making each day it flew for Hollywood, however. That's when I realized how Mike could afford to buy the new whale-tail Porsche he was driving.

Besides supporting offshore oil platforms, in their smaller ships Mike's company flew executives and wealthy people around the LA basin. They also did news, real estate and advertising photography flights. The job Mike gave me was not quite as glamorous as flying in a Hollywood movie, or acting as an air taxi pilot for the wealthy and famous. I was assigned to fly tourists to Catalina Island. It was going to be my only job, a steady gig.

Before I could start I had to get trained. My uniform-of-the-day as a civilian helicopter pilot was short sleeve collared shirt, blue jeans and Chuck Taylor model Converse All Star tennis shoes. I brought a ball cap and my military shades. All decked out I probably looked like the pilot who had buzzed my car in the LongRanger at the McDonnell-Douglas plant gate. When I reported for work, Mike hooked me up with one of the other company helicopter pilots for a familiarization course in the Bell LongRanger.

My instructor pilot was younger than me by probably ten years. I asked him how long he had been flying helicopters. He said, "Since I was sixteen." By the look on his fresh, young face that meant he'd been flying probably two years. It turned out I wasn't far off. He told me he'd never flown an airplane. Starting off flying in helicopters is unusual, mostly because it's an expensive way to learn the basics. I had started off flying airplanes at his age, and then learned to fly helicopters in the Marines. He said he learned to fly helicopters first because his Dad had owned a helicopter. He had gotten his helicopter pilot license when he was seventeen. I knew by the way he handled himself around the aircraft on the ramp that he must have flown a lot in the period before we met. When he found out from Mike I was a military guy he volunteered that he had never flown anything but civilian helicopters. He bragged though about the few hours of "heavy" time he had in a Huey. He said he hoped to fly the Huey for Mike full-time one day.

I gave the young instructor his due. I didn't tell him I had flown that very Huey. I didn't tell him I probably had more time in Hueys than he had total time in helicopters. I also didn't tell him that I had even more time flying the CH-53 than in the Huey. The '53 weighed four times as much empty as that Huey did full of fuel and people, so I didn't consider the Huey a "heavy" bird. I didn't tell him that. Neither did I note that I had been passed over for promotion. That instead of pinning on the rank of major I had instead gotten a 'pink slip' for my twelve years of service. He probably wouldn't have understood that anyway. This morning my experience didn't matter much to me. Much as I hated leaving the Marine Corps I was already gaining personally from the experience. It had humbled me. I needed that. It was manifested this morning. I didn't brag and make a fool of myself with that young instructor. I just shut my pie hole, listened and learned. It was refreshing being with this enthusiastic, fresh young pilot. I spent some time affirming his justifiable pride in the experience he had. In return he taught me what I needed to know about the helicopter I would be flying. Just as important he taught me about flying as a civilian. He was better than me at what I needed to know. I paid attention to what he taught.

The LongRanger transition course started in the hangar break room. We filled a couple cups with coffee and sat down with the pilot operating handbook he had grabbed from the helicopter we were going to fly. The helicopter was the metallic blue one I had seen as it zipped over my head a few days before. He had probably been the pilot who buzzed me. He said that when we were done training I would have to fly a "part 135 check ride" with an FAA examiner. I didn't know at the time that part 135 of the Federal Aviation Regulations governs air taxi operations. I was going to be checked out as a taxi driver. I would come to find out that the similarities between me and a cab driver would be many. Among them: I would work and be paid by the day. People I carried would take me completely for granted. I would be little more than a control unit for the machine taking them to their destination. People would not want to talk to me. People would feel superior to me, even if they themselves were scum. They would remain oblivious to the fact that my bad driving could end their life. There were other similarities but there were differences too. The major ones were that I would make less money than a taxi driver, and that no one I drove around would tip me.

My young instructor knew the FAA examiner I'd fly with. He also knew exactly what I needed to do to pass a check ride with him. "His rides are always the same," my young instructor said. We sat at the table in the break room and went quickly through the manual. Our review would only cover those things I would need to know to start and operate the helicopter, and those questions I would be asked by the FAA examiner. The book review took about two cups of coffee. Then we went out on the ramp. I followed behind him as he did a walk around inspection of the helicopter. A LongRanger is just a stretched Jet Ranger. I had been trained in the Jet Ranger from the people who built them at Bell Helicopter in Texas. I knew a lot more about the machine than my instructor did, but my young instructor did a better job with me than I would have teaching him. He didn't waste time on minutia as I would have. He just focused on what I needed to pass the check ride.

I looked forward to flying a small ship again instead of a forty-two thousand pound behemoth CH-53. Because all my helicopter time to date was with the Marines, I had never flown a helicopter in anything except a flight suit. It felt odd to be preparing for a flight in blue jeans and tennis shoes. It would be interesting interacting with unarmed passengers for a change, too. My passengers would be focused on making their time in my helicopter part of a vacation. In that I would soon share their interest.

When we were done looking over the helicopter, we untied the blades and jumped into the cockpit. There were no linemen or fireguards like I had become accustomed to in the military. We were the whole crew. He let me start the engine. It was a little different than the Jet Ranger. I would get used to it. Then we called Long Beach Airport Control Tower for permission to fly in the local airport traffic pattern. They directed us to an area away from the airplane traffic. Then they left us alone to do whatever we wanted. That included some normal and steep approaches to a closed runway. We did all the standard string of maneuvers I would be expected to know how to do if I were to fly people around in the machine. We didn't do any emergency procedures except simulated engine failures. These were benign. He never rolled the throttle to idle unexpectedly. Rather, he gave me the opportunity to roll the throttle to idle on my own which resulted in textbook autorotations. I felt completely at home in the bird within forty-five minutes. He knew it. So we taxied back to the parking ramp where we had started. I landed where we had taken off and rolled the throttle to idle. Then he surprised me. Without saying anything to me he climbed out. Just before he unplugged his headset he said, "Take it around the patch a few times. I'll see you when you're done."

Then he unplugged his headset, ducked as he walked under the turning rotors and left. He never turned around, just walked into the hangar.

Watching him walk away I suddenly realized that in all my years of flying helicopters I had never flown one by myself. I had always had another pilot in the cockpit with me. Even when I was working on getting my Navy wings I had another student fly with me on the flights the training command called "student solos." I felt exactly as I had the day my father threw me the keys to the family station wagon and asked me to go to the grocery store and buy some milk. It was the first time I had driven a car by myself. Here was that day repeated.

I rolled the throttle back up on the LongRanger. The idling blades whirled faster and blurred as they reached flying speed. I glanced across the instrument panel and checked the caution light panel. It seemed strange not announcing my intentions or observations to a copilot. I surprised myself with a laugh as I pulled up on the collective. With no one in the aircraft but me the skids lifted lightly off the ground. The helicopter seemed to dance at my touch on the flight controls. So did my spirits. I called the Tower for takeoff and got the same clearance as before. The dancefloor was mine. I pushed the cyclic forward, picked up altitude and airspeed and for the rest of my career as an air taxi pilot I enjoyed myself immensely.

The next morning I flew with the FAA inspector. It turned out that the questions he asked were the same ones my instructor told me the inspector would ask, word for word. The instructor told me, "He's going to ask you if it's okay for a passenger to put a wet wig in a plastic bag and carry it onboard. If you're smart you'll play dumb on that one and the oral part of the exercise will be over." I thought I had misunderstood him. "Why would an FAA employee ask me something like that?" My young instructor smiled slyly. "The FAA Inspector who does our check rides heard somewhere that a wet wig in a plastic bag could cause spontaneous combustion. That makes it a hazardous material. It may be totally bogus information but if you'll just play dumb and act like you don't know that, he'll spend the next thirty minutes telling you why it's so. Suddenly he'll realize that he's taken up all the time for the oral exam talking about his pet question. The oral will be over and all you'll have to do is fly."

That is exactly what happened. The FAA inspector was like many employees of his agency I have met since. He was a stuffy, officious bureaucrat -- full of himself and short on personality and humor. The collar and the rest of his starched white shirt had fit him when he bought it ten years before, but it was now a couple sizes too small. The wattle around his turkey neck was squeezed so tight by the collar that it turned his face and balding head pink. His tie was several inches too short and badly stained by spilled food and drinks over the years. The pattern and color of it were both long-gone out of style. I would have bet my paltry first paycheck that this man could have told me to the hour how much longer he had to be a government functionary until his retirement. I would have bet my second paycheck that he'd be dead of a coronary within two months of that date.

I met him in the lobby of the helicopter service with the same vigor Mike showed me when I came through the front door. I need not have bothered. His limp handshake gave me the creeps as well as the firmer impression he was less than thrilled to meet me. I led him back to the break room and offered him coffee. He declined, sat down and opened his briefcase on his lap. He reached in and then handed me a three page government form. "Fill that out," he said with an air of self-importance. "I want to see your pilot certificate and your medical certificate."

I gave them to him. He began to write on a notepad. I worked on the form. We finished writing at about the same time. I didn't know it, but half my oral exam was now over. I had thoughtfully remembered to place the copy of the operator's manual on the table for the convenience of the inspector. He picked it up and opened the cover. He turned a few pages and then rested his finger on the item at issue.

"What kind of helicopter is this?" he asked.

"This is a Bell 206 L-3 LongRanger. It has an Allison 250 C-30 engine."

He looked up under his bushy eyebrows and over the black frames of his glasses. "I didn't ask about the engine did I?"

I learned the lesson. From then on he asked the questions. I just answered them. They were all just about as easy as it turned out.

"So can you carry children?"

"Yes."

"Do they have to have a life vest if you're over water?"

"Yes."

"What's the minimum fuel you must have on the aircraft when you land on a day like today?"

"Twenty minutes remaining." That was a cinch, I thought. I wondered if they were going to get harder.

"Can you carry hazardous materials in the helicopter?"

"Yes." I could have elaborated myself into trouble but let the opportunity pass.

"Can you carry a wet wig in a plastic bag?"

There it was already: *the* question. Startled it came so soon I struggled to keep a straight face. I wanted to say, "That's it? That's an FAA oral exam? In the Marine Corps I would be answering questions until the sweat on my brow mixed with blood!" Then I recalled I wasn't in the Marine Corps anymore. I'd always be a Marine. It was in me to my bone marrow. But now I had to adjust to real life. Dealing with this FAA guy was part of the adjustment.

My instructor's advice came to mind. I could almost see him winking at me. I recovered from my shock at the ease of the exam. Still, it was easier to put on my baffled look than it would have been in my military days.

"A wig, you say? In a plastic bag?" I looked at the ceiling, wrinkled my brow. "Er..I...I don't know." I stuttered and looked at him in feigned surrender. "Can I?"

The inspector slowly grinned. "I told you, I'm asking the questions," he said. "But in this case..."

He went on for over thirty minutes about the construction of wigs. I felt he had a deep personal knowledge of the subject and suspected by the bad comb-over on his pate he had come by the information through long and careful research. He outlined how plastic bags are made, their chemical composition and how they react to wet wigs. I think he believed what he was saying. I didn't. Even so, I nodded as though I was really learning something.

"Is that so?" I said. I added later, "I never knew that!" I lied boldfaced as I said several times, "Hmmm, that's interesting!" He finished up his discourse and I added with a flair a final, "How in the world did you learn all that?" He was about to tell me when he suddenly blanched. Maybe it was an act, but his pink head grew a little pale. He snapped his fat wrist up before his bulging eyes to read his cheap wrist watch.

"Oh, my gosh!" he exclaimed with what sounded like genuine surprise in his voice. I really couldn't tell if it was serious. "We'd better go flying! I don't have much time before I have to be back at the office!"

I supposed he had to get back to the office in order to get his full hour off for lunch. So I put down the coffee cup and relieved him of the flight manual. With it we walked out to the helicopter. We passed my young instructor. I was a step behind the FAA inspector. I quickly tapped the top of my head. My instructor smiled and gave me a quick "thumbs up."

Thirty-seven minutes after I hit the starter button I was tying down the rotor blades: check ride complete.

The day of my FAA check ride also turned out to be my first day on the job as a Catalina Island Shuttle pilot. I knew almost nothing about what my duties would entail. The FAA inspector had left without saying good bye. So with my FAA paperwork in hand saying that I had passed the check ride I reported to the office of Chief Pilot Mike. He stood up and walked over to a local flying map pinned to his office wall. He pointed to our location on the Long Beach airport. Then he put another finger from the same hand on "Queensway." It was an area at the nearby Long Beach harbor named for the regal passenger liner, "Queen Mary." Queensway was a tourist spot. "The Queen" was the main attraction as she was permanently berthed there. I could see between Mike's fingers that after takeoff I could follow Lakewood Boulevard almost to the harbor. Once I got there, a target the size of the Queen Mary would be hard to miss.

"At the bow of the Queen there's a helipad hanging out into the harbor. It's marked with an 'H,'" he said unnecessarily. "Get some lunch. Then take 24 X-ray over to Queensway and land. Look for John. You can't miss him. He'll tell you what to do."

I would find that Mike's mission oriented orders were always brief and to the point. He wasted no time. I liked that. I replied with, "Wilco." That's pilot-ese for "will comply." It seemed appropriate.

The company helicopter "Two Four X-ray" was in the hangar when I left for lunch. When I came back it was sitting next to the helicopter in which I had taken my check ride. Like the snappy blue and gold LongRanger, Two Four X-ray was similarly configured. It had a white background paint job with several shades of yellow and brown stripes. "Earth tones," a name that could only have come from California, were "in" at the time. All the Southern California interior decorators were using those colors. To me that word mix meant "shades of brown." Like everything else in California, the name and the paint would be dated by next week. But to the modern Californian who made up probably ninety percent of our customers, our earth tone helicopter looked really good right now. Customers would notice.

I noticed the floats. There were sharks in the Catalina Channel. I brought the operating handbook to lunch with me. I made sure I knew all about them before I finished my hamburger. When I got back from the lunch stop I did a careful preflight inspection. I ran my hand over the words "Island Shuttle;" white vinyl letters on the earth tone (brown) tail boom. I smiled. No more olive drab for me. No more "MARINES" painted in four foot tall flat black letters on my over-sized fighting machine, the CH-53 "Sea Stallion." This was my ride now.

I'd be working next to a luxurious old British ocean liner. I had seen it from the air passing over it in the Marine helicopters I had flown. Even from altitude it looked grand. It had carried the wealthy and powerful of a past generation. I would come to meet their modern counterparts quite often on this new job. Flying across the channel was pricey. That didn't stop people of lesser means from flying. But the very wealthy people always flew to Catalina Island. The never took the more plebian channel boats.

Beside the Queen Mary, Queensway was home to Howard Hughes' famous giant transport plane, the *Spruce Goose*. It resided in a unique dome shaped building overlooking the harbor in which it made its only flight, a takeoff and landing. Between the Goose and the Queen, tourists relaxed in a park between the two. They inevitably gathered at our fence to watch the comings and goings of our helicopter. Just being there was the perfect way to lure them for a ride. The trip to Catalina Island was beautiful, and often resulted in them springing for the round trip when their Catalina visit was through.

Another spot from which we flew was the nearby harbor town of San Pedro. It was a picturesque spot. Between Queensway and San Pedro we flew over the Long Beach Navy yard and the San Pedro Channel. It was a trip of about five miles from Queensway to San Pedro. Besides being a beautiful spot to linger on a pleasant California day, San Pedro was home to many bistros and shops. It also supported the northern end of the

Vincent Thomas suspension bridge that spanned the ship channel. Tourists at San Pedro were drawn to the passing ship traffic always plying the narrow channel. They walked the little streets that led to the big bridge. And then they spotted our helipad. From restaurants along the channel they watched the helicopter come and go.

The helipad at San Pedro was actually under the main span of the bridge. I still think it strange that commercial helicopter operations were allowed to take paying passengers for a flight under a bridge. It was an act that would have lost me my Navy wings had I done so in a military helicopter. But the FAA was okay with it, so that is the way our business was done. We left from or returned to Catalina via Queensway and San Pedro. They were the three points of our triangular route. I would come to know each leg very well.

After my post lunch preflight inspection was complete I untied the blades. After takeoff I turned west. Even before I passed the airport boundary I saw the Queen Mary in the distance. I followed Lakewood Boulevard until the helipad came into view near the grand ship's bow. The pad was large enough for two or three LongRangers to land at one time. A singlewide trailer house was placed on the inland edge of the pad. The other three sides of the helipad were bordered by the water of Long Beach harbor. I made a conservative, slow approach to the pad. Two-four X-ray came to a hover over the big "H." I bumped the cyclic gently and slid to the edge of the pad to leave room for other helicopters to come and go. Then I deftly landed and rolled the throttle to idle. I started the stop watch on the clock. During the two minute engine cool-down cycle I looked at my surroundings. Looking out over the instrument panel I saw somebody standing behind the sliding glass door of the singlewide. He had white hair, a white mustache and wore wrap-around sunglasses. His arms were crossed. I would see him like this watching my many takeoffs and landings in the coming months. It was John, my new boss. He was the manager of the Catalina Air Shuttle Service.

I wondered if the company would use an acronym like the military always did for such things. "I work for 'CASS,'" I might say. I found out later that John didn't like "military stuff." So nobody I worked with called the business anything except, "the shuttle." John was an anomaly. He dressed the part of a young man who spent a lot of time at the beach. With his straight, white shoulder-length hair and white mustache he looked like a very old hippie. I found out later he was only ten years my senior. Once I saw him close up I would have bet on him being at least twenty years older than me.

He waited until I had the helicopter blades tied down to come out and meet me. He slid open the door of the single wide that served as an office and slowly strolled out in my direction. He wasn't in any hurry. He never was in a hurry all the days I worked with him. Besides the wrap-around sunglasses, he was clad in a collarless t-shirt and Bermuda shorts. They, like his helicopter, were earth tone. He wore leather deck shoes, not flip flops. I guess he had some sense of propriety. Only once or twice, and then only on the coldest of days did I see him wear a pair of blue jeans. Hot or cold, he never wore socks.

As he got closer I could see in his face that he had seen a lot of sun. His skin was the color and appeared to be the texture of old leather. There were deep creases and wrinkles in his face. His visible skin was all the same dark and deep pecan hue. Though shoulder length and straight his hair was professionally cut in a longish version of a page boy. All of his hair was snow white: on his head, his eyebrows, arms, spewing from the neck of his t-shirt and sprouting from his upper lip. His mustache was as long as the chief pilot's but straight, not bushy. Like Mike's mustache, John's went well past the corners of his mouth and lapped well below his lower lip. Unlike Mike's, John's mustache never bore a hint of a smile in it, even on those rare times he might have been smiling. In the time I came to know him, the full gamut of John's expressions ran from grumbled displeasure to the occasional chuckle. In any case his mustache never seemed to move.

From my first meeting with him to my last he had a commanding presence I came to respect. Despite the first impression he gave by how he dressed, he conducted business with the bearing of a bank president. He almost never showed any emotion in his face. Still it was always clear to everyone who worked with him when John was not pleased. He had long been a helicopter pilot and now he was a manager. Although he had much more flying experience than time in management, he was most certainly up to running this air taxi service. He most often spoke in such a quiet voice I had to listen hard to hear him. I almost missed the first word he ever said to me. He rendered it as I stepped away from my job tying down the rotor blades.

"Hi." He said.

"Hi." I replied.

He reached out a hand, shook mine and said, "I'm John. Come with me." Then he turned and walked back to the trailer at the same relaxed pace by which he had walked to the helicopter. I had to slow down to keep from passing him. We both stepped through the sliding door into a passenger waiting area. He let me in and pulled the sliding glass door closed behind us. When the door was closed he remained facing the harbor. I had to lean forward to hear him when he said, "A helicopter is coming in here in a couple minutes. Get in the front and fly with Ed. He'll tell you what you need to know."

"Okay," I replied.

Then John turned and walked toward the door to a room at the far end of the singlewide. It was his office. It too had a sliding glass door that faced the helipad. He left the office door open as he disappeared into his warren. I turned and looked at a lady who was standing nearby. She was wearing a company t-shirt, leaning on a podium near the door out to the parking lot. The plastic tag on her shirt said her name was Catherine. She looked like my mother. She was about the same age, slender with brightly dyed red hair and blue eyes. Her job was to handle waiting customers of which there were currently none. She had seen the whole exchange between John and me. She looked at me and shrugged. "That's John," she said.

A few minutes later another shuttle service helicopter arrived, hovering for a moment above the "H." Then it landed. Catherine and I went out the sliding door and walked toward it. The pilot gave her a "thumbs up" signal and she ducked under the turning rotor. I followed her. As she walked past the cockpit she pointed to the left front seat and looked at me. I climbed in as she opened the back door for several offloading passengers. They were coming back from their morning on Catalina. She herded them into a little clutch, keeping them between the door and the nose of the helicopter. Nobody walked toward the tail rotor. Then she closed the door, ducked down in an exaggerated fashion and walked past them and past the cockpit. She got another "thumbs up" from the pilot as I took the left front seat and buckled my seatbelt. The passengers all imitated her as Catherine ducked the rotor like it was going to chop her head off. It was a perfectly exemplary way to get a bunch of untrained people safely out of the rotor arc intact. I was impressed.

I put on a headset that was hanging from a hook between me and the pilot. I saw the intercom button on the floor. Later I would point it out to hundreds of passengers. The pilot I was with didn't need to show me. I stepped on it. "Howdy!" I said. "I'm Paul."

The pilot smiled broadly and said, "Howdy to you, too! I'm Ed." Catherine had already told me that Ed was a moonlighting LA cop. He flew police patrols in a little Schweizer helicopter for his real job. He looked like a cop. He told me I looked like one, too.

"What makes you say that, Ed?"

He pointed to my head. "The hair," he said. "I figured you were either a cop or in the military or something." I confirmed his speculation replying, "Marine." I hadn't learned to say "former Marine," yet. I noticed he didn't look like a Marine, though. He had apparently spent a little too much time in the donut shop over the last couple decades, I supposed. He wasn't fat, but he didn't look like someone who was going to win any physical fitness competitions either. Like me he wore a ball cap and sunglasses, a t shirt and blue jeans although his shirt didn't have a collar on it. Mine did.

"We don't have anybody to pick up here. I have some across the harbor who are going to Catalina, though." He adjusted his cap. "Hey, 'you ever flown under a bridge?" He laughed as he smoothly rolled up the throttle, pulled up on the collective until the skids cleared the concrete. Then we skidded sideways across the pad. As we slid toward the edge of the pad he pushed the left pedal and swung the nose into the desired direction of travel. We'd be going westbound and parallel to the Queen Mary. When he got to the edge of the helipad and pointed the right way he nosed the helicopter over to accelerate. We did so quickly and left the pad low and fast. Low over the water alongside the Queen we gained both speed and altitude. Tourists along the railings looked down at us as we passed. We were close enough to see them smiling and waving. I waved back.

Ed pulled the helicopter up into a sweeping climb over the stern of the ship. He rolled out at an altitude slightly higher than the ship's smoke stacks and headed past the dome over the *Spruce Goose.* There on the other side of the dome lay the Long Beach Navy Yard. Among the cruisers and smaller ships stood the mighty battleship New Jersey. I got a little twinge looking at our country's proud and mighty fleet and felt just a little lonely for a moment. Ed broke my short pity party to point to the distant Vincent Thomas Bridge.

Ed was smooth on the controls. "That takeoff was pretty hot," I said smiling. He smiled back and then laughed. "I guarantee you'll be doing it just like that. This is a cool job, Paul. Easy. All you have to do is fly and be nice. Everybody is going to Catalina to have a good time and probably to get laid. Either that or they're coming back from having done one, the other or both. You'll meet the occasional asshole, but they're rare. Just cut off the intercom system and pretend the headset doesn't work. That's how I handle 'em." He pointed to a small toggle switch on the panel I had not noticed before.

There were no flight controls in front of me. The collective on the left side had been removed. I could see the pedals. A clear plastic box covered them so no one could step on them. Over the stub of pipe where the cyclic would normally reside was an opaque, plastic box. A couple silver snaps held it in place. Ed saw me eye the little box and its flimsy construction. "Watch out for the passengers. They'll step on that plastic box. Then they pop those snaps and catch their heel on the cyclic stub," Ed warned. "Watch the big, long legged men especially." I looked at the plastic box again. "That cover doesn't work at all," Ed continued. Some big-footed, football player-sized dude pulls his foot back and rests it on that cover and the snaps let loose. Then you have a hundred pounds of force on the bottom of your cyclic. It'll snap the stick right out of your hand." I'm sure my eyes widened. "The first guy did that to me really got my attention. We pitched down so fast it took both hands for me to pull the cyclic back. I lost a couple hundred feet before I realized what had happened. Good thing I had a little altitude or we'd have all have been fish food."

Note to self, I thought: *Watch out for the cyclic stub.*

Throughout our flights together that day I found out lots of similar tricks and traps from Ed that could help me avoid an unpleasant, first-hand learning experience. I had flown long enough to know that all the mistakes you can make in a helicopter had already been made by someone. I just didn't know what they were. I certainly didn't need to repeat them. So I pumped Ed for all the pointers he could give me. Some were pretty arcane; they were things I had never before encountered.

"Watch out for Champaign bottles. Partiers will stick one in their carry-on. About the time you get your takeoff started, bang! Out comes the cork. It sounds just like an engine compressor stall. The first time it happened to me I thought the engine had quit. The passengers in back popped the cork just as we took off. I thought we were going in the harbor. 'Scared me to death." He looked at me and winked. "Just be ready, it'll happen to you too, I bet."

After my first takeoff from Queensway with Ed and for the rest of the day I kept thinking, *"You're not in the Marine Corps anymore, boy."* It resounded when we landed under the Vincent Thomas Bridge. That was a first for my flying career. Four passengers were led out to the helicopter from a singlewide identical to the one at Queensway. The leader was a kid in a company t-shirt. He was probably about college age, but he looked like he was about twelve. His hair was flaming red and his white skin and freckles shaved half a dozen years off his age. Like Catherine at Queensway he too did the thumbs-up-and-duck entry under the whirling rotor blades. I decided that redheads make good ground crew people.

Without meaning to, Ed pointed out a skill he had developed as he evaluated the oncoming passengers. "That fat gal there weighs two ninety if she's an ounce. Her daughter is young, but she's pressing one forty. It's a shame to let a child get fat like that, 'specially a girl. She'll get zits and no dates. 'Probably turn into a lesbian or something." He chuckled a little, then went on with his weight calculations. A man who looked like he might be the fat lady's husband was shouting over the helicopter noise at another man who might have been a relative or friend. They walked out together behind the girls.

"Together those boys are four hundred pounds, say four twenty. You're one eighty-five. I'll call you one ninety." He must have been looking at my bathroom scale. He was dead on. "I'm not going to tell you what I weigh. You can do the math if you like. He glanced down at the instrument panel. We've got four hundred fifty pounds of gas. With our basic weight we could carry another five hundred fifty five pounds of gas or ass. Speaking of gas, I don't leave this spot with less than four hundred pounds. That gives us a round trip here to the fuel truck and a little to spare. I'd hate to run out just shy of the fuel truck, know what I mean?" He winked at me. I noted that when he winked it meant I had just been taught something valuable. Ed winked a lot that day.

I was impressed with his ad hoc weight and balance system. He did the arithmetic all in his head. When the last passenger was strapped in, the red-headed kid with the freckles handed Ed a little clipboard though the sliding glass window in the pilot-side door. I leaned over and looked at it. It had a form filled out with all the calculations Ed had just done in his head. Around two of the passenger weights the kid had put a circle and a little note, "Yeah, right!"

"She said she weighs one-fifty. Well, maybe the top half. Not the bottom half. No way. She says her girl weighs ninety pounds. Closer, but it shows you a skill you'll have to develop. When you're done flying here you can get a job guessing people's weight at the county fair."

"Most people won't step on our scale." He looked at me solemnly for the first time that morning. "Most of them lie." He glanced over his shoulder to see that the passengers had their seatbelts on. "I can't blame them. I would too. They just give the ground crew their weight. You have to do the real weight and balance calculations. I can't truthfully say you won't ever takeoff over gross weight. But I'm telling you and you can take it to the bank, you're putting your *life* not just your pilot certificate on the line if you do. This little bird will fly heavy time after time and then one day all of a sudden, she won't. She'll either splash into the channel on takeoff or something will break. Worse, something you did to the machinery flying it heavy might just break on my watch. *I'll* end up in the drink. So do us both a favor. I'll respect the machine if you will. Promise you won't fly over the maximum gross weight, and I'll do the same."

I raised my right hand and nodded. He covered the collective with his left hand, clasped the cyclic stick with his knees and stuck out his right. I shook it. Then he put his hands back on the controls and rolled up the throttle. I knew why he was serious about his advice on flying a heavy load. I was new to civil aviation, but I didn't just fall off the back of a turnip truck. I learned early in my Marine Corps flying career that it was best to obey the rules. They're usually right, and they're most often written in somebody else's blood. I had no intention of having them re-written in mine.

Taking off from beneath the bridge at San Pedro was just as new an experience for me as the landing. Ed picked the helicopter up into a hover a foot or two off the pad. He looked at the torque gauge. It measures how much power the engine is delivering to the rotor drive system. The heavier the aircraft is, the more torque is required to fly. When you know what you're looking at you can tell how close your weight and balance calculations are by looking at the torque gauge. Ed stepped on the right rudder pedal and smoothly swung the nose around a one hundred eighty degree arc. We were now pointing right down the San Pedro ship channel toward the open Pacific Ocean. Ed carefully checked the gauges and caution lights. For my benefit he said, "No caution lights are on except 'floats armed.' We have plenty of torque available and we've got the gas to get home." I nodded once in agreement. Then he nudged the cyclic stick forward and we scooted down a concrete boat ramp that led to our helipad, and across the water of the ship channel.

We slipped out of the shadow of the Vincent Thomas and into the afternoon sun. As we picked up speed we flashed past the customers at the restaurant tables alongside the channel. We climbed briskly until we were above the altitude of an approaching auto transport ship. I could see it was coming up the channel to join a number of similarly shaped vessels. Several were tied up to the dock between us and the Long Beach Navy Yard. They looked like modern versions of what Noah's ark must have looked like. They were huge box shaped vessels almost as tall as they were long. From the side of each ship a gangway stretched from the ship to the quayside. Out of one of these ships a line of little, brightly colored cars were lined up and following each other into a vast parking lot. There hundreds of lines of dozens of cars each spread out across the dock.

Ed pointed to the oncoming car carrier. "You have to pay attention to the ships moving up and going down this channel. It would be bad news if you scooted out here just as a ship was passing by. You'd be surprised how fast something as massive as a container ship can move. You might think you had it beat and then 'whamo!' It would be like hitting a mountain. They move a lot of air too, so just getting close to one can make for a wild ride."

We turned toward Catalina and rolled out over the vast import car parking lots. Now I could see them in detail parked one next to the other. They were inches from each other, side by side and nose to tail. Their colors reminded me of a glass bowl full of colorful M&M candies. I wondered how the drivers got in and out of them. It looked like there wasn't space between them to open a door.

Beyond the car transport ships and parking lots was the Long Beach Navy Yard. We flew alongside the jetty protecting it from the open ocean before angling away toward Catalina. The Yard wasn't busy today. Ed saw me looking at the New Jersey.

"It's a big boat isn't it?" Before I responded I thought about his offhand comment. The New Jersey wasn't a boat. In Navy vernacular she was a ship. A battleship: the gallant "Black Dragon," with BB-62 painted on her prow. She was the last of the mighty Iowa class battleships. Maybe Ed knew the phenomenal power of her tremendous main batteries. They fired shells eighteen inches in diameter and probably six feet long. Each weighed at least a ton. I thought about how those tremendous guns had protected Marines ashore from the War in Vietnam back through World War II. Then noticed Ed had called "her" an "it." To Marines and sailors ships were always referred to in the feminine.

Then Ed said something that brought me back to my role as a civilian helicopter pilot.

"I'm glad they parked it there. That's right on the way to Queensway. It has a great big helicopter landing pad on the back. If this engine quits when I'm anywhere near it, that would be a good place to go. If I screw it up the sailors are probably pretty good fire fighters."

I nodded and directed my attention back toward Catalina.

"Yes Ed, sailors are good fire fighters." I was still thinking like a Marine. Ed was thinking like a good helicopter pilot. He was planning what to do in the event something went wrong anywhere along the route. I had been sight-seeing, lapsing into days forever past. I realized I had to start thinking like Ed. Let the passengers enjoy the view. With that unintended lesson from Ed, I really focused to get my head in this game.

As we crossed the Catalina Channel Ed caught me looking down at the floats mounted on the skids. I looked at the arming switch on the instrument panel. "I'd hate to have to land on these floats," he said. "But I'm glad we have 'em." He pointed to a trigger under the collective. It was mounted near the throttle where I usually rested my hand while flying. "I don't want to hit the float trigger by accident," he said. "Flying with floats takes a little more attention than flying without them." Then he taught me the techniques I needed to know to use them should I need them.

"Once the throttle is open, double check that it is fully open. Then arm the floats." He had already moved the float arming switch to "ON" before we took off from San Pedro. "Check the light when you arm the floats." He pointed to a one inch square lighted button next to the arming switch. Inside the square were the words "Floats Armed." It was not illuminated but I could tell the words were yellow. "Whenever that light is on, always put your hand here on the end of the collective." I noticed that position kept his hand far away from the float actuation switch.

He smiled. "If you lose the engine, lower the collective and arm the floats. If you have to land on the water those floats will be a welcome sight. Don't touch the trigger until you are flaring to land. If they go off early you'll stop flying right there. When you pull the trigger the floats go off with a bang. They're fully inflated in about two seconds. A pilot from the competing service had to land here in the channel using them once." Ed pointed vaguely in the direction of the channel passing five hundred feet below. "They worked fine. A boat was nearby. Everybody stepped out of the helicopter and into the boat and nobody even got their feet wet."

"What happened to the helicopter?" I asked.

"It floated for a while. When they tried towing it to shore with a boat it flipped over. The float bags eventually broke and it sank like a stone. After that they couldn't have gotten it back if they had wanted to. The water's at least a mile deep from here to Catalina.'

It gave me the shivers at first to think about how deep the water was below us. Then I recalled my experience flying over the ocean in the Marine Corps. I was reminded that if the water was deep enough to cover your head it didn't really make any difference how deep the water got after that.

I looked out at the island. Leaving San Pedro it had been an indistinct lump in the distance. Now I was able to see the white line of waves breaking along the rocky cliffs. Trees on the island looked like indistinct splashes of green. Ten minutes later everything about the island stood out in stark detail. Passing the town of Avalon on the south end of the island we slowed. Ed lined up to land on the sea plane ramp south of town. He slid into a high hover moving across the parking ramp, simultaneously kicking the pedals to drive the tail around opposite the direction of our approach. He set the aircraft down like a feather, rolled the throttle down and punched the clock.

"Welcome to Avalon," said Ed.

Once I had done it a while, the job was indeed easy. Four early mornings a week I drove to Long Beach airport. I would preflight the helicopter and takeoff for Queensway. Then I spent the rest of the day flying the triangular route from Queensway to Catalina to San Pedro. If there weren't enough people to justify a flight, I'd just hang around whichever pad I was on and wait. I didn't even have to make the decision to launch. Somebody at Queensway did that. Usually it was one of the redheads or whoever else was working the passenger desk that day.

Cooling my heels left me time to walk around each base. When I had to wait around at Catalina after the first flight of the morning, I often had Huevos Rancheros at the Buffalo Nickel Restaurant. It was next to the passenger terminal at the seaplane ramp at Avalon. The island had a herd of buffalo that had been breeding there since they were left by a Hollywood film crew back in the thirties. Ground-up hunks of them were for sale in the form of buffalo burgers at the Nickel, thus the name of the restaurant. For breakfast it was always eggs over easy, tortillas and refried beans for me: Huevos Rancheros.

After breakfast I took the short walk down the road that ran along the base of a cliff from the seaplane ramp to the shops in Avalon. I really liked hanging around the town. It is built around a small but deep, semi-circular harbor. The buildings are tiny and close together to take advantage of the limited real estate. The town looked like a movie set or a street in downtown Disneyland, too small and charming to be real. There were always foreigners and people from outside California wandering in and out of the shops. There were also lots of Angelinos and Southern Californians as. I guess it made people coming over from Southern California feel at home since they had all probably been on a movie studio tour or to Disneyland several times at least.

I soon got to know most of the locals who worked in the shops and cafes. A mellower lot I never met. I really liked to walk out on the dock at the harbor, too. The water was crystal clear. I could see how the island sloped down steeply into the depths beyond. Around the pilings there were always lots of colorful fish, some of them quite large. I enjoyed my stays on Catalina, but I never got too distracted to do a flight. If I had passengers, the agent at the seaplane ramp would call my pager. Sometimes it didn't go off for hours, though. I had lots of time to meet people, watch the fish and enjoy the town. I also learned how to relax and enjoy life day by day. I will always be thankful to Catalina for teaching me to do that.

The ramp and passenger terminal at San Pedro was a neat place to hang out as well. I never wandered through the town because I rarely stayed at San Pedro for long. Just the same, it was fascinating just standing under the Vincent Thomas Bridge on the edge of the helicopter parking ramp. I was always captivated watching the big cargo ships lumber past so close I could almost touch them. Few of the vessels that passed were shaped like the classic ocean-going freighter. Instead, most looked like immense floating boxes, or tubs full of semi-rig trailers: container ships. The crews working on them passed close enough to the helipad for me to see the expressions on their faces. Although I couldn't make out the conversations, I could often hear them talking to one another, often in languages other than English.

It was also novel for me to look up and watch cars rolling across the suspension bridge above my head. Bicyclists and pedestrians crossed the bridge as well. While doing so, a number of them were clearly surprised to look down and discover a helicopter parked below them. They pointed at the helicopter and talked excitedly when they saw it. If they were walking toward the San Pedro end, some of them came down to take a closer look. I happily provided them a tour of the aircraft. I saw a number of them buy tickets either right after the tour or later when they had more time. I saw with my own eyes how being nice to people was good for business. In retrospect, in looking up at that bridge I should have been thinking more like a helicopter pilot than a marketing director. I soon found out that there were more hazards in landing under a bridge than I had supposed.

The incident that finally turned the light on for me happened shortly after I started the aircraft to carry a load of passengers bound for Catalina. I rolled the throttle up, came to a hover and swung the nose around to point it toward the channel. Just before takeoff I checked the gauges when suddenly a terrifying roar grabbed my attention and froze my hands on the flight controls. It was a petrifying sound. My mind raced as my eyes flashed over the instrument panel. The gauges were perfectly normal. I turned my head to check the sound's origin. It was definitely coming from the main rotor.

In my mind I immediately pictured a blade delaminating, its aluminum skin peeling away from the structural spar that gave it strength. If that was what was happening it meant the blade was about to come off. A friend of mine quite miraculously lived through such an event. He was just starting the helicopter and was still on the ground when it happened. He said there was a tremendous roar accompanied by vibration so severe that it pulled the controls from his hands. When it was over he was lying outside of a totally wrecked helicopter, still strapped into his seat.

Thinking about my friend's accident, I figured I would be lucky if I got the helicopter back on the ground intact. The roaring sound from the main rotor of Two Four X-ray was unabated, continuous and terrifyingly loud. Surprisingly though, I still had control of the aircraft. The cyclic moved smoothly as though nothing at all was wrong. I lowered the collective gently. The roar didn't increase or decrease. There was no vibration in the controls or the airframe. The helicopter just settled softly on the pad as if nothing was wrong at all. I was still ready for the blades to depart the rotorhead, however. If that happened and the helicopter didn't just explode it would most certainly be shaken to pieces. So I snapped the throttle right through the idle stop to the closed position. There would be no two minute engine cool down this time. I wished I had a rotor brake. I didn't have one on this helicopter. That meant my terrified passengers and I had to sit there while the rotor coasted to a halt. The roar diminished somewhat as the rotors slowed. I looked up to see what was causing the noise but the blades were still a blur. I looked over my shoulder at the passengers. They were all white with fear. Their eyelids were fully opened, eyeballs distended toward me.

Since they were all wearing headsets I clicked the intercom switch on the cyclic stick I held and said, "I think we're okay. Just sit tight with me and we'll let the rotor blades coast to a stop." It was a smart move on my part. I think a couple of the people were about ready to bail out and run for the terminal. Running in a panic from an operating helicopter is a good way to leave shorter than you arrived. We were probably safer inside anyway if things did start flying off. Even at low RPM, blade chunks carry a real punch and fly quite a distance.

As the rotor slowed, the roar began to diminish. Now when I looked up I began to see something formless and black flash by just over my head. The roar increased and decreased as the object passed by the cockpit. When the rotor had all but stopped I began to see that the object appeared to be glued to one of the rotor blades close in to the rotor mast. I suddenly recognized it. It was a giant, black plastic garbage bag! Someone had probably dropped it from the bridge. It had landed squarely in the middle of my rotor system. I could not see how that could have happened unless something had been in the bag to cause it to plummet straight down. Even so, hitting my turning rotor from two hundred feet up or so was a pretty slim possibility. But that has to be what happened. I wondered what was in the bag, and what damage it must have done when the blade struck it.

"That was scary folks," I said unnecessarily emphasizing the obvious. "I'm sorry. It looks like we hit a trash bag. It sure makes a lot of noise doesn't it?" They all readily concurred and when I laughed, they did too. I tried not to let on that it had scared me as badly as it scared them.

Scared or not though I did what any pilot should do when something goes wrong. I kept flying the aircraft. I think the passengers were happy that I did. They were relieved when I said it was okay for them to think it was a scary event. I finally climbed out of the cockpit and opened the passenger door on my side of the helicopter. The company agent came out and led the passengers back to the terminal. I got a ladder and climbed up the side of the helicopter. As I climbed I took my time. I did an especially careful examination of each main and tail rotor blade before I determined that the bag must have been empty. I didn't see any damage at all. The bag may have come off the bridge, but it wasn't aimed at me. I thought of it as a stray bullet. They don't have to be aimed at you to kill you. Aimed or not though, I had apparently dodged this one.

When I was done with my inspection I waved for the passenger agent to bring the customers back out. I was moderately surprised when they all came back again. I think it was my attitude and apparent calm that gave them the confidence to climb back aboard with me. As they came out I doffed my ball cap and bowed, one hand sweeping toward the passenger door.

"Ladies and gentlemen, welcome. 'Anybody here want to go to Catalina?" One, then another, then all of them raised their hands. They smiled and climbed in, perhaps a little sheepishly. By the time I started the helicopter again they were ready for the ride. As I lifted the aircraft into a hover I keyed the microphone to talk to the passengers. "No more adventures today folks, okay?" They all laughed and began to enjoy themselves. I was back doing what I was paid to do, be nice and drive safely. As the San Pedro breakwater slipped past us I turned and gave them a thumbs up, which they all returned with a smile.

From then on, whenever I landed or took off at San Pedro I looked up through the rotors to see if anybody was up on the bridge. While the rotors were turning and often when they weren't, I watched for anything someone might pitch out of a passing car. I saw plenty of projectiles hit the water in the ship channel. Most of them were probably bottles and cans. None of them belonged in my rotor system. A full one zipping through the rotors and the window above me could take my head off. I don't know why I hadn't thought of worrying about dropped objects before. I too had often been tempted to throw stuff out of the car while driving over long spans of water. Certainly other people would have the same temptation. There would be no malice in it. But the next time I encountered something off that bridge it might be the stray bullet that found its mark. Another note to self: Watch for dropped objects when you're flying below where people are. It was one of many lessons I learned flying to the island.

I was beginning to think like a civilian helicopter pilot. The lessons I had learned about flying helicopters in the Marines formed a strong foundation for the ones I was adding every day I flew to Catalina. I had often practiced techniques in high powered military machines that I used every day in earnest in the smaller, and much lower powered civilian helicopter I flew to Catalina. Enjoying the easy life flying back and forth across the Catalina Channel I was completely oblivious to the fact that more pieces were falling into place in my life. This fork in the road I was forced down was being paved with Valuable experience. One would soon lead to another. I didn't know it yet, but they were all leading me in the direction that answered my forgotten prayer.

The first time I landed at Queensway without a flight to do, John came out of his office and said, "A clean helicopter is a happy helicopter." It was the only time he ever had to ask me to wash and clean the helicopter after that. In the bushes next to John's office there was a shed with all the cleaning supplies I'd need. I poured liquid soap in a wheeled mop bucket. I gathered up a roll of water hose and pushed the bucket out to the helicopter with a long handled brush. After filling the bucket with water I got busy with the brush. While I worked I thought about my Marines.

There had always been a full time maintenance crew that took care of the job I was now doing. I had always walked out to the aircraft, flown a trip, returned to base and walked away. What came after that was the job of the maintenance men and the aircrew. That included washing the bird.

As I scrubbed the LongRanger I was in a world of my own. I remembered trying to help the crew clean the aircraft once after a flight. They made it clear that they didn't need officers hanging around helping them do their job. But now I was both the pilot and crew. I understood how those enlisted Marines had felt. I wanted to focus on the care of the machine I flew. I know it was just cleaning and not mechanical maintenance. Now, like my Marines had always done their jobs well taking care of the helicopter, I would do it, too. I didn't notice the sunshine or the cool temperature or even that it was a nice day. Instead I thought about where I had been, and how different it was from where I was now.

I was flying happy citizens, not combat troops. As I washed the helicopter my mind drifted back to other times. Flying straight and level over the ocean to a resort island was enough of a thrill for anyone I carried now. But I still longed for the type of flying that was falling farther behind me into the wake of time. I didn't have to do aerobatics to dodge bullets anymore. I would never again swirl into high G turns to land quickly in little, dusty landing zones. As I hosed soap off the windows of my little air taxi I remembered landing in the desert dirt of Twenty-nine Palms Marine Corps Base near Palm Springs. Our landings were something only we Marines beheld. Huge machines stirred up rolling clouds of talcum fine dust. It would swirl through rotors and roll through the aircraft, a shamal of desert brown. We settled hard into the desert sand as the crew chief lowered the ramp in the back of the helicopter. The dusty light entered first, followed by the shadow figures of the Marines. Behind the dust that swirled into our cockpit came the rank smell of dirty Marine infantrymen. It was an honest smell like a hay barn, or machine oil or an old saddle damp with horse sweat. It was an honest smell only unpleasant to the fully civilized or those who would never be warriors. It would arrive with the infantrymen and linger a while after they departed. These experienced fighters came up the ramp on the run, the muzzles of their rifles pointed rifles down. As the ramp closed we were pulling like rising dragons, rising swiftly out of the dust cloud me made as we took off. Often from behind us came the visceral roar of the men we carried aloft with us.

I laughed as I continued my chore. Now in my little air taxi my passengers strapped in slowly and awkwardly. They moved like confused sheep, herded here and there by our passenger agents. They would laugh, or blanch with concern as they took their seats. Ignorant of concern, in their giddiness they paid no attention to the need for a seatbelt or headset. Again, our passenger agents cared for them like children. Unlike my Marines, these holiday riders smelled of cocoa butter, suntan lotion and perfume. It was not unpleasant. But it was not yet for me.

I slopped suds onto my little brown and white island shuttle. Ringing in my memory was the sound of heavy machine guns as they banged away in the cabin behind me. Spraying tracers and incendiary bullets I could smell the ether from the open ammunition cans. The raw smell of gunpowder burned my nostrils. The concussive thud of each bullet leaving the gun, the clang of its brass case falling on the aluminum floor of the Sea Stallion was music.

When I was done with the soap and water I went back to the shed to find more cleaning agents. Inside the air taxi I wiped down the leather seats. When I was done the aircraft look and smelled like a new limousine. The instrument panel and the arm rests glistened. But in my mind I was with my mates. I was in a uniform at a helicopter squadron, not in blue jeans in the shadow of the Queen Mary. My mind was months and miles away.

Then the sliding door to John's office slid open. I didn't notice his approach. It was slow and quiet. He stopped to appreciate the beauty of the day. Seabirds drifted by. He watched them. A little girl waved at him from the bow of the great luxury liner of a time gone by. He noticed and waved back. After a while he walked toward me again and stopped a few paces behind me. I caught his movement out of the corner of my eye. Leaving my reverie I glanced back at him. He was facing me, but was still looking up at the ship. I glanced up too, either not seeing or ignoring the little girl John was watching. He said nothing. So I turned back to the cleaning supplies at my feet. John walked up beside me and bent to pick up the roll of hose. His shadow fell across me. I stood and turned. His tossed the hose away toward the shed and stepped up close to me. He looked up at me through his dark sunglasses. His mustache twitch.

"Look here, Paul" he said. He brought up a hand and pointed at his mirrored sunglasses. "Look right here."

I was a head taller than he, so I had to look down. He was suddenly uncomfortably close, well inside my space.

"Right here. Look right here." He emphasized by pointing his index finger from my sunglasses to his. I could see myself reflected in the blue funhouse mirrors of his civilian style wrap-around shades. He slowly reached up with both hands and took off my sunglasses. I drew back a bit and squinted as the glasses came off of my face. Since I got to pilot training as a second lieutenant I had always wore sunglasses on bright sunny days. I liked the military aviator style glasses like the ones John was now holding. The sun was very bright. But I managed to hold my focus on him. I couldn't see any detail in his eyes, but I could somehow tell that they were focused on mine.

"Hmmmm," he mumbled. A moment later he moved with a start, as though he had found what he was looking for. He stepped back a pace, reached down with his left hand and folded my glasses into his right. "Stay right here," he said. I started to ask why but he put a finger to his lips. "Stay right here, Paul" he repeated.

Then John turned and walked past the helicopter, off the pad and out into the grass between the helipad and the Queen. He stopped. And like a professional baseball player drew his arm back. I knew exactly what he was going to do but I couldn't even shout, let alone stop him. In what seemed slow motion he pitched hard and threw my sunglasses out into the harbor. I watched incredulous as they floated over the water, spinning and flashing in the bright sun. Then they splashed into the flat calm water in the shadow of the Queen Mary.

I stood frozen, disbelieving what I had just seen. I regained my voice as John turned back toward me. "What did you just do?" I shouted at him. He walked calmly back toward me. "John, those were my best pair of sunglasses! What am I going to wear now?" He stepped up close in front of me again.

"I liked those glasses, man! What did you do that for?"

John just stood before me. He folded his hands behind his back and waited. Deeply distressed I looked past him at the dissipating ripples in the harbor. I wondered if the glasses were too far out or the water too deep to retrieve them. For some reason I felt as though something had been torn out of me. I wanted to punch John very hard in his face, and he knew it. But he kept his hands behind him, not concerned at the damage I could do him.

It shouldn't have been such a traumatic event. John knew it would be. That was why he did it. Somehow he knew what I had been thinking as I washed the helicopter, deep in thoughts of a life impossibly long gone for me now. As I clasped my fists he reached out with both hands and put them on my shoulders. He gave me a shake. Then he pointed again to his eyes.

"Look here, Paul" he said. He took his hands off me and pointed with both hands to his own sunglasses. I focused on them, could see them through his own dark shades now that mine were lying in the harbor. I could still not see his eyes in detail but rather as dark orbs behind the blue glass. His eyes were again searching my own. Then he reached up with both hands and took off his sunglasses. I saw his eyes clearly now. He now squinted. His naked eyes were looking straight into mine. It occurred to me that it was the first time I had seen John without his shades on. It was the first time I had actually seen his eyes.

I thought it strange, like seeing my grandfather for the first time without his glasses on. His eyes were a deeper brown than his deeply browned skin. It may have been the sharp lines at their corners that made his eyes look tired. But in them there was a gentleness. I sensed a quiet and unspoken compassion there. He seemed to know that my heart was hurting. I sensed that he probably understood its reason better than I. His eyes scanned mine for a moment. As they did so, I no longer felt uncomfortable. Instead, I began to feel the onset of a certain peace I had not felt since I left the Marines. I felt his empathy. I felt as though he knew something about me from firsthand experience that I knew neither about him or myself. I felt as though we were both warriors who had fought and bled together. We had a bond I didn't yet understand. He knew what it was.

He drew back a little, stood a little straighter. And then he gave me his glasses. I looked at him and then down at the glasses.

"There," he said. "That's better."

I took a deep breath. His mustache rose up a little and his white eyebrows fell a bit.

"Wear them," he said. He reached down and took the glasses. He opened them and fit his own sunglasses on my face. The world turned a lovely shade of blue. I looked above his head at the harbor. He squinted hard against the sun as he evaluated my reaction.

For me it was a new world. It was as though I had been blind but suddenly could see. I looked up at the sky and around the horizon. It was beautiful. It was the same world, the same surroundings I had seen through my military glasses. It was the same day I hadn't even noticed when I stepped out into it to wash the helicopter. Now it seemed different. Better. The world was no longer greys and browns but a more natural blue. The sky was clearer. I could see things I had missed before. The sun no longer glared off the buildings across the harbor. The passing boats stood out in their detail. Light ceased to reflect from the surface of the harbor. It appeared instead in its depth. For the first time I could see past the shining surface of the harbor. I had never noticed before that surrounding the helipad, not far beneath the water were big rocks. I was sure that if I looked closely I could see the fishes swimming among them. Perhaps I might even see the glint of my own sunglasses in the distance.

I turned in the direction John had gone when he threw them in the harbor. I walked away from him and headed for the edge of the water where he had just stood. From behind me I could hear him say, "I know what you're thinking, Paul."

I kept walking until I stood in the grass near the water's edge. "They're gone, Paul. Let them go. They weren't doing you any good anymore." I looked at the place where they had landed. It was dark there, and deep. There was nothing there to see. I raised my eyes and over the harbor, out beyond the harbor to the distant stone jetty.

"Wear those," John said. I turned around and looked at him. He stood bare-faced and squinting. His hands folded back behind him. I walked over and stood again before him.

"You're not in the Marines anymore, Paul." He pointed at me with his chin. "Wear those. You'll see things differently. They're better for the flying you do now, anyway. You'll see things that are farther away. You'll see a lot of things you'd have missed looking through those military glasses."

He took a step closer to me and stopped. He started looking me over with the skill of a drill sergeant. His eyes moved slowly over me. He started at my head and stopped at my feet. His eyes slewed back and forth across me. Then he looked back up at my face. He reached out with one hand and took hold of my collar. He shook me back and forth a little.

"I don't like collars. Our passengers don't like collars. Tomorrow, and from here on out I want you to lose the collars. Wear a t-shirt. No logos, no smartass sayings on them. Just a colored t shirt." He released my collar and dropped his hands. Then he raised one back up and pointed his index finger at my nose. "No collar. 'Got it?"

I nodded. "Got it. No collar. Wear a t- shirt."

He nodded back. His index finger stayed extended, like he was holding a pistol he was about to use. He stared at my blue jeans. He pointed his pistol barrel finger at them. "Blue jeans. Lose them. Wear shorts. It's not cold." Then he stepped back a pace or two. "Bermuda shorts." He pointed to his own. "Like mine. They sell them all over. Get some tonight." My shoes displeased him as well. "Those are military shoes. You ran in those when you were an officer candidate, didn't you?"

I blushed. How did he know? I didn't say anything.

"Deck shoes; do you know what they are?" I nodded in the affirmative.

"Have you ever worn them?"

Somehow he knew I hadn't worn deck shoes, either. It was a rhetorical question for him. He knew somehow that no self-respecting Marine of my day would wear deck shoes. Only Californians and the effeminate would do that, and I didn't fit either description. Besides, I'd be laughed out of the squadron.

"No, of course you haven't worn deck shoes. Buy some. Canvas or leather will be fine. Don't wear those tennis shoes. And never come here wearing boots, either. Not ever." Then he added as though having forgotten to say, "...and don't wear socks."

He squinted at the sun and then at me as he examined my head. "You look like a storm trooper." He leaned this way and that to see just how short my hair was cut on the sides. "Short hair makes me nervous. Slack off. Grow your hair out."

He nodded at me. "Okay. That does it. Did you get all that?"

I nodded back. "Got it," I said.

"Okay." He turned slowly back toward the trailer. Halfway there he stopped and looked up at the Queen Mary. The little girl was gone. A sea bird floated overhead. I watched him watch it as it wheeled and flew back toward the harbor. He saw me looking at him.

He looked over his shoulder at me. "This isn't the Marines, Paul. This is real life." He turned his head back, put his hands in his pockets and slowly walked into his office. With my new sunglasses I could see through the reflective material on his office door now. I saw him sit down at his desk, his back to me. He put his hands behind his head and leaned back in his wooden desk chair.

Turning back to my task I pushed the bucket with the brush back toward the shed. As I finished the job I had started, I stopped now and again. I looked up at the Queen. For the first time I noticed people touring the decks. Nobody looked back at me. I wondered how it looked back in her early days when people moved across her decks on trips between continents. All the generations of people she had seen, all the voyages she had made and now here she was. Surrounded by boulders that served as a breakwater I wondered if she felt like she was in prison. She was still grand. The people who visited her, who stayed the night or celebrated their weddings on her still recognized how special she was. People were not crossing the Atlantic onboard her. But they were still boarding her, still living a part of their life within her. They were still climbing her stairwells, sleeping in her cabins, still flowing through her like life's blood. So I came to believe that in this change of her life she was still important. She was still meaningful and vital and alive.

It struck me that she and I were in some ways alike. Leaving the Marines left a void within me. I was mourning as though someone I loved had died, or that a lover had divorced her heart away from me. Today though, I could see through my blue sunglasses that the healing was beginning. The void was ever so slowly filling in.

I went back to my task. When I had finished and put away the cleaning tools and potions there were still no passengers to carry. So Instead of sitting in the office and drinking coffee, I stayed out on the edge of the helipad admiring the sailboats that drifted slowly past. *They choose a destination and they set a course,* I thought. *The people onboard are really just there to enjoy the ride. They trust the captain to get them where they are going. They don't get involved in how that's done. They just enjoy the ride.*

Behind me the redhead slid the door open and called my name. I turned to see what she wanted. She whirled her finger in the air. She smiled brightly as always. "Four for Avalon, Paul. Enjoy the ride!"

And I did.

With summer approaching the weather got hot. The sky was clear and blue. Not a breath of air moved, not at Queensway or probably anywhere else in Southern California. Catherine had sent me out with a light load in the morning. The takeoff had taken all the power the engine could generate. The climb to altitude proved that any takeoff after this one would take some skill to accomplish if there was any load onboard at all. Add a few more degrees of temperature and a couple hundred extra pounds and a taking off from the Queensway pad would be a real challenge.

I flew back toward Long Beach into the rising sun rose though. With each minute it climbed so did the temperature. Along with the heat arrived a particularly heavy load of passengers arrived at Queensway happily planning for a day on Catalina. As I turned to make my final approach to Queensway, Catherine called on the radio.

"We have a full load for you, Paul." That was not what I needed to hear. After landing I shut down and walked inside to see what I had to carry. I fretted a little when I saw one guy probably six inches taller than me step on the scale. The digital readout flashed through three hundred pounds as he stepped on, but settled down to a number starting with a two. Nobody else in the group was suffering from anorexia either, apparently. Hauling this group was going to take some savvy.

Catherine totaled up the weight column on her little clip board and figured out the center of gravity calculation for me. Then she handed me the clipboard and looked at me. The look said, "Can you do this?" She pointed to the bottom of the weight column. I knew the charts in the book said I could do it. But not the one that said I could hover with a heavy load on that hot a day. Catherine didn't need to know how the watch was built. She just needed the time.

"Yup," I said. "I can do it." Without saying, "You're the pilot," she shrugged.

So here's how the watch was working for me today with Bell's LongRanger helicopter. Normally when a helicopter takes off, the only lift it has is produced by its rotor blades. Its jet engine compresses the air, mixes it with fuel, adds a spark and the resulting sustained explosion produces the energy that turns the rotor system. Both the rotor blades and engine turbine compressor blades generate more power when the air is cool. Simply put, the air molecules cluster closer together in the cold. The opposite is true when the air is hot. The air molecules stand farther apart. Consequently fewer of them strike the engine compressor blades or rotor blades. That means the engine makes less power and the rotors make less life.

What that meant for my takeoff with this heavy load on this hot day at Long Beach was that I was going to have to find some more lift somewhere. In order to do that, I would have to perform a maneuver called, "the maximum performance takeoff." As the name implies, taking off would require the maximum performance of the rotor blades, the engine and the pilot. The maneuver is performed by taking advantage of "ground effect."

Ground effect forms when the cushion of air produced by the rotor blades buoys the helicopter off the ground. In the current hot and heavy circumstances I was facing, the rotors weren't going to buoy us up very much. I only expected them to be able to lift us into a hover of perhaps a couple inches of altitude. Not much, but that would be enough to allow me to produce some "translational lift."

Translational lift occurs when the helicopter is going fast enough that the entire rotor disk flies. The blades would fly individually, but the whirling rotor disk would add to the lift by acting as a circular wing. It doesn't take much speed to create translational lift: fifteen or twenty miles an hour will do it. At that point both the blades and the rotor disk too start flying. The pilot can tell when it happens. The controls start to vibrate. The extra lift the rotor disk provides drops the engine torque required to keep the rotors going around. The pilot has a gauge to see when that happens. It is not surprisingly called the "torque gauge." When the needle in the torque gauge drops, the savvy pilot pulls up a little on the collective. The engine is then being asked to produce all the energy the hot air molecules going inside it will allow. Keep doing that until the helicopter is flying and that is how a maximum performance takeoff occurs. Simple.

Done right, the maneuver would make it appear today as though the LongRanger was going to fly very low off the helipad and into the water. Done wrong, that is exactly what would happen. So before I left the air conditioned comfort of the passenger lounge, I explained to the passengers what the properly done takeoff would look like today. I told them not to be alarmed. I told them it would be fun. And we would get to see what the Queen Mary looked like on the harbor side from down below the railings.

John stood in his office door listening while I talked to the passengers. I couldn't see his eyes behind his new blue glasses. His moustache and eyebrows remained unmoving. I could only guess what he was thinking. I turned toward the passengers and pointed to the door. "Let's go to Catalina," I said cheerily.

As soon as the last of the passengers was seated and Catherine had checked their seat belts were fastened, I started the engine. Once the rotors were fully up to speed I checked the instrument panel for the final time. Then I looked out the windscreen. Catherine now stood behind the sliding door to the passenger lounge. She smiled and gave me a thumbs up. John stood behind the sliding door of his office. He watched, passive, his hands behind his back. I pulled up on the collective.

You might think it odd for me to say that I was comfortable with the situation I was in. I really was. I had done maximum performance takeoffs a thousand times. I had done them with students, simulating hot and heavy conditions by limiting the power I allowed them to use. And I had done them "for real," loaded down with Marines and their equipment. Loaded with Marines I took off from dusty desert mountain plateaus. Temperatures there often hovered near a hundred and twenty degrees. These max performance takeoffs were the real deal. Do it right, the helicopter flies. Do it wrong, the helicopter settles.

Settling wasn't so bad in a wide open field of grass with a new Navy flight student. There the helicopter would just settle until it bounced a time or two on the grass. Then we would either stop and try again, or skip a couple times and fly away. Settling in a cloud of desert dust was far different. By the time the collective was moved up an inch the windshield might just as well be painted brown. This became an instrument aided maximum performance takeoff. A mistake ever so slight would have resulted in the payment of life insurance policies. Settling there would have had commanders writing letters to bereaved families. But since I was here to do this one I can vouch that all those ones before it came out alright. So would this one.

Obviously, settling off the pad at Queensway was not an option. It would have resulted in me and my passengers going for a swim. So I planned not to settle. One way to settle on takeoff was to pull the collective up and demand too little power approaching translational lift. Then the helicopter would just run out of lift as it left the pad and splash into the water. After that the laws of physics, gravity and buoyancy would take over.

The other way to settle was to pull the collective up too much. Doing that would demand more power than the engine could produce. Once the engine on a helicopter produces all the power it can, demanding more than it can produce causes the rotors to slow down. We call that "rotor droop." I thought it was a good term because when the rotor droops, so does the helicopter. Drooping causes settling. At Queensway settling causes swimming.

The students I flew with were constantly getting themselves into situations where they started to settle. My job as an instructor was to let them get far enough into it to see that it was bad. Then I had to show them how to gingerly use the flight controls to adjust power and the nose attitude to get the helicopter to fly. I helped them turn many a settling situation into a smooth takeoff. I had a perfect right to believe that on this day at Queensway I could do the same thing.

As I expected, it took all the engine power to hover. The torque needle read one hundred percent when the skids came off the ground. Two inches of altitude later the LongRanger stopped climbing. That's all the altitude I was going to get. I moved the cyclic stick ever so slightly to the right, simultaneously slightly depressing the left pedal. The helicopter slid past John's office and the nose swung to the left until it pointed just left of the Queen Mary. I stopped the helicopter over the grass on the farthest edge of the helipad from the ship. I could see John leaning against the window to watch me.

I looked at the flag laying limp against the bowsprit of the Queen. The water along her harbor side looked like a mirror. In fact the water of Long Beach harbor was glassy smooth clear out to the jetty. There would be no help from the wind. I checked the gauges. The torque needle bounced around the hundred percent mark. I pushed forward on the cyclic almost imperceptibly. The helicopter started to move slowly toward the Queen. It moved at the speed of a cow grazing as it came off the grass and onto the concrete pad. Passing John's door we were up to a stroll. The helicopter settled perhaps half an inch or so. The torque needle flickered down.

I moved the collective up to demand the last erg of torque from the engine. The settling stopped and speed began to pick up quickly. As it did, I began to feel the aircraft vibrate ever so slightly. The leading edge of the rotor system was gaining translational lift. I pushed further forward on the cyclic, still demanding maximum engine power with the collective. The aircraft accelerated even more, but it didn't settle. The speed continued to increase. The edge of the pad was coming up fast now. The rotor vibration increased, meaning that the rotor was gaining more translational lift. There was still not enough lift yet to fly away. I was not concerned, even the grass on the Queen's side of the pad raced under the skids.

Just as suddenly the rocks around the pad disappeared behind us. That's when we began to settle. I expected that. I pushed farther forward on the cyclic. The helicopter followed the downward slope of the heli-pad, down toward the water. As the helicopter dropped it gained speed quickly. Translational lift increased until the controls ceased to vibrate. The torque needle dropped. Now I had spare power. I pulled up on the collective to demand all the power I now had. With the cyclic I directed the extra power downward and behind us.

Behind us was terra firma. We now skimmed across the water like a seabird. We were perhaps two feet above the harbor and still picking up speed. The passengers were shouting and screaming and laughing. I heard no panic. We still weren't climbing but we sure weren't settling. So far as the helicopter was concerned, the smooth water was as effective at helping provide lift as the boost I had been getting hovering over the concrete pad. Concrete or water makes no difference to the helicopter so far as ground effect is concerned.

From Catherine and John's perspective they could see our rotor downwash leaving contrails across the surface of the harbor. By the time we disappeared behind the Queen, John knew we were going to make it to Catalina.

Inside the helicopter the passengers were still hooting and laughing. They were enjoying the thrill of scooting across the water so low and fast. I know that I enjoyed it just enough to stay low an extra moment or two, holding off on climbing a bit longer than I needed to. Finally, as the Queen Mary passed along our right side I pulled the cyclic back. The nose rose slightly and the helicopter began a steady climb. As we climbed past the altitude of the Queen's smoke stacks I rolled into a gentle turn toward Avalon.

John was a fine pilot. He knew exactly what I was planning to do when I scooted the helicopter over to the far edge of the pad. John knew, and Catherine probably suspected that there was going to be no room for errors on that takeoff. In John's shoes I probably would have demanded the pilot offload a passenger or two. That he didn't do that expressed better than words that he had a great deal of confidence not only in my skills, but in my judgment. That doesn't mean it was easy for him to watch. I am certain it was not.

As the helicopter moved toward the Queen Mary at the bovine-like start of the takeoff run, he began to mumble to himself. "Go boy..." The helicopter built speed as it edged near the end of the pad and he mumbled louder. "Go boy!" Then the helicopter disappeared over the edge of the pad. He clenched his fists and shook one in my direction, sucking air through his teeth. His expert eye knew we weren't settling for a wet crash landing. He knew I was seeking the ground effect of the surface of Long Beach harbor. When we disappeared behind the Queen leaving twin trails of disturbed water from the rotor thrust, he threw his fist over his head and said it again: "GO boy!"

He shouted again so people outside the trailer could have heard. "GO BOY! Yes, Yes! Yeeeeeeeessssss!" He danced a little jig out of his office and into the passenger lounge. Catherine joined him and clapped her hands together.

"Did you see that?" he asked her. "Now *that* madam, was one fine max performance takeoff! Damn, that was fine!"

As John danced smiling toward the back door, in her enthusiasm Catherine ran over to the passenger desk and picked up the radio microphone. She always called me when she thought I was past the jetty. This time when she pushed the transmit button she said, "John said for me to tell you that was one fine takeoff!"

I heard her. I was in no hurry to reply. I knew John would *never* want her to tell me that. I also noted that in her excitement she had held the transmit button down on the microphone for a few seconds. In the background I heard John say, "Doooooon't tell him that!" Then the mike clicked off.

After that it was probably a one way conversation aimed at poor Catherine to discourage her from complimenting the pilots. I knew that, so I didn't reply to her radio call. Perhaps John would think I hadn't heard her…or him. Perhaps he wouldn't give Catherine as bad a chewing out for letting on that he liked what he saw. So I just shut up. I got no follow up call from Catherine, either. I was halfway across the channel before I dared to call Queensway again. Even then, it was just a standard and brief, "Two Four X-ray is mid-channel."

John must have left the building, or at least the room because Catherine replied.

"Hey, I just wanted to let you know I've never seen John so excited. He was dancing around in here like a cheerleader. I *really* think he was impressed by that takeoff. I know *I* was."

I didn't say anything. I just clicked the mike switch twice. That signal means, "received and understood." I smiled all the way to the island.

As I came to know John better I also came to know his wife and kids. They all lived out on the island so they often rode back and forth with me on the helicopter. John's wife was a sweet lady. She was a slender, tanned California girl with a wide, toothy smile and shoulder length, sun bleached blonde hair. Like her husband she looked like she spent a lot of time outdoors. She was much more open and approachable than her husband. She liked chatting with me as she sat up front on the flights from Catalina to Long Beach. She said that before he started working for the helicopter service in Long Beach, John had worked in Alaska. He was flying a helicopter supporting the National Park Service up there. He met a pretty blonde park ranger and married her. She of course, had been that park ranger. After they married they lived in Alaska where she became a mom. Then John got a job working for the helicopter service in Long Beach. When he started managing the Catalina Island shuttle operation John and his family moved to the island. They really fit the life style of Catalina. Imagine "laid back." That's Southern California. Add valium. That's Catalina.

Part of my job included taking the boss to work. When I carried the first load of paying passengers to Catalina each morning, John was often passenger number one for the return flight. He'd always sit up front with me. He was usually pretty quiet during the ride. The channel was often dead calm in the morning. Sometimes it was gray and misty and the visibility was not good enough to see more than a few miles ahead. Other mornings however, the air was clear as crystal. On days like that, the glassy water of the Catalina Channel mirrored the snow-capped mountains and the sun rising behind them east of the LA basin. When that happened, the flight from Avalon to the beach was stunningly beautiful. Poetry and song came easy to my soul.

One early morning there were layers of high clouds above the mountains. The sun rising behind them turned each layer a different color of orange, yellow and purple. Each color was doubled by its mirror image on the channel. It was breathtaking. John sat next to me, his hands crossed in his lap. I thought that like me he was enjoying the splendor of the sunrise. He didn't say anything. I understood how he might be speechless – if it was someone other than John. What I didn't notice was the channel boat headed toward us at an oblique angle. He wordlessly pointed it out by nodding in its direction. This one was cutting a long "V" across the glassy surface. All day long the channel boats plowed back and forth between harbors along the coast of Southern California and both ends of Catalina. They were filled with tourists and mail and supplies for the people who lived on the island. If you don't go to Catalina by helicopter, you go by channel boat. This one was long and low slung with a line of portholes down the side. I thought it added a certain beauty and charm to the overall image God displayed for John and me.

John had been quiet the whole flight, which was usually the way he liked it. If he didn't want to talk, well that was just okay by me. As we closed the distance to the channel boat though he stirred a little bit. I dared a glance his direction. He had a half grin on his face, a gleam in his eye. I saw his right foot move slowly toward the intercom switch on the floor. I half expected him to quote the poem, "High Flight." "Oh I have slipped the surly bonds of earth…" But he quoted no poetry. Instead he stepped on the intercom button and said, "There was a day I could have put a rocket through any window on that boat."

I believe that if I had I been asked what John was about to say before he said it, I would n-e-v-e-r have predicted *that*. I turned and looked at him in disbelief. He now displayed a full up smile, the first ever I had seen on his face. It might have been described as "a toothy grin." He turned his head slowly toward me, like an owl. "I may not have told you, I flew two tours in Vietnam supporting the Navy SEALs. I shot thousands of rockets. I really could put one in through a window if I wanted to. I did it plenty of times."

When I regained my composure I just said, "No John, you never told me that." I mentally dipped down into my well of experience to remember my own encounters with the Navy's elite Special Forces, the SEALs. As a Marine who calls all sailors "squids" let me sum up my assessment of the Navy's SEALs for you. The SEALs in my opinion are the toughest soldiers on the planet, bar none. They make the grittiest Marine combat veteran look like a sissy by comparison. That is not something this or any other Marine would say lightly. They're tough, the SEALs. I would not under any circumstance want to tangle with one. I'm glad they're on our side. The pilots who support them may not be able to eat nails and spit bullets like the SEALs can, but they certainly take the SEALs to places I would never want to fly. I came to the immediate realization that my "old hippie" boss was anything but a hippie. He had fought with SEALs for two full years in head-to-head combat in Vietnam.

During my Marine Corps days I flew out a number of times to support operations of one kind or another on San Clemente Island in my venerable CH-53 helicopter. San Clemente is the island just south of Catalina. It and the waters surrounding the island are off limits to all but military personnel. One reason it is off limits is that the south half of the island is a bombing and naval gunfire range. The north end of the island has an airfield on it. The airfield personnel keep a dock with some wooden whaleboats there. They are used to retrieve supplies from ships anchored offshore. They are also there for the pilots. Rather, they are there to retrieve pilots when they eject into the ocean. That has happened on more than a few occasions, too. Jets practice taking off from and landing on carriers at that airfield. It is called "Field Carrier Landing Practice," or "FCLP." If during an FCLP something goes wrong, an engine quits or catches fire or something else cataclysmic happens, pilots sometimes end up in the water. That's when the whale boats go out and get them.

One time I heard that a Phantom jet crew was doing night landings on San Clemente's airstrip when something went terribly wrong. As the aircraft landed and then took off again, both engines suddenly burst into flames. The aircraft looked like a meteor streaking into the night trailing flaming fuel behind it. Shortly after passing the shoreline of San Clemente Island the crew pointed their dying jet out toward the middle of the Pacific Ocean and ejected. They came down in the water no more than a mile offshore. By the time the whaleboats got to them the sharks had gotten there first. Catalina and San Clemente are home to a wide variety of very large sharks. Tigers and Great Whites are among the two less friendly varieties.

I tell you all this because San Clemente is where I saw my first Navy SEALs. I had flown a Naval Gunfire Spotting team out there from Camp Pendleton. They were slated to do a day of work with the gunners on a Navy frigate. They asked me to wait at the airfield until they were ready to go home later that afternoon. So I did a little sightseeing while I was there. A sailor was with me that brisk morning when we walked down to see the whaleboats. We noticed a number of hard-bodied men wearing nothing but tiny Speedo bathing suits lying around on the dock. Oddly I thought, they lay very close to each other. Most had their heads on each other's legs or midsections. As we approached they looked to me like a bunch of hairless harbor seals. Their familiarity with each other however, reminded me of the kind of guys who hung out at bath houses looking for other guys that hung out at bath houses. Their bathing suits were almost too small to qualify as such, little more than jock straps really. The hair on their heads was civilian length. That alone was a flight in the face of most hairless Marines. So too were the faces that also sported moustaches way out of even the Navy's loose regulation for facial hair at the time. Being a Marine I saw them as an undisciplined looking lot. Caring not if they heard my opinion, in a conversational tone I made my observations clear to the enlisted sailor I was with.

He instantly went pale and snapped his head toward me. He looked at me with a look of fear. His eyes flew wide open. "Shut up, sir!" he said.

Now even in the Navy where things are pretty loose, enlisted men are not generally allowed to tell commissioned officers to "shut up." I figured this petty officer had either lost his mind, suffered from Tourette syndrome or he had an iron-clad reason for having me expeditiously shut my mouth. In any case, I waited until we passed the bath house gang before calling him to account.

"Sir, sorry about that but I may have just saved your life! I at least saved you an ass whipping! Those men would just as soon kill you and feed you to the sharks as look at you! It wouldn't matter to them!" He was very excited about what had almost occurred. When I saw him glance fearfully past my shoulder it appeared he was still not quite sure I was out of the woods. I on the other hand, was confident I could handle this crowd if it came to whipping someone's ass. I assumed my best John Wayne stance. "Is that so, sailor? We'll bring them on. Who in the hell are those guys anyway?"

We were well past them on the dock now. The sailor looked nervously over his shoulder at them while shushing me. The men were still lying quietly on the dock, dozing. They didn't seem to pay us any mind although I had the feeling at least a couple of them were casually interested in the substance of our conversation. They may have suspected that the now hushed conversation was probably about them.

"Sir, you don't understand. Those men are SEALs."

I had heard the SEALs were pretty tough, but didn't have any first-hand knowledge regarding how tough. I looked over the excited sailor's shoulder and could see that one or two of the Speedo clad guys were now looking our direction. They had heard their name mentioned. They had also picked up on the sailor's tone of voice, and possibly mine. They were alert now. They were attuned to any threat. SEALs are that way.

The sailor pointed to them while he was looking at me. "Captain, they just got finished swimming around this island!"

Now it was my turn to grow pale. The petty officer saw my eyes widen. Looking at me he could see I was getting the picture. "Yeah," he emphasized. "Now you know what I'm talking about, don't you?" He grinned, shrewdly.

I looked away from the petty officer and noticed thankfully that the SEALs who had seemed interested were getting disinterested again.

"Yes sir," the petty officer continued. "They swam around this island." And then he added with emphasis, "at night." I stopped breathing. "With explosives strapped on their chests," he continued.

I coughed. "Holy crap," I said. "Why?"

He told me about the training exercise they had just completed. They were charged with setting explosives on a guarded beach on the other side of the island. They entered the water there at the whaleboat dock and swam around the island, the long way!

Even in the middle of the summer the water is icy cold, It was winter now. The water was probably a bone-chilling forty five or fifty degrees Fahrenheit. They had been swimming in it all night. I wondered how they stayed alive. Hypothermia was only part of the issue. I had flown around San Clemente Island many times. Like the water around Catalina, it was clear and deep blue, like aquamarine glass. I had often seen exceptionally large sharks hunting along the rocky shore. I pictured them gliding among the floating kelp beds that spread like a carpet on the surface in some places. All along the cliffs I saw the blue waters wash up and explode into plumes of spray.

Looking again at the pile of sparely clad men there on the dock, I quivered. Swimming in the water around San Clemente would have paralyzed me with fear. Then I considered what it would be like to be in those waters at night. I decided to end my whaleboat tour and get myself past the SEALs, back on dry land. Walking back to my helicopter I had to concur with the Petty Officer. Without a doubt, men like that would indeed kill me without a shred of concern. I thanked him for telling me to shut up.

I respected the SEALs after that. I knew that they were as fearless, brave, and possibly as mentally unstable a group of warriors as existed in modern times. They trained, and fought like men who had nothing to lose. Like myself I could not imagine them outside of life as a soldier. All this brings us to John. Visualizing him shooting rockets at the channel boat, John was just doing what a pilot for the SEALs would do. He had not flown in combat for a long time. But quietly resting behind those shades and under that long, white mane was a warrior. On that beautiful morning crossing the Catalina Channel I discovered that I had much to learn about this most interesting aspect of this unusual man. I knew why he had my number, too. He had helped me learn some important things about myself and about this new and unregimented world I had entered.

The freedom I felt in flying by myself was the best part of my job. I felt unfettered in a way I had never felt flying as part of a military flight crew. On one morning in particular, that independence I began to seek might very well have killed me. I took off from Long Beach airport where we parked the helicopter at night. It was a fine, clear Saturday. I could see Catalina Island clearly as soon as I was high enough to see past the buildings that surrounded the airport. I spent a few minutes at Queensway taking on the first load of tourists. Twenty one minutes later I dropped them off at the passenger terminal at Avalon. Nobody was standing there ready to go to the mainland that morning. Everybody wanted to go instead from the mainland to Catalina. So the company called me to fly back empty to San Pedro to pick up another load of customers.

I was flying this morning using the ADF (Automatic Direction Finder). The ADF is a navigation radio. It works by tuning a radio station at a known location and following a directional needle on the compass which points to the radio station. I didn't need a directional needle on a clear day like this. But I did take advantage of the other function of the ADF. It worked well as an AM radio. Los Angeles had the hottest oldies station one could find on the AM dial. This morning as I rocketed toward San Pedro I couldn't have picked a better play list had I been the DJ of the station I was listening to. As I left Avalon my headset was filled with classic rock and roll.

I left the island heading toward the distant Vincent Thomas Bridge. The wind was light and the water calm. Since I was solo I decided to drop down low over the water and enjoy the ride. I ignored an important lesson I had learned long ago. "Altitude is life." It gives a pilot time and options to deal with an emergency, distraction or an unexpected event. Altitude also keeps you clear of obstructions you might hit by flying low. I knew what happened when an unseen wire or tree branch swatted a low flying helicopter out of the air. I had seen first-hand the results of low level runs ending in shards of torn metal, cabin interior, charts and electrical wiring scattered along the ground. I had seen broken rotor blades and dead people as shapeless lumps among torn, burned and twisted aluminum.

This morning I forgot the full margin of safety that altitude allows. I focused only on the hazard to low level flying posed by obstructions. Over open-ocean I convinced myself, obstructions were not an issue. I had no passengers onboard to terrify with a low level run to San Pedro. I forgot the part about altitude leaving a margin for errors in judgment or unexpected events. So I was confident that under the circumstances it would be safe to fly as low and as fast as I wished. Doing that would be a rare treat.

So I took off from Catalina with a song in my heart and rock and roll in my headset. Once I cleared the boat traffic around Catalina, I dropped down in altitude. I dropped down a lot. I was careful to descend slowly. I took it especially easy at the bottom until finally I was flying fast and stable above the glassy surface of the Catalina Channel. I kept my eyes outside, never referencing the flight instruments. From experience I knew that I was only ten or twenty feet above the lapis colored water.

Flying like that I was no more than two seconds away from flying into the water. One slight mistake would kill me before I could comprehend the event. I didn't couch it that way in my mind any more than a speeding driver sees himself dead in a wrecked car he's driving. Going fast in almost any vehicle is an adrenalin addict's dream. Cruising that low at a hundred and twenty miles an hour makes the world seem like a blur. I focused all my attention into staying exactly on altitude. I had convinced myself that there would be no obstructions on the flat water. I never conceived that streaking along on a course perpendicular to mine was a whale. Beneath the channel he was probably doing the whale version of what I was doing in the helicopter. Then, right about mid-channel he decided to increase altitude or from his perspective rapidly decrease his depth. By the time he reached the surface he was already climbing much faster than I could.

From my perspective he appeared without a ripple of warning. The whale blasted out of the ocean right in front of me. The instant I saw him I knew what he was. I also knew he was too close to dodge. In the span of a single human heartbeat he appeared. In the second he was filling the space in front of me. He was as wide and as long as a submarine launched Polaris missile. In fact, that is exactly what he looked like coming up out of the ocean. As he continued to rise my blood ran cold. My perception of time slowed to a crawl. As my helicopter closed the already narrow gap between us I could see that I was about to hit a California gray whale. It seemed to slowly fill my windscreen. Its size utterly dwarfed my little mosquito of a helicopter. In a third heartbeat my field of vision was filled with a gray wall. Seawater wicked off of it. It was covered with dark gray and white barnacles. It rose up so fast that I knew that I could not climb over it. I was overcome with a sense of calm knowing that despite my best efforts this was where I would die.

An attempt at a hard climb from this meager altitude would put the tail rotor in the ocean. The tail rotor would then be torn from the tail boom. The aircraft might have time to spin quickly to the right before slamming into the whale with the helicopter's broad side. Too hard a turn would be just as bad. The main rotors blades would strike the ocean. This would tear the transmission from its mounts and break the helicopter up into smaller chunks. These would hit the whale like a giant shotgun blast. So in the last split second I had before I died I decided to try both deadly maneuvers simultaneously. I executed a steep climbing, fast rolling turn.

I pulled briskly back on the cyclic. At the same time I pushed it smoothly but hard to the right. That rolled and climbed the helicopter. I added right pedal to make the turn as vigorous, balanced and as smooth as I could. Had I looked to the right at that moment instead of fixating on the whale, I probably would have seen the rotor tips kick up spray. Instead I watched the whale move through space. I could almost feel the animal before me.

I judged our mutual climb rates, our mutual turns. He had apparently turned a fluke to begin a gentle roll to land on his back. As he continued toward the apex of his broach, his belly and that of the helicopter must have gone parallel. The bottoms of the skids of the helicopter must surely have passed within inches of the belly of that flying animal. I held my breath ready to be smashed to smithereens. Even if he fell away from me, the slap of a barnacled fin could still send me and my helicopter out of control into the channel.

Both of us continued to pitch up and roll over now on slightly opposing courses. My body temperature went from icy to hot. As I waited to see if I would die I realized that I could do no more. I held the controls where they were. Whatever was destined to happen would happen. Meanwhile I watched as more sky and less whale began to fill the windscreen. As the helicopter pitched nearest the vertical I began to think I might yet survive. Then Catalina began to appear again to my right side. The island represented a reverse of course away from my doom. It represented a reprieve. I was still not dead. I supposed that meant that the whale was falling away from me now. The nose of the helicopter fell back toward the horizontal. I rolled the helicopter left and looked through my door. Beneath me was a huge frozen explosion of water. It looked like a picture of a depth charge that had exploded beneath me. The water was frozen in place and time. Everything stopped and I saw a whale. He was laying in the middle of the frozen, foaming explosion of water fanning out all around him. From snout to fluke he was entirely exposed. He lay motionless in a hammock-shaped hole in the water. Azure water pushed away from him like a wave moving in all directions. On the margins, the placid water of the whole Pacific lay blue and impossibly deep around him.

For that instant I looked down into his wide, brown eye. I can see it still. His eye was the size of a basketball. The look of it seemed to say he was terribly startled. I knew that he was looking right back at me, right into my eyes. In that moment, the whale and I were of the same species. Whatever he was thinking, I was thinking. We were both momentarily there in the cosmos, amazed and communicating the emotions we shared in that single second. His emotions of fear, reprieve, relieved anxiety and joy were mirrors of mine. We were brothers who knew how close we had come to death.

And then the water closed over him. In the swirling, foaming sapphire whirlpool that closed around him the air followed him down. The clock began to tick once again. I was climbing still, focused on the swirling pool. The spreading foam rushed away from the center of the explosion as I did a quick circle above the foaming eruption of ocean. Clouds of bubbles boiled up from the deep. A line of them streamed down from what could have been the bottom of the channel following the whale's sounding. Although I could probably see down a hundred feet or more into the crystal sea, even the shadow of the whale had disappeared into the darkness of the deep. I am astonished to this day that propelled by his powerful flukes, he probably plummeted for the bottom faster than a dropped anchor could have gone there.

I finally rolled out of my turn into level flight. The helicopter was still climbing at an impressive rate. In a moment however, I leveled off. Pointing once again toward San Pedro I made the rest of the trip at a significantly higher altitude. In the remaining minutes flying to my destination I had time to think. I had started out my morning doing something I had been trained never to do. I knew from experience that flying that low is treacherously risky. Yet I ignored my gut instincts and my training. Instead I followed both my ego and my id. I knew better. Once again I gained a valuable insight into the man I was becoming. I repeated a lesson I had already gained from past experience. What did it matter that I had learned the lesson as a Marine. I did not have to re-learn such lessons as a civilian pilot. Once again I only dodged a sudden, watery death by the direct intercession of God. I silently thanked Him for sparing my life again and promised faithfully not to do something so stupid ever again.

I also took a moment to thank Him for what I learned from my last look at that whale. It was a significant thing. I had come close to the soul of a magnificent fellow being. I felt that I now knew that everything on this planet, even man and whale, is somehow linked. I clung to that heady realization as I stayed at a safe altitude until it was time to descend to land at San Pedro. Once the engine was shut down under the Vincent Thomas Bridge I began to chuckle. The blades coasted slowly to a stop. As they did I was thinking about how the accident report would read if someone had actually witnessed the collision. I was certain that I would be talked about by helicopter pilots as long as there were helicopters to fly. I also wondered what Brother Whale would tell his pals as he wintered in the warmer waters of Mexico. He might never breech again.

The flying to Catalina was fine, but any job can begin to drag. Boredom will set in unless you find something every day that changes and keeps you interested. For me that change came with every new load of passengers. I came to enjoy interacting with the customers as much as I enjoyed the flying. Taken as a group, I generally carried helicopter loads of happy, horny people across the channel between Long Beach and Catalina. It made for some fun and sometimes unusual passenger interactions. During my time flying the LongRanger across the Channel for example, some of my passengers couldn't even wait for the flight to end before they got randy. There was the couple who boarded for the ten minute flight from San Pedro to Long Beach. That's it; it was a ten minute flight to take them from under the San Pedro Bridge over the Long Beach Navy yard and land at Queensway. This young couple had gotten off the helicopter at the wrong stop coming back from Catalina. So they waited at San Pedro for me to return from a trip to Catalina for their short trip to Queensway. After I offloaded all my passengers from Catalina beneath the bridge, the couple boarded. No other passengers were making that trip so they got to ride solo. As it turned out, that's exactly what they were waiting for – privacy.

I could tell the couple was romantically inclined as the passenger agent led them out to my running helicopter. They kissed and hung all over each other as they walked out. The girl was attractive with big sunglasses, long hair, a short skirt and skimpy top. He was in beachwear too: a longish bathing suit and tank top shirt. Both wore beach sandals. Under the watchful eye of the agent they climbed in the back and strapped in next to each other in the rearmost seats. I heard their seatbelts click. I glanced over my shoulder as the door closed and the red-headed agent departed. They were not looking back at me. I faced forward, I wound up the throttle for takeoff and brought the helicopter to a hover.

About the time I started my takeoff run toward the San Pedro ship channel I thought I heard the seatbelt buckles click again. I was busy guiding the helicopter down the boat ramp and low across the water though. I didn't turn around to check that the passengers were still belted in. As I reached the altitude I wanted for crossing the Navy yard I felt the helicopter's center of gravity shift from right to left. Before I could turn around to see why, I heard the young man in back holler, "Hey, slow down!" I glanced over my shoulder. I saw the young man's naked back and buttocks and the young ladies bare feet above his shoulders. Thereafter, I averted my eyes.

I know I should have told him to put on his seatbelt. It was a federal regulation, for goodness sake. But in keeping with the moment I decided to let the strict enforcement of that regulation wait. Per the young man's request I slowed down trusting he would not. Slowing the helicopter was all in keeping with their safety, of course. I didn't want some sudden movement on my part to cause the un-seat belted couple to accidentally fall out of the aircraft. I continued my slow flight with a slower-than-usual approach to the Queensway helipad, too. As I began the descent to the helipad I heard their seatbelts click again. I thought it safe to check and looked around to see that they were both safely belted in. They both gave me a "thumbs up."

They were both laughing uproariously as I landed. The passenger agent opened the door for them to get out. It was probably a spontaneous gesture when the young man reached over the back of my seat. He stuffed a twenty in the pocket of my shirt. Then he stepped out of the helicopter. He and his girlfriend both gave me a little low wave as they walked past the cockpit. After they were clear of the rotors he turned back and mouthed a "thank you." Then the couple left the helipad and disappeared behind the sliding glass door of the passenger lobby. I'm sure as I took off to end my day back at the Long Beach airport I left behind me a pair of satisfied customers.

Another time a strikingly beautiful young lady asked the passenger agent at Queensway if she could sit in the front seat for the ride to Avalon. That wasn't uncommon. The front seat has the best view and there was usually a little more room up there than in the cabin when I carried a full load. Before I took off she asked me if there was a way to isolate our conversation from the passengers in back. I told her "Sure," and pointed to the switch on the radio panel that said "Intercom Isolate." She smiled. After takeoff she glanced over her shoulder. Then she reached up and flipped the switch.

"Can they hear us?" she asked.

I shook my head. "No, ma'am."

She turned around and double checked, asked anyone sitting behind us, "Can you hear us?" She got no response. I suppose the rear passengers were all just enjoying the view and chatting among themselves. They could hear each other over their headsets. They couldn't hear us.

I could feel the attractive lady looking at me. So I glanced her way. She had one eyebrow raised and an impish look on her face. She winked at me. I smiled and asked if she was enjoying the ride. In response she asked me if she could perform a service for me I had never had anyone offer to do for me in flight before. Taken aback, I don't think I said anything. When I failed to respond she said we'd both enjoy it. I'm sure I blushed.

When I got back a little presence of mind I told her I was both flattered at the offer and very seriously married. I thought that would be enough to discourage her. I was wrong. I tried to come up with alternate ways to explain I meant it when the original "no, thank you" didn't work. I didn't bother to explain to her the sequence of events that would undoubtedly result if I accepted her offer. She seemed oblivious to the fact that although the passengers behind us couldn't hear us, they most certainly were not blind. I thought in a rush about what they would see, what they would say. I could imagine what my boss would say about two minutes after the passengers told him what happened when their pilot lost his mind. I didn't have to imagine what the FAA safety inspector who took my license would say. He would never get a chance to revoke my certificate because I would be dead when my wife found out why I was fired.

The attractive passenger next to me shrugged when I turned her down again. Then she turned and looked to the left out the window. In a moment she slipped her right hand across the collective and rested it on my thigh. Looking down I thought, *she has very lovely hands*. In fact I told her so. I also noted that the people sitting behind us might take umbrage at her distracting me like that. She turned and looked at me with a wry smile and shrugged again. I told her that if she kept distracting me like that I might lose control of the helicopter. She smiled. Then I gave the cyclic a little shake. The aircraft responded with a quick roll left, right roll and back to level. I don't think the passengers behind us noticed. But the pretty passenger up front quickly withdrew her hand. I saw her grow a little pale. Her head whipped around as if to see if the helicopter was going to stay upright.

I took that moment to put my chin on my chest and close my eyes for a moment. "If you do what you're apparently planning I might just fall asleep."

I opened my eyes, looked at her and smiled. Her eyes were very wide open, a trace of panic in them.

"And if I fall asleep, you'll have to fly this thing." I turned my smile into a serious look of concern.

"Do you know how to fly?"

She pulled her whole body away from me as though I'd slapped her.

"No, of course I can't fly!" she said angrily.

I could see that this line of logic had gotten through to her. In fact she kept to her side of the cockpit for the balance of the flight. I glanced at her a couple times. She scowled and looked away from me when I did. I had been married long enough to know what "the cold shoulder" looks like. I chuckled to myself.

After a few minutes I pointed to the "isolate" button and asked, "'Mind if I turn that back on?" She snapped her head toward me and stared daggers at me. Then she turned her head away. "Fine," she replied. Once again, being an old married guy I understood what her "fine" really meant. I flipped the intercom switch back on.

"Sorry about the turbulence there a moment ago, folks," I said to the people behind us. "I think we passed through a little patch of hot air." My pretty passenger stared more daggers at me but didn't say anything.

When we got to Catalina she had her seatbelt off before the passenger agent got to her door. She was out of the cockpit like a shot when he let her out. As she walked away she didn't even look back. I have to say though, she looked pretty good walking away from the helicopter. It's probably a good thing for me that I never saw her again.

I had not been working long flying the Catalina Channel before I determined that at least half the people who sail boats to Catalina believe they should take all their clothes off for the greater part of their sailing trip. It got to be academic for me to reply in the affirmative when my passengers noted that the sailors on the boats we passed were all naked. Most of my regulars knew that's how things are done in the Catalina Channel. They lived on the island; most owned boats. They certainly sailed naked themselves. The regulars only pointed out the unusual naked people to me.

I never flew much higher than five hundred feet. At that altitude, one Catalina resident sitting next to me for the ride to the island started laughing.

"What's so funny?" I asked. He pointed down at the sailboat we were approaching. All I could see was a lone sailor sitting sideways in the cockpit of the boat.

"That guy, he's wearing nothing but a straw hat."

The sailor must have heard us approaching. He didn't look back at us and he didn't look up. He just took off his hat and placed it on his lap. After we went past, my passenger observed that he put his hat back on his bald head.

"Something is going to get sunburned on him today," my passenger said.

"But on which end?" I asked.

Another regular flier with me was an employee of Southern California Edison. Edison was the power company for Catalina and that end of the state of California. He went with me to the island on business every week or two. He always flew up front. We came to know each other pretty well as we chatted amiably on the trips. He was always interested in the people I met on the flights. We were on the way out to the island when he said he agreed that the Catalina set I ran across was a particularly peculiar and interesting crowd. He assured me that Catalina Islanders were unlike most other Californians he had met. When I agreed and told him stories about the naked sailors I encountered though, he disbelieved me.

I assured him it was so. He said he'd have to see that to believe it. I got busy during the landing phase and didn't have time to say anything more to him until I had landed the helicopter. The agent at Avalon came out and opened his door for him. As he stepped out I asked him if he'd be on my last flight back to Long Beach that evening. He nodded in the affirmative.

"I'll prove it to you that most people sail naked to Catalina."

He gave me a half smile. "We'll see," he said. Then he hung up the headset on the hook above the instrument panel and left.

Our conversation gave me something to think about while I flew back and forth waiting for my Edison guy and flying day to finish. The sun was not very far above the island as I headed out from Long Beach with my last load of passengers. As I taxied in to drop them at the Catalina Terminal I saw my one and only passenger waiting for the last ride home that day: Mr. So Cal Edison. He smiled all the way out to the aircraft. I could tell that he too had been thinking about our last conversation. He strapped in without assistance, closed and locked the door like the pro traveler he was. Then he put on his headset and slapped his knees. "So, are we gonna' see any naked sailors?

"I'm willing to bet some money on it," I replied.

I rolled up the throttle and lifted the helicopter into a hover. I kicked the tail around toward the island and pointed the nose toward Long Beach. I pushed gently forward on the cyclic and dipped the nose and pulled up smoothly on the collective lever to gather speed. We scooted low and fast across the parking ramp and out over Avalon Harbor. Normally at that point I would climb pretty briskly to cruising altitude. In this case with just my one seasoned passenger aboard I stayed low. It was fun being low. It allowed us to better check out the boats that were making for the island in the last of the daylight.

The shadow of the island was long and dark as it stretched out toward Long Beach. Several sailboats heading toward us still caught the sun further out in the channel. Their bows pointed toward us, their broad sails broached to catch the offshore breeze. Each reflected the sun off their wide canvas spread of sail. I suspected they were all probably intent on dropping anchor in Avalon Harbor for the night. Running with the wind with their sails swung wide, the cockpits of each boat was blocked from our view.

I adjusted our heading slightly to line up on the closest boat to us. A mile ahead of us now I made small adjustments to pass close by. Knowing that we would be almost abeam before we would be able to see the cockpit of the boat in clear detail I lined up our flight path so my passenger could get the best view of the cockpit of the boat. Just before we passed it I impulsively made a wager with Mr. Edison. I speculated that there were probably two naked people onboard this sailboat. I further speculated that they were a man and a woman and that at the moment they were assuming the position of mating dogs.

I really had no idea whether or not that was going on. I even told him that I had not seen the boat on the inbound leg. It was on my part an irresponsible bet made on a wild guess. But it was still a bet. We were drawing very close abeam now, the cockpit still barely behind the sail. "C'mon, man! Make up your mind. Twenty bucks to you if I'm wrong. What do you say?"

He looked at the boat and instead of taking my wager said as the cockpit fell into his line of sight, "You're a pervert, Paul. You've gotten twisted flying horny passengers back and forth all day." And then we passed the boat. The obstructing sail passed behind us and there it became apparent that I was correct in every regard.

The startled lady and gentleman on the sailboat had no time and probably by then no inclination to stop what they were doing. Maybe they would not have done so even if they had known we were approaching. From my perspective the only shame in the whole incident was that my passenger didn't take me up on the bet. I could have used a quick twenty bucks.

The boat flashed past and I began to climb. Our hunt for naked sailors was done. Edison whipped his head back until the boat was out of sight behind us. Then he spun his head back toward me. Clearly nonplussed he looked at me with his eyes much wider open now.

"How in the world did you know?" he asked.

I leveled off at altitude. "I just know," I told him, grinning. "I always know."

Another of my regulars was a seemingly bored, unfriendly and long faced lawyer who went back and forth between Long Beach and Catalina on a regular basis. He was actually a nice looking fellow. He was mostly bald with a stately, well-trimmed Prince Edward style beard. His tepid personality was complemented by a routine that never seemed to vary. Besides always remaining aloof, he always wore a Navy blue or black suit to do his business out on the island. He always traveled on the same day every week, out in the morning, back in the evening. He always carried a thin black valise which he kept on his lap as we flew. He held it close as though it contained something valuable he thought I might steal. He always sat in the front with me. Most people sat in front because they enjoyed the view, or enjoyed talking to the pilot. I think this guy did so in order to limit his contact with lesser beings than himself. In the back he might have had to sit right next to or – perish the thought – talk to someone. Up front he only had to deal with me. With me he said little or nothing. And up front he had the extra space between us allowed by the manufacturer for the radio panel and the collective. It kept us apart. I think he would have liked it better if there had been a wall between us instead.

Despite his aloofness, as he put on his headset I always greeted him like an old friend. I tried to get him talking by pointing out the beautiful view or the occasional pods of whales we passed. I even tried getting him interested in looking for naked sailors. He never responded. He never even smiled. He didn't look at me or even in my direction during the trip, let alone converse. I thought that perhaps he was scared of flying. But during flights when we went through some bumps and rough weather it didn't seem to bother him. I concluded that he was just a dreary person with nothing in his life that interested him except his work.

He most certainly had no sense of humor. I knew that because I had told him some of my best jokes on our trips. He never cracked a smile. Then one day I told him one of my many lawyer jokes. That's when things changed. The day I told him my first lawyer joke was the first day I heard him laugh. After that I had a new lawyer joke for him every time we flew. I could tell after a while that he looked forward to it. He got a little more animated after that. The last time I saw him he was walking away from the helicopter, his valise held tightly under his arm. I had just told him a new lawyer joke I had heard. I still tell it. It's one of my best. He was laughing as we landed and wiping his eyes with the back of his hand as he left. I like to think that in the time we flew together that maybe I made his life a little better even though he never really said so.

One windy day I stood in the passenger terminal at Avalon. Waiting with the service agent for customers to show up I looked out the big window and across the channel toward Southern California. Sailboats skidding across the channel toward the island were all healed well over on their sides. The stiff and gusty wind filled their sails full to bursting. Flying back and forth that morning I noted that the wind had made the channel extremely choppy. I knew that the wave height would increase and the ride for boaters would only get worse. The passengers on all the boats I passed were already getting quite a ride. Sailboats plunged and heaved, their bows often plowing up water. Smaller motor vessels seemed to bounce from wave to wave. Even the big channel boats plunged and wallowed and rolled heavily. I pitied those poor passengers on those channel boats. Their plans for a nice outing at Catalina for the weekend probably went over the side with their breakfast and lunch, and maybe even last night's dinner.

After a while standing at the passenger counter I saw a happy looking group of ladies and gents approach. They looked like members of the sailing set. At least they were all dressed in nautical looking clothing. Most had light jackets or sweaters tied around or draped over their shoulders by the sleeves. They all wore sun hats and sunglasses. As they paid for their flight I struck up a conversation with them and asked them about how their day was going. They confessed that it wasn't going the way they had planned. It seems that they had started out their journey to Catalina from Long Beach in a friend's sailboat. They told me that their trip started out well. Then the wind came up and with it, the waves. The ride got rough and soon they had gone from feeling miserable to feeling seasick. Before long everybody was throwing up. That is, everybody but their friend the captain. Adding to the unpleasantness he made fun of them. He seemed to take pleasure in how rough the ride was. He ribbed them about their inexperience and how uncomfortable they all were. Not yet mid-channel they all suggested he turn back for Long Beach. He would have none of that. When he refused to return they couldn't wait to get to Catalina and dry land.

They came ashore pale and shaken. They said their captain teased them mercilessly. When they arrived they asked the boat owner if they could stay the night and wait out the choppy conditions. He happily refused. He called them "landlubbers" and "sissies." He shamed them and told them that he was leaving shortly in order to make it back to Long Beach before dark. They knew that they would have a short day on Catalina and then an even more miserable ride back to Long Beach. He added to their misery when he told them that they could remain if they wanted to, but that their only option beyond returning with him was to take the channel boat. The channel boat, he smirked, would still be wallowing its way back to Long Beach full of puking passengers while he was back home drinking cocktails.

They resolved as a group to stay on Catalina, anyway. The arrogant sailboat captain left them on the dock at Avalon with a final, "So long, suckers." The captain's newest former friends retreated to a waterside restaurant to decide on what to do to get back to Long Beach. That's where one of the group saw one of our fliers advertising helicopter service to Long Beach. They decided at once that they would beat their arrogant captain back to Long Beach and go in style, to boot.

As they told me their story, one of them asked if I could find the arrogant captain's sailboat on the way back. They wanted him to know that they had found a way to trump him. This group constituted a full load. No one else would be put out by any delay that searching for the sailboat might cause. So I said, "Sure, I'll try." We took off across Avalon harbor and climbed into the wind. I checked in with the passengers on the headset and asked them to help me. They would have to identify the boat for me.

As it turned out I had no trouble finding it. The Channel was so rough by then that most sailboats around Catalina had sought safe harbor. There was only one boat mid-channel. I could see only one person in the cockpit. As I flew past I could tell by the laughter and shouting from my passengers that it was indeed the boat we sought. I began to circle it.

The passengers waved and shrieked. I could see the captain looking up as we circled. He must have been trying to figure out what I was doing. I am sure that from that distance he couldn't make out who these people were in the circling helicopter. Then one of the women got a unique idea to let him know who was up there. She unbuckled her seat belt, dropped her shorts and pressed her bare bottom against the door. I couldn't see what the lady was doing behind me. I could see by the captain's gestures that he suddenly understood what was going on above him. That got the passengers laughing uproariously.

I looked over my shoulder to see what was going on in the passenger cabin. When I saw the lady's bare bottom pressed against the door, I must have blanched. Pressing on the door like that I was amazed that she had not already popped it open. I saw in a flash as from a distance a semi-naked woman plunging the five hundred feet from my helicopter into the Catalina Channel, screaming all the way down. I gently rolled the helicopter level. Since they were all wearing headphones I mildly suggested that the lady pull her pants back up, sit down and buckle her seat belt. Without argument she merrily complied. As she did so I told her that I appreciated her quick thinking and ability to communicate with the sailor below. I also told her that dropping her bare fanny into his boat was probably not what either of us wanted to do that day. She agreed to keep her pants up and bottom buckled in. Her friends laughed all the more. I circled the boat once more and headed back to Queensway.

When we landed one of the passengers reached over my shoulder. He shook my hand and then handed me a twenty dollar bill. When they made it to the door of the passenger terminal they all waved crazily, saluted me and blew kisses. I returned the salute and took off backwards until I was over the harbor. Then I stepped on a pedal to cause the bird to swap ends, scooted across the harbor and headed back to the Long Beach airport to end my day.

I came to love my job because I came to love people in general. I loved flying with the pretty ladies, the rich, and the tourists from all over the world. I loved the vacationers, the people with business or businesses on the island. I got to know the Catalina regulars and their families by name. Most were seasoned veterans of the Catalina Shuttle. I flew many a first time helicopter rider. Some were white - knuckle terrified when we started. I tried to get them to sit up front with me so I could take special care with them. I told them what to expect and talked them through everything that was happening as it happened. I engaged them in conversation as we crossed the channel. Through them I got to revisit my own first experience in flying. My day was always better when they ended up having the time of their lives. I do not recall a first time passenger stepping off the helicopter who in the end didn't enjoy the ride. I learned how to make people laugh, and how to be diplomatic in dealing with people who were difficult. Most important for me was that I learned to enjoy real, regular people. I was beginning to see in me where the Marine ended and where I began.

Good as it was for me and for John's business, there was a critical element missing in flying to the island. The job did not pay enough. Southern California was one of the most expensive areas of the country in which to live. With what I was being paid I couldn't even afford the tiny house I was renting without dipping into our savings each month. It was also hard to swallow that I was scraping by when the managers were doing very well. Mike drove a brand new Porsche. Mike's partner asked me out in the parking lot at the hangar to show off the new Mercedes he'd just bought. Later the same week he showed me pictures of the swimming pool he put in his back yard. A business is supposed to make money. I had no problem with that. Mike and his partner didn't share it with those who made it for them, though. Working for selfish people like that didn't sit well with me. Especially when I couldn't afford to buy shoes for my kids. I was resolved to get a little more pay for my efforts.

Make no mistake, the job was wonderful. It was one I would gladly have done for the rest of my flying career. But I had three children to raise. I hoped to help them through college one day. With the Shuttle's meager pay I'd never be able to do that. I didn't want to rent a house all my life either. It was just another one of the financial goals I had to abandon to work for the pay I got at the shuttle. So one day when I was cooling my heels at Queensway I walked into John's office. He was fussing with some papers piled up on his desk. They might have been invoices. I saw a couple checks. It looked like they were coming in, not going out. They steeled my resolve. I stood silent for a moment waiting for his attention. I didn't get it. He didn't look up.

"I need to talk, John."

Still he didn't look up. "Yeah?" he said.

I told him I needed a raise - that I couldn't afford to stay on with the pay I was making. He seemed to not hear me. I told him I was eating up my savings just living in Orange County. I told him, "I don't need the money for myself. I need a raise just to make it, John. I need it to take care of my family."

He looked up at me from under his eyebrows and half snorted, half chuckled. Then he stood up, walked around the desk. He looked like he was headed for the door. I stopped him.

"John! I'll make you an offer."

He turned around enough to look over his shoulder. "What offer," he shot back.

"Double my pay and I'll never leave here."

John shook his head and turned back toward the door, walked through the passenger lounge, got in his car and left.

2 GOING TO TEXAS

I am glad I took the Catalina flying job. It brought my real career objective back into focus. I wanted to fly before I want to join the Marines. The Marines were initially a means to that end. I joined the Marines because I wanted to be a pilot. I didn't intend to stay in. Then I became a Marine and fully bought into the Marine Corps ethos. That was enough for me. Flying was secondary to being a Marine officer. After ten years I had no other aspirations except to stay in the Marine Corps. Then my Marine Corps career ended suddenly. I was scared. I lost the career I intended to pursue for another decade, maybe two. Now I had a family to care for and no idea what I would do if being a Marine was no longer an option for doing that.

Looking for security I could have fooled myself. I could have succumbed to taking the job at McDonnell-Douglas. I could have told myself that it *did* have to do with aviation. I could have abandoned my desire to fly to the siren song of good pay and stability. It almost lured me away from what I really wanted to do with my life. Had I not been buzzed by that helicopter, had I driven straight home and presented Linda with my plans to work for McDonnell-Douglas I might never have flown again. Catalina helped me remember why I joined the Marines. It reminded me that I loved to fly. That day I came home with two job offers I needed Linda's gentle nudge. She got me pointed down the right road. Soon she would do so again.

Catalina was a training ground for me. In the LongRanger I honed the skills I had acquired in the past. I also acquired flying skills there that I would soon need in similar machines, in a very different job. In the Marines I flew tremendous, over-powered helicopters. There was no comparable equivalent to them in the civilian helicopter market. Flying to Catalina I flew small, marginally powered ships. The Catalina ship was constantly loaded to the weight limit with fuel, passengers and baggage. I flew most flights with just enough fuel to get the job done. With nowhere to land *en route* but the Catalina Channel I did dozens of fuel computations in my head on every flight. I learned to manage every drop of fuel I carried. I did that accommodating for changes in wind, weather, company objectives and requirements as well as passenger needs and desires. My destinations were all challenging spots to land. Each took a different sort of finesse and good judgment to land and takeoff safely. These were all skills I mastered flying to the island. They were skills that important now, would soon quite literally save lives. The first of them would be my own.

Sometimes the weather was perfect on the Catalina Channel. But it could change very quickly. Often it changed before my eyes while making a single transit. Dense sea fog would form behind me as I headed toward my next destination. It would close the door to a return in the event something went wrong ahead of me. Worse, sometimes fog began to boil up around me. Flying into clouds would turn a routine tourist flight into a race for survival. The helicopter had only the most marginal of instruments for flying in clouds. Entering them and staying upright would be only half the challenge. There was no way to get out of them anywhere on my route. My only option for safely making an instrument approach was the Long Beach airport. Getting there in a helicopter equipped like the Shuttle could easily take longer than the rest of my life.

Another challenge that faced me on the island route was the arrival of the unpredictable and vicious Santa Ana winds. The weather guessers never did a good job predicting their arrival. That was not an issue. As an experienced pilot I had learned never to trust a weather forecast. The guy making the forecast had nothing to lose. I never heard of a weather forecaster being fired for being absolutely wrong. After a few times being lied to by "weather guessers" I learned how to effectively make my own predictions from the same data the paid forecasters used. I was usually pretty good at it. But that data didn't help me the first day I met the Santa Ana winds over the Catalina Channel. They are a spectacular and usually unpredictable phenomenon. They just race into the Los Angeles basin unannounced. I had lived in Southern California long enough to know what to expect. Hot winds would roar out of the desert east of Los Angeles. Moving with the speed of a hurricane the desert winds raised the coastline temperature from a comfortable seventy or eighty degrees Fahrenheit into the triple digits almost immediately.

The first time they caught me flying the island route I never knew they were coming until I saw them. I saw them coming though. When I knew what they were heading toward me, I got the same feeling you might get opening your bedroom door to discover a Bengal tiger waiting inside for you. Crossing Long Beach Harbor, at their leading edge they tore a line of whitecaps from the surface of the water. They hit the Catalina Channel all at once on a line stretching north and south as far as I could see. They acted like a fifty mile wide snow plow as they moved out behind whitecaps that leapt up before them. The water was calm where I was at the moment. But behind the Santa Ana winds waves just jumped up vertically. As the edge of the snow plow neared, I could see the waves ahead were bigger than my little LongRanger was tall.

The winds were moving toward me at almost the speed I was moving toward them. Turning away to avoid them was not an option. They would catch me before I could land back at Catalina. Before I could land at Avalon they would blow me into the face of the island. In the turbulence they would create rising over the island, even landing at the airport on top of Catalina would be impossible. Crashing on Catalina was no choice at all. I pointed the helicopter toward San Pedro and prepared for what I knew was coming.

I looked at the fuel gauge. Based on a guess I determined I had plenty to hold to my course and land at San Pedro. There the winds would have become steady. I would be facing into the wind. I tried to be confident. And then the forward edge of the approaching winds hit. It was terrifying. The ride became as if we were on a rodeo bull. A couple of times the helicopter was completely out of my control. That lasted an eternal minute as the turbulence pushed the little helicopter around as though it were in a boiling pot. And then things smoothed out a bit. I regained a semblance of wings level. Except for a few odd slams up or down or sideways I knew we would be okay. Then I looked down at the channel. I was barely moving. I drove faster to work on the interstate than I was heading toward San Pedro. That extra fuel I had a moment before all disappeared as I calculated our groundspeed. With a little luck I would still make it without cutting into my final fuel reserves. But things had changed for the worse and they could change again. It wasn't just because of the hike in temperature that I began to sweat.

I pressed on. Ahead of me the crew at the San Pedro terminal under the bridge was describing a scene from a film about hurricanes. Being low on fuel suddenly became second in priority behind being able to land and stay upright. The winds passing under the bridge created treacherous air currents. The bridge created a funnel, a giant venture that narrows and speeds up the air passing through it. Wild air currents whipped around the bridge supports. As I headed toward them I watched how they tore at the San Pedro Channel under the bridge. Seeing how they raced around the giant bridge supports I formulated a plan to avoid these winds. As I approached I could see a path on the channel that was flat calm. The winds moved so fast on either side of a bridge support next to the helipad that they left a calm void downwind of the support. The void reached out across our helipad and well down the channel. I rolled the helicopter into the void and followed it.

When I landed I kept the throttle wide open. We wasted no time getting the passengers unloaded. They were all too happy to leave. The crew closed the door and left me sitting on the pad like a doomed man. They knew I was about to takeoff downwind. They didn't want to be anywhere nearby when I tried. I knew immediately that I was not going to turn the helicopter's tail into that wind. I would spin down the channel like a top. So I decided to take off into the wind. That would mean flying under the bridge. On the other side I would pop out on a short leg to the fuel truck at the Long Beach airport. Fuel was now priority one again. And the fuel gauge was not giving me any time to bolster my courage. I got busy.

I lifted the helicopter into a stable hover and slid out into the channel. When I slipped out of the calm behind the bridge support the wind hit me and I was once again on the rodeo bull. Although I was bucking around at zero ground speed, the airspeed went from zero to seventy knots instantly. I moved the cyclic forward and gained groundspeed slowly. By the time the airspeed needle hit its limit I was back to moving at a near crawl across the ground. As I watched the last of my fuel burning away I flew directly back to the airport. Nobody else was crazy enough to be flying that day. Even the airliners were parked. So the Long Beach Tower gave me latitude to do whatever I had to do in order to get back on the ground. Having learned the lesson of wind shadows at the San Pedro Bridge I landed in the wind shadow of our hangar. Had I not done so, the rotor would never have stopped spinning even though I had the engine shut down. It was just one more lesson I piled into my book of lessons that day: Never fly a helicopter that doesn't have a rotor brake.

In the coming days I told John repeatedly that although I enjoyed working for him and that I wanted to stay, I needed better pay. He had a couple kids of his own so I expected he knew that with a family to feed pay was a serious issue for me. I told him another time that we certainly couldn't make it at all financially without Linda's teaching job. Despite all the pleading, John listened but said nothing. I grew increasingly irked that he appeared not to care. Then one day he passed me on the helipad. He asked me how much pay I wanted. I had told him many times before by that point. So I reminded him. I thought it was a start to negotiations. But he didn't say anything to me about pay after that. There wasn't a counter-offer that day or any other.

The calendar pages turned toward summer. Linda and I came to some conclusions. I finished my Master's degree. Linda and the boys were about to finish school, too. We decided that with no further word from John that it was time for me to move on. I talked to a recruiting officer for the Navy Reserves in Los Angeles. Despite my being passed over for promotion by the Marines, they had a commission and a flying slot for me. I would fly gunships at Point Mugu Naval Air Station, north of L.A. They were even going to bring me on as a lieutenant commander. That was the equivalent of a Marine major, the rank for which the Marines had passed me over.

I was flattered. I would also be flying still, and flying gunships at that. I also shopped around and got a full-time civilian job lined up. The job was one working with another aircraft manufacturer in Los Angeles. It was a desk job, not a dream job. So I would be flying with the Navy. Making a salary and benefits with a civilian employer would get us into a house. We'd even save for the kids' college again. I was due to start both of these jobs at the end of the summer. So we decided I would quit my

Catalina flying job early enough to take the family on a long summer vacation. First we would take the boys on a rambling tour of the west. Then we would circle through Texas and visit relatives. After that it was back to Southern California where we would settle into whatever new, as-yet-unseen opportunities blossomed for us.

When I gave John my two weeks' notice he ignored me. I asked him if he heard me. He didn't reply. So I dropped a business envelope with my notice in it on his desk and went back to work. I said no more about it and neither did John. A week later I asked him if he had a replacement in mind for me. He let my question go without comment.

When I left the airport for Queensway on my last day of my last shift, I looked out at the channel. It was foggy. I knew I wouldn't be going across to Catalina until it burned off. So I landed at the Queensway pad and shutdown. I washed the helicopter as the fog began to burn away. Then I walked into the terminal. John had stayed the night. He was there drinking coffee when I came in. There were no passengers waiting. I poured myself a cup and told the baggage handler that I was glad he was working today. Since this was my last day the stop gave me a chance to thank him for his good work and to say goodbye. Across the room John suddenly exploded.

"This is your *what*?!" he shouted. I had never seen him lose his temper so quickly. I had made it plain that I was quitting, that this would be my last day. So at first I thought John was kidding me. Then I recognized his anger was both genuine and irrational. I waited for him to calm down. When he did somewhat I asked him if he had reconsidered raising my pay so I could afford to live. He shook his head and told me he was paying me too much already. That was the final straw for me. I turned for the door and said, "Well John, I guess there's nothing more to talk about then."

I walked out to the helicopter and stood facing the Queen Mary. The fog was beginning to clear. John never came outside. I wasn't going back inside. About the time I could make out the outline of Catalina, the Dispatcher leaned out the door and told me some people were waiting for me at Avalon. I flew the rest of the shift and never talked to John again. When my shift was done I flew back to Long Beach airport. In approaching the parking ramp I flew an orbit across the McDonnell-Douglas parking lot and zoomed over the same corner where I had been sitting in my sports car when someone did that to me. I scooted across the runway, onto the parking ramp where I picked the helicopter up each morning. I hovered there a moment and carefully turned the nose of the machine toward the fence. I set it down oh so gently, rolled the throttle to idle and started the clock.

As the engine cooled I looked up and noticed a man in a suit. He was hanging on the airport fence on the McDonnell-Douglas parking lot watching me. I waved. He waved back. “Okay pal,” I said out loud. “It's your turn.”

The vacation was wonderful. We traveled light, took it slow and stopped whenever we desired. We stayed an extra day or two if we wanted to do so. In some cases we saw sites I had only seen from the air. In others we saw places we had only driven past in the rush to get to a new duty station during my Marine Corps career. There was no duty station waiting for us now though, no date we had to be anywhere in particular. My family and I were happier than we had been in many months. We stayed a couple nights on the rim of the Grand Canyon. We took pictures of the kids at the Meteor Crater in Winslow, Arizona. We drove through the beautiful mountains of western New Mexico and stayed at Cimarron and Santa Fe. We worked our way into West Texas and ate Tex-Mex food in El Paso. We crossed the border for the day and did some shopping in Mexico. Back in America we saw Texas' highest mountain, Guadalupe Peak. Then we drove northeast across the arid, flat prairie to Lubbock where we visited my brother Mike and his family. He was working on his doctorate there at Texas Tech. We had such a good time together that Mike loaded up the wife and kids and followed us to Dallas. We all stayed a couple of nights with our older brother Steve and his family. We spent weeks like that visiting with family and old friends all over Texas. Everywhere we went there was a reunion. I didn't have the slightest idea that it was really a homecoming.

When I graduated from college I married Linda. In a couple of months I was commissioned a new lieutenant. We were preparing for our trip for me to start my career in Quantico, Virginia where new lieutenants learn how to be lieutenants. My Mom saw her baby flying out of the nest. Being a first generation American of Irish parents she often waxed poetic. Sometimes she had wisdom handed down. Sometimes she made stuff up that sounded like old wisdom. I'm not sure which it was when she told me as I was leaving, "One day you'll find yourself in your own backyard and you'll know then, you can never leave home." If she meant I would come back to her house to live, I believed she was wrong on that score. I was ready to get out and see the world. If she meant that things change when you leave home there was surely no disputing that. Things did change. I saw that every time I came home on military leave. After a couple weeks in Texas I was about to find out what she really meant.

Over the years and the babies we started bringing with us, everybody knew that my leave time in the Marines meant our stays were always just visits. So we visited and then we and our relatives and friends all went back to our regular, day-to-day lives. Coming to Texas this time things were different. Our relatives knew we could stay if we wanted to. They treated us like that's exactly what they expected us to do. My Mom's wisdom hit the mark. I was finding out, you might leave home, but you *can* come home when the traveling is done.

Linda and I had not seen our families in three years. I was a Marine headed from one coastal duty station to another on the opposite coast. The twins were toddlers then. Our third son hadn't even been born yet.

Now we were back in Texas and they were spending time with two grandmothers. I think the boys received at least three years' worth of hugs and kisses. I recalled time with my own grandmother. I remember how much I loved her loving me despite the required pinches on the cheek she always had for me. Grandmothers, aunts and their friends all doted on our kids. The boys played happily with their cousins. They became friends with this blood kin they had never met. Linda too was visiting with relatives now. She was no longer a military wife just passing through. She was home, part of her civilian family. Surrounded by those who had loved her since she was a little girl, I began to relish what was happening to us. We were blending back into the family. For the first time in my life my Dad was my friend. I was no longer just one of his boys. He knew that I had unconsciously honored him by choosing the same path he followed into manhood.

He joined the Marines, and so did I. He fought in the Pacific Island campaign of World War II. I was immensely proud to brag to my fellow Marines that Dad's sixth island landing was on that iconic Marine Corps battlefield, Iwo Jima. I never saw a shot fired in anger. That meant nothing to Dad. He bragged to his Marine veteran friends that his son was a Marine pilot and an officer. He could not have been more proud. When I was not promoted and was given six months to leave the Marine Corps he fought a good fight to get the decision reversed. Without my knowledge he wrote letters to the Commandant of the Marine Corps and Secretary of the Navy on my behalf. The letters certainly stirred things up in my last weeks as a Marine. Although they didn't change the ultimate outcome, they did prove where my Dad stood so far as I was concerned. And his efforts showed the lengths to which he would go to in order to prove it.

While I was home, we developed the kind of friendship I had seen that he shared with fellow Pacific War veterans. The Marine Corps was a proud part of our past. I had seen that bond when he invited me to a veterans' affair one time when I came home on leave. More substantial, our common past made for a stronger bond between my father and his adult son. It was a bond built on love as always. Now it was also build on a bond of mutual respect.

Linda, the boys and I spent the final days of our vacation in Austin. Linda's sister, her husband and their two little boys lived there. When we were dating in college, Linda and I spent a lot of time enjoying the hills and lakes around Austin. It was a nice place to be. By the time we got there on our post-Marine Corps vacation we could feel time catching up with us. We knew we would have to head back to California soon. Summer would come to an end. Linda and the boys would go back to school. And I would start my new job and process into the Navy reserves.

The weeks we traveled had been fun. But with all the visiting we never had any time to ourselves until we got to Austin. There the pace slowed down. We were happy for it. The time in Austin gave us a chance to catch our breath. One weekday morning before we were due to head back to California Linda's sister and family left the house to us. They had summer activities to do. They left early, careful not to wake our boys. For the first time since arriving in Texas we had a house to ourselves, quiet time. It was early in the morning. I made a pot of coffee while Linda made us some toast and cut up some fruit. The morning sun brightened the breakfast room windows. The kids remained sleeping as we enjoyed the quite company of each other.

I shared the newspaper with Linda. We drank our coffee as we thumbed through the newspaper section by section. As I did I realized that I was going to miss this peace, our family and the beautiful Texas Hill Country. I became aware that I was not just upset that our vacation was ending. I was not looking forward to returning to California at all. In trying to stir up some enthusiasm I thought about the plans we had for our return. There was promise of finding a home in a nice neighborhood. It would probably be near the old neighborhoods where we had lived not far from the Marine bases. It was pretty there in Orange County. Linda still had her teaching job there at a high school. She was valued and had a good chance to grow in that position. I'd commute to work. That was certain. And I'd commute farther to fly with the Navy. That was life in Southern California. Both jobs were ones I could enjoy. I thought about the kids. I was unhappy that they would grow up in another state entirely from their cousins here in Texas. Once they got into school in Orange Country though they would be happy. They would lose their Texas roots. They'd become Californians. We'd all become Californians.

The glow of the early morning seemed to dim for me at the prospect. I hadn't even left the Lone Star State yet and for the first time since I left it as a new lieutenant with a new bride I was getting homesick for it. Lost in my reverie I was unaware that Linda was watching me. I put down the sports page and picked up the want ad section. When I visited Texas during duty station changes or while I was on leave here I never looked at the want ads. In scanning them this morning it made sense to do so. I no longer had a set of orders to carry out, after all. I no longer had a date to, "report no later than." Looking at the want ads it occurred to me that we didn't really have to go back to California at all. I was a free agent. The only obligation I had was to my family and myself.

I dropped the paper and looked across the table at my bride. She had her chin in her hand, a devilish look in her eye and a half grin on her face. I realized she had been watching me for some time, and waiting.

I returned the smile. "What?" I asked.

"You've been doing a lot of thinking over there."

I nodded. "I have."

"I've got a proposition for you."

"The kids *are* still sleeping," I noted.

"Not that kind of proposition," she said as she wrinkled her nose at me.

I crossed my arms. "Okay. I'm open to your proposition. Shoot."

With her next words a new course became clear the moment she said them. The best things that happened to us always happened that way: quickly and unexpectedly. She got a questioning look on her face.

"Wanna' move here?" she asked.

I supposed she had been feeling and thinking the same things I had been as I flipped through the Austin paper. Knowing Linda, she probably thought them first. I looked down at the sections of newspaper piled before us on the kitchen table. In front of her and wide open was the section listing houses for sale and rent.

I picked up the want ads again. It was a pretty thick section. It appeared to be well populated with jobs. I didn't look at what the jobs were listed there. I just noted there were plenty of them. Had I paid closer attention I would have realized they were mostly positions open for restaurant workers and lawn care people. What I saw though, was what I wanted to see: a reason to stay, a reason to say, "Yes."

I picked up and put down the paper again. Linda was still looking at me for an answer.

"Sure," I said confidently.

And that was it. I had no second thoughts after that. California could well have slid into the sea with that word, "sure" and I would not have missed it. I knew at once that I would have no second thoughts later, either. "Sure," never felt better than it did that Austin morning.

Linda stood up, came around behind my chair and wrapped her arms around my neck. She kissed me sweetly behind one ear.

"Kisses are good for luck," I said. I turned my chair around and sat her on my lap. I kissed her on the mouth. She returned it warmly. She pulled her head back and took my face in her hands.

"The kids *are* still sleeping, you know." I knew what she meant. "Wanna' get lucky?" she asked.

The question was rhetorical. "I already am."

She looked into my eyes with a very serious countenance.

"'Want to get lucky, again?"

I didn't need to answer. She stood up, opened her robe and took my hands. She put them inside her robe and said, "Well? What are we waiting for?" I didn't have an answer for that. She led me to the bedroom and into another chapter of our life together. We were going to Texas.

We dropped off the boys in Houston with Linda's mom. Then we flew back to California. We took a cab to our little rented house in Irvine where the 280ZX in the garage would provide us the ride back to Texas. I called the movers who had the bulk of our household effects in storage. I asked the lady who answered the phone how soon I could have them pick up the rest of our effects in Irvine and move them to all to Austin, Texas.

"Tomorrow morning, if you'd like," she said. She asked where our stuff was going. "Address unknown," I replied. "We don't have a house there yet."

"Oh, that's no problem," she responded sounding unconcerned. "We do these moves all the time. We'll find a warehouse in Austin. You can call for your furniture and such whenever you're settled."

Check off one big step toward Texas. But we still had a lot of work to do. We'd kept our moving boxes. I raced out and bought other packing materials we'd need. Linda started emptying cabinets and getting what little we had in our house ready to move. We stayed at it all day and most of the night. When the movers arrived we had everything ready for them. They worked fast. By lunchtime we were standing in an empty house. I had our suitcases squirreled away in the back of the Z car. We spent the afternoon giving the place a good cleaning. Then we checked into a hotel for the night.

The next morning we had places to go. First, we met the landlady and gave her the house keys. Then Linda dropped me off at the hotel. I had some phone calls to make while she headed out to slip the cables that kept her in California.

My first call of the day was to a Navy Commander who was waiting for me to sign a commission in the Navy Reserve. He picked up the phone like he had been expecting my call. Before I could say anything he told me I could swear in as a reserve lieutenant commander whenever I was ready. After that I could start flying at the Point Mugu Naval Air Station. His end of the line got quiet when I told him I changed my mind. When he realized I was serious he got upset with me. I heard him out until he insinuated that perhaps I hadn't been so good a Marine after all. I kept my cool. Then in almost as few words I said, "Thanks, sorry," and "'see ya'." Then I hung up the phone. He didn't call me back. So ended my career as a sailor, U.S. Navy Reserve.

By then Linda had arrived at the Irvine School District Office. The High School was closed for the summer. The school district office on the other hand was open all year. Many of the people there knew and liked Linda, or so she thought. It's not me boasting to say that she was an up-and-comer in the district. Aside from my personal observations her colleagues had told me so. She was named teacher of the year in the high school the first year she taught for Irvine. After that she became a mentor, and not only for new teachers like herself. She was put in the position to do workshops and special "teach the teacher" projects. Teachers her parents' age admired her and learned from her. They too had told me so. I was proud of her. She was leaving a promising career. But she was confident about leaving.

Understandably when Linda pulled into the District Headquarters parking lot she was anxious. She hated that someone might be upset with her decision to leave the school district, let alone on such short notice. Sad to say though nobody got upset. When Linda entered the building she bumped into the Superintendent's administrator. It was the same lady who made arrangements with Linda to receive her Teacher of the Year award. When Linda told her she was going to resign and move back to Texas the administrator turned her over to a functionary to get the paperwork started. There was no effort to convince her to stay. She didn't take her to the superintendent. She didn't even ask why Linda was resigning.

Linda spent the last hour of her employ with Irvine School District standing at a counter filling out forms. People she knew passed by. She greeted them. Nobody even returned her smile, let alone stopped to talk. By the time she got to the last form in the stack she was no longer concerned with disturbing anyone with her resignation. She checked the block at the bottom of the form that said, "Send the proceeds of my California Teacher's Retirement by check to the address listed below." She wrote her mother's address in Houston. She was done.

The call to the Navy behind me I called my soon-to-be employer, the Norton Aircraft Factory in Los Angeles. The lady in personnel listened to the same reasons I told the Navy recruiter I wouldn't need the job after all. She just replied with, "okay," and "good luck." Then she said, "bye-bye." I pulled the phone from my ear and looked at it. "That was simple," I said aloud. As I hung up the receiver I also slipped the last cable that anchored me to the west coast. Linda was on her way back as I gathered our packed bags and headed for the hotel lobby.

I checked out of the hotel and dragged our bags outside into the fresh California sunshine. Across the driveway a bench in the shade of a manicured tree looked inviting. I took a seat surrounded by brightly colored pots of flowers. Southern California is rife with flowers. But none of them ever seem to have a bouquet. Today however, I noticed the air smelled of fresh orange blossoms. I recalled that smell greeting me as we drove into Orange County, California for the first time a decade before. That day seemed a lifetime ago now. Perhaps I only noticed it when I was getting a fresh start. As I crossed my legs and took in the sweet scent of oranges I noticed my cute wife rocketing up the hotel driveway in the Z. She pulled up near the bench and spooled down the window.

I stood up and walked toward her. She was smiling but as I got close I could see tears on her cheeks. I reached in the window and wiped them off with my thumbs. I took her face in my hands and kissed it. She pulled away and looked down. Her lower lip drooped in a pout.

"Adios, Irvine School District," she said. I opened her door and helped her out of the car. I gave her a big hug.

"'You change your mind?" I asked.

I felt her shake her head. "No way," she said muffled up close against my chest. We stood for a moment like that, wrapped up in each other's arms. Then she gathered herself up and looked me in the eye. She wiped away a last tear and said, "Let's go to Texas."

We'd have time to talk about what had happened in the coming hours, and we did. Ten minutes later we both felt better accelerating up the on-ramp to the I-5. Irvine and Orange County fell behind us. A short trip north toward Los Angeles took us through the sweeping eastbound turn toward Riverside. In heading out of Los Angeles we both remarked at how quickly we had brought our California chapter to a close. We came to the mutual conclusion that our departure from California was clearly meant to be. Our sixteen military moves over twelve years had all been grueling. Arrangement for them took days and even weeks. Leaving California this time though for what we knew was a final time, a move that would complete change our lives, took little more than a full day.

California and all the living we did there was history. In leaving we visited no one. The friends we had made in the Marines had mostly written us out of their lives months earlier. A former Marine was a former friend to them it seemed. Some of them had moved on to other duty stations. Others had just let us go. We didn't drive past the Marine bases for one last look. I don't recall seeing Marine helicopters passing overhead. If they flew by I don't remember even looking up. Linda and I were both looking and moving forward.

We were out of Riverside and through the Banning Pass well ahead of the rush hour glut. When we joined Interstate 10 eastbound through Palm Springs I noted that we would not leave this highway until we were in Houston. Linda nodded and replied, "I can't get there soon enough." I saw that as a mandate. As we drove into the afternoon she told me how hurt she had been at the school district.

"I know exactly how you feel, baby," I replied. She knew I did. She'd been there for me when I was passed over for promotion. It was a hard time. I hoped I could be a help to her in getting over the cold shoulder she got that morning.

"You'll get past this, Linda. You'll get settled in Austin and you'll forget all about Irvine."

I wasn't making that up. I had learned over the past year that when you get knocked on your butt you get back up and get busy. Regrets don't help you get back on your feet. I looked over at her in the seat beside me. She rested her arm on the window sill. Her head rested in her hand. Her long blond hair was floating around her and in and out the window. There were tears in her eyes.

I smiled at her. "No regrets, now girl," I said. She smiled back at me. "If it hadn't been for you girl, I'd probably still be living in the past waiting for something good to happen."

She reached down with her other hand and took mine and pulled it into her lap.

"You're the best thing that ever happened to me," she said. She looked down the road as though looking into the future. "Houston's not so far away, really. Is it?"

We traded off driving during our fuel stops. One drove and one dozed. We had gone back and forth across the country our whole married lives spelling each other like this. After a career as a Marine I was good at getting the most from catnaps. Linda was less so. I knew as it got late I'd do the bulk of the driving. That was okay by me. When we stopped we fed the Z car premium gas and ourselves sugary drinks, coffee and bad food. Day turned to night as we crossed Arizona. We intended to spend the night in Phoenix. When we got there we just pressed on for Tucson. Between those cities we drove under a canopy of brilliant stars. The midnight desert air was cool and crystal clear. We kept the windows down and smelled the desert creosote bush and mesquite.

I took the wheel in Tucson. Linda looked tired. I may have looked tired too, but I felt rested. We'd done this before, driving all night or until it made no more sense to keep going. I'd know when that happened and get a room for the night. For now I was good to keep going. Linda was ready for a nap. As we left Tucson she dozed off. I spooled up the windows as the dark mountains to the east of Tucson beckoned us on. Coming down on the New Mexico side of the mountains the engine RPM dropped off as the car sped down toward Deming. Passing the little town in the far distance I could see Las Cruses. It sparkled through the windscreen like a luminous diamond. A dozen times I'd driven and flown this route across the New Mexico desert. I knew how the road dipped down over dozens of miles into the valley before me, rising again as it approached Las Cruses. There were no headlights or tail lights on the ribbon of absolutely straight interstate highway before me. We were alone racing into the narrow circle of the Z-car's headlights. The moonless night left a dome of stars from horizon to horizon. I craned my neck looking at them. When I glanced down at the speedometer I was shocked. I was doing ninety-five. It felt like we were crawling. I remembered the last time I had let the Z car's reigns out. A California State Trooper gave me a speeding ticket for eleven miles per hour over the limit. I shook his hand. I was doing three times that. "Keep it at the speed limit sir," he said politely. "That thing you're driving is a ticket magnet."

I chuckled then and I was chuckling now as I contemplated racing into the darkness at a mile and a half a minute. I was not worried about the car's performance at high speed. I knew it was powerful, fast and handled well. For no good reason I felt alert and very much in control. I glanced at Linda. She slept peacefully beside me. There would be no objection from her if I let the reigns out again. I was already cruising in high gear. The RPMs were stuck at a comfortable cruise. There was room under the accelerator and lots of RPM left to use. If I really wanted to see what this car would do, this was the time to do it. So I did.

The RPMs came right up. The speedometer needle climbed until the needle rolled over the top of the case. With RPMs left to burn I buried the speedometer needle buried in the far end of the gauge. The ride was smooth and the car handled like the racecar it was. The engine delivered power without a twitch. The cool desert air satisfied the engine's radiator and kept the oil and coolant temperature right where it would be idling on a parking lot. I felt as though we were flying. The now not-so-distant lights of Las Cruces grew and spread across the windscreen. I recalled them doing that when I flew this route at night in a Marine Corps H-53. That night I was going not that much faster than this.

I never let off the accelerator until a set of headlights appeared on the horizon. Then I backed off and put the car in neutral. The Z still raced up the miles long slope toward the city like a projectile shot from a cannon. Even with the engine now idling I could not believe it took so long to coast to a reasonable speed. When we reached the first signs of life along the highway outside the city I put the car back in high gear.

We glided around the curve of I-10 that led to El Paso. The highway mile markers counted down into the single digits. Past the curve and leaving Las Cruses a large cutout highway sign in the distinctive shape of the State of Texas appeared ahead. It was a landmark, brightly lighted with the words I longed to see. I nudged Linda and read the sign.

"Welcome to Texas!" She opened her sleepy eyes and sat up.

"Almost home!" she said.

"'Half-way there, actually." She looked at me incredulous.

"Los Angeles to El Paso is the same distance as El Paso to Houston, honey. Texas is a big place."

We picked up the boys from Grandma and settled in Austin. The realtor who rented us our house was a prince. He was a diminutive gentleman with thick glasses and an equally thick Polish accent. When I filled out the rental application he noted that I had not listed a work address. I told him I was currently unemployed. The irises of his eyes loomed big in his glasses as he bit his lip. He asked where Linda worked. I told him she didn't have a job either. He slid his glasses down his nose and looked over the top of them as though he could see me. His eyes immediately looked tiny. I thought he was probably wondering why a crazy person was trying to rent one of his houses. My supposition was incorrect. He chuckled and told me I looked like somebody who wouldn't be unemployed so long. Perhaps he admired my chutzpah. He rented us a house.

Unfortunately his supposition and mine about my employability was wrong. I looked for months and couldn't buy a job. My Polish landlord and I had both incorrectly suspected that a former Marine officer with a Master's degree would be snatched up by some smart employer. So not finding a job immediately was not just a surprise. It was a humbling learning experience. Fortunately, Linda and her sister were both teachers. With her sister's network and a few introductions Linda got a job pretty quickly. She had to drive clear to the other side of town to work. At least the job she had made enough money to pay the rent.

For me, not finding a job was mortifying. I made finding work my full-time occupation. I spent all the daylight hours traveling around Austin looking for work. Naturally, the airport was the first place I went. It was also the place I returned to most often. I found out that there were exactly four operators in the City of Austin flying helicopters. Three of them were at the airport. There was a small air ambulance operation at the hospital downtown, too. They called themselves "Lifeline." I thought the name rather clever for a hospital helicopter program. They flew a LongRanger from their hospital helipad. I visited them and filled out an application. I got a cold reception from a guy who said he was their Director of Operations. He looked briefly at my resume. He asked no questions. I could tell he was not impressed. I suspected my application and resume were in his trash can before I got back to my car. So much for Lifeline.

There was also a LongRanger working from a rented hangar on the back side of the airport. I found out that it was flying as an executive ship ferrying rich people around. A couple locals flew it for them. It turned out the pilots were moonlighting full-timers from the Army National Guard unit on the field. The Guard unit was the third operator of helicopters in Austin.

I still knew something about the military, so I went to the Guard unit to meet the pilot moonlighting on the LongRanger. He wasn't there. But an operations specialist by the name of Sue was. I got his name from her, as well as a phone number at the hanger where the helicopter was parked. She gave me directions to the hangar. It was one of the smaller ones on the airport. One wall in a hangar that had a single door that opened outside the airport fence. It opened onto a small, sun-bleached parking lot. Phone calls to his number apparently went to an answering machine in the hangar. I left a half-dozen messages. None were returned. Neither were messages I left at his Guard unit. "I gave him your last three messages," one sergeant said. I got her message pretty plainly. So I had no other choice. I tracked him down. I stalked him. To do it I staked out the hangar door where the LongRanger was parked.

I started the stakeout by passing by the hangar several times a day after dropping off job applications elsewhere. I added time there by eating my lunch in my car in the shade across the parking lot near the hangar. The first week doing this I was there every day. I never saw the door open or a car even parked nearby. I finally resolved to spend the whole day there. That's when my luck changed. It was after lunch time in the heat of the day. From my shady spot I saw a pickup truck swing into the hangar lot and park right where I would have if I flew that bird. Out of it stepped a guy ten years older than me. His hair was slicked back. He wore standard issue military pilot sunglasses. He was dressed in faded blue jeans, a western cut long-sleeved shirt with snap buttons and a set of cowboy boots. A regular ranch hand gone helicopter pilot. He was shorter than me by a head and probably fifty pounds heavier.

I got out of my car and left the door open a little rather than close it and spook him. He reached down for a clip on his belt that held a wad of keys. He fished for one to lock the driver's door. That's what gave me the time to close on him. With that accomplished he turned toward me to spit out a large wad of chewing tobacco on the parking lot. He was clearly surprised. He looked around to see where I had come from. Then he saw the car in the shade. In a flash I could see he knew who I was. I was the guy he had been avoiding these weeks.

Knowing he was trapped he turned back and grabbed a bundle of maps and chart updates he had left on the hood of his truck. He was clearly making up a plan of escape. I was having none of it. I walked toward him to extend the time I'd have before he shook me off.

"Hi! I'm Paul Stone," I stated in a friendly way I wasn't really feeling. He blinked and wrinkled his brow, like a bad actor doing the part of meeting someone he didn't know. The actor said, "Paul who?" He knew exactly who I was. He'd surely deleted each of my numerous messages on the hangar message machine. I bet he'd made sport of shooting my messages at the Guard into the office trash can. Still, I helped him out of his predicament. I played nice.

"I'm the helicopter pilot that's been leaving you messages about flying the LongRanger."

The furrows left his brow. Now he badly acted the part of someone who just realized who I was. I left my hand extended. He took the opportunity to shake out the right key to open the door that was behind me. He didn't shake my hand. He did take the opportunity to look me up and down. Then he found the right key and stepped past me.

"Hi, Paul," he finally replied in not unfriendly manner. "'Name's Vince. What can I do ya' fer." His accent was pure Texan. I could tell he was overdoing the country boy talk. He was clearly uncomfortable. I'm sure he was piqued at having been stalked. He didn't wait for my answer. He just struggled with the lock on the door. I figured it gave me at least another twenty seconds to make my case.

"I just moved here to Austin." I thought maybe it would help to play the military card. "I just got out of the Marines. I'm looking for a helicopter flying job. People here at the airport tell me you're the guy to go to for some help with that."

To his obvious relief he finally got the lock open and the key out of the door.

"What did you fly?" He asked as he grabbed the door knob. He opened the door and wedged his leg inside the door to keep me from following him. Smart move on his part. I surely would have done so.

"53s," I said. "I flew the big Sikorsky transports." The Army didn't have them so I spoke a language he'd understand. He smirked, and I knew why. He gave me the short version of what Chief Pilot Mike had told me that day at the Long Beach airport.

"'Too big. 'Can't use you."

I edged my knee against the door to keep him from opening it enough to scuttle inside.

"I flew Jet Rangers for the Navy as an instructor, too."

He saw I was holding the door.

"Too small. We're flying a LongRanger here."

I didn't give up. "I just left a job in California flying an L-3." I already knew it was exactly the same ship he was flying. He stopped pushing the door against my knee for a moment. For the first time since I caught up with him I thought I had a chance. I thought that maybe I would at least get an invitation inside. He pondered my answer for a few seconds. He didn't invite me in though, even though the door remained half open.

"How much total time you got?" he asked.

"Thirty five hundred hours," I said proudly. I knew that was a good number of hours for a commercial pilot to have. Most military aviators my age had at least a thousand hours less. I wasn't sure what to think when I saw him suppress a smile. Then he pushed the door firmly against my knee and wedged through the space it opened for him.

"Sorry, Stone. Our insurance won't let us hire anybody with less than four thousand. Come see me when you pick up a few hours."

He left off the word "sonny." I heard it just the same. He also left off any suggestion about where I might go to pick up some flight time. When I let the pressure off the door he knew he'd trumped me. Without anything further to say he pulled the door shut behind him. He locked the deadbolt behind him. I could almost hear him sigh in relief.

"Game over," I said to the closed door. I was crestfallen. Standing in the bright sun staring through the small wired-glass pane in the door I watched his receding silhouette. He moved away down the hall like a lost opportunity. The silhouette finally blended with the darkness inside and disappeared. I turned away slowly and walked back to the car feeling very much alone.

The fourth and last helicopter operator in Austin sold Jetrangers. Aside from the passenger terminal, theirs was the biggest and easiest facility to spot on the Austin-Mueller Airport. "We sell Jetrangers." That's what the bold sign on their hangar with the Bell Helicopter logo said, anyway. I had done my homework. I found out that the owner was a man with an Army background. He had flown Hueys in Vietnam. Here in Austin he had started and grown a thriving business selling any helicopter his customers wanted. It was only lately that he had gotten his Bell Helicopter dealership. Evidently the dealership came with a sign. His sponsors made him a Bell helicopter dealer.

In the coming years this man would become a good friend and mentor. I didn't know it then. Despite his resistance to my approaches, from the time I met him I saw that potential. On the day I arrived at his business though, this first time looking for employment, he was just one more person in Austin who didn't have any kind of job opening to offer me. To his credit he gave me a good deal of his time. He offered what counsel he had for a guy in my situation. During my weeks unemployed I visited with him a couple more times. He offered his reflections on leads I was trying desperately to develop. As my job hunt continued week after week I didn't have to tell him that things weren't going well. He felt for me. I know his concern was sincere. There was nothing he could do from his own business' perspective, however. He was flummoxed that he could neither help nor point to someone who could employ me elsewhere. I told him I'd sweep the hangar for him until a flying or sales job came open with him. If he couldn't afford minimum wage I would work for free. He was impressed with my drive. Perhaps that is what made him my friend for all those years since that time. Still, he didn't give me a broom to push. I was just happy he didn't say the line I was hearing almost every day now; "I'll keep your resume."

Without a prayer of flying helicopters in Austin I drove around the perimeter of the airport to the executive air terminal. That's where all the private airplanes arrived and departed. It was pretty busy with everything from single engine trainers to business jets passing through each day. I hadn't stopped before because there was nothing for me to fly there. The terminal just provided service to transient aircraft. This time though, I parked out front and went inside anyway. I asked the lady at the desk if I could speak with the manager of the facility. I was not wearing a suit. Instead, I dressed like a lineman because that was the only job I could expect my visit to garner.

The manager arrived in due time. Actually, he kept me waiting longer than was courteous, even for an obvious job applicant. I'm not sure about his initial impression of me. My initial impression of him was not very flattering. Words like "officious," "bully," and "dull" all came to mind. He wore a coat and tie. Neither looked like it belonged on him. He'd have looked more at home in coveralls. He led me into his office. The walls were covered with what looked like framed awards. Taking a moment to read a couple I could see what the frames contained. There were a couple of continuous employment awards. I deduced he had been in his current line of employment for at least five years. Bravo for him. He also had what looked like diplomas from courses he'd taken. There were titles like "Phillips Petroleum Fuel Handler – Basics," and "Hazardous Materials Handling," signed off by vendors' representative who taught the courses.

He sat down in the narrow space behind his desk. He didn't offer me a chair because there was not enough room for one on the other side of his desk. I saw no reason to beat about the bush making small talk. He clearly wasn't interested in doing so. So I just came right out and asked for work as a lineman. I told him I had lots of experience working on airports and dealing with customers. I was sure that my background and education would be my own worst enemy. So I referred only to my last employment flying the line for the Island Shuttle. With one well thought out question about what else I had done in my career he could have rolled up my attempt at employment like a rug. "Over-qualified," he would say. I'd heard that before. I didn't understand it.

Instead of asking me anything about myself though he just opened a drawer. He withdrew what I had come to know well as a standard employment application. I had filled out quite a few in the past weeks. He handed it to me. I thanked him for it and for his time and took it home. I filled it out that night, just as I had filled out dozens of others on all the nights since we had come to Austin. This one was cleverly written enough to reap the information the manager used to say, "You're over qualified." He said it the next morning when I caught him in the lobby and delivered it to him personally. I took exception. I had nothing to lose, and no bridge to burn with him. I wanted to know exactly what that meant. "With respect, sir," I said trying to be polite, "how can a person be over qualified for a job? If a job applicant knows how to do a job and will work for the pay, what's the problem?" He just gave me *the look*. It said that someone with a brain and experience would replace him one day. He didn't want that someone to be me. Austin being the state capitol, in applying for jobs as a bureaucrat I saw that look a lot. He just shook his head at me. He wasn't inclined to debate with me.

"Sorry," he said. I know he wasn't. So I left.

After weeks and then months spent looking for work I was having trouble keeping my spirits up. I figured that staying active and searching diligently would be better than sitting at home feeling sorry for myself. I kept up the same pattern every day. During the day I picked up applications. In the evenings I filled them out. Meanwhile I searched the want ads. They grew boring. I found out that some want ads run continuously. They make the same low paying job look newly posted, exciting and easy to get. I wager these places do that because they cycle through employees regularly. If you have an education and a record anywhere except with the police, even those jobs are hard to get.

I spent a lot of my searching time downtown. There were lots of white collars on the streets around the capital at lunch time. I followed some of them to see where they worked. I found that a fifty story bank building resembled Austin's want ads page. The same thing was repeated on every floor just as the same ads were repeated in every want ad column. Lawyers and lobbyists, CPA's and state agencies I'd never heard of were piled in layers from the parking lot level all the way up. None of the offices offered employment.

The place to find government jobs was through the state job banks. I spent time there, too. Near the largest of the job banks downtown was a car lot in which I could park for free. I'd get there early and keep my spot there all day. Knowing I might meet my next employer while dropping an application I always dressed neatly. I even kept a suit in my car. Several times when I turned in an application I was asked to come back the same day for an interview. That's when it paid to have my suit handy, or so I thought. In the building with the job bank was a large public bathroom. There I'd brush my teeth, put on some deodorant and splash on a little aftershave. Then I'd don the suit. At the appointed time I was ready for the interview and looking like it. That plan never worked out though. I got no job offers. I didn't quit.

I came to know the resources available in the state library, too. I researched every committee, commission and office holder with an office in Austin. During my research I found out that Texas had its own aviation agency. They didn't fly airplanes. They helped inspect, repair and develop the state's airports. Working there would be fine for me. When a job posting popped up there for an airport inspector I jumped on it. Reading the qualifications I saw I met every one. I had the standard state employer's application at hand so I walked the eight blocks to the Texas Aeronautics Commission. It was housed in an art deco office building that looked nothing like it dealt with aircraft, airports or anything having to do with either one. I walked through a wide lobby to a wooden door with a small sign on it. "TAC," was all it said. On the other side was a long hallway with offices on both sides. The first one on the left had no door. Behind a heavy oak desk sat a secretary. She was my age, plain looking and completely disinterested with the fact that I was standing four feet from her. She was typing. She didn't even look up from her typewriter. I saw that she had an "in" box on the corner of her desk. It was so marked.

"Excuse me," I interrupted. "I have an employment application I would like to submit." She stopped typing. Without looking at me she reached out with her right hand and took the application from mine. Almost before it had settled in her inbox she typing again. I shrugged my shoulders and left.

The rejection letter almost beat me home. When I got it I stood in the driveway and thought about my options. I decided that going back to places I had already been bore the only promise I had at the moment. It occurred to me that during my days stalking Vince the LongRanger guy that I saw a lot of activity behind the fence at the Army National Guard facility at the airport. I decided that I would drive back to the airport and see what lay behind the fence there. I made it my first stop the next morning.

I was surprised to find the gate to the parking lot stood wide open. There was no gate guard either. So I parked on the lot like I belonged there, got out of the car and walked in the front door of the National Guard facility. It wasn't hard to find the recruiter. A sign near the door pointed the way down a well-lighted, windowless hallway. At the end of it was an open door with an Army logo and the word "RECRUITER" posted on it. I'd seen one just like it many years before just before I joined the Marines. I stepped inside to find a portly, bald and camouflage clad Sergeant First Class sitting behind a standard gray metal government desk. The nametag on his uniform read "Garza." I introduced myself. He flashed a wide grin and said, "Howdy, and welcome to the 124th Cavalry." I asked him where they kept the horses. He took the crack in stride. "They're out back," he chuckled. "They look a lot like helicopters."

"Well, how about that, Sergeant Garza. It just so happens that I fly helicopters." He waved me toward a government style metal arm chair in front of his desk.

"We'll shoot, looks like we've already got a match. So, what can I do for you?"

I gave him my now polished biography. I told him frankly what I had been doing over the passing weeks and now months. I was happy to share my frustration with the only person who had even expressed interest in me in the past weeks.

He was looking at my resume as I spoke. "You're a jarhead?" he said with some excitement in his voice. "Hey, I was one of them once. 'Got out after 'Nam and joined this outfit."

He looked up from the resume from under his eyebrows. "You're wondering, 'What's a Marine doing here in an Army uniform,' right?" He didn't wait for me to answer. "Well, welcome to the National Guard where nobody is what they seem."

He asked me about my military career and what I had flown in the Marines. I told him. Although I figured it would be the deal killer, I also told him I had been passed over for promotion from captain to major. I didn't see any reason to waste our time if being passed over made a difference to him or the National Guard. When I said it he just laughed. That caught me by surprise.

"You've been passed over? Big deal! Hasn't everybody?"

That really confused me.

"Let me tell you how the Guard works. Our facility commander last year was a lieutenant colonel. He's been in the Guard his whole career. He got passed over for full bird. No colonels eagles for that hombre." Garza chuckled. "He coulda' retired. Probably shoulda'. Everybody thought he would. Well, he didn't. He took a warrant."

I wasn't following him. Garza could tell.

"He became a Chief Warrant Officer Two!"

That would be CW2 on a scale that topped out at 4. Colonel to CW2 was a huge rank reduction. CW2 was also a rank usually held by guys half a colonel's age. I was wondering how it would feel to slip back up so far in the rank structure when Sergeant Garza said, "Now he works for the guys he used to command. 'Flies Cobras in my troop in fact. Now that he's a warrant officer he told me he should have done it sooner. He's having a fine time. Now he just flies. No paperwork. None of the bull crap he had to do as a commissioned officer."

That sounded good to me. I knew Army warrant officers were specialists. Warrant Officer pilots just flew. Commissioned officers – lieutenant through general – did the paperwork. They were in command. They paid for it by not flying much. I asked Garza where he fit in the Guard.

"I'm a full-timer," he replied. "I do this gig full time here during the week. I get a salary for it. I'm still a part-timer, too. That's what will get me my military retirement. I do weekend and summer drills just like all the other Guardsmen. I get paid for them just like you would."

Getting paid to work in Austin and fly helicopters was a brightening prospect.

Garza saw my eyes brighten. He went on. "In the Marines you and I called Guardsmen, 'weekend warriors." He smiled broadly.

"And we still do," I replied, smilingback.

"We *are* weekend warriors, Paul. But we do special duties during the week sometimes, too. We make some money and gather a few retirement points. And when times are good here we've got guys who make a living at it. Extra duty includes flying assignments. We'll fly to an airshow to do a display, or work with the police somewhere in the state looking for people growing dope. 'Things like that."

I was catching on. The Guard was looking like the first glimmer of hope for employment of any kind I'd seen since I got to Austin.

Garza went on. "I'm a weekend warrior in a cavalry unit. We've got OH-58 Scouts and Cobra gunships."

The OH-58 was just an Army green Jetranger. I knew the Cobra gunship from my days as a Marine. The Army flew a slightly different model, but both the Army and Marine version had a three-barreled, twenty millimeter Gatling gun and rocket pods. Garza was speaking my language. When he slipped into Army-eze he saw it on my face and he translated it to Marine..

"This is a cavalry unit, so we got troops here instead of platoons, ya' know?"

He saw that I understood that.

"Marines got squadrons?"

I nodded.

"I knew that. Well, cavalry's got squadrons, too. And we 'doggies' in the cavalry had 'em before the Marines!"

"Doggies" or "Dog-faces" are what Marines derisively call soldiers, rather like they call Marines, "Jarheads."

"Those Army cavalry squadrons rode horses. Now we ride helicopters."

The Marines didn't have cavalry so this organization of squadrons was all new to me. "Hey, you was a Marine. Us Marines are brothers, right?"

I smiled and nodded again. And for the next couple hours, Sergeant First Class Garza, Texas Army National Guard, formerly Sergeant Garza, USMC showed me around the facility and filled me in on how things work at the Texas Army National Guard. He took me out on the flight line and showed me the helicopters they flew. A dozen or so of the unarmed OH-58's were lined up on concrete pads. The Army Cobra gunship were better armed than the Marine version. They had two racks on the stubby wings for anti-tank missiles.

There were a couple faded green Hueys out there on the ramp, too. They looked very old and well worn. Garza said that these were being replaced soon by the new Army Blackhawk.

"In the Army, Warrant Officers do all the flying. Commissioned officers do all the paperwork. If you decide to join, you might want to keep that in mind."

I didn't really care at that point what position I held. I just wanted work. Walking back into the building from the flight line Sergeant Garza introduced me to someone I'd met before. It was Vince, the guy who had shrugged me off at the LongRanger hangar. Today however he was wearing the same uniform Garza wore only Vince's uniform bore the rank bars of a senior warrant officer on the collar. Vince turned out to be his last name. In short order I was told that CW4 Vince would be the person I'd turn my application over to if I decided to join the Guard.

I didn't see any reason to delay the process, so I asked Mister Vince for an application package. I already knew that Warrant Officers in the Army are called "mister." Mister Vince led me to his office and handed me a folder filled with forms. He was only a little more forthcoming than he had been at the LongRanger hangar.

"Fill them out and get them back to me," he said. "Then we'll talk."

Brief though it was, that response and bundle of government forms represented a positive change in my employment prospects. Having no other hot leads I went home immediately and got busy filling out the forms. The work supplying information to the Guard took days. I filled out a thick stack of papers, got finger print cards and passport pictures made. I copied my whole Marine Corps record at least twice and referred to it in filling out other forms for the Army. Most had to be done in quadruplicate. When I finished I turned them in to Mister Vince. He took the neat stack of forms and said, "I'll call you." If he did it would be the first time ever.

I left. And then I waited. I didn't wait long, though. Never one to make a phone call when a personal visit will do, whenever I passed nearby the Guard facility I checked on the progress of my application with Mister Vince. After a while it got to the point that as soon as he saw me we would say together, "It's in processing."

Another month went by and then another with no word from the Guard. I stayed at it looking for work every day. It had been four months since we moved to Austin and I had not gotten so much as a second interview at any of the places where I applied for work. I couldn't help it. I became depressed. I was running out of ideas and we were running out of money. Since my unexpected career change from Marine captain to unemployed civilian, I was finding out the hard way that God sometimes gets your attention by placing you in trying circumstances. He was certainly getting my attention now.

One night after Linda and the boys were sleeping, I sat at my desk in a spare bedroom that served as an office of sorts. It was where I always spent my evenings filling out job applications. The room was full of unpacked boxes. I had finished looking through the want ads for the third time that day. I had read them all before. Most of the open positions were the same as they had been for the past weeks. I had probably applied for them all. That evening I had already filled out a couple more applications for jobs I didn't want. I still would have taken any of them just to have a job. I looked at the pile of applications I would deliver tomorrow, knowing most were probably destined directly for a garbage can somewhere. I checked the bank balance again and got the sick feeling I got every time I did that. Checking account low, savings lower.

I walked down the hallway and looked in at my boys as they slept. I stepped in quietly and rubbed each little head. They were at peace. They believed in me. It never occurred to me standing there in the dark bedroom that millions of fathers for thousands of reasons couldn't do what I was doing at that moment. Only a couple years ago I would have given anything to be able to do what I was doing there. Not so long ago I was away on foreign shores out of touch with my precious wife and children. And now here I was standing in the boys' bedroom, listening to them breathe, feeling sorry for myself. I missed the blessings I had in rich abundance sleeping there before me. I missed all the other blessings I had, too. All I could think of was how I would be able to keep feeding these little boys, keep paying the rent.

I walked downstairs and out into the backyard. I took a seat on the picnic table out in the middle of the yard and looked up at the night sky. All I saw was blackness. I missed the reminder the stars offer of how miniscule we are, how unimportant our troubles seem on such a vast scale. I missed how little time we really even spend here on earth. The twinkling lights in the heavens had left their source before man's first ancestors were born. My time on earth was less than the blink of an eye on that scale. Yet all I saw from my post on the picnic table was the dark night and the endless void above me. There was no prayer on my lips. There was no God there for me. I just groaned. Here I was, tough, smart, capable, young and experienced and all of it counted as nothing. I had shouldered this whole burden myself, as though I was the one who determined whether or not I got a job, whether or not I drew the next breath.

Then I realized quite suddenly that in the year since I had been passed over I had missed something far more important. I had missed God. I had never asked God for help. I had in fact never even recognized Him at all. With that sudden realization I was ashamed of myself. How could I have ignored Him? I was not raised that way. Where was my faith? I looked up at the bedroom windows across the back of my house. Behind them slept my wife and my sons, my greatest gifts. They were protected and safe. My depression shifted toward remorse that I had forgotten to thank God for them. Tears gathered in my eyes and I moaned aloud, "Oh, God I am so sorry." I looked up at the sky again and this time noticed the stars. "I am so sorry I forgot you. I know now. You've shown me that I need you and it took this long for me to notice."

I hung my head in shame. "I'm sorry, Lord," I prayed. "I thought I could do it all myself. I thought my life was my own, that I did what I did on my own. I know now it all comes from you. You knew all along I'd come to you, that I'd tell you I cannot carry this burden by myself. And you're right. I can't. I can't do anything without you. I am weak. Saying that doesn't come easy. My pride makes it hard for me to say. You've shown me and I can't deny it. I need you. I should have asked for your help sooner. I'm sorry I didn't. I'm asking you now, Lord God. I need your help. Please help me."

I sat there on that picnic table with my head hung low. All alone I cried and prayed until I was spent. Then, my prayers said and wiping the tears from my eyes, I stood and walked back into the house. There was no brilliant flash of light as acknowledgment that my prayer had been heard. I didn't really expect one. I didn't really expect anything -- not a job, not a change, just more of the same failures following failures. I was cried out and exhausted walking through my dark living room. I walked into the bedroom, undressed slowly and quietly and went to bed. As I slid beneath the sheets and lay down next to Linda, I felt a weight I had carried come off my shoulders. I knew I might pick up that burden again tomorrow. Still for the rest of the night I would sleep unburdened. I pressed close to Linda. Tomorrow would be another day.

I slept exceptionally well. In fact I didn't even hear the alarm the next morning. When Linda scuffed my head and woke me I sat up feeling like something good was just about to happen. I told her so. Nothing had changed in my situation. I was still out of work and going broke. I couldn't explain why I just felt hopeful this morning. I knew somehow that this new day would lead to something special. Even coming home from another fruitless job hunt I felt that way. Walking up the front steps I opened the mailbox. Inside was another letter from the Texas Aeronautics Commission. The letter was not one of the form letters I had been getting. It was one that had been drafted by someone. A Mrs. Scarsdale asked me to ignore the rejection letter I had received earlier. She asked that I please contact her if I was still interested in a job there.

I called her the next day. She said another position had come open. When she described it I found the new job was more interesting, offered a lot more autonomy, and paid better than the one for which I had been rejected. I took the job of course. Shortly after that a colonel, the commanding officer of the National Guard unit in Austin, invited me visit the Guard facility and talk to him. He asked me if I would like my commission back. He had a captain's slot that was open. In not too long I would go before a promotion board, he said. After that it was more than likely since they needed a major too, I'd be a major pretty soon. I thought about what the colonel was telling me. I had another chance at promotion to major that the Marines had not given me. Having a job was great fortune. Getting offered two in the same week I could do simultaneously was like a miracle. It really was a miracle. I just didn't have the eyes to see it yet. That time would come.

With the opportunity offered to make captain and then major with the Guard, Sergeant Garza's words came back to me. Perhaps a commission was not the best idea for what I wanted out of the Guard. I wanted to fly. Besides, things had changed for me since I left the Marine Corps. The rank of major was not important to me anymore. If it had been, I would have changed trouser colors and joined the Navy at Point Mugu. Besides the additional pay we could sure use after the long dry spell, it was my desire to fly that drove me now. When I visited with the facility commander I asked the colonel for a warrant. It surprised him that a Marine knew what an Army warrant officer did. And it surprised him more that I asked for it with a commission in the offing. He smiled. Then he addressed me as warrant officers are addressed. "Mister Stone," he said, "You're not as dumb as most Marines I've met."

He put me into Sergeant Garza's cavalry troop. I got a slot as a Chief Warrant Officer Two (CW2). The captain commanding the troop made me his instructor pilot in the OH-58 helicopter. It was a perfect fit. The OH-58 was the Army's version of the Navy's TH-57 I had flown as a Marine Corps flight instructor. The Guard even recognized my Navy time as an instructor in TH-57s. They counted it hour for hour toward designation as an Army Instructor Pilot. Now I had not one job in aviation in Austin, Texas. I had two.

The jobs that shared my time were perfectly symbiotic, thanks to my boss at the Aeronautics Commission. He was a retired Air Force colonel, a Phantom pilot with the improbable name of Lance Casey. His name not only sounded like a fighter pilot's, he looked the part. He was a white haired, tall, slender and mustachioed Texan. His work attire consisted of a Stetson hat, a western cut suit, a bolo tie and highly polished alligator cowboy boots. As a former military pilot himself he fully supported me any time I wanted to spend time flying with the Guard.

Yes, God had been listening that night I spent in despair in the back yard. It took me a while to know He had just been waiting for me to ask Him for help. Unfortunately I quickly recovered from the humbling experience of being out of work. When things are going well it is easy for us to take the credit. And in short order that is exactly what I did. As I got comfortable with my new life I grew lazy. God likes to hear from us even when things are going well. At first I made it a point to thank Him for my new blessings. But as He knew I would, I forgot about the grace with which He had showered me all my life. I should have known he had something waiting for me that would put me back on track with Him again. God loves us. One of His finest traits is His patience. He was certainly patient with me.

As He must have known I would, I lived my new life circumstances as though I was the one in control of them. My new professions made me happier than my Marine Corps career in almost every respect. I worked my two jobs in happy harmony. Together they brought in all the money we needed, with Linda's salary just another blessing I took for granted. Unlike when I was a Marine I spent time at home now. After work and on weekends I was with my family. For the first time in my life I had time to be a good husband and a good dad.

Linda and I also found and bought a very nice house in South Austin. I missed the seemingly serendipitous circumstances that got us into it. I missed that gift of grace. The timing was perfect as God's timing always is. Before we got to Austin the housing market was off the charts. We couldn't have afforded a house there any more than we could in California. Houses couldn't be built fast enough to meet the need. About the time we arrived in Austin though, the housing market mysteriously died.

Foreclosures were soon common. Banks owned houses they couldn't sell. A bank owned the place we wanted. In order to get it off their books they accepted our ridiculously low offer. So we got a place worth roughly twice what we paid for it. It was a huge custom home. It had a big yard and trees just right for a trio of happy boys to play in. And it was also located two blocks from the boys' school and a five minute drive from Linda's. We just moved in and lived life thinking how lucky we were. I missed yet another tailored miracle I'd been handed. I must have been numb to the constant miracles that were occurring. They seemed so common now. So like a spoiled child I just figured that was the way life was supposed to be.

After all I had been through in the two years after I left the Marines I was living life like nothing could go wrong. I either ignored or forgot how life could change in a moment. We got some reminders, though. Sadly, Linda and I both lost our mothers to cancer that year. We watched one slip away and then the other. If I had been a Marine major at that time, our mothers would not have known our sons, their grandkids. Neither would Linda and I been there for them when they were sick. Living in Austin we were there for their last days. And we were with them at their passing. Even in their loss God had been good to us.

I missed seeing that blessing. I focused on the day-to-day. Work, the kids' school and social events, paying the bills and living the good life we now had was enough to fill our days and nights. Then one day in reading a book I picked up, I stumbled upon an old book marker. On it was printed a prayer. It had been spoken by a soldier long ago on the morning of a great battle. "Oh Lord," it began, "this day if I forget thee, do not thou forget me."

It struck me that in living my new life as a civilian, I had forgotten God once again. I closed my eyes right then and said that prayer from my heart. Fortunately for me God replied. He sent someone to me who changed my life yet again. In doing so he me back on track in his service. The guy he sent was no angel. He was a Navy pilot.

3 A NEW DAY

Life was a bowl of cherries. I had been working for Colonel Casey for five years. I was sitting at my desk one morning when the receptionist called me. I had a visitor. She sent him down the hallway to my office. When I rose to greet my visitor, in stepped my alter ego. Aside from the short, clipped moustache he looked like I must have the day I arrived to interview with McDonnell-Douglas. He had a close military haircut. He wore a sharp looking new suit that fit him perfectly. His shoes were shined like mirrors. Shaking his hand I introduced myself and offered him a seat in front of my desk. I pulled another up in front of him and sat down. A short silence ensued while I waited for him to introduce himself.

"You don't know who I am, do you?" He smiled in a rather devilish way, as though he knew a secret I would discover shortly. I took a careful look at him. I thought I vaguely recognized him from somewhere in our past. Then it came to me.

"Well, actually I think I do recognize you. You're a military officer in an interview suit. My guess is you're a Naval Aviator. You're too secretive to be a Marine so that makes you a squid." That's what Marines jokingly call sailors.

He smiled broadly. "Not bad for a jarhead," he replied, returning the jest with the Navy version of the same ribbing.

"Yeah, I'm a squid alright. I was also one of your flight students in Pensacola."

He could see I didn't remember him. "My name is Arlen Johnson, late a submarine hunter in our United States Navy."

I rubbed my chin, feigning recognition that I still didn't feel. "Oh, yeah Arlen. I do remember you. You're the student who wore the green flight suit and white helmet. I believe you had a sweat bead hanging off your chin last time we flew, right?"

He laughed out loud. During my time as a Marine flight instructor I flew with over seven hundred flight students: Marines, Sailors and Coast Guardsmen. During the three years I flew as an instructor some students stood out. Most like Arlen, did not. Even my flight logbooks recorded only the name of the first of perhaps three student I might teach each day. The other two were forgotten even to my logbook. During those three years every one of those students I flew with wore a green flight suit and a white helmet. Learning to fly was hard work for them and they all sweated, often profusely. With six or eight hot months flying in Pensacola each of those three years, my students and I probably sweat gallons. It dripped from our noses and chins and into our eyes. We wiped it away and we flew.

Arlen particularly enjoyed my joke about the sweating student. At what turned out to be the end of his Navy career he too had been an instructor. He flew in the same training squadron where we met. Today I had plenty of time to help Arlen. I started by listening. I started where he told me he had been the top student in his flight school class when he got his wings. "It got me a plum assignment out of flight school. I was assigned to the first Navy helicopter squadron to fly the new SH-60 Seahawk." That made him a submarine hunter. I knew they usually worked off the back of a guided missile cruiser. Those guys spent a lot of time deployed away from their families. "Haze gray and underway, as the sailors called it. Arlen told me that besides his normal deployments he had volunteered for several additional deployments into harm's way as well. He was good at his job. He was dedicated. He thought that would have made him a shoo-in for a promotion. He figured he was due a tour ashore. So he went to Pensacola. There he'd be home every night for the two year Navy tour as a flight instructor. The Navy thought otherwise, I suppose.

I went to Pensacola for the same reason: to be with my wife and babies. The Marine Corps promotion board didn't like that, either. Leaving Pensacola I made it back to the fleet. Then my career ran up on the rocks. Arlen didn't see the fleet again. He was passed over for promotion there in Pensacola. He was discharged without fanfare. Then he moved to Austin. He liked Austin. He met his wife at the University of Texas there before they started a life torn apart by Navy deployments. This morning in my office he looked like I had back when I needed a job in Austin. He had no idea that I had walked every step of his journey myself. Taking care of citizens who needed jobs in aviation fields was now my job.

"Arlen," I said, you came to the right place. I'm going to help you find a job." And that is exactly what I did.

I had this under control. My catharsis in the back yard five years before did not come to mind. I was going to do the driving (I thought). I didn't ask God for help or ask Arlen if he had done so. I didn't even know if Arlen believed in God. It didn't matter. I just jumped in with the intention of taking over. Now that I had control of my life again it never occurred to me that I needed help anymore. I could accomplish anything I wanted to do. In retrospect I can't believe I was so arrogant.

Before he left my office I asked Arlen how he had found me. It was an unlikely chain of events. It was just like the unlikely chain of events that always seemed to guide my own life. Arlen said that he had heard my name mentioned on his last assignment. One of the more senior flight instructors at the training squadron was a Marine. He knew me, knew I was in Austin. "Look him up," he told Arlen. "He might have a flying job for you."

"Is that what you want, Arlen? A flying job?" Suddenly my cockiness got a slap in the head. I didn't know he was going to be much more specific.

"I want to fly for Lifeline," he said looking at me quite seriously. He couldn't have known the situation. "Lifeline Air Ambulance" was located at the Brackenridge hospital a half dozen blocks from my office. Both the Director of Operations and the Chief Pilot flew Cobra gunships in my National Guard unit. I knew they had all the pilots they needed. So I told Arlen, "Take a number, shipmate. Everybody who flies helicopters in this town wants that job. That includes most of the local National Guard pilots I fly with. I think they have all applied there and been turned down. I applied there myself when I first got here. They didn't even call me back."

If he had looked crestfallen I probably would have shut up right there. I could see he had no plan to quit, though. He knew his objective. And I had told him I would help. So I said, "Look, Arlen. I may have spoken too soon. Do you have a resume?"

He took a business envelope out of his inside coat pocket and handed it to me. "Funny you should ask," he replied with a grin.

"Okay," I said reaching out and taking the envelope. It was unsealed. "This is a good start. Don't get your hopes up," I warned. "Pilot turnover there is almost nil. They have a stack of these a mile high."

He looked undaunted. I wished I had been just a typical state employee at that moment who dodged work. This was going to take some work.

I looked at the envelope and bit my lip. "Give me a week." I had a Guard drill scheduled for the coming weekend. I'd talk to the Lifeline pilots who flew with me at drills. Maybe I could make something happen for Arlen. At least I'd try.

"If something comes up sooner I'll let you know. Meanwhile, keep your hopes up and keep looking on your own. First one to find you a job the other guy buys the coffee.

"That's a deal," he said. Then he left.

When he was gone I slid his resume out of the envelope, unfolded it and gave it a quick look. His qualifications were impressive. He had a lot of flight time, including time in light helicopters. He had more ratings than I did on his license. Even so, I knew that it was unlikely his resume would get even the cursory glance from Lifeline management. I bet his skills were as strong as his qualifications. I wasn't betting on Lifeline. I was going to look elsewhere for him. San Antonio, Houston and Dallas had jobs with EMS operators. If he wasn't settled in Austin yet maybe he'd be willing to move. I thought it only fair to check them out. I shook my head as I walked back to my desk. I dropped the resume in the "in" box. It would be part of my job for a while I bet. *Lifeline...we'll see.*

During my next Guard drill I looked up my friend and fellow Guardsman, Anthony Rosso. He was a longtime Army pilot. He had flown the first models of Cobra helicopters in Vietnam. He was no braggart. In the years I served with him I heard a few of his war stories from others, but never from Anthony. He was most certainly a warrior. Was also a leader. He looked and acted like it. Even in his green military flight suit he looked neat, fit and in command. He was a swarthy Italian, short in stature and slender. Though physically diminutive he had a big, masculine personality. He was old enough to have earned the gray in his neatly cut, otherwise jet black hair. His coal black, pencil thin mustache made him look like a classic rake, a villain, a pirate or most certainly an attack helicopter pilot.

During our weekend drills he wore the distinctive black Army cavalry hat with his flight suit. No one challenged his right to do so. We had all seen the chest full of medals on his dress uniform. I recognized among them a Silver Star and Distinguished Flying Cross. Those medals were given sparingly and only for great valor at substantial risk of the wearer's life.

Until I offered him Arlen's resume I had spoken to him very little about his work at Lifeline Air Ambulance. I knew that he was their Director of Operations; he was the top dog. I bragged that he had been my flight student. He looked at me with a twinkle in his eye, one side of his mustache revealing a little smile. He flipped the envelope open and looked over Arlen's resume. While he looked it over he said, "You know Paul, you'd make a good air ambulance pilot. If we had a position open I'd recommend that you apply."

I thought he was being polite. I smiled. "Not likely Anthony. Thanks. I've got a good job. Besides, I applied there a few years ago. I guess I didn't make the grade."

His face didn't change. He read on, nodding as he finished Arlen's resume. Then he looked up. "He looks like a strong candidate." But then Anthony switched subjects again. "You said you applied? I don't recall ever seeing your resume go across my desk."

I described the time I had come to Lifeline's quarters at the hospital and spoken with the pilot on duty. "It's probably been five years, Anthony. I can't remember if the pilot I spoke with told me he was D.O. (Director of Operations), or if I just assumed that he was. When I gave him my resume and application though, I could tell he wasn't going to call me back. I don't think he liked me much."

Anthony knit his brow. "Who did you talk to?"

I chuckled. "I can't recall his name. I caught him up on the helipad. He was pretty disheveled looking, as I recalled. Not someone who emitted the milk of human kindness, to be sure. And he had an unusual name." I tried to recall it.

"Jolly," Anthony replied. "His name is 'Jolly.'"

Anthony got a dark look on his face but didn't say anything.

"Is that guy still flying for Lifeline," I asked.

"Yes," he replied crisply. "He's still one of our pilots." Arlen's folded resume still in his hand he crossed his hands behind him. He looked down and rocked on his heels. I could tell something was on his mind. He looked up at me and drew breath as though he was going to say something. Then instead, he stepped off down the hallway. A few paces away he said over his shoulder, "I'll let you know what we can do for your friend."

The next week Arlen and I started a tradition. We met for coffee at the little café across the street from my office. I told him I'd planted his resume. I hadn't heard anything that week or the next about it. We'd have to see what came of it. I didn't tell him I thought his chances were for working at Lifeline were hopeless. Meanwhile, I started beating the bushes around Texas for other Emergency Medical Service (EMS) flying jobs. I had new ones for him to consider at each weekly coffee clutch we shared. He was thankful for my efforts. Arlen was stubborn though. "I'll wait for Lifeline," he said confidently.

To my surprise, several weeks later Arlen called me. He said he was scheduled to interview with Lifeline. I was surprised and happy for him and told him so. When he got the job, he gave me the credit. I told him I may have cracked the door open for him. I knew that he got the job at Lifeline based on his own merits. I believed every word I told him, too. I didn't know it at the time but Arlen didn't believe any of it.

During the next few months I found out from Anthony that Arlen had turned out to be an exceptional air ambulance pilot. His skills notwithstanding, I know now that he was meant to get that job. Whether I helped him or not he had to be destined for it, although I didn't know that then. Neither did I know the role Arlen was destined to play in my own life as a consequence of being a pilot for Lifeline. I had not yet matured enough to know then that certain things in life are supposed to happen. We play a part in how they happen, although we are only actors on life's stage. We don't write the play. We certainly don't direct it.

The hospital where Arlen now worked was a short walk from my office. He and I visited each other pretty regularly during the first weeks he worked for Lifeline. Sometimes we met for breakfast, other times for dinner. It depended which shift he was beginning or ending. If it was dinner we hit Austin's and Arlen's favorite, the "Texas Chili Parlor." It was over near the state capitol building. If it was breakfast we walked right across the street from my office building. "The Hill Country Smokehouse," was noted for breakfast tacos and good coffee.

Initially, Arlen was pretty busy learning the job. We discussed his training. He enjoyed setting up scenarios he had mastered and asking me what I would do in the same situation. He seemed impressed that I often came up with ways to solve a problem that hadn't occurred to him. "You're still the master instructor," he said to me one scenario he had hope would stump me.

"No I'm not, Arlen," I replied sincerely. "I'm just a helicopter pilot."

He would have none of it. "You should have applied for my job," he said. "You're a natural for it."

"'Doesn't pay enough, Arlen." I took a big bite of breakfast taco. "Besides, I can't stand the sight of blood." I smiled, doffed my coffee and changed the subject.

After his training was done, Arlen started flying shifts. He flew a week of days, took a week off and then flew a week of nights. We had a lot of coffee and breakfasts and dinners together. We also got to be good friends. I was fascinated by some of the situations he described in which he found himself. He was doing things with the helicopter I had never done. It seemed exciting. I knew he was getting good at it, too. I was happy for him. He was clearly enjoying his new job.

Then while we were at breakfast one morning he surprised me. He said that flying an air ambulance wasn't all as rewarding as he thought it would be. When I asked why, he said, "It's the crew."

I didn't know what he meant. I knew he had great stick and rudder skills. I was sure he could fly a helicopter through a keyhole. But when he said he was having problems with the crew, I wondered what he meant.

"They say I don't have any empathy." I remained silent. He finished his coffee and put the cup down. "I guess what they mean is that I don't understand their part of our job. But they're wrong, Paul. I understand it. I land. They pick up the bleeding body. I fly home. What's to understand?"

I knew there was a lot more to what was bothering the crew about Arlen. I couldn't tell what it was because I don't think Arlen knew.

"So what part of the job requires your empathy?" I asked.

"I'm a pilot. I just ignore what's going on back there."

"Maybe you need to ignore less and participate more." He didn't seem to make the connection. "Everybody on a team likes to think the rest of the team is involved," I said. "I'm sure they expect you to know what they do. Maybe it would help if you pitched in once in a while, ya' know what I mean?"

He looked at me with anger in his eyes. "You sound like a nurse, Paul! In fact you sound just like a nurse I work with. I'll tell you what I told her. I don't give a damn about the medical crap." He broke eye contact with me but he was still charged up. "I'm not a paramedic. And I'm sure not a nurse. I'm a captain on an air ambulance helicopter. I get everybody to the scene and I get everybody home. I don't do medicine."

Now I could clearly see where Arlen's problem lay with the crew. But I was missing something bigger, something I wouldn't see for many years.

"They think that flying that mission, controlling that helicopter is done by a voice vote. They act like it's a democracy up there." He locked eyes with me again. "I can tell you one thing, Paul. And you'll know just what I'm saying here. You're a Marine pilot, or Army, or whatever the hell you are. You're military so you know. If a military flight crewmember told me how to fly like they do, that would be the last flight they ever flew with me."

His coffee cup was empty. He held it up until he got the waitresses attention. It didn't take her long to refill it. She left in a hurry, too. He gulped some down.

I thought that perhaps Arlen hadn't made that transition from his Navy career yet, but he didn't need to hear that just now.

In listening to Arlen's woes I didn't realize what was wrong. He didn't know, either. Arlen had been to his first, "bad call." He wasn't really mad at the crew. He was mad at himself. He had done all he could to help someone. But despite his probably heroic efforts, the patient's outcome was unsatisfactory. Someone had died. Maybe it was a child. Bad calls weren't always children, but children were more often than not involved when a call went bad.

But I didn't know these things that day when Arlen and I met in the Smokehouse. I just knew my friend needed help. I had apparently been a person he could turn to when he was confused or needed advice. Today I could be nothing but a willing listener. So I listened.

After he was spent I paid the tab. He nodded his thanks.

"Hey, Paul," he said as we stood to leave. "I need you to help me out."

"Sure, Arlen. Anything, buddy. What can I do for you?"

He looked off to one side and then the other. Then he looked at me and squinted. "I want you to go on a ride-along."

I'd never heard the term. So I asked him: "What's that?"

"It's just like it sounds, you ride along with me. You sit in the copilot seat while I fly. You just watch."

My face remained neutral. I didn't say anything as he continued. "I'm allowed to take guests with me on my shift."

He expected me to say something. I didn't.

"Heck, Paul, it's a pony ride. We do it all the time. You'd just climb into the copilot seat and see how I do my job."

I thought about it for a minute before asking, "Who else have you carried?"

"I haven't invited anybody before today. But you can't imagine how many people fight for the chance to do this. We have medical people, hospital folks like ER techs and social workers. The high and mighty administrators never come, of course. Neither do the nurses and doctors from the hospital, l unless a nurse decides she wants on the team. Then they get all friendly with me and the crew. I can see it coming now. They get one of my medical crew to sponsor them and guess what? Next thing I know they're up in front with me. And I'm always getting schmoozed by cops and fire fighters to take them along. They're all adrenalin junkies, anyway."

He glanced over my shoulder to see if any of the other patrons were paying attention. Apparently they weren't. "We get the occasional reporter as well. Did you see my picture in the paper last week?"

I hadn't. "So you're famous, huh?" I smiled at him.

"Heck, no! I hate it! I wish they'd all mind their own business and let me mind mine."

I got a flash of déjà vu. Was it Ebenezer Scrooge said that? I couldn't remember.

I asked the obvious question on my mind. "So if you want to be left alone, why call me out to do this with you."

Arlen looked at me like I was stupid. He slowly shook his head back and forth. "So you can see what I'm doing wrong, of course." He suddenly looked serious again. "You won't believe this, buddy. But if the crew makes a big enough stink about me and this empathy thing, I could lose my job. I didn't join Lifeline to get fired, Paul."

He wasn't smiling anymore. "I need you to help me out and see if you can tell what's going wrong. I appreciate your advice. You understand what I'm saying. But you have to see what I'm doing for yourself."

I was thinking Arlen looked pretty pitiful, maybe even a little desperate. In my own skull the wheels were turning. *I might be able to help him, see what he's having trouble with.* Selfishly I thought: *Maybe this would also be an opportunity for me to see something new.*

At that moment I was not thinking about the time decades ago when being an angel was all I wanted to do. I was not thinking of the prayer I said as a little boy to that effect. I was not thinking about my friend Jack Harrell who even then I believed had died in Vietnam flying an air ambulance mission. Perhaps I was too settled into where I was in my life at the moment. I had gotten sedentary, smug and happy with my circumstances. Taking a trip on an air ambulance helicopter was as foreign to me as taking a trip to India would have been.

I think he saw the wheels stop turning. He looked suddenly hopeful.

"Please," he said. I knew he was serious. Arlen never said, "please."

What could it hurt? I was forming the words to tell him I'd go when he said suddenly and with confidence, "Good! I signed you up for this Thursday when I go on nights. Meet me at Brackenridge at seven PM."

I went to work as usual on Thursday. When the day was done I left my car in the parking lot at work and hoofed it up Red River Boulevard to the hospital. In the distance I could hear the helicopter making a racket as it made an approach to the helipad from behind the trees in the park across the street. It flew into view, nose up and tail swinging across Red River before settling on the helipad. From down the street I could see the rotors flashing like a strobe in the afternoon sun. The helicopter seemed to squat on the concrete pad which sat on a parking garage a story above street level. It was now in plain view to anyone passing the hospital or walking up to it.

My destination was in the parking garage located below the helipad. That's where Lifeline's crew quarters were located. But a little flash of adrenalin caused me to alter that destination. As the rotors slowed to a stop a group of people raced out to the aircraft. They reminded me of a pit crew at a road race. The helicopters sliding doors on the side of the fuselage as well as the cockpit door flew open. People in surgical scrubs leaned inside the wide cabin. People in dark blue flight suits disembarked.

I stepped up my pace. I wanted to see what was happening up there. But before I was another block closer, everyone surrounding the helicopter was gone. From where I walked up Red River the irregular squares of the cockpit windows now reflected the sunlight at me. I squinted. The drooping rotors and sad-eyed look of the cockpit made the helicopter look like a pathetic, abandoned basset hound. Instead of following the driveway into the garage below the helipad I continued walking along Red River. Beyond the parking garage a steeper driveway angled up behind the helipad. It terminated in a circle that brought cars and ambulances up to what I would find later was called, "the loading dock." It was the entrance to the emergency room for people driving up in their cars. But it was also where the ambulances brought their charges.

The main lobby doors of the emergency room reminded me of doors you would see at the entrance to a classy hotel. They were tinted glass and bronze metal. But off to the right of them at the end of the loading dock was a pair of more simple glass doors. They were clear glass with stainless steel fixtures, hinges and handles. A rubber mat extended out about ten feet from the doors. Above these was a small white sign with red letters that said, "EMERGENCY." I stopped under a large awning that stood above the doors to the main entrance to the emergency room. Inside the main doors it looked like a hotel lobby. Everything in view was polished wood and metal. It could have been the Brackenridge Hilton were it not for the people in scrubs who stood behind the admission desk. I didn't know that I was looking at "triage," the place where the sick people first saw someone interested in getting them treated. It was also the civilized face of the Brackenridge Hospital's trauma center.

Turning away from the hospital I looked out toward the park across the street. Behind it loomed the beautiful Texas State Capitol building. But there before me on the helipad, overlooking Red River Boulevard sat the Lifeline helicopter. This was a Bell 412, a four bladed and updated model of the Hueys I had flown in the Marines. This one looked like it had been gutted. By that I mean it literally looked as though the internal organs of the beast had been forcibly yanked out. A bloody sheet hung creased and crumpled from an extended stretcher that was attached to the helicopter cabin floor. The stretcher that swung out at a ninety degree angle from the aircraft had straps and belts hanging from it. What looked like IV tubes and bags lay about on the cabin floor. Inside it looked as though whatever order had once existed within had been chaotically disturbed. It appeared as though the crew had run away from the helicopter as it died a bloody death.

I was used to green helicopters. The red of the blood I saw was accentuated by the largely white backdrop of this helicopter's primary color. As I stood there looking at the helicopter, a city ambulance swung up the driveway to my right. Passing the helicopter the comparison was stark: two different vehicles, same paint scheme. The truck raced a little too quickly and a little too close past me. Its tires squealed a little as it turned and came to a stop under the awning in front of the Emergency Room. Then the ambulance's backup alarm beeped as it backed toward the innocuous clear, double doors with the "EMERGENCY" sign above them.

The driver spilled out leaving the engine running and his door standing wide open. Doors swung open behind the ambulance. In a minute, two paramedics were quickly pushing a stretcher load of patient toward the innocuous doors. When they stopped briefly on the rubber mat I noticed one of the paramedics reach out to punch in a code on a keypad I hadn't noticed earlier. The doors popped open, swung away from them and they disappeared inside with their patient. The doors closed quickly behind them.

I walked to a stairwell near the helipad and down to where I was to meet Arlen at the Aircrew Quarters. He told me the crew had a small apartment at the end of the stairwell and on the first floor of the employee parking garage. I walked down a flight of concrete stairs and knocked on the door marked simply "Quarters." Arlen opened the door and led me inside. Things were busy. It was crew change time. The pilot who had apparently been the one who abandoned the helicopter upstairs was gathering up his laptop computer. He looked at me over his shoulder and said, "Hi, I'm Skip." Then he finished his business, put the laptop under his arm and edged past me and out the door.

Arlen pointed me to a closet past the little galley kitchen. "Get one your size," he said. Then he walked into the next room, a tiny office. He sat down in front of a desktop computer and began typing on the keyboard. Inside the closet I found a rack of blue flight suits hanging. On a shelf above them were half a dozen big eared white helicopter helmets of various sizes. I picked a flight suit about my size off the closet rack and then found a helmet that fit. When I stepped out Arlen said to the computer screen, "The bathroom's around the corner. Get dressed and we'll go upstairs."

When we popped back up at the top of the stairwell we were looking right into the nose of the Bell Four-Twelve. I paid a little more attention to the details and the differences from the old Hueys I flew in years gone by. For instance, the Four-Twelve had two extra blades, total of four. It also had one extra engine, total of two. Together they made the Four-Twelve faster than the Huey by twenty or thirty knots. The four narrow blades also took away the iconic "thump-thump-thump" for which the two bladed Huey was known. I noted for the first time that the Four-Twelve paint scheme prominently displayed the Lifeline logo on the side. It was enhanced by a trace heartbeat of an electrocardiogram painted down the side and tail boom. On the side of the aircraft a large caduceus was painted, the serpent twined staff of Hermes that represents the practice of medicine.

The medical crew came out of the hospital with an armload of supplies about the time I reached the cockpit with Arlen. I supposed the off-going crew was still inside with their patient. As they got within earshot, Arlen introduced me to the lady who would be the flight nurse for the night shift. Mary looked too small for her flight suit, and too young to be a flight nurse. She had cropped blonde hair, narrow frame black glasses on the end of her nose and perhaps the smallest pair of combat boots I had ever seen. Next to her was our flight paramedic, Karl. He looked a little like John Lennon, not the less for the round frameless glasses he wore. His uncombed brown hair hung over his ears and collar. He was a head taller than Mary but still shorter than Arlen and me. He followed Mary around placing medical supplies in drawers and pouches in the medical cabin. I got the impression that in the medical cabin, Mary ruled the roost.

The medical crewmembers were both pleasant enough. They greeted me warmly and made me feel welcome. They were clearly focused on getting the mess cleaned up that the last crew had left them. I wondered how long it would take them to get the aircraft back into service. I watched them work as Arlen did a standard pilot's preflight of the Four-Twelve. As the helicopter medical cabin appeared to be coming back together I ventured a few questions about the equipment and supplies they were working to put right. They seemed surprised and then pleased when I asked them their function as individuals and then as the medical crew on the helicopter. They became increasingly more open about telling me things about the equipment in their medical bags and in the helicopter cabin. I had never seen any of it before. I was amazed at how much equipment they packed in their medical kits.

There were two particularly large bags and several smaller ones laid out on the helipad. The large canvas bags had a dozen zippers and pouches built into them. The crew opened and stocked the bags pouch by pouch. In doing so they removed, tested and stowed their specialized equipment. I could quickly tell that I was far too limited in my knowledge of emergency medicine to understand the function of most of it. I had much to understand about the function of a flight nurse and flight paramedic, too. I wanted to ask, "Who does what?" I knew my visit was not about hounding the medical crew, though. So I watched quietly…mostly.

I wondered if Arlen ever watched the medical crew do their preflight inspection. Did he know the function of any of this equipment any better than I did? Perhaps I was asking questions that led to answers to Arlen's empathy problem. I had to give Arlen some consideration though. *How in Sam Hill could a pilot ever understand the job of the medical crew?* I thought.

Having finished his preflight, Arlen walked up behind me and tapped me on the elbow. He pointed to the left cockpit door, the copilot's seat.

"Put your helmet up there behind the seat and climb in."

He wanted me to see the cockpit, but he wanted me to know what I would have to do when a call came in. He wouldn't have time to coddle me while he was busy on his side getting the helicopter started and ready to fly.

When I was seated I practiced strapping into the seat belt and shoulder harness. He stood on the step on the skid cross tube and explained how things on my side of the cockpit worked. I noticed that he called the cockpit, "the business end of the helicopter." Ignoring the Intensive Care Unit in the cabin behind us, I realized that Arlen was probably less than half right.

Speaking from my years of flying experience, this Four-Twelve had the most impressively equipped helicopter cockpit I had ever seen. It had dual pilot controls. I rather hoped, but didn't expect, to fly it from the left seat. I wondered if Arlen ever let the medical crew fly. For some reason I doubted it.

The instrument panel on each side of the cockpit and the console between the pilots was remarkable. It could very well have come out of an airliner rather than any helicopter I ever flew. The instrument panel even contained a sophisticated autopilot and color weather radar. I had never seen either of those in a helicopter before. I looked overhead at the electrical control panels as Arlen stepped down and walked around the nose to his side of the aircraft. He stopped and plugged in a Ground Power Unit (GPU). The big black female end of this electric power cart mated to the male prongs of another plug located in the nose of the helicopter. As I looked back at the dozens of circuit breaker buttons overhead, Arlen flipped a switch on the GPU. Then he stepped up into his side of the cockpit and hit two battery switches and two electrical inverter switches.

Everything inside came to life. The sounds of whirring gyroscopes and humming power converters, radio cooling fans and medical equipment behind me all mingled into what sounded like a living thing. As Arlen leaned into the cockpit from the skid step, he flipped switches on his side of the overhead panel. The aircraft and the helipad lit up like a powerhouse in the gathering twilight. All the lights inside and outside were on. There were medical cabin lights that lit the back cabin like a surgical theater. Outside, the helicopter had masked spotlights I had not noticed before. They seemed to point in every direction. The helipad was bathed in white light like some dark spot on a highway would be as Lifeline landed near a traffic accident. Experienced as I was in flying helicopters, I still felt like Dorothy meeting the Wizard of Oz at that moment.

Karl leaned into the cockpit from the medical cabin. He pointed out to me three swivel seats in the cabin that backed up to the cockpit. "Here's where the crew sits," Karl said. "These seats can move the full length of the cabin so we can stay seated and have safe access to every inch of the patient's body."

He pointed to the switches in the cabin that he and Mary would use to control the medical cabin lighting. They could dim them down or brighten them as the need arose.

Arlen paid little attention to what the crew was doing or what Karl was saying to me. Personally, I was fascinated. As Karl went on with his explanations I could see Arlen got a little piqued. He interrupted, rather rudely I thought, to show me how the radar worked. Karl backed away and went back to his own business. I took another mental note.

Done with the tour of the pilot's equipment, Arlen went through his preflight checks. His hands moved confidently over the switches and throttles. He explained that the checks he was doing would allow him to start up and get going faster when a call came in. He said he could get the helicopter started and off the helipad in under three minutes. I was incredulous.

"How can you do that so fast?" I asked.

"By doing these checks now, and by knowing how to start this thing from practicing it a hundred times. Learning to start this aircraft is like a quick draw."

He demonstrated where his hands would go as the engines started. The swift movement of his hands from the overhead panel, to the fuel pumps to the throttles to the engine start switches reminded me of the quick and purposeful movements of a skilled martial artist.

He reset all the switches and throttles, looked at me and said, "That's how you do it." Then he swung his body out of the seat and hopped out of the aircraft.

As we walked away from the aircrew still busily readying the cabin, he explained how a call comes in.

"We get the call from dispatch on our radios and voice pagers. Our radio call sign is 'Lifeline One.' We have a LongRanger stashed in a hangar at the airport to back up the Four-Twelve. When the Four-Twelve is down for maintenance and we're in the LongRanger, it becomes 'Lifeline One.' Technically, there's no 'Lifeline Two.'"

He explained that one helicopter provided all the EMS helicopter service available to the citizens of Austin.

"Besides working with Austin EMS, we also support emergency medical services in thirteen counties surrounding the city. After Lifeline, the EMS helicopters nearest to Austin are in the most populated Texas cities. The closest of them is in San Antonio."

San Antonio was a hundred miles to the south of Austin.

"Isn't that a lot of work area for just one helicopter, Arlen?"

"Yeah," he replied, seemingly without concern. "That's why we average three calls per twelve hour shift. But I've already done six calls on a couple shifts."

I thought about how busy the crew would be doing six calls. I wondered how many calls must have been missed when the one helicopter available was on another call. Then I got a sudden shock. *With a call volume that high we could get a call any minute!*

I told Arlen about my sudden realization, but he seemed unconcerned. He stopped at the edge of the helipad and looked out at the park across the street. I looked at my watch. We had been on the pad a half hour already.

"How can you do that many calls in twelve hours?" I asked.

"Well, most of them are short hops right here in the Austin area. I log between point two and point five flight hours on a lot of the local calls I fly."

Aircraft flight time is measured on a 'Hobbs meter,' a clock in the cockpit that measures the time that the engines are running while the collective is raised. It measures 'hours of flight time' in tenths of an hour. Each six minutes of flight time is one tenth of an hour, or "point one." So a twelve minute long flight would be two tenths of an hour, referred to by pilots and mechanics as, "point two."

"On some of those calls we just load the bleeding body and go. That doesn't take long to do. I don't even shut down the engines. Unless it's a hospital transfer or a scene call that takes a long time, I can be out and back in forty five minutes, sometimes less."

I looked baffled. "A scene call?" I asked.

"Yeah, we do scene calls and hospital transfers. Somebody dials 911 and we go to the scene of the call. It can be trauma, like a car crash -- or medicine, like a heart attack."

I got another twinge of anxiety. I pointed out the fact and asked him if it bothered him having that anxiety. "That's EMS," he replied. Then he turned toward the stairwell and led the way toward Quarters. Looking over my shoulder I noticed that the medical crew was still working diligently zipping up and stowing their medical bags.

"Isn't there something we can do to help the crew?" I asked. Arlen was already a couple steps down the stairwell to Quarters. I heard his answer echo down the stairwell. "Nah, they'll be okay."

As it turned out, no calls came in while the crew was still on the pad. When they came back down to Quarters, Arlen and I were on the couch watching TV. The nurse went back in the little office on the other side of the room and started working on the computer. The paramedic grabbed a frozen dinner out of the freezer and plopped it in the microwave. Quarters included a small but efficient and well stocked kitchen. *Not bad digs*, I thought. But as I lay back watching T.V., I found that I had developed a case of butterflies in my stomach. I labored to eliminate the constant feeling that we would be called out. I wondered what it would be like to live like that twelve hours a day.

Despite *my* case of nerves the crew seemed calm. They watched T.V. or got up and walked outside. They sat down at the computer, or chatted with each other as the night progressed. They seemed perfectly relaxed. I thought it ironic when the paramedic stepped outside to smoke a cigarette. I suspected that was how a number of his patients earned a ride on Lifeline. The nurse got up once and went upstairs to visit the emergency room. It seemed that neither of the medics paid much attention to me. Perhaps it was because I was Arlen's guest.

Arlen never moved except to go to the bathroom. He just sat with me watching mind numbing T.V. programs one after the other. It got dark and then it got late. Still no calls came in. Finally the nurse came back to Quarters from the hospital and excused herself to the bedroom down the hall. With her disappearance, I missed an opportunity to talk with her and find out what Arlen needed to learn about flying EMS. While the paramedic sat and watched T.V. with us I further ignored what I was tacitly there to do, help Arlen. I suppose I was remiss because I let my own anxiety get the best of me.

Arlen looked like he was dozing. So I got off the couch and excused myself to go back up on the helipad. As I climbed the last few steps to the pad I could see a white glow of light to the west of the hospital. The last glow of twilight had long since faded. As I stepped up on the pad I could see that the glow was coming from the State Capitol dome. Only two blocks away it was illuminated now by lights mounted on the lawn below. The dome looked like its own source of light. The helicopter was also brightly lighted. Blue-white mercury lights low on the brow of the helipad illuminated it like a billboard. Perched above a parking garage, passing traffic could see it. Glowing above them as they passed it must have seemed to them as it did to me. It looked powerful, like an archangel is powerful. *A guardian archangel*, I thought.

As I stood looking at the helicopter, behind me a car came up the driveway from Red River Boulevard and stopped in the hospital driveway. I watched as it came to a stop under the covered overhang in front of the tinted glass doors of the emergency room. A man got out of the car and walked into the hospital like he knew where he was going. I looked at the other doors where the ambulance crew had disappeared. I wondered where those doors led. If I had been more on the ball I would have gone back downstairs and asked Karl the paramedic that question. That may have led to where Mary was, and a tour of the emergency room.

That night I let that opportunity to learn about Lifeline pass, too. I didn't know it then, but in stepping through those ambulance doors I would have been standing right in the middle of where I needed to be to see what Lifeline was really all about. It wasn't about helicopter flying. It was about rendering emergency aid to very sick and injured people. The pilot was just part of the means of getting sick people where they needed to be. Those doors led to trauma rooms, medical treatment rooms, teams of emergency room specialists, doctors with every medical specialty I could imagine and many more I could not imagine at all. That tour would have been as interesting as a flight on Lifeline. I didn't know that then. Apparently, Arlen didn't know it either or appreciate it enough to show me.

I stayed up on the helipad for a while, walked around the helicopter and watched traffic pass on the street below. The brightly illuminated helicopter showed clearly that it was something of which the hospital administration was justifiably proud. As a pilot though, I thought about how those lights along the edge of the pad would kill the crew's night vision. What did I know? I was just a kid on his first pony ride. All I was supposed to see was the pony. Still, I couldn't help that I was still a pilot. I looked over at the capitol dome. It too was something of which people were proud. As a pilot I noticed that although it was brightly illuminated, the details on the dome were becoming indistinct. I looked straight up. I could see a couple of stars directly overhead. But at any angle they disappeared. A layer of cloud and mist was forming above Austin in the cool of the evening air. *Great*! I thought. *The weather is coming in. Now we won't launch at all even if we do get a call!*

I left the helipad and walked back downstairs. Just as I opened the door to Quarters the EMS pager went off. I froze, not knowing what it was. The shrill alarm that blasted through a speaker system in the ceiling of the Crew Quarters would have raised a dead person to a stand. I pushed in the door with my shoulder and held my ears as Arlen and Karl stood up from the couch. They walked calmly toward me. To my left down the hallway the bedroom door flew open. Mary suddenly appeared in the hallway looking rudely awakened. She blinked widely and pulled up the zipper on her flight suit as she closed the bedroom door behind her. Then, she too headed my way. When the alarm ceased, I heard the EMS Dispatcher's voice come over the speaker system in the Quarters ceiling. It reminded me of the powerful public address system I had heard often on the flight deck of Navy ships. Those speakers were powerful enough to be heard inside a helicopter above the noise of running aircraft. I was sure the speakers in the ceiling at Lifeline had been taken off of one such ship. The Dispatcher's voice sounded calm to the point of being bored. "Lifeline One, hospital transfer."

The paramedic pushed a button that silenced the pager and pulled it out of the amplifier that piped it through the speakers in the ceiling. He clipped the pager to the utility belt he wore around his waist. He picked up a radio and put that in a holster on the belt. A computer printer buzzed and spat out a sheet of paper. The nurse grabbed it, looked at it quickly and headed out the door. I followed her. The pilot and medic followed me.

"Burnet," she said without turning around as she mounted the stairs two at a time. When we all reached the top of the stairs the crew moved more briskly and with purpose. But they didn't run. As I climbed up in the copilot seat, I felt like I had never been in a helicopter before. I was all thumbs buckling the seatbelt and shoulder harness. I felt as though I had been swept up by a torrent. I picked up the helmet from a hook behind my head and had difficulty buckling it on. When I finally got the snaps to work I lowered the microphone to my lips. By that time Arlen had already donned his helmet, started both engines, rolled the throttles up to flying speed and sat looking at me, waiting. My headset came alive.

"Are you ready?" he asked. I couldn't believe we were ready to fly while I was barely ready to close the door. The crew answered Arlen as one. "Ready!" I grabbed the door handle, closed it and looked at him. I nodded. "Ready," I said into the microphone. He looked over the instruments and then Arlen looked out ahead of the helicopter. He pulled up on the collective without finesse. The helicopter responded and rose briefly while Arlen pushed sharply forward on the cyclic. The Four-Twelve pitched rapidly forward. It climbed smartly as it roared over the helipad railing and past the brilliant mercury lights around the rim of the helipad. As we passed them we passed into what looked for a moment like pitch blackness. It took a moment for my eyes to accommodate the city lights that raced by as we flew down the street that paralleled the helipad. We continued to climb, heading down Red River Boulevard toward the Colorado River that wound through downtown. When it passed below us, Arlen snapped the aircraft into a turn that oriented us to fly west past the center of the city. Over the river we stopped climbing. We had not gotten very high. I was still looking up at the buildings of downtown Austin as we headed upriver toward the black Texas Hill Country west of town.

I had flown here in Austin for years now with the National Guard. But I would never have dared to fly through downtown so low as Arlen did in Lifeline One. Besides the noise complaints that would have been awaiting me when I got back, I would have met a red faced colonel who would have grounded me, at the least. I also knew that on the western edge of Austin the terrain rises sharply into hills several hundred feet above the city. Hitting one of them or flying into a wire stretched over the river was a real possibility when flying this low. But it appeared Arlen was perfectly at ease with this fact. As it got darker west of town he climbed slightly until he maintained an altitude I figured about equal to the highest of the hills ahead. He was certainly below the height of the antenna towers that topped a number of them.

Since takeoff, my ears had been assaulted by constant radio traffic from several radios at once. I tried to sort them out. I recognized Arlen's calls to the Austin airport air traffic control tower that was not far to the east of the hospital. On one radio, Karl was giving the EMS Dispatcher a report that we were *en route* to the City of Burnet. Mary was on another radio. She was getting an update on the patient's condition from Brackenridge, the receiving facility. In the cacophony of radio traffic Arlen switched frequencies to contact Austin Approach Control. The last of the four radios blared EMS dispatch information and conversations between the city's ambulance crews. As we left the city limits behind, I checked the mixer switches. All the switches were up in the 'on' position. That was why I could hear all of them simultaneously. I moved to flip down the medical radio switches but noticed that Arlen had all his mixer switches up, too. He was listening to all the radios just like I was. It was maddening, but I left them all up to listen to how Arlen and his crew managed the flight.

Although I followed his lead on switch positions, I turned down the volume knob on my switch panel. *How can anyone distinguish what's being said?* I wondered to myself. I noticed as we left the city that the haze I had seen earlier had thickened considerably. The lights in the distance faded. The windscreen grew increasingly dark. I saw Arlen raise his left hand off the collective and without looking up he adjusted six rheostats on the overhead panel. He did it quickly and precisely. Each knob set the level of brightness of the different panels of cockpit lights. Each panel in turn dimmed: his instruments, then my instruments, then the engine instruments, the overhead panel, the lower panel. Last, Arlen shutoff the eyebrow lights below the edge of the instrument panel. The cockpit was much darker now. The lights outside seemed to brighten. It didn't improve my situational awareness much.

I could hardly tell where I was. What appeared to be stray disconnected lights were sprinkled over the hills before us. Lines of red and white lights from the head and tail lights of cars defined the highways. But even having lived and flown here I was a little disoriented about which highways we passed. It became increasingly difficult for me to navigate as we moved into the mist and the darker country west of Austin.

I knew Arlen was following the river because it looked like a black strip bordered by the lights from the houses on the hills on both sides. As he followed the river west out of the city the glow of its lights faded behind us. Arlen dimmed the lights on the panel yet again. Even as my eyes adjusted I could barely make out the terrain I knew we were flying toward. I wondered how he knew where it was. I started to get the uncomfortable feeling I was about to go from overwhelmed and confused, to suddenly dead. I felt as though we might be flying directly toward a black hill, one Arlen couldn't see any better than me. Instead of saying anything I just reached for the bottom of my seat and held on. Things were happening too fast. For the first time in a long time I was completely overwhelmed by what was happening in a helicopter. I knew I was behind the aircraft and way out of my league. If this was EMS flying, I was less than a rookie at it. Pin pricks of light continued to pass across the windscreen and through the black mist below us.

I looked at the instruments. The altitude Arlen flew was unwavering but the attitude gyro and directional gyros told me Arlen was slaloming through the hills like a skier whisking down the side of a mountain. Only this event was like skiing at night with no lights, whisking crazily between the dark trees. We were too low for me to see any distant checkpoints. The instruments were the only way I could orient myself to our location. The heading indicator said we were flying due west. The radar altimeter on the pilot's side blinked its yellow "LOW" warning light from time to time as we passed over high terrain I never saw. I noticed that although I was using the instruments, Arlen never looked at them at all. I noticed that he took a casual glance at the engine instruments from time to time. We might as well not have had an attitude indicator, airspeed indicator or altimeter for all the attention he paid them. I supposed that meant he could see. I leaned forward to look out at the blackness. There was nothing to see. So I leaned back and took a firmer hold on the bottom of my seat.

The radios continued to blast at us. The chatter of air traffic faded as we flew low over the hills and got further away from Austin. Patient status reports, ambulance dispatch calls and radio traffic between ambulances and supervisors were still loud and clear, though. I keyed in on these for a moment. The city ambulance crews and the Dispatcher chatted casually about life threatening injuries and illnesses. The ambulance crews were providing care and transport to hospitals. Sometimes the ambulance calls were animated. I could hear a siren in the background of a radio call as the crew gave a patient update to Dispatch. Dispatch always returned the calls sounding detached and bored. Often all they said was, "Received, Medic Fourteen," as though they could just as easily have said, "What do you want me to do about it?"

Dispatch occasionally called us as we headed west. They asked for our position and ETA (expected time of arrival). Even the crew always knew where we were while I was mostly lost. They answered the call for Arlen. Except for giving our position they sat silently behind Arlen and me. I turned around and looked into the dimly lit ambulance cabin. There Mary and Karl sat in their tall, narrow seats with their backs to us. The nurse looked out one door. The paramedic looked out the other. From my perspective, the big windows in the sliding doors could have been painted black. I wondered how they knew where we were by looking out the back when I couldn't tell where we were by looking out the front.

It wasn't until we neared the town of Burnet that Arlen and the crew started talking to each other. Arlen updated the crew on how long it would take before we arrived at Burnet hospital. He reviewed how we would approach the hospital helipad and land. Then the nurse and paramedic shared information with each other about the patient we were heading out to pick up. I gathered for the first time that the patient we were transferring was an elderly lady. The staff at the hospital in the city of Burnet had apparently determined she could receive better cardiac care in Austin.

The crew of Lifeline was all business at this point. The medical crew spoke about "the patient" in a way that could have been substituted with the phrase "the unit." Most of the terms they used were completely foreign to me. It might as well have been the language spoken in a doctoral level college math or engineering class so far as I was concerned. I barely passed high school algebra. As the medical crew spoke I could pick out the prepositions and some of the adjectives. The nouns and verbs eluded me. From what I could understand this was one sick lady we were flying out to Austin. I felt a good deal of concern for her. Listening to the conversation by the crew and lack of it from Arlen, it sounded to me like I was the only one aboard who was concerned for her. Everybody else on the helicopter was functioning in a completely detached way. They were doing their job as if they were computer controlled.

From a pilot's perspective I silently questioned what we were doing flying at all. Visibility was dropping when I was up on the helipad at Brackenridge. I didn't see Arlen get an updated weather forecast or even look up at the sky on his way out of the Crew Quarters. How did he know what the weather would be like in Burnet? Approaching the little town there were no stars visible now. I knew we were below an overcast layer of clouds. I had no way of knowing how far below it we were. We cruised at low level above the terrain the entire trip. I was constantly concerned about flying into it.

The safest method I saw for getting out to Burnet, Texas tonight was to fly using the instruments. That is what I would have done. We would have filed an instrument flight plan. Then upon takeoff we would have talked to air traffic control. We would have been in contact with them the whole way to Burnet. We also would have flown at a safe altitude well clear of obstructions. We would have been watched by someone on radar until we flew an instrument approach to the Burnet Airport. Instead we flew alone without any assistance or navigational help from anyone. We were entirely on our own. None of this appeared to concern Arlen or the crew one iota.

During the whole flight across the dark countryside, I sat there in the cockpit of a helicopter feeling completely out of control. I felt more like a terrified passenger than a commercially certificated instrument helicopter pilot. I wondered why we wouldn't choose to fly higher, use instruments and fly an instrument approach. After all, the aircraft we were flying was one of the most capable instrument helicopters I had ever seen. It had two full sets of instruments in fact. It also had dual communication and navigation radios. And there were backups for everything on the panel. I recognized the autopilot. I knew it cost a quarter million dollars and was most commonly used on business jets. It might as well have been a paperweight. Arlen never touched it.

I knew for a fact that Arlen was a well-trained instrument pilot. Heck, I trained him. Confused as I was at the moment he still could have utilized me tonight as a copilot. Instead, he never said a word to me during the whole flight. He risked sawing us in half with a wire strike by flying low level in the dark at a hundred and twenty knots. Flying into a hillside that fast would have been no prettier. I knew from experience that there were many hills and wires along our route, too. So why did we take the risk? My experience and judgment could not and would not have allowed me to attempt to do the trip this way. It was all crazy and completely outside the bounds of everything I knew about flying a helicopter safely.

We finally came out of the blackness and intercepted a north-south highway and turned north. I recognized it as U.S. 281. Arlen gained no altitude whatever as we roared over the few cars on the highway. Their headlights played out weakly along the road. I looked down at them and realized they were driving through fog. In the near distance I picked out the weakly blinking green and white Burnet Airport rotating beacon. I guessed that it wasn't foggy, or at least not *as* foggy there as it was where we were. *You may survive after all*, I thought. *This is good. At least we can land at the airport to pick up the patient.*

I wondered if the patient was in an ambulance waiting for us. Otherwise, I really didn't know what to expect when it came to the medical end of the mission. As we closed the distance to the airport beacon we began to wander off the highway and away from the airport at an oblique angle. I looked over at Arlen. It surprised me to suddenly see his face jump out of the darkness in stark clarity. He had turned on the "Nightsun," a powerful pilot-controlled spotlight that hung beneath the cockpit. White light filled the aircraft and wiped out any night vision I had acquired during the trip. I looked forward. We seemed to be flying inside a cloud of superheated plasma. The beam from the spotlight reached out in front of us from under the nose of the helicopter and up into the night. The beam was indistinct and fuzzy in the mist.

Since once again there was nothing I could see outside, I glanced at the instruments. I couldn't feel it, but the instruments said we were turning and descending. I wondered if Arlen was aware of it. I wondered if he was possibly suffering from vertigo. I calculated how long we could hold that rate of descent before we hit trees or terrain. I figured we had less than a minute before impact. Then I saw Arlen look out the door to his right. "That's where we'll land," he said.

I looked down at Arlen's hands as he manipulated the flight controls. His right hand on the cyclic appeared to be deftly controlling the aircraft. His left hand was wrapped around the collective. There his thumb rested on a switch shaped like a Chinese coolie's hat. He pushed the coolie hat switch to the right. The beam of light from the Nightsun followed, swinging in the direction he was looking. In the swing of the fuzzy white beam I saw a car moving along a road angling away from us. A couple red lights drifted past on my left mounted on an otherwise invisible and nearby tower. I had a disjointed orientation that left me wondering if we were still turning or upright and level now. Arlen pushed forward on the coolie hat switch and the searchlight beam suddenly moved smoothly down. The radar altimeter's "LOW" light glowed solidly yellow on the panel in front of him. I began to faintly make out the flat roof top of a building and the irregular shape of a grove of trees. I certainly saw no suitable landing site for our helicopter. Arlen announced to the crew, "We're on final approach."

"Ready!" the crew answered.

I noted that the cyclic moved toward my stomach. The needle on the airspeed indicator dropped toward zero. When we had almost stopped, in the void I saw four blue lights on the ground. They marked a spot far too small to be a landing area for a helicopter this size. The landing point was also completely surrounded by trees and wires. Our descent told me that Arlen was indeed going to attempt to land on the tiny patch of asphalt between the lights. As we descended, the spotlight illuminated a complex cluster of power lines and poles. The ones I could see were only a few feet away from the tips of our rotors as we descended among them. I wondered how many black wires I missed seeing. I could no longer help myself and asked, "We're really going to land here? It's not as big as the helicopter!"

Arlen just smiled. Before I could complain further, 'land here' is just what we did. To my surprise no pieces of wire, rotor or wood whirled around us as we set down. Just before he killed the spotlight I could see that the part of the pad surrounded by blue lights was made of concrete. It was larger than the footprint of the skids and smaller than the helicopter. Beyond the concrete the hospital had added asphalt around its edges. That increased the pad's size slightly. Still, when the skids finally rested on the concrete the remaining dimensions of the rotors and tail dangled far outside the circumference of the paved area of the tiny helipad. There was no security guard present, no fence preventing someone from walking up to the helicopter or into the tail rotor. I looked around outside. "It's still too small for a helicopter this size." Arlen laughed.

After that watching the crew disembark was like watching a kind of syncopated ballet. Each movement of the dancers seemed carefully choreographed. They stayed close to the helicopter as the rotors slowed. Then they unloaded their medical equipment in a regimented fashion, slung their packs over their shoulders and left. They headed across the parking lot toward the brightly lighted ER. As the crew punched in the door code and disappeared inside the hallway beyond I removed my helmet. I followed Arlen's lead. I hung it up on a hook behind my head. Then I opened my door and unstrapped my seat and shoulder belts. We both climbed out. I joined him as he walked around the helicopter. He handed me a flashlight as he took a powerful lantern from a spot where it was mounted on the medical cabin wall. He examined the aircraft for leaks. I looked for rotor damage. Neither of us saw anything to worry about. That surprised me more than him. I was sure the blades would have been a few inches shorter. He put the lantern back in its place and turned to me.

"Give me my flashlight." I did. Then he said, "I know this came at you fast. My first EMS flight scared me to death." He gave me a serious look. "We are trained for this. It's a different kind of helicopter flying. Believe it or not you get used to it."

I shook my head from side to side. I kept my thoughts to myself as we closed the doors to the helicopter. We walked into the hospital through the door the crew had taken. It turned out to be the ambulance entrance. The emergency room was small. So too was the hospital. There were only three or four treatment tables in the room. Each was separated by a blue cotton drape. Steel and glass cabinets lined the walls of the room. It was brightly lighted and smelled as all hospitals do of antiseptic. I was surprised to find that nobody was there: no patients, no medical staff. We walked right through the ER and out into a hallway on the other side. I didn't have to ask directions. Arlen apparently knew where he was going. I followed him as we turned down one corridor and another. In a minute we entered the Cardiac Care Unit (CCU). People in scrubs at the nurses' station never even looked up as we walked past them. I guess they'd seen a lot of dapper pilot types in their flight suits pass through there before.

The lights in the CCU were much dimmer than in the ER or even the hallway. Inside there was a dissonance between the beeps of heart monitors, the sounds of hissing oxygen and puffing of several respirators. An occasional sharp, rapid fire electronic alarm beeped or made a unique warbling tone. I suspect the nurses in the CCU knew what each alarm meant. They didn't seem in a hurry to mute them. Several heart monitors were visible at a glance in any direction. They all appeared to be attached to someone. I never saw a patient. I never saw anything in the CCU rooms more than a lump under the covers. Each room had a lump in it. *Busy place*, I thought.

A pane of glass was the front wall of each room. The nurses could see all the patients and their heart monitors at a glance. Our crew was standing in one of the rooms with several people in scrubs. They all appeared to be assisting someone in the middle of the pack. I suspected the one in the middle might have been a doctor. They were all paying attention to the far end of the lump under the covers. It was the point where all the IV drip lines and respirator tube seemed to meet. Hoses and wires were all attached to machines or various sized bags of fluid. There was even a tube leading to a bag of fluid below the bed. I knew that was for urine. I couldn't remember what the system was called until somebody mentioned "the Foley." *That's it. A Foley catheter: right,* I thought.

I stepped close enough that I could hear plainly what the medical people were saying. Again, except for picking up on "the Foley," they might as well have been speaking a language with which I had only a passing familiarity. There were lots of metric fluid measurements tossed around. Strings of medical terminology were connected by verbs and prepositions. I recognized what could have been the names of medications. I didn't know what they were for. I was too new at this to grasp the specifics about what was happening here. I knew things were under control. Like my position on the helicopter, I felt much like a passenger on a conveyance headed for an unknown destination. Once again, I felt out of place. Everybody else involved with this patient except Arlen and I seemed deadly serious and busy. Arlen just quietly crossed his arms and watched the goings on in the crowded room. He looked like someone waiting for a train, ready to board, waiting to leave.

The total lack of response by the patient gave me the impression that she was already dead, unconscious or at least oblivious to what was happening to her. Then one of the nurses said her name. She addressed Mrs. Somebody as though she were sitting up and conscious. That confused me because there was no indication she was even alive except for the activity indicated on the heart monitor. The nurse began explaining to her what was going to happen next. Since I had no idea what to expect myself I stepped closer to listen. I could see white hair in tight curls. I could not see the lady's face. I noted the roundness of her belly and her general shape. I expected to at least see bare hands, feet or even skin. But I saw nothing but white hair, a white blanket and lots of tubing.

Mary, our flight nurse disconnected the respirator tube as I watched. The respirator gave a loud sigh before one of the other nurses turned it off. Then Mary connected a blue football shaped device to a translucent tube that disappeared into the area where I supposed the lady's face was hidden. Mary began squeezing the blue football rhythmically. I was stunned with the realization that now Mary was breathing for the lady under the covers. She quite literally had the patient's life in her hands. One of the nurses stepped out of the room and grabbed a rolling hospital gurney from the hallway. Our stretcher was on it. She pulled it back to the door of the patient's room. Everyone but Mary did a little shuffle to get the gurney into the room and beside the bed. The doctor left as all the other medical people became preoccupied with moving the patient to the stretcher. Except for the flight nurse, everyone began pulling up the corners of the sheet on the lady's hospital bed. Someone counted to three. Then they all struggled, strained and then half lifted, half dragged the lady from the bed to our stretcher.

In another minute we pilots were following the lump on the gurney. The flight crew and the hospital staff members all left the CCU alongside the gurney. As they rushed through the hallways I was struck by how all the devices and bags and tubes and medicines keeping her alive were all aboard this little gurney. The heart monitor rested between the patient's knees. Most of the little medicine bags for IVs rested on her belly. A little infusion pump connected them to needles in her arms. The whole gurney at that moment was a mobile CCU. I watched the green screen on the heart monitor record each heartbeat. Rigged up that way it appeared we could have pushed her all the way to Austin. Two minutes later her stretcher was beside the open sliding door of the helicopter's medical cabin.

Karl asked me to help lift the stretcher with the lady on it. We raised it onto the rotating stretcher platform that was mounted on the floor of the cabin. That was the first time since I arrived for the ride-along that I felt like something other than useless baggage. Mary had climbed up into the helicopter. She was stowing the monitor on a rack and pushing buttons. Another nurse from the CCU pumped air into the patient's lungs with the blue football. Then Mary leaned out of the helicopter and took over the breathing for the patient again. That's when Karl surprised me. He started talking to the patient, too. He was so gentle. He had been all business since we left and now suddenly he was gentle and kind. He sounded as though he was speaking to his own grandmother. He used the lady's first name. As the nurse in CCU had done he too told her exactly what was about to take place. Then he swung in the swivel mechanism with her stretcher aboard and locked the aircraft stretcher into a latch on the floor of the cabin. As he did so the sheet fell covering the patient away from the stretcher exposing the lady's hand. For me it was the first evidence I saw that we were carrying a person.

I took note of how soft and pretty her hand looked. It rather made me think of my own mother's hand. Her fingernails were painted and polished. She wore no rings. Her skin was pale. Thin blue veins made it look like white lace. Then I saw her fingers move. They twitched just a little at first, then more frantically. It appeared she had dropped something or that she was searching for something. I thought perhaps she was just looking for something to hold onto. So instinctively, without really thinking about it I took her hand in both of mine. She grabbed my fingers with the vigor of a drowning person offered a hand at the last second before going under for good. It startled me. I took the paramedic's lead and called her by her name. I told her that we would take care of her and that she didn't need to worry about anything at all. Then I stroked her hand, patted it gently and put it back under the sheet. As I released her hand I could feel her grip loosen. I kept my hand on top of the sheet until I could tell she had calmed down. I gave it another pat through the sheet before helping the paramedic close the sliding door.

I felt a little embarrassed, as though someone had just told me that my fly was open or that I had food on my chin. Nobody looked at me strangely, though. Nobody said anything to me at all. Perhaps they hadn't noticed. They just went about the business of getting ready to leave. The hospital people took the gurney and backed away from the helicopter and we, the crew of Lifeline One all strapped in. In far less time than it should have taken using a checklist the rotors were turning. The Nightsun startlingly popped on again. In another moment we lifted straight up past the power pole covered with wires. We scooted along behind the beam of the searchlight across the tops of a grove of oak trees and out into the blackness.

The trip back to Austin was less terrifying than the route to Burnet had been. I supposed that if we flew the same route back we'd likely miss the same wires, hills and towers we had missed on the way to Burnet. Instead we flew a parallel route along the crests of the hills. Flying a little higher this time my heart rate stayed closer to normal than during the first flight. I got a little better perception of our whereabouts. Going back I could see the shape of the hills silhouetted against the glow of the distant lights of Austin. It was also reflected off the low clouds that had gotten thick enough to obscure the stars all the way home. Shortly I began to pick out landmarks I recognized. We crossed the Capital of Texas highway that circled the city. In the distance I could see downtown and the Capitol dome. As it passed by Arlen's window on approach to the hospital helipad I felt a wave of relief. *I won't die in a sudden meeting with terrain on this trip after all,* I thought to myself.

When we landed I looked at my watch. It was difficult to believe that we had left the Crew Quarters just over an hour ago. It seemed like we had been gone most of the night. I was exhausted. A few scrub-clad people waited with a gurney at the foot of the ramp leading to the helipad. When the rotors stopped they helped the crew unload our patient. They disappeared into the utilitarian set of ER doors as I unstrapped from my seat and shoulder belts. I opened the cockpit door. I did everything slowly. I felt weak inside as though I had just flown a combat mission. In the seat next to me Arlen went through the routine of filling out the aircraft paperwork. Then we climbed out and spent the next twenty minutes or so fueling the aircraft. At Arlen's request I retrieved the medical oxygen from a wire cage at the end of the gurney ramp. A heavy, man-sized green tank was mounted vertically on what looked like a refrigerator dolly. It looked like a bottle of industrial welder's oxygen. When I got it to the helicopter, Arlen had finished refueling. He used the green tank to top off the medical oxygen tanks on Lifeline One.

With the return of the oxygen tank the pilot duties were done. Arlen never made a move to check on the patient. I would like to have known how she was doing. I was a guest. I didn't bother him. Instead I followed him back downstairs to the Crew Quarters. When Arlen entered the flight details into Lifeline's computer I noted the patient's name. She could have been somebody I knew. I lived on a farm out near Burnet. She could have been my neighbor. I didn't recognize the name, but I knew I would remember it. To me, her name had music in it. She was special for some reason I didn't understand. Knowing her name made me smile.

To the crew, she was a patient who critically needed a high level of cardiac care. To Arlen, she was nameless. I got the impression that to him she was little more than baggage. I watched him work for a minute. Then I went back to the couch. When he got done with the paperwork he didn't want to talk about the flight. I was too tired and probably too disoriented with the flood of stimuli to push him.

Since I was told that the average number of flights on a shift was three, I knew that I could expect at least two more flights before the shift was over. I wondered if I could handle even one more flight, let alone two. The crew came in after I had been settled on the couch for a while. They didn't look tired at all. They dropped their paperwork on the desk in the office, excused themselves and went straight back to the bedroom. Then Arlen did the same. I stared at the T.V. The volume was turned all the way down. A minute later I shifted to keep my booted feet on the floor while I reclined on the couch. I must have immediately fallen into a deep sleep.

I didn't have to worry about another flight. Around dawn I woke up with a stiff neck and back from the half sitting position in which I had slept. There had been no calls. I stood up slowly and stretched. I walked to the back window of Quarters and looked outside. The buildings downtown were already gray with the light of dawn. I hadn't been awake long when the next day's crew came in the door one by one. When everybody from my crew woke up to change shifts, I changed out of my flight suit. I thanked my hosts and got out of everybody's way.

I felt dopey, dazed and confused as I walked down Red River Boulevard toward work. I'd be the first one there today. Unshaven, grubby and in need of a hot cup of coffee, it would be a long day. It was Friday. I would have time to think things through today and during the weekend. Despite my weariness I marveled at what I had just seen. If one trip like that with all that frequent fear and confusion was a slow night, I wondered what a busy night would be like. Certainly it must be an unending stretch of terror spanned by moments of fierce anticipation. I couldn't imagine doing that for a living.

A couple days later Arlen asked me to meet him for an early breakfast before work. "The hospital cafeteria makes some great hashed browns," he promised. I left the house before dawn and got to the crew parking garage just in time to find the helicopter departing on a call. I knew Arlen was at the controls. I parked and walked upstairs to the helipad as the helicopter disappeared behind the buildings of downtown. I turned to go to my car. Then, on a sudden impulse I turned around and walked past the helipad and into the main entrance of the hospital. Just like any other visitor I stepped up to the information desk and asked for directions. I remembered the name of the lady we had transported. I smirked wondering why I remembered.

"*She was your first patient*," a little voice inside told me.

"First and only," I mumbled in response to the little voice.

The volunteer at the desk told me she was still in the hospital. "She's been moved from CCU to the floor," she said. I suspected that meant that she was in a hospital room.

"She's on the cardiac care floor, room four fourteen," the volunteer offered. I thanked her and got on the elevator. I got off on the fourth floor. Across the hall halfway to the nurses' station I saw an open door. I didn't have to check the room number. Somehow I knew she would be there. I never saw her face that night I flew with her. Still, I knew her as soon as I saw her through the half open door. She was sitting up in the bed. She was a pretty, white-haired lady with glasses. She had her makeup on. She looked like someone's best representation of a friendly grandmother. She was smiling and talking to two ladies a little older than I. They sat in chairs next to the bed. I stepped in and tapped on the door.

"May I visit a moment?" I asked.

The ladies all turned and looked at me with curiosity, but welcomed me in. I introduced myself by my first name to the lady in bed. The two ladies sitting beside her turned toward her as if to get an explanation of who I was. Looks were exchanged that said, *I don't know who he is. Do you?* I walked past the two bedside visitors a little unsure of myself.

"I just wanted to make sure you were feeling better." I looked down more in embarrassment than for any other reason.

Not quite sure why I would care she politely said, "I'm feeling much better, thank you." Her voice trailed off leaving. "Who are you?" hanging in the air. I wondered still how to tell her how I met her. I asked myself what I was doing here in this stranger's hospital room. Then I noticed her hand was lying on the bed in just about the same position relative to me as it had been on the helicopter stretcher. It still looked soft. It was a little rosier than that night. Her nails were still polished and pretty. She wore a wedding set on her finger now. It must have been a day for acting impulsively. So impulsively I reached down without asking and took her hand in both of mine.

"'Feeling fine. That's good!" I said. "That's wonderful!" I meant it too. Then, before I could say another word I looked up to see her face light up in sudden recognition.

"You were the one!" the lady said. She looked at her visitors with excitement and I knew at once that they were her daughters. Their faces suddenly flashed with the same recognition as though they had already met me before.

"This is the angel I told you about!" the old lady said excitedly. She reached over with her other hand and clasped my hands with both of hers. I was speechless. My jaw hung open as I tried to form some words of response. The effort was hopeless.

"You are the angel, aren't you?" she asked. Before I could do more than stammer she continued as though she had just won a lottery. "I told my girls that after my heart attack I felt like I was in a dark and frightening place. My chest hurt so badly. I felt like I couldn't catch my breath. I could hear people talking around me. They all seemed so glum and hopeless. They were so concerned and I just wanted to tell them I was alright, but I couldn't say anything. After a while I could hear the heart monitor. I knew I must be in a hospital. I couldn't open my eyes. Somewhere during all that confusion I suddenly felt like I was falling. I thought maybe I was going to die. I tried to reach out and catch myself. That's when I felt *your* hands."

She took my hands up off the bed and shook them. "I told the girls that I knew I had been caught by an angel. It was you, wasn't it?"

I still just stood there speechless, my hands caught in hers. Her grip was warm and soft, and firm. She looked into my eyes. I didn't know what to say.

She smiled. "I can see I've embarrassed you. I'm sorry. Why, you don't have to say a word. I *know* it was you! I told my girls, I said I would hold that hand again in heaven, never this side of it. I said that, didn't I girls?"

I turned my head. One of her girls, then the other nodded. Then both stepped up and hugged my neck. Their mother released my hand and I hugged them back, first one daughter and then the other.

"Now that you're here," the older lady said, "... well, I think perhaps I was wrong."

I turned back toward her.

"Wrong about what, ma'am? About being an angel you mean." I could feel my face warming, blushing.

"No, no. Certainly not. I was wrong about not holding that hand again this side of heaven!"

"Oh yes...about that...I..." I didn't know what else to say. I started feeling especially uncomfortable and out of place.

"Your hand was so warm and so strong," she said sweetly. "You caught me on death's doorstep. I'm sure of it. And when you let go I knew I was going to be alright." She turned to her daughters. "Didn't I say that girls?"

"Ma'am, I'm no angel," I cut in defensively.

The women would have none of it. "Well if you're not one you were sure working for one that night," the grandmother said. The other ladies effusively agreed. They had tears in their eyes now. Their faces were so happy and their smiles bright. I told them I had just been a rider that night. I wasn't part of the crew. The crew was taking care of her. I just happened to see her hand and thought it needed holding.

"Just like today," I said as I picked it up and then set it down on the bed with a pat.

The grandmother just brushed off my explanation with a wave of her other hand. "You'll never make me believe that. That moment I felt your hands I knew I was going to be alright. I knew God wasn't going to take me just yet. I knew I would see these sweet girls and my grandbabies again. And as you see..." She raised both hands up, "Here I am."

I had to laugh. "And so you are." I laughed out loud. It came from my belly and made me throw my head back. I wiped a tear from my eye. It might have been the laughter. "And I am so glad to see it. I hope you get out of here and get home to see your grandbabies soon."

That gave me the opening to extract myself so I bowed out. I wished them well and said goodbye. I took one last look, smiled and waved at the lady in the bed before I left the room. She waved back. I heard her say, "God bless you!" as I headed up the hallway toward the elevators.

I didn't realize then just how much he already had.

4 THE LAST CHANCE

After my visit with the patient and her family I was actually relieved that I missed my rendezvous at the hospital with Arlen. I spoke with him on the phone a couple times over the next two weeks. We couldn't get our schedules to match. Actually, I made sure my schedule didn't match his. I found reasons to be busy because I didn't want to talk to him. It took a week or two after the flight to come to grips with why I didn't want to talk to him. When I knew, I wasn't overly anxious to tell him.

Part of the problem was that he had called on me as his instructor and mentor. He asked me to help him. I was supposed to put my finger on a problem he had. Now that I knew what it was I didn't think he would like what he heard. Part of the problem was my own. I lost some confidence in myself in doing something I did well: fly helicopters. When I agreed to the ride-along it wasn't just a pony ride for me. I flew helicopters for a living. I was as comfortable in a helicopter cockpit as I am in my bathtub. But during that one EMS flight I had been completely overwhelmed. I felt like a neophyte. The experience on Lifeline One caused me to question just how capable a pilot I was. I realized as we swooped into the hill country that night that I didn't know what I was getting into. I thought a flight with Arlen would just allow me to evaluate him. I had plenty of experience at doing that – evaluating pilots. Instead, I found that the cockpit of an EMS helicopter was nothing like any helicopter I had flown. When I left the crew quarters I was tired, dazed and confused, completely overwhelmed. I hadn't even seen the blood and tragedy for which I had tried to prepare myself. We hadn't flown back to back calls. All I had done was a simple hospital transfer. Yet I came away shaken and traumatized. I felt like a coward. I didn't want to admit that to Arlen, either.

I had come to another conclusion that surprised me. EMS flying wasn't just hazardous, it was dangerous. The difference between the two was that hazardous situations don't necessarily kill you. Hazards can be recognized. When those hazards are purposely avoided the hazards go away. When a pilot and crew just ignores hazards and plows on anyway, that's when a flight becomes dangerous. At that point survival becomes a matter of luck. Sooner or later luck runs out. From my perspective and level of experience flying helicopters, everything about the flight on Lifeline One was dangerous. Arlen appeared to violate every rule of caution I ever learned about flying. I was stunned that he was comfortable with such cavalier and dangerous flying. It made me re-evaluate what I knew as the right way to fly. After the reevaluation I came to the same conclusions I had before my ride-along. I also came to the conclusion that flying at Lifeline was unnecessarily risky, probably dangerous.

I didn't want to tell Arlen all this. I doubted he wanted to hear it. I also thought he would think less of me. So I retreated within myself for a while. I knew Arlen was very good at what he did. I had heard that at funerals of lots of my flying friends. "He was a great pilot," someone would say. And in the cartoon bubble above my head would be the words, "If he was so good how come he's dead?"

EMS was different from any flying I had ever done. Because we were very different helicopter pilots I didn't feel I had the right to tell him more. I saw what he *wanted* me to find even before he finished his preflight inspection. The crew had already told him. He was indeed apathetic. I personally learned in the first conversation with the crew that apathy, as well as sympathy were critical elements in dealing with his crew and the patients he carried. I also noted that Arlen was also probably egotistical and self-centered. I didn't really know him well enough to be sure. And I certainly didn't know him well enough to tell him that. Doing so would probably end our budding friendship. I didn't want that to happen.

So I retreated. I went back to life as I knew it. I went back to work. My job demanded that I travel all over Texas. I did that to avoid the office. It kept me at arm's length from Arlen and our cups of coffee at the Smoke-house. As a husband and a Dad there were more than enough activities to keep me away from Arlen. School band concerts and PTA meetings, Cub Scout meetings and Little League games all filled in the cracks. Also, Linda taught high school. Teachers were expected to attend Friday night football, baseball or basketball games. We went to many of them. Linda teaching high school kids also left us with no lack of babysitters. We took advantage of that for frequent dinner dates and movies. It's how we had remained lovers and friends. It also offered an escape from ever having to address what I saw at Lifeline.

After Lifeline I shifted back to normal. Weeks went by. I was busy and happy. I could see myself keeping the job I had. I'd retire from the State job and the National Guard one day. We were already paying off the house. One day the boys would move off to college. Maybe a few years later we'd retire to a lake house. Perhaps we would stay right where we were. I remember telling a friend, "The only way I plan to leave what I've got going now is in a box carried by six of my friends." Maybe that's why life took a dramatic turn. It always seemed to do that when I thought I was the one holding the tiller. You'd think I'd have gotten smart enough from my life experience to expect it by now.

And life changed. It started its new course when I arrived at work. I parked my car in the usual place, a lot a block from the state office building in which I worked. As I walked around the corner heading for the front entrance to the office building, I spied Arlen. In his blue flight suit he was hard to miss. He was sitting on the front steps looking across the street at the café. Lost in thought he didn't see me coming.

He looks tired, I thought. *He probably just got off the night shift.* I stepped up next to him before he noticed me.

"Hey, sailor. Are you looking for a date?"

He smiled, turned toward me wearily and reached out a hand. He stood up as I shook it.

"You know why we kept Marines on the ship don't you?"

I looked at him from under my eyebrows waiting for the punch line.

"So we wouldn't run out of dance partners."

I smiled widely. I left my defenses down. In truth I was happy to see him. "Yeah, I probably knew that. So what are you doing sitting on the front steps? You don't have an empty coffee can."

Austin's pan handlers often sat on the sidewalk in front of our building with an empty coffee can waiting for people to drop in money. There were probably desperate people among them. In Austin though, it was as likely some of them just didn't want to work for a living. Collecting free money from passersby seemed like a good idea. "Keep Austin weird." It was a slogan the left side of Austin loved and much of the city represented. Even the panhandlers fit in.

"You know we have chairs inside," I continued. I started up the steps to open the door for him. He held up his hands as if to stop me and shied away from the door.

"I'd rather buy you a cup of coffee if it's all the same to you." He pointed to the diner. "Do you have the time?"

I scratched my head. He could see I was a little perplexed.

"We can do it another time if you'd like." He knew I wouldn't turn him down. I stuttered a little. "Of course. Sure. We can do a cup. Let me drop my brief case, get some face time and then I can go. It'll take maybe ten minutes. Are you sure you don't you want to come inside?"

He looked at me with a strange, knowing look. Like he possessed some secret that might come out if he followed me in. He shook his head slowly. "I don't think I need for your boss to see me."

I shrugged. *Why so cryptic?* I wondered. "Have it your way," I said. I pulled the door open and disappeared into the building. When I came back out I apologized for keeping him waiting.

"I made some spare change," he said, jingling a few coins in his hand."

"I don't want to know."

Arlen pointed across the street to the café. "Coffee," he said. "It's on me, Marine."

We took a booth where we could look out on the street. With the business day underway there wasn't much traffic on the street or inside the diner. All the government workers were in their offices droning away by now, except me. The waitress appeared. We waved off the breakfast menu in favor of coffee.

"Black, please. Times two," said Arlen. He didn't say anything else until she returned with two porcelain mugs full of steaming coffee. She put one down in front of each of us and evidently got my pal's unspoken message that we wanted to be left to drink it. After she left he looked over his shoulder as though to check to see everyone was out of earshot. Then he grinned conspiratorially.

"I don't want to get you fired when I try and recruit you."

"So that's what the free coffee is all about? You want to recruit me for what, to steal state computers? Help you rob a bank? What? "

He swigged his coffee. "Nah, there's no future in that. I want you to apply for a job."

My brow wrinkled. "What kind of job? I have a job. A couple of them in fact."

He twirled the coffee mug slowly on the table in front of him. Then he changed the subject. "What did you think about the ride-along we did?"

He knew I'd be uncomfortable with that. He let me stir uneasily as I thought about how to answer him. He wouldn't take excuses. Every one that popped into my head sounded lame even to me. I took another second to frame my words and slugged down a swallow of coffee. There would be no more dodging. If he wanted to hear it he was going to hear it all.

"Well Arlen, candidly…it scared the hell out of me. We were flying on a dark night in instrument conditions at a daytime low level altitude. I spent most of my time waiting to hit a wire or a hill. I felt like I was on a roller coaster about to come off the rails."

Arlen chuckled.

"I thought you'd lie and tell me you liked it." He took a swig of his own coffee and collected his thoughts. Then he put down the cup and said, "My first night flight at Lifeline I felt just like that, too: scared. You'll get used to it."

I caught the use of the contraction that inferred present tense. I *will* get used to it.

"Arlen, do I gather that you expect me to do another midnight ride so I can get used to near death experiences?"

He smiled and replied, "You're pretty quick! You must have been an English major in college."

"Yeah, you know I was. And you did Journalism. It's why we are pilots. We couldn't get real jobs with those degrees. We're digressing here however, Arlen. So let me clear things up for the record. Thanks but no-thanks. I don't need another ride along. I'm not interested in building up my tolerance to flying low level at night." I paused, "Besides, that's not what I was there for anyway, was I?"

"No, that's not why you were there," he said with a lopsided grin on his face.

"You were having trouble with your crew, remember?"

"Yep."

"And you wanted me to help you identify what the problem was, right?"

"Yep."

"And I welched on the deal and didn't tell you what I saw."

"Yep, again," Arlen replied.

"I didn't want to tell you what I observed or what I thought the problem was…or maybe still is. Did you know that?"

"Of course I knew that. I knew when I asked you I'd have to pry it out of you. You didn't want to hurt my feelings. That's why the crew liked you."

I was getting confused. "What does the crew have to do with all this?"

He deflected the question. "You're a hard man to catch when you don't want to be caught."

"I can be illusive."

"Yes, you can. This isn't the first morning I tried to ambush you at work, ya' know."

I didn't know. And I didn't know what to say to that. Another lame excuse came to mind. I swallowed it. Arlen sipped his coffee. He set his cup down and crossed his arms on the table. He looked outside for a second and then back at me. He got a serious look on his face. "I have to tell you, Paul. I brought you on that ride under false pretenses. I know that I've had some issues to work out with the medical crews. But I already know those problems are constant. They're stirred up by the friction of the job. You'll see. "

I was really lost now. "What are you getting at Arlen? False pretenses? What am I going to see?"

He looked down at his coffee. "I had to give you a reason to be there on that ride. I knew I had to make it about me or my crew wouldn't have seen what I have been telling them about you. That flight wasn't about me and my crew, Paul. That flight was all about *you* and my crew."

I opened my mouth to say something. Then I shut it again when I realized I didn't know what to say.

"Yeah, I knew that would catch you. You didn't know they were watching you, did you?

I shook my head. "No, Arlen. I didn't know that. Why would they be watching me?"

Arlen put his finger down in front of me to make a point. "Long before you got there to Quarters for that ride-along they knew your bio. Thanks to Tony Rosso and me they know all about you. We put together a summary of your flight time and experience."

"Where'd they get that?" I asked incredulously. "I never gave anybody a resume."

Arlen crossed his arms again. "You know anybody named Vince?"

I was shocked. The guy who dodged me from the National Guard like I dodged Arlen had given them my flying record. I didn't like that. "What's Vince have anything to do with this?"

"Well, Anthony Rosso knows him. And anything Vince and Tony didn't know, I filled in. The crew knew you before you showed up. At least they knew your bio. They knew a lot more than what a resume can tell. They knew you got me my job at Lifeline. You and I both know you should have taken it yourself. That's not your style though, is it, shipmate?

The question was rhetorical.

"That was what got Mary's interest. She was the one who convinced me to take you with me on a ride-along. Karl took an extra night shift to go along with Mary's plan. Did you know Karl is a former Marine, too?"

I was speechless.

"We've all been looking for another pilot. Anthony's leaving. One of our pilots is taking his place."

I nodded. I heard during a Guard drill that Anthony Rosso had been replaced as Director of Operations at Lifeline. I didn't know any more than that.

"That's going to leave us short one pilot. Our medical crews have a vested interest in who does the driving for them. After you left Quarters after your ride-along, Mary and Karl both came to me and told me, 'He's the one.' They've pretty much sold you to the rest of the medical crews."

This was happening pretty fast for me. I held up one hand. "Wait a minute, Arlen. The one? I'm the one for what? Flying at Lifeline? Are you kidding me? I can't fly that job. It scared the crap out of me!"

"I know," said Arlen. "Like I told you, it scared the crap out of me, too. But I got used to it."

"Yes, you said that. But here's another thing I didn't want to tell you. I didn't know how. But here it is. That job is dangerous. You selected it. I didn't want to spoil your fun. But if I had some spine I would have tried to convince you to get a job like mine. You're going to kill yourself at Lifeline one day."

Arlen took no umbrage. "Paul. I have a wife and two kids. I didn't survive flying helicopters so far by being stupid. Neither did you. Come on. Think about it. How many dangerous things have you done in a helicopter?"

I said nothing.

"You got trained to do dangerous things. Good training limited the risk. Is what we do risky? Sure. I knew Lifeline would be risky too. And it is. What you haven't seen shouldn't surprise you. I got trained very well to fly EMS. I learned the job. It's just a different kind of flying. You can bet it requires all the skills you already have. We'll just have to hone them to a finer edge."

What he was saying made sense. He could see me mulling it over.

"You can do this job, Paul. I know that. I know by your reputation that you fly a helicopter as well as anyone I know. But that's only part of the job. The crew picked up on something more important than that. At least they think it's more important. Do you know what it is?"

I held up both hands now to slow things down. "Okay, okay. Hold on a minute, Arlen. Let's stop here. You're saying you want me to fly with you on Lifeline?"

He nodded. "You're slow, but you're catching on."

"And that flight was sort of an interview?"

"Nope, that comes later. That flight was for the crew to take a look at you and see if they even wanted you to interview."

I shook my head. "This is not what I was expecting today." I gathered my thoughts. "All I did was hold onto the seat and wait to die. If I hadn't been in shock I'd have cried out like a little girl for you to land and let me off. What in the world did your crew see in me that makes them want me to apply for the pilot job?"

He swigged his coffee, turned and held his cup up for the waitress to see. Then he turned back to me with a gentle look in his face. It was not one I was accustomed to.

"It was your heart, man. They saw your heart."

I shook my head again, still not getting it.

"Mary and Karl told me the next day that you have 'a good heart.' They both saw you take that patient's hand. I did, too."

Arlen gave me time to think about that. He looked out the window at the office building where I worked. I looked at the building, too. I could see my office window. I remembered that smiling grandma shouting blessings after me. I remembered how special that moment was to me. But I was also thinking about how I had finally gotten my life on an even keel. The job I had across the street there was easy and fun. It paid pretty well, too. It certainly paid better money than Arlen was making. I'd gotten regular promotions working over there. I was already flying for the National Guard, so I didn't need to slake my flying habit. The Guard paid me to fly, too. Working for Lifeline I'd always be just a line pilot. There would be no promotions. Line pilot was the job description and the end of the line for me if I chose to work at Brackenridge. With the state job, unless I got hit by a bus I'd probably live to be old and then retire. I thought about the routine I had fallen into. Life was just where I wanted it. Why would I want to change that?

I could feel Arlen looking at me now. I turned my head and looked across the table at him. Before I could say anything, Arlen said, "They're going to announce the job opening tomorrow. There are going to be a lot of applicants. There are lots of good pilots out there. Lots with EMS experience."

He wasn't doing anything to encourage me with that line. In fact that gave me one more reason to let the opportunity pass.

"Management will probably find someone better cut out for the job than you."

I wasn't expecting him to say that, either. He saw it in my face, saw my pride rising up. It was just what he wanted.

I slugged down another swallow of coffee. "So why should I apply then?"

He leaned toward me. "I think you will want to. I think you will want to know if you're really good enough. I think you will want to know if you can even beat the stiff competition you're going to get. The winner gets the job offer."

"And if I apply and get the job offer?"

He just shrugged.

"That's your call. Take the job or let it go. But you'll never know if you're good enough if you don't apply."

I looked back at the State office building. "The pay probably sucks too, right?"

"Yep," Arlen confirmed. "It sucks. You'd take a pay cut for sure...*if* you got the job."

He knew he had me. He waited patiently until I looked back across the table at him.

"So how do I do that? Apply, I mean."

He zipped down his flight suit a few inches to withdraw a business envelope. He dropped it next to my coffee cup.

"'Thought you'd never ask."

I had a fresh haircut. I was wearing my best suit. My shoes were highly polished. I looked like a job candidate. And I was stuck in rush hour traffic on the way to the hospital. I spent the time crawling toward Austin thinking about how it had come down to this. Today was the last step in the pilot application process. By close of business today, at least the management of Lifeline would know if I'd have the job offer or I wouldn't. All that was left now was a meeting with a committee of crew members. They would have the last word about who got the pilot job at Lifeline Air Medical Service.

Arlen kept me abreast of my progress throughout the application process. There had indeed been dozens of pilot applicants for the position flying for Lifeline. Sorting the applicant's resumes and applications took Lifeline's management two weeks to finish. Most of the pilots who made that cut had more experience than me. There were a lot of them. Some had flown combat in Vietnam. Some had flown at other air ambulance services. Some had never had a break in their flying experience. Some had all those qualifications. I had none of them.

The initial sorting of applications was a brutal process. Most applicants got phone interviews. Most of those phone calls were followed by a letter promising to keep their resume on file. They never even met the management face-to-face. After that, probably a dozen applicants including me, interviewed personally with the administrative director. Of those, five pilots – including me - went on to fly with a guy with the implausible name of Jolly Pearson. He was the guy I had met on the helipad when I first moved to Austin. He's the one who probably never showed my application to Anthony, his boss at the time. It turned out that Mr. Pearson was also the one who replaced Anthony Rosso as the new

Director of Operations for Lifeline. I asked Arlen about why Anthony had been replaced. "Anthony needed to go," was all Arlen said. He would not elaborate.

Now it would be Mr. Pearson who would make his cut on the surviving pilot candidates. He would examine our flying. All five of us would fly with him in the company LongRanger. I don't know where I fell in the order of flight candidates. I was assigned a time mid-morning to meet Jolly at the airport. Ironically, I knew just where to park. I parked in the same lot where I had staked out Vince, the moonlighting National Guardsman. Lifeline's LongRanger was parked in the hangar right next to the LongRanger I staked out. I went through the front gate of the flight line building this time. Walking out on the ramp I saw that the office door in the side of the Lifeline hangar was propped open. Stepping inside, I saw Jolly Pearson for the first time in five years. He looked much as I remembered him: unkempt. He didn't look up from what he was doing, trimming his fingernails with a pen knife. He was leaning back in a desk chair, one dirty boot up on the desktop.

Since he ignored me I got to look him over. The negative impression held. His hair was cut too short on his forehead and too long everywhere else. It was thin and oily looking, dark and shot with gray. It needed combing and trimming. The thinness and color matched his beard, which I presume he grew to hide a prominent double chin. As I stepped toward the desk he looked up from his manicure. Then he slowly drew his unpolished boot down from the desktop as he folded the blade of his knife. When he stood up behind the desk I couldn't help thinking: *"dumpy."* He was a head shorter than me and overweight by at least fifty pounds. As he stood up the zipper of his faded blue flight suit strained at the waist. I could tell that he gained most of his current weight since he had gotten the flight suit.

"'You Stone?" he asked. I responded in the affirmative. I set my headset on the desk to extend my right hand. He ignored it and turned toward the hangar door behind him. Obviously expecting me to follow him. "Shut the door behind you. Bring your headset. We'll go flying."

I followed him through the cool hangar and out into the sunlight where the Lifeline LongRanger was parked. It had the same paint job as the Four-Twelve down to the caduceus and EKG heartbeat line down the side. LIFELINE was painted boldly in dark blue across the doors. It was currently configured with two pilot seats and two sets of flight controls in the cockpit. In the ambulance configuration, a LongRanger's copilot seat was replaced with the foot of a stretcher. Knowing that I was the pilot-in-command and Pearson's guest of honor, I opened the right pilot's door. I hung my headset from a hook located in the same place we had one in the LongRanger I had flown to Catalina. I flipped on the battery switch and checked the fuel level. A glance around the cockpit began my preflight inspection of the helicopter.

I got the sense Jolly didn't want me to do that inspection but he didn't stop me. I didn't care much what he thought in that regard. I didn't get into anything I flew before I conducted a careful preflight inspection. I wasn't concerned. I could see that the machine was well maintained. I climbed up the side of the helicopter and looked down into the area around the transmission. It was clean as a maiden's honor. Jolly stood by the left door, arms crossed looking up at me. The sun reflected from his cheap-looking dark sunglasses.

"'You know Austin Executive?" he asked.

I told him I knew it well. It was a small airport about ten miles north of the Austin-Mueller airport where we were currently standing. Austin Executive had a single runway. West of it was a single hangar. Several sun bleached little airplanes were tied down outside. There was rarely any activity there.

"Well, that's where we're going."

Ten minutes after I finished my inspection, Jolly, the LongRanger and I were on a right downwind approach to the runway at Executive. Just before I lowered the collective to descend, Jolly rolled the throttle to idle: a simulated engine failure.

"Take it to the ground," he said. That meant he didn't want me to roll the throttle back up before we landed. This would be a touchdown autorotation. There would be no room for mistakes. Jolly had rolled the throttle off at a point far enough away from the runway threshold that I knew I had to stretch the glide just to make the runway. I did that by pulling up on the collective slightly during the descent. Doing that slowed the rotor to its minimum speed. The loss of RPM created the extra lift I needed to reach the runway. Had I just left the collective fully down I would not have made it. That didn't happen. When I rolled out on runway heading I was still a couple hundred feet in the air. The runway numbers swished underneath us. The runway was made.

I gently pulled back on the cyclic and fully lowered the collective. The nose rose smoothly and steadily. Rotor RPM rose too, as the helicopter slowed. I had more rotor RPM than I needed for a soft landing. The aircraft slowed and settled. Just before touchdown I let the cyclic move forward. The nose came down even with the horizon. When the aircraft was level I pulled up smoothly on the collective. The aircraft hung motionless over the runway and then settled gently to the surface. I lowered the collective. I didn't say anything. I had impressed myself. I had not shot a touchdown autorotation in a LongRanger in years. This was a sweet one. Jolly only said, "Roll up the throttle and takeoff."

For nearly an hour I flew around the Austin Executive airport traffic pattern with Jolly. Most of the time he sat with his arms crossed. He commanded and I performed. He set up scenarios and had me fly the helicopter within their difficult and narrow bounds. During each scenario he would introduce one emergency procedure after the other. He would block the pedals with his feet and announce, "Stuck pedals." He turned off the hydraulic system and had me make approaches to a hover. The manufacturer's handbook said to fly a hydraulic failure to the ground.

Jolly knew how difficult it was to hover without hydraulics. So he said, "Land to a hover." And that's what I did. Then he turned the hydraulics back on.

He rolled the throttle to idle time after time in every possible circumstance: in a hover, during a normal takeoff, while flying low and fast. We were still the only aircraft operating at the Austin Executive airport when he gave me the scenario that would normally and by-the-book crash the helicopter. We were sitting in the middle of the width and length of the runway. We were facing into a light wind. Jolly told me to assume there was a power line tower in front of me two hundred feet tall. I had to takeoff vertically to clear it. At two hundred feet he wanted me to transition to forward flight and proceed to the hospital. I turned and faced him for a moment. He stared impassively forward. I thought for a moment he was checking my knowledge of the Helicopter Operator's Manual. In it is a chart known as the "height/velocity diagram." It shows the pilot the combination of height and speed at which the aircraft will probably crash if the engine fails. I reminded Jolly that a vertical takeoff above forty feet puts the helicopter in "the Dead Man's Curve." That's the part of the chart for performance of the helicopter in a hover. It shows you that you will crash if the engine quits in a high hover. I told him that if the engine failed while I was performing this maneuver we were in short, toast. He ignored the warning. I asked him if I could takeoff under the power line.

"No."

I asked if I could lift into a hover, back up a significant distance and then takeoff over the power line and stay outside of the Dead Man's Curve.

"No."

"Can I takeoff parallel to the power line and then climb to a safe altitude to cross it?"

"No."

I knew what his answer would be. But I was thinking of another option to avoid a vertical takeoff when he held out his hand to stop me.

"Look, I know about the Dead Man's Curve. Just takeoff vertically. It's your only way out."

I knew that the exercise was academic. No experienced pilot leaves one way out of a given situation. I knew this was just a training scenario. There was no real power line there. If I had enough altitude I *might* be able to get some forward airspeed if the engine really quit. I *might* salvage a safe landing. I didn't like the "might" part of that equation because there was a "might *not*" side of it, too. Since Jolly was calling the shots I gave in.

I lifted the helicopter off the runway into a low hover. I checked the engine, rotor and torque gauges. Everything looked normal. Then I pulled up on the collective until the torque needle reached the red dot marking its limit. Since we were low on gas and the helicopter was light, we rocketed straight up. As we approached two hundred feet and I was ready to push forward on the cyclic I felt Jolly roll the throttle to idle.

The wire-in-front-of-me scenario instantly took a back seat to surviving this stupid trick Jolly had just performed. I did what helicopter pilots do when the engine fails. I pushed the collective fully down. Smack in the middle of the Dead Man's Curve the helicopter did just what it was supposed to do. It fell like a piano. We were going to crash just like the manufacturer said we would. I didn't want to crash. So I pushed the cyclic smartly forward. That dumped the nose down. Way down. With a windscreen full of runway, Jolly and I were both looking straight at the white line down its middle. It looked like we would dive straight into the ground. Doing that bought us some airspeed. Airspeed in this situation was life. With some airspeed and some luck I *might* gain enough rotor RPM at the bottom to slip out of the Dead Man's Curve. I might recover and land the helicopter somewhat intact. One way or the other we would know in about a minute. If we didn't kill ourselves.

The forward, and downward vertical speed increased. Going forward wasn't happening fast enough, however. So on the way down I got unconventional. We needed rotor RPM in a hurry or it was going to get ugly in that helicopter pretty soon. So I did something else the manufacturer says you shouldn't do. I began to roll the throttle back on. Doing that causes the engine to twist the drive shaft leading to the transmission. The torque gauge reads how much twist that is applied to the driveshaft. In this case the needle in the torque gauge zipped around the case toward the limit mark. Passing the limit is called an "over torque." Doing that will seriously damage, if not destroy the drive system of the rotor. But hitting the pavement would do that, too. And that is just what was going to happen if I didn't do something fast. It was just a matter of physics, gravity and time. So I kept the torque needle on the red dot and kept winding up the throttle.

We needed rotor RPM to parlay for lift. And we needed lift to keep from crashing. Slowly increasing the engine speed was giving us both RPM and lift. The rotor was speeding up. But I knew it wouldn't be enough by the time we hit the ground. That's when I planned to get even more unconventional. As we dove at the ground I had no idea what Jolly was thinking. I just knew his hands were nowhere near the controls. That was good. If he grabbed the controls he would not let me do what I was going to do. Keeping one eye on the torque needle and the rotor RPM I started to pull back on the cyclic. The nose came up until we were nearly parallel with the runway surface. I raised the nose a little more. The vertical speed slowed. Rotor RPM was building. It was still too low to hover though, so I pulled back on the cyclic some more. I was trading all of what little airspeed I had gained for a further reduction in our descent rate. Then, still rolling the throttle on, I steadily pulled up slowly on the collective.

The torque needle stayed on its upper limit. The rotor RPM speed needle dipped dangerously low. The blades passed by so slowly that I could see each as it went past. With the collective up, each blade was at its highest pitch. They were biting the air for all the lift LongRanger rotor blades were designed to produce. One blade went by and then the other. But the descent stopped. We were maybe a foot above the ground. I held the aircraft there as the throttle finally reached the full open position. The torque needle quivered at its limit until the rotor sped back up to its normal speed. Then torque dropped back into the normal range. The helicopter sat steady and undamaged hovering a few inches above the ground. A maneuver that started as a certain crash ended in an uneventful hover.

I set the helicopter down on the runway and looked at Jolly. His hands hovered above the cyclic and collective. I wondered how long they had been there. Jolly's eyes were so wide open behind his sunglasses I could see their white orbits. His jaw was slack with astonishment. It was the first time since we started flying that he looked anything other than put out or bored. He turned his head slowly like an owl and looked at me.

"What in the hell did you just do?" he asked.

"A 'Low RPM Recovery,'" I replied as though everyone who ever flew knew how to do one.

"I've never seen that done. Where did you learn to do that?" Jolly had relaxed his hands and put them back in his lap.

I knew he was an Army pilot in the past. "I don't think the Army does them. They teach that to instructors in the Navy. When a student screws up an autorotation we used that maneuver to get ourselves out of an otherwise untenable situation."

Jolly was no rookie to flying helicopters. He had to either be extremely competent or just plain crazy to let me - an unknown pilot – handle an engine failure inside the "dead man's curve." After rolling the throttle to idle in a two hundred foot hover I was willing to bet on the latter. That doesn't mean I was going to let him kill me or bend the machine I was flying. If I had just handed him the controls and let him crash the helicopter, no one would have any been better off. So I kept flying and did what I could. The low RPM recovery caught him off guard. I was sure he wanted to know how to do one. I knew he was too proud to ask me to show him. He looked thoughtful for a moment. Then he looked back at me.

"Was that one of those...situations?"

"Untenable, you mean?"

He nodded. "Yeah. That."

I nodded back. "Yes, sir. I think that was one of them."

I knew that was the telling maneuver. I just didn't know what it told him. For better or worse I suspected the ride was done. I was right.

"Let's go back to the hangar," he said. I nodded to him, looked around for traffic and made the radio call.

"Austin Executive traffic, Copter eight five Tango X-Ray departing the pattern to the south, Austin Executive." Then I took off. I headed back to the Robert Mueller airport downtown following Interstate 35 through the center of town. While we flew back I paid attention to what I was doing, and to what Jolly might yet do to me. I figured he had one more simulated engine failure in store.

The return flight was uneventful.

I landed the helicopter where I had taken off in front of the hangar. Then I shut down the engine and stopped the rotors with the rotor brake. As we got out of the aircraft he said, "You're free to go. I'll take care of things here."

So I left. I walked straight into the hangar without comment. Jolly didn't stop me to offer any of his own observations. I doubt he would tell Arlen anything positive about the ride. He did tell Arlen that there were just two pilots left for consideration, though. There was me, and there was my National Guard buddy, Brad Wright.

Sitting in traffic on the day of my final interview I thought a lot about that flight with Jolly. I was sure that if his vote counted on who would fly with Lifeline, Brad was the one he would choose. Jolly probably didn't like either of us. But then Jolly probably didn't like many people, anyway. Brad had cleared all the same hurtles I had. And Brad was better qualified for the job. Like me, Brad had plenty of time in OH-58s. That equated well with time in a LongRanger. Brad also flew the Huey at the National Guard. In fact, he was an instructor pilot for Hueys there. That made him a lot more current in them than me. Jolly would know that Brad would consequently have no trouble in a transition to the Four-Twelve. He couldn't be so sure about me. Apparently though, I made Jolly's cut. So today was the day. The interview at the hospital was the last step in the selection process.

I looked at my watch. I was making adequate time. Brad was slated to interview first. He was probably starting his interview about now, in fact. He would do well. At the Guard unit everyone thought Brad was a great pilot and good human being, including me. I was sure the interviewers today would sense that. We were told that the interview would be with a nurse, a paramedic and a pilot on the Lifeline program who had not met us yet. The flight with Jolly measured our flying skills. This last wicket today would focus upon our judgment, character and personality. Brad had plenty of all of them. Backed up at a traffic light I wondered how I would match up with Brad there. I came away from the traffic light not entirely sure I wanted to beat Brad at this last step, even if I could. He wanted the job. I just wanted to get the offer. That would be enough for me. I considered what it would mean to turn the job down today in favor of Brad. *That is unnecessary,* I thought. *Even if I win I don't intend to take the job. Whether I come out on top or not, Brad wins.*

I was just in it for the competition. From the start Arlen had said it. "Go through the process. At least you'll know if you could have had the job if you wanted it. If you don't apply and compete you'll never know." As I pulled into the parking garage next to Quarters I took some comfort in how this day would end. Regardless of how the interview turned out, after today I could say I had run the full gauntlet. I had my concession plan ready. My boss at the Aeronautics Commission never knew I interviewed let alone flew with Lifeline. After I let go of this new job opportunity I'd go back to work like I'd never had plans to do anything else in my life. I'd continue along the path I was on, keep my stable job with the State of Texas and say goodbye to Lifeline. Back at the office I'd call Linda.

"The better man won," I'd say, sounding a little disappointed. "Life goes on. It's a dangerous job flying nights and bad weather with no instrument flying allowed. Those air ambulances have a terrible safety record. I'd be exposed to all sorts of disease. I might even have brought some disease home to you and the boys. Besides, the pay was way too low. We'd be broke in a year." Actually those were all the reasons I had already given Linda for not filling out the application in the first place. When I told her that the evening of the day Arlen gave me the application, she would have none of it.

"You most certainly *will* fill it out, Paul. You fly helicopters. You do it well. It's one of your gifts. You apply for that job, baby. If it's meant to be, you'll get the job. If not, you won't get the job offer. You have to apply."

I should have expected no less from her. Linda had always backed me. In every scheme, no matter how hair-brained; in every challenge in my life since we met, Linda backed me like that. She always had absolute confidence in me, especially when I lacked it in myself. She was sure this was the right thing to do from the moment she heard about it. After the process got started she was sure I was going to get the job offer. "And then you're going to take the job," she said resolutely.

I argued that I probably wouldn't make the first cut. Then I got past Jolly's check ride and was chosen to interview. I was running out of excuses for not getting the offer. The evening before the final interview, over dinner Linda looked across the table at me and narrowed her eyes.

"What?" I asked.

"I think you better plan on a job change." She smiled at me, then went casually back to her dinner. I thought about that smile of hers as I parked the car in the hospital garage.

I was on time. Brad was well into his interview by now. I was supposed to meet Jolly at the Crew Quarters. He would take me to the room in the hospital where my crew interview would take place. There I would meet the pilot, nurse and paramedic who had just spoken with Brad. I hoped they got a good first impression of me. I wondered how they would see me and what they would think. I dressed nicely, anyway. Maybe they'd remember that. "The number two choice, remember the one who didn't get the job? Now *he* was a sporty dresser!" they'd say. I smiled. And I thought about Linda's smile again as I knocked lightly on the door of Crew Quarters. I could hear voices inside. Evidently no one heard me knock. I knocked harder. Still no one answered. I opened the door.

It looked like a party was going on in there. It was packed with people. A wave of heat poured out as I stepped inside. There were certainly too many people in there for anyone to be comfortable. They were all animated, talking and laughing with each other. A few people were in street dress. Only the duty crew wore flight suits. Arlen said there would be a monthly crew meeting that morning. I suppose everybody stayed around afterward to visit. They didn't all see each other often. After all, they only worked three to a shift.

It was clear they were all friends. I thought that maybe they stuck around to take a look at the two pilots who were coming in for the interview. Since one of them would be their next pilot and with so few pilots on staff I suppose they had cause to be interested. If they were interested in me I saw no evidence of it. I didn't feel ignored, exactly. But I was surprised that I didn't draw any attention from anyone.

They probably think I am a hospital administrator, a county EMS employee or something, I thought. *Maybe they think that pilots looking for jobs dress more casually.*

Besides the flight crews, there was an ambulance crew in Quarters. They wore white uniform shirts with the distinctive red paramedic patch on the shoulder. There were also several people in scrubs. I couldn't tell what they did in the hospital since everybody up there from the doctors through the guy who mops the emergency room wore scrubs. Since everybody was making small talk in their little groups I looked for a spot to sit down to wait for Jolly. I'd get the interview done and be on my way back to work. A couple of days might go by before the committee would announce whom they had selected. Arlen would probably call me. Then I'd call Linda.

I couldn't get her devilish little smile out of my mind's eye. That's why I was grinning as I found an open space on the couch. It was the same place I had dozed away the last of the night shift during my ride-out over two months ago. A drowsy, disinterested looking lady in purple scrubs occupied the other end of the couch. She acted like she was watching TV. It was on and making noise but I knew she couldn't see or hear it any better than I could. There were half a dozen people standing in front of it. I sat down beside her and took advantage of my orientation tucked in the corner to look at her more closely. She was svelte and looked like she kept herself in shape. She was nicely built and not at all bad to look at. Pretty in a rugged, outdoor sort of way, I'd say. She had wavy, shoulder-length dirty-blonde hair. The color might have been natural although the highlights might have come out of a box. With her dark tan on her arms and face, the sun may indeed have had some influence on the brighter highlights in her hair.

She had the look in her face and her eyes of someone who had seen a lot of life. I would have bet some of it was on the harder side. She apparently took no notice of me at all so far as I could tell. I snatched a glance at what appeared to be enamel pins on the lapel of her scrubs. I quickly recognized them as military in nature. I leaned forward a little. My interest did nothing to disguise where I was looking. Neither did it tell exactly what I was looking at. There was a miniature 101st Airborne Division "Screaming Eagle" emblem on one of the enamel pins. Below it she had a miniature Bronze Star medal. It had a little gold "V" on it. I knew that military medal was awarded for valor in combat. Below that was a little Purple Heart medal. That's only awarded for being wounded in combat. For some soldiers it's the last and only medal they receive because it is awarded when a wound is mortal, too.

Noticing my interest in her chest, the lady turned her head toward me. She didn't appear to think I was admiring her enamel pins. I smiled at her, believably, I thought. It didn't change the challenging look on her face though. Not even a little bit. She clearly didn't expect me to say out loud what I was thinking, either.

"If I recognize that hardware you're sporting on your scrubs there ma'am, you are one tough flight nurse! You didn't get those awards around here I'm sure."

She realized what caught my interest then and her face softened a little. "I'm not a flight nurse," she said. "I work in the ER. I'm just down here to kill some time on my break."

I nodded. "And if I'm not out of line, may I ask where you got the 'Screaming Eagle' pin and the awards for valor?" She glanced down, put a light touch on the pins. I spotted it as a loving touch. Then she removed her hand and straightened herself. She half turned toward me and pointed to the pins. "These medals are my brother's. He was killed recently in Mogadishu, Somalia." She told me that as though she'd said it a few times before. There was no emotion in how it came out. I was set back a little. I took a second or two with it. I remembered the Blackhawk helicopters that had been shot down in Somalia. They were supporting US Army Rangers going after a warlord in the city of Mogadishu. The city, the whole country really was in total anarchy. Landing the 101st there had been President Clinton's first opportunity to show he had some spine. It was supposed to prove that he knew something about being commander in chief. But he had virtually no understanding of how to command from a military perspective. He had given the Rangers an impossible mission and far too little backing. There was no armor to support them. They should have had a carrier offshore but instead they had no air cover. In the end, all they had was some little helicopter gunships supporting far too few Rangers. When the inevitable debacle occurred, the Rangers were overwhelmed. Their vicious, last ditch street fighting marked America's memory of the event. Clinton pulled out the survivors. He chickened out. The warlord he was seeking laughed at him, the Rangers and the mighty United States. He took the credit for running the Americans out of Somalia.

Before they left, the 101st fought their way into the city to rescue a Blackhawk crew that had been shot down. With great valor against immense odds they recovered the crew, the dead and then fought their back way out. The Rangers used a number of unarmored vehicles to reach the crash site. It was like the charge of the Light Brigade: a mission by brave men doomed from the start. Everybody in Mogadishu it seemed, including women and children, fired at them. Many of the Rangers in those vehicles died bravely. They killed scores of their enemies in the dying. One of the Airborne Rangers who died there must have been this nurse's brother.

Every Marine I know respects the 101st Airborne Division, especially me. I had met the families of heroes before. So with this ER nurse I knew what to say. "I'm sorry you lost your brother. He was a hero." I didn't mean for it to sound stilted or trite, but to me it did. So I apologized. "But I'm sure you know he was a hero."

Her face softened a bit more. "Yes, he was a hero. I'm very proud of him."

"I'm sure he'd be proud to see you remembering him by wearing those medals of his."

She looked directly into my eyes. I didn't blink.

"Thank you," she said. "Yes I'm sure he would." She extended her hand and introduced herself. "Nancy."

I smiled, took her hand. "Paul, I'm one of the pilots being interviewed this morning for a job here with Lifeline."

"That's interesting," she said as though it wasn't. "Why would you want to fly here?"

I looked away from her and thought about that for a moment. It may have been the first time I had been asked to put it in words. Why *would* I really want to fly here?

"Well, to tell you the truth the opportunity came to me suddenly. I really didn't think I wanted to after I went out on a "ride along" one evening. I thought I'd never want to do this after that flight. It was very different from any flying I've ever done. And it was very different from what I thought it would be. Then a couple days later I met the patient we carried. I talked to her and her daughters. I felt connected somehow, like I knew them. It was like they were family. It was a good feeling. When the opportunity presented itself to fly here after that, it surprised me. But I realized that I had wanted a job like this since I was a little boy. I guess I was drawn to it. I just didn't know it. I think I want it because I have something in common with your brother."

She raised her eyebrows. "Really? What's that, military service?"

"Well yeah, that. But that's not what I was thinking. I was just thinking, "service." It's what he gave his life doing. And I think it is what we both were put here for, to serve. I think it is what all of us were put here for, really." She looked up at me through her eyelashes as if to say, "go on…" I smiled. "You know, to serve other people. I like the idea that this job is a lot about doing something good for people."

I'm not sure what reaction I expected from her. Probably none at all. I had the same feeling I got after I held that lady's hand on the helicopter. I felt like I had said too much. Let too much of myself out for a total stranger to see. I hadn't really meant to. I felt like I was blushing a little bit. I noticed one side of her mouth curled up, like she wanted to smile but had forgotten how. I wasn't sure how to read that. So I asked, "Does that sound corny?"

She just looked at me, at my eyes. One then the other, as though she were looking for truth. Then she said, "No. That doesn't sound corny."

I found out a few weeks later that Nancy was a charge nurse in the trauma center. When she was working charge, everything that went on in there hinged on her. When the place was on fire as it frequently was, this was the lady the whole ER staff relied upon to put it out. She was one of the most respected nurses at the hospital. She was tough, unflappable, professional and probably as cool under fire as her brother must have been earning that Bronze Star. Lifeline's crew members held her opinions in high regard. She was their mentor. She had worked the ER since before most of the flight nurses on Lifeline were wet-behind-the-ears nurses just out of school. She had taught most of them their trade before they went on to fly with Lifeline. The flight paramedics too had all given patient reports to her. They saw her face many times when they were still EMTs bringing their patients into her ER in an ambulance.

I also found out much later that it was no accident that there was a seat open on the couch. The ambulance crew I saw included a pair of Lifeline flight medics doing their ground shift on the ambulance based next to Lifeline Quarters. Most of the others in scrubs or street clothes were other flight paramedics or flight nurses. No one spoke to me because they wanted me to speak to Nancy. She had been planted there on the couch by her colleagues. They wanted to find out what kind of people these two pilot candidates were. She was there to ask the real interview questions before I even saw the committee. I don't know if Brad, the other pilot candidate spoke to her. I suspect he did. Clever folks these EMS crews.

The morning after the interview Jolly Pearson called me at work.

"Can you meet me at the hospital parking garage at noon? We can have lunch."

"Sure, Jolly."

"Good. I want to talk to you about the job."

"Okay..." I waited for him to elaborate, tell me I had it or I didn't. He hung up. I found myself staring at the phone.

"I guess I'll see you at noon," I said to the dial tone.

When I parked in a slot below the helipad, Jolly was waiting. He was leaning on the wall outside the door to the Crew Quarters. As I got within earshot he pointed to the garage exit.

"That way," he said as he pointed to the ramp I had just driven up to park. I presumed that meant we were walking.

He didn't make small talk as we walked. He just informed me we would eat at the Italian place right next to the hospital. I got the impression this was going to be a short meeting. He exhibited the lack of charm I had come to expect from him. This time though, I saw it as the beginning of a meeting that contained no good news for me. I was okay with that.

The lunch rush had beaten us to the restaurant. The only table available was a two top against one wall. We took it and picked up the menus that were standing between the condiments and napkin holder. Before I had opened it a waiter came and asked what we wanted to drink.

Jolly said, "I'll take a smoked turkey sandwich and water."

Then Jolly looked at me, knowing I hadn't seen the menu.

"You want to split that with me? It's a big sandwich."

I nodded thinking, *what am I supposed to say?*

"Put that sandwich on two plates," Jolly added.

I asked for water too. The waiter looked at us like he was resisting the urge to roll his eyes. We looked like eaters who could put away a couple turkey sandwiches and a pizza besides. "*Cheap!*" is what he was thinking. I know he was thinking that because so was I.

The waiter just nodded, took the menus from us and stuck them back where we had gotten them. He brought us our water, which we drank while we waited for the sandwich. It was uncomfortable for both of us just sitting there. I couldn't really drive the conversation, either. I wasn't sure what Jolly wanted to talk about. So in lieu of any stimulus to the conversation from his side of the table I asked him about his career.

As I suspected, Jolly was a topic Jolly didn't mind bragging about. He even appeared to be moderately animated. He told me he had been a flight instructor in the Army at Ft. Rucker, Alabama. That is the home of Army aviation. Then he said without prompting that he didn't like teaching students. I thought that odd for an instructor to say. But then he noted how most of them were, "just stupid." I wondered if he had ever been a student. Then he said with some relish that he "got promoted" to a job at Ft. Rucker giving check rides to the other instructors. I guess his superiors figured other instructors could take his negative attitude. He didn't have to instruct them, after all. He just gave them check rides and oral exams. That he liked. "I was a real hard ass." I believed him.

The sandwich was slow in coming so he told me about his next assignment: Alaska. I figured he had probably gotten it due to his skills as a brilliant conversationalist. I would like to have talked to him about the EMS job, but this was Jolly's show. It was his invitation. I didn't think it was my place to bring up why he had invited me there.

He didn't talk at all about his civilian flying career, flying EMS or more particularly about what it was like working at Lifeline. He just talked about his time in Alaska. He elaborated about why he liked the flying there. The biggest reason was because he spent most of his time flying solo. No surprise there. I had never flown in Alaska so I listened and nodded. I was in no hurry. I had all day. Then the sandwich came. What little small talk there was, ended as we ate our respective sandwich halves. Contrary to what Jolly told me, it was not a big sandwich after all. I think the waiter added some chips to the order just to fill the plates a little. He dropped off the meals and gave us some more water.

In no time Jolly's sandwich was gone. Then he polished off his potato chips. Without any preamble he mumbled past a mouthful of chips, "The job's yours if you want it."

I had eaten a few potato chips. He pointed to the ones left on my plate. "You gonna' eat those?"

I shook my head and threw an open hand towards them. "Have at 'em. I'm done." I wasn't done but I was in a giving mood by then. As he reached for the last of my chips I said, "The pay is too low you know." I wiped my lips with my napkin and put it down next to my plate.

Jolly continued to reach across to my plate and pop my potato chips into his mouth. "Well, I can't do anything about that. The pay is what it is." He picked up the last crumbs of potato chips off my plate by mashing them under his thumb. Then he put his thumb in his mouth and withdrew it clean of potato chip crumbs. He wiped off his thumb with his napkin. "So do you want the job, or not?"

My ego had gotten me into this. It almost got me out of it right then and there. Jolly was such a cretin. I couldn't imagine what it would be like working for him. He also seemed so nonchalant about the offer. He presented it like I could a take it or leave it. I believe he expected me to say, "no." I almost did so. Instead, I took a minute before saying anything in order to maintain my cool. This was the negotiating stage I never got to at McDonnell-Douglas. The interviewer at Douglas was cordial. Jolly wasn't. I was straight up with the Douglas guy. But I wanted to let Jolly hang for a while. I recalled a tactic I had abandoned in interviewing at Douglas. I figured it would give me some more time to calm down and collect my thoughts. "Can I think about it?" I asked.

He didn't seem to recognize the tactic. He probably hadn't read the book on how to negotiate with a future employer. "Yeah," he said. "You can think about it. Just don't think too long." He put his napkin on his plate. When the bill came he told me how much I owed in order to pay for my half of the sandwich. When he put down his half I noticed that he stiffed the waiter. As Jolly left, I dropped ten bucks on the table and followed him out. I resolved that working for a philistine like Jolly was worth putting on the list of "cons" in considering Lifeline's offer. When I finally turned down the job I would do so personally with Jolly – over lunch. We'd order our own entrees. And I would buy them.

Arlen was waiting for me in the parking garage when Jolly and I got back to the hospital. He looked a little surprised to see me. He knew I had been offered the job. He thought I might very well turn it down immediately and leave. When the D.O. climbed in his oversized diesel pickup truck and unceremoniously rumbled past us out of the parking garage, Arlen signaled me with a head nod to follow him. We walked through the Crew Quarters. I waved to the duty crew and smiled. They looked up from their magazine and the TV respectively and smiled back. Arlen slid open the back door and we both stepped out onto the back porch. He pointed to the picnic table that sat under the shade of a nearby tree. We sat down opposite one another.

"Well?" he said.

"Nice lunch," I said. "Turkey sandwich and water. Half a turkey sandwich, actually. Cost me two and a half bucks." I rolled my eyes. "Where did Jolly go to charm school, by the way?"

"He usually makes me pay, too." Arlen said through a crooked smile. "So?"

"So, what? You know he offered me the job."

Yes, he knew. "…And?"

"Pay's too low. I told you that when you told me to apply. I can't take that kind of pay cut."

He put his chin in a hand and waited for me to say what I was thinking.

"I went the whole route, Arlen. I proved I could do it. It surprised me a little that I was selected. Particularly after that ride with Jolly. I have no idea what he thought of it. Did he tell you I had to do a low RPM recovery to keep from crashing the helicopter?" Arlen had been a Navy instructor. He knew the maneuver. He shook his head, 'no.'

"He never told me how I did."

Arlen spoke through his fingers. "He said Brad was better."

"Ouch," I replied.

"He only said that because you're my friend, Paul. I also knew he'd especially put you through the ringer because of it. I'm sure Brad got an easier ride."

I shrugged.

"As for the low RPM recovery, he never mentioned it. He never would. You know he wouldn't admit that you saved his butt."

"He's that way, huh?"

"Oh, yeah," Arlen replied. "All the time. It's just his ego talking. So don't worry how he thinks you did. You have to use a kind of reverse psychology working with Jolly. We all do it. The fact that Jolly said nothing about you told me and the committee that you did better than he expected. And if it's any comfort, the committee thought you were the best candidate hands down. Unless Jolly said you were a dangerous pilot or something, his vote on whether or not to hire you was irrelevant."

I thought about that. The committee had spent a couple hours with me. They asked me how I'd react to a couple scenarios. Then they spent the bulk of the time with me talking philosophy. By the end of the interview they were giving me pointers on how to do the job. I figured that meant I'd garnered their approval. In the time I spent with them I left feeling as though I liked them. I knew they were good people. They would be good to work with. Too bad. I was going to miss them.

Arlen knew I was thinking the offer through. He was patiently sitting with his elbow on the table. His chin rested in his hand.

My mind was made up. I didn't see any reason to soft soap what I had to tell him. So I just gave it to him straight.

"When you gave me the application you said at this point, *if* I didn't get cut..."

Arlen blinked. "Yeah. Well you didn't get cut."

I went on, "...I could make the decision to turn down the job."

Arlen nodded once.

"Okay. So I made the cut."

Arlen nodded another time.

Then I let my ego do the talking. I completely forgot what I had told Nancy the charge nurse about being here to serve other people. Instead I remained completely pragmatic. I listed for Arlen all the same reasons I had given Linda for not applying. The job was dangerous. Then there was the exposure to disease and all the rest. My arguments were both logical and incontestable. Arlen didn't interrupt me or try to argue any point I made. So I concluded my comments. "And to cap it off, Arlen I just can't get past the pay. Taking a pay cut that big would make things tight around our house."

Arlen still made no effort to say anything. I was beginning to wish he did. So I added, "I have three boys. I would like to help them through college one day. How am I going to do that on a Lifeline pilot's pay? I have to think about my family."

I felt like I was arguing a point I didn't really believe. By that chin-in-hand posture I didn't think Arlen believed me either. After a few seconds he dropped his hand to the table and crossed his arms. He looked at me with an intensity that surprised and then startled me. The

Arlen I knew, the arrogant sailor and proud and capable pilot seemed to become someone else.

"Paul, a long time ago you said a prayer that is being answered today."

I blushed. I knew the prayer of which he spoke. I remembered the day as a little boy I had asked to be an angel. Had I told him of that prayer? *How can he know that?* I wondered. *No*, I decided. I had never told him. I don't think I even told Linda. I told no one. So how could he know?

"You know your prayer was heard. This is the answer. If you really want what you asked for, this is your last chance to have it. I think if you turn this down you will regret it. You'll refer to this day for the rest of your life as, 'the day I should have followed my heart.'"

Then Arlen stood up, stretched his arms and walked back into Quarters. I followed him with my eyes. As the sliding door to Quarters closed I knew with certainty that this decision was a crossroad in my life. My whole life had been about getting here today. On an impulse I bowed my head.

If this job is my calling, God...if this profession is the one for which I was being prepared, I accept it. Show me the way. I will follow.

With those words a great burden fell off my shoulders. I stood up and went back into Quarters. The flight crew was gone. The T.V. blared at no one. Arlen stood across the room. His back was to me. His hands were crossed behind him. He was looking at a map of the local flying area pinned on the far wall. He had seen it a million times. Still, he seemed immersed in it just the same. I slid the door closed behind me. In a voice loud enough for him to hear me across the room I told Arlen, "The pay is lousy." He did not react. "I'm not sure I can keep paying my bills with pay that low." Still there was no reaction from Arlen. I smiled. "If the pay is still this low a year from now you may have to go through the interview process again."

Arlen chuckled.

"But if the D.O. will agree to that, then I'll take the job."

Arlen turned around. His hands were still folded behind his back. He wore a crooked smile, too. He took a couple of steps toward me and reached out to shake my hand.

"Welcome to Lifeline," he said. "Jolly will agree to your terms, I'm sure. I'll tell him that later."

"Why later?" I asked.

"Because I just called him. I already told him you'd take the job."

I followed through and bought Jolly lunch. I ordered a pizza and two turkey sandwiches. When he had eaten his fill I struck a deal with him. It was strictly verbal, but I planned to hold him to it. "Since the pilot pay is so low, as part of this employment deal I want you to let me use the off-duty helicopter." He raised his eyebrows. "I want to earn my CFI, Double "I" and ATP." The Certificated Flight Instructor, Instrument Instructor and Airline Transport Pilot certificates are the top bar in a helicopter pilot's professional field. Jolly understood that. He had those certifications. He could understand me wanting them. I know he didn't believe I would follow through in getting them. A lot of study, a lot of training and some arduous check rides must be accomplished to clear those bars. Once I started flying for Lifeline he never expected me to have the time or focus to follow through. So he made the deal. He even shook my hand on it. Why not? He could make a promise I wouldn't keep. Even if I followed through with the work required to get the ratings, the preparation, tests and check rides were all on me. And the cost of letting me fly the helicopters would be on the people of Travis County. It cost Jolly nothing. Otherwise he would never have agreed.

The way I looked at it, Jolly had just given me a raise. I knew that the flight time to get those ratings would have cost me thousands of dollars. The value of those ratings in future ventures might be worth many times those thousands, too. To the great surprise of Jolly I did follow through. During my shifts that first year with Lifeline I spent long hours between calls studying. I crammed for the FAA tests. I was already well skilled at my craft of helicopter flying. I also became a technical expert on each of our helicopters. Soon I knew them both like the engineers who designed them.

I took the written exams for the ratings one by one. I scored well on all three. Then I surprised Jolly. I arranged to use my off time to practice. I took the off-duty aircraft a number of times and flew them in instrument and other operations I rarely got to practice in flying EMS flights. Usually I flew the LongRanger. But sometimes I got the Four Twelve. Our paramedics were always anxious to fill the copilot seat while I practiced. They liked to fly, especially when there was no pressure to do their medical voodoo. They watched out for traffic and learned a little more about how pilots do their jobs. They were also becoming my good friends.

I practiced until I was positively ready to face the FAA examiners. The first flight exam came during an annual check ride. The examiner offered to wind my helicopter instructor check ride into the annual Lifeline check ride we all had to take anyway. Our FAA examiner and I went out in the LongRanger for the ride. When I came back I was a freshly checked company pilot and a newly minted helicopter CFI. Jolly seemed a little miffed, as though I had taken advantage of him. He proved it when he made my next check ride harder to accomplish.

The Instrument Instructor and ATP rides were going to be more complicated. They would be done in the Four-Twelve. Jolly complicated the process by telling me that he wasn't going to take the Four-Twelve out of service for me to take the check rides. We had to do them in between calls. If I was in the middle of a check ride when a call came in, I'd have to abandon the check ride and go on the call. I wondered how that would float with the FAA.

Further complicating the process, no one in our local FAA office was authorized to do the checking. So the FAA sent us a guy from an office in Louisiana. There, helicopters supporting the offshore oil fields are thick as flies. The inspector I got had a lot of experience in bigger helicopters. He was okay with working the check rides into the work schedule. When I met him, I knew he wasn't going to budge on the standards. That was fine by me. I was prepared. I'd either do a terrific job or I wouldn't get the ratings.

The inspector planned to stay for two days to get all the checking done. He figured we could get interrupted some and still do the check rides. During the morning of the first day, Jolly filled in for me. The examiner sat me down in one of the bedrooms and grilled me. He opened up the helicopter flight manual to page one and started asking questions. Four hours later he nodded his head and said, "Okay, that part is done." Jolly turned the Four-Twelve over to us and the check rides began.

My nurse and paramedic sat in the back seats in case a call came in while I was being examined. The FAA examiner occupied the copilot seat. I prayed there would be no calls until we were done. We flew to Austin Executive, the quiet little airport where Jolly had flown with me during my interview at Lifeline. He watched how I flew and how I worked with the crew. They acted like the professionals they were. I knew they were back there behind me pulling for me, just hoping I would do well.

The examiner peppered me with questions as we went round and round the airport traffic pattern. He simulated every emergency he could do safely. I didn't have to execute any low RPM recoveries. But I scraped off a lot of metal from the bottom of the skids. And I grooved lines in the runway pavement in long strips doing single engine landings. When we were done, I flew over to the Austin municipal airport and shot a couple instrument approaches. I was getting pretty tired by then. So the examiner said, "Let's call it a day and finish this tomorrow." I didn't see it as negotiable. So I went back to the hospital and landed. As we dropped off the FAA examiner a call came in. "No rest for the wicked," he said with a smile. I guessed I had done okay up to now.

The next morning started with another call. It was a short one. When I got back to the hospital the FAA guy was waiting. I topped off the fuel, gathered my crew and off we went to Robert Mueller Municipal Airport across the highway from the hospital. He told me that one of my holding patterns yesterday looked about as ragged as I was at the time. So he had me do another one. Having had a little rest, my air work was apparently a more to his liking. We took two turns in holding. As I turned the aircraft inbound to the airport to shoot a final instrument approach a trauma call came in. I looked over at the examiner. He looked excited. "You're done!" he said. "Let's go!"

He was now just a ride-along visitor for me. I focused on my job while he listened to the cacophony of radio calls. He reminded me of myself on my first EMS call with Arlen. He looked overwhelmed. The call was in response to an injured eight year old boy. He had gotten his legs pinned under his Dad's boat when it slipped off of some blocks. It was a fishing boat with a heavy outboard motor on the back of a V-shaped hull. Lucky for the little boy, the soil beneath the boat was soft. His little legs bent but didn't break. We landed in the boy's very large back yard. The examiner was well into being part of the call. He helped carry the little boy on the stretcher. I could see the guy had a good heart. In doing so, I realized what the crew had seen in me the night of my first call. Being a good air ambulance crew member first requires a concern for others. *This FAA man would probably make a good EMS pilot*, I thought. Whether I had passed my check ride or not, at that scene he passed mine.

We closed the doors, started the engines and I looked over at the FAA guy. He was smiling ear to ear. "You ready?" I smiled back. He gave me a thumbs up. I pulled the collective up briskly. The Four-Twelve shot up vertically like a climbing eagle. I pushed the nose forward. In a moment we were cresting the hills west of Austin.

At my suggestion the FAA man followed the patient and crew into the ER. When he came back to Quarters he could not say enough about how exciting it was to be an EMS pilot. He never stopped talking about it the whole time he filled out the paperwork to award me the ratings I sought. I was now both a helicopter Airline Transport Pilot, a flight instructor and an instrument instructor. It was the end of my first year at Lifeline. I had accomplished the objectives I bartered for. A couple of weeks later, Lifeline doubled the pay of all of its pilots. Now I had no good excuse to leave. By then, I thought I'd never want to.

5 THE SCHEDULE

Arlen stayed positive. He liked to say, "Just do the math. You should be happy working here. You do it so little. Everywhere else you work for the man two hundred and ten days a year. If you work for yourself you do it three sixty-five. We only work a hundred and eighty days a year. We should be paying the county for this job!"

I did the math. As a drone in a cubicle working for the state I was paid to work eight hours a day. I multiplied that by the two hundred and ten days of drudgery per year. The total effort came to *seventy*, twenty-four hour days of work per year. We EMS pilots worked twelve hour shifts. I multiplied those one hundred eighty days of swashbuckling and flying carefree through the clear blue by twelve hours each day. It worked out to *ninety,* twenty-four hour days per year. I pointed that out the twenty extra days we worked to Arlen. He was unapologetic, even when I told him I had failed to add the regular Lifeline staff meetings we attended. On shift or off we were always being called in to meetings. Even if we were on our break days, there was no excuse and no reimbursement for those meetings.

We also did flight training for free. Training days came when Jolly wanted to do them. They happened on his schedule, which usually meant during our off days. Arlen also ignored how we spent our duty days. There were clear blue days, of course. There were sunrises and sunsets. In the Texas Hill Country they were as beautiful as beginnings and ends of daylight get. But we also dodged thunderstorms, ice and turbulence. People have lots of car accidents when it rains, or snows or when the roads ice up. So we flew into lots of rain, lowering clouds and poor visibility. There were times when we slept in the helicopter waiting to fly home because worsening weather stopped us from returning to the hospital. Getting to the scenes, we flew into weather no pilot in his right mind would fly through. Arlen also forgot to mention the bird strikes, mechanical failures and in-flight emergencies we encountered. Most importantly, Arlen didn't mention the stressful decisions, the traumatic life or death decisions and the guilt EMS people deal with every day.

Guilt lives with us. People died despite our best efforts. We all tried unsuccessfully to keep our emotions at bay. Despite our professional patina, each of us at Lifeline took personal responsibility for the souls put in our care. Families trusted us with their loved ones. Sometimes they expected the impossible of us. Sometimes too, we expected the impossible of ourselves. It was easy to say, "It was their time." But our patients were grandparents and parents, siblings and progenies, lovers and friends to someone. Their families touched us in their mourning. When horrible injuries happened, our hands were the first to render aid and sometimes the last pair to hold theirs on this earth. We knew that they were never our purview to cure. We only tended them until we brought them to higher levels of care. Then we pressed on with our tasks taking care of those we met each day. Whether they died or recovered, we generally never knew. We wondered if we could have done better for our patients. We did what we could, and we filled the margins of what we could not do for them with guilt.

Guilt's companion is fear. 'Fighting on through fear,' is a definition of courage. If so, we courageously pressed on with our jobs accompanied by the stink of blood, vomited booze, burned flesh and bladder and rectal drainage. While my crews took our patients to the ER, I often took the lead and washed that effluent and smell out of the helicopter. Later I would wash it out of my nostrils. My car reeked of it sometimes. I took it home with me to be washed out of my flight suits with strong detergents. I never forgot those smells. They haunt me still, and flash back at me. The smell of animal blood and fresh meat does not differ from that of humans. I remember snips of events I thought I had forgotten when on my farm I catch the smell of urine, feces, blood or dead livestock.

There was a time that, despite all the cleaning we did, the Four-Twelve carried the faint smell of blood and death. I attributed it to the fact that almost every day somebody spilled their life's blood into our aircraft cabin. I came to think of the smell as a consequence of our occupation. Hospitals smell like antiseptic. Lifeline One smelled like blood. On hot days the scent was especially strong. We left the Four-Twelve's sliding doors open to dispel it. Then as the weather cooled we found that we still had to crack the doors open to circulate the air in the helicopter cabin. We finally had to acknowledge that something dead was inside the aircraft somewhere. No one - pilot, medic or mechanic - could put a finger upon where. Then came the time for a comprehensive mechanical inspection on the Four-Twelve.

Every area and individual part of our helicopters was inspected regularly. The inspections were based on the calendar, and upon the number of hours we logged flying it. Some areas were inspected less often. It was during one of these more comprehensive inspections that our mechanics discovered the secret to the growing odor that had long hidden in our aircraft. It had to do with the chemistry of human blood. Metaphorically, blood may be "thicker than water." But biologically, warm human blood is actually quite thin. While it is warm, it flows easily though us and outside of us. Spilled blood gets everywhere. It moves like liquid mercury and seeps through the tiniest of cracks. Then, like the tissues it feeds, dead blood decomposes and mortifies.

The floor of our aircraft was supposedly sealed to prevent blood leaking beneath the aircraft's cabin floor. That's one reason inspections beneath the floor were infrequent. But the sealant on Lifeline One cracked. The cracks were so tiny as to be almost invisible. But over time, small amounts of warm blood found those cracks.

The mechanics who removed the cabin floor for a scheduled inspection later related to me what they found. Blood that had dripped down into the closed belly of the aircraft covered the structural ribs and runners and the aluminum inner skin that composed the belly of the aircraft. As it mortified and deepened, it covered the flight control rods. It worked itself into the fittings and the angled bell cranks that connected the control rods together. They said that pulling the floor off of its rubber seal was like lifting the lid of a not-so-long buried coffin. Those who were in the hangar when the floor was lifted up, ran from the hangar in mostly unsuccessful attempts to keep from vomiting.

The mechanics would have none of it. They backed away from the hangar and called the chief paramedic. The job of cleaning out the belly of the Four-Twelve was left to him and a few volunteers. It took them two days. During those days, fans blew the smell out of the hangar while the cleaning crew wore moon suits, respirators, rubber gloves, splash guards and clear plastic masks on their faces. One paramedic told me he swiped eucalyptus vapor rub under his nose before putting on his respirator. He said it killed the smell. It was a trick he learned working in the morgue during his medical training.

I had no similar trick for masking or washing away the memories of the trauma and human misery to which I was exposed. What it cost each of us to effectively do our jobs was hard to quantify. We all ignored as best we could the price we paid and how we paid it. My optimistic comrade Arlen stayed positive with his emphasis on how much we were paid by the flight hour. There were days - he pointed out - when we didn't fly at all that, "We got paid to do nothing," There were also many days that I would log less than an hour of total flight time. On those days he would quote our daily pay and add, "We made hundreds of dollars to do four tenths of an hour of flying." But we often logged three flights in plus or minus one hour of flying, too. The county got allot out of us in a short amount of flight time.

I flew one trauma call where I logged two round trip transports. I hauled six patients to the trauma center. In doing so I logged only four tenths of an hour of flight time. During those twenty-four minutes I twice landed at the scene of a head-on collision. Two men in a beaten up, rusty old van were "Driving While Intoxicated" (DWI). DWI, DUI or "Driving Under the Influence," "Driving Impaired" all result in someone driving who should not have been behind the wheel. I found out later what it meant for the pair in the van. Their blood samples contained cocaine, marijuana and large amounts of alcohol as well. The driver of the van certainly had no business driving. He was speeding along a winding four lane road in the hills west of town when the combination of intoxicants in his blood caused the driver to pass out. In doing so he lost control of the van. He drifted out of his westbound lane. Moving at high speed the van crossed through the passing lane. It then went through the aptly named suicide lane that separated eastbound from westbound traffic. The van made it through the first eastbound lane before it hit another van head on in the last lane carrying traffic.

The oncoming van was occupied by a poor Hispanic family of five. Their van was being driven by Dad. Upon impact, he and Mom who sat next to him, folded over the dashboard. The instrument panel was driven downward snapping their femurs. Two of the children in the back seat were strapped into seatbelts. But their parents' bucket seats were blasted off their rails by the frontal impact. The seats traveled backwards and smashed their children's legs and torsos against the bench seat. Their baby sister's car seat was placed between the two older children. It was not properly attached to the middle of the back bench seat. The sudden stop sent her unrestrained baby seat flying forward like a cannonball. The seat and the baby girl it contained sailed through the hole where the family's windshield used to be. It miraculously missed the coke head's van somehow. It hurtled down the highway before hitting the ground. It tumbled over a hundred yards into a ditch. The seat came to rest on top of the baby, leaving her face-down in the water-filled roadside ditch. She would have drowned there. According to the coroner though, she was already dead before she could drown. She didn't make the flight with us back to the hospital. She rode in the coroner's wagon.

My first twelve minute round trip that day carried the two surviving children. They were stacked on one side of the cabin. The intoxicated citizens who unfortunately both survived were stacked on the other side. While I flew them to the Brackenridge Hospital trauma center, fire fighters pried Mom and Dad out of the tangled wreckage. The parents got the benefit of my next round trip flight. Twenty four minutes was all I logged for the day. I made some serious money per flight hour. The hospital got a bump in their patient load, too. The hospital, the city and the county didn't make any money though. There was no accident or medical insurance onboard either van. The citizens of Austin and Travis County picked up that tab.

I even did one patient transport flight where I logged two takeoffs and two landings with no flight time at all. We were dispatched to a T-bone car accident. Someone ignored a stop sign at a busy downtown intersection. He plowed into the driver's side door of a lady who had expected everybody to obey stop signs. My destination, the accident, was less than a mile from the hospital pad. The wreck snarled traffic so badly that the ground ambulance could not take the patient to the trauma center as quickly as she needed to go. I had the collective up for maybe two minutes before landing in the intersection downtown. I left the motor running while we hot-loaded the patient. Then I lifted the collective for another two minutes. When I landed at the hospital the Hobbs meter hadn't even clicked over a tenth of an hour – six minutes. Yes, I did a call and logged zero flight time. If that was all the flying I did that day I logged no flight time, two landings and got a day of pay for doing it. I think the hospital and Lifeline billing department got paid for that one. I wonder how the city billed the lady's insurance company for the flight time, though.

The administrators at Lifeline above Jolly's rung on the ladder wore suits and had offices. They worked regular hours. I believe that they occupied much of their time planning meetings. I know that they took up much of our time holding them. Their meetings were always called to conveniently fit into their schedules, not ours. I sat through many of them after having flown all night. If I had just finished a night shift and was due to start my 'off' cycle I was expected to stay for the whole meeting. If I was scheduled to fly that night they cut me loose early so as to avoid cutting into my FAA required eight hour rest cycle. The rest cycle started the moment I left the meeting. It didn't take into account the time required for my commute home, nor the meal both before and after a nap, as well as the shower that came before returning rested and ready for another night shift.

There were regular meetings that took place the first Wednesday of every month. Then there were special meetings which happened whenever the administrators wanted to have them. We occasionally had emergency meetings, too. I never went to one that constituted an emergency as I understood the use of the word. then I worked for an emergency service that knew what a real emergency looked like.

The regular meetings were opportunities for us to visit with our comrades on different shifts. We brought donuts. I think Jolly even brought some once. Usually those meetings covered topics that rated talking about. They were always longer than they needed to be. Special meetings covered issues and passed information that could not wait for a regular meeting. Most of the information passed during special meetings could have been passed to us by posting a memo on the crew bulletin board. Sometimes the management did write a memo. Then they had a special meeting to pass it out and read it to us. Only *then* did they post it on the crew bulletin board. Especially when it came to important issues like improving race relations, preventing sexual harassment or keeping your car out of management assigned parking spaces a special meeting was required. That insured a personal emphasis was made by management regarding the issue.

The administrators never flew with us. They never stood a shift with us. They never visited us at Quarters or asked our opinions or advice. They only addressed us as a group, never individually. They did that at meetings. Mostly they did it when they had to or when we did something they weren't happy with. Although most of us did heroic things rather regularly a meeting to recognize such an act would have been worthwhile. But we never had a worthwhile meeting.

Mostly though, meetings wasted our time. Worse, they wasted our personal off time and they didn't pay us for it. One of our more outspoken nurses once challenged the managers about utilizing our off time without compensation. One of Jolly's deskbound bosses happened to be in the room. The nurse had the audacity to ask Jolly if we were going to be paid an hourly rate when we came in on our own time for meetings. Jolly exhibited no empathy as though he had never flown the line. He just looked at the perpetrator and said, "That's why we pay you a salary." Jolly's manager grinned widely. After that I was certain that Jolly was going to remain the Director of Operations for Lifeline for a long time. He and his decisions regarding the crew apparently fit the style of Lifeline's management perfectly.

Flying for Lifeline was in some ways much better than if I flew for a competitor. With Lifeline I lived in the same city where I worked. That wasn't the case with many of the pilots and medical crew members I knew who flew for other air ambulance companies. Those aircraft were often staffed by people who lived far away from their work base. I worked half the year, plus meetings and training of course. Pilots at other programs did what I did in that respect. But they had a long commute every time they had to go to work. Whether for their shift or attending meetings or training they drove. Sometimes for hours. I worked a week 'on,' and a week 'off.' Other air ambulance services did two week shifts. So far from home they were away from their families for the whole two weeks. They packed a bag with what anyone would pack for a week or two away from home. Then they hit the road. Some crews lived in a cheap hotel. Some lived in a "crash pad," which was usually a single-wide trailer or a dumpy apartment shared with one or two other crew members. If they didn't live in a hotel they brought their own sheets and towels. Everybody working away from home brought incidentals like laundry soap and even their food. If a crash pad was ever cleaned it was done in desperation by some resident crew member who couldn't stand the filth any longer. Then they skipped sleep and used their off-time, elbow grease and their own money on cleaning agents to return their living space to hygienic standards. Even so the places didn't stay clean for long.

Those of us working for Lifeline lived in the Austin area. My commute to work for shifts, meetings and training was about thirty minutes. Between shifts we slept in our own beds. I was grateful for that. I was also grateful for the facilities at the hospital base where I worked. "Quarters," where we sat out our shift was a two bedroom apartment. It was located at the foot of a stairwell below the helipad. We kept the place clean. But the hospital housekeeping folks augmented our efforts. Cleaning crews dropped by to spruce things up pretty regularly. They left the cleaning supplies in the bathroom where we could get at them. We didn't have to buy our own.

We ate well there, too. We collected a monthly fund to keep the kitchen stocked. The new guy was responsible for hitting one of the big box grocery stores and buying what the crew continuously added to a list on the fridge. The pilots and paramedics wanted sugar and carbs. The nurses wanted rice cakes. We always had plenty of both. We also brought in homemade food from our own kitchens. Casseroles, pans of lasagna and racks of barbeque ribs were not uncommon to the kitchen of Lifeline. Texans in general and many of our staff in particular pride themselves on their ability to barbeque. So the crew purchased a nice gas grill. We kept it on the porch out back. We had some good cooks working at Lifeline. In no time my waistline served as testimony to that.

Lifeline belonged in Austin because Lifeline belonged to Austin. The pilots and helicopters belonged to Travis County. Our quarters, helipad and the nurses belonged to Brackenridge hospital. Our paramedics worked for Austin Emergency Medical Service. It was often a cumbersome arrangement, but it worked. Other EMS services worked like gypsies. One company was noted for working their crews out of cheap, portable house trailers. They often showed up without notice. They just pulled up their trailer based program into one of the outlying towns around Austin and got down to business. If business wasn't good they just as quickly pulled their trailer and their operation and moved them to another town. In my travels with Lifeline I saw how they did business. They were most often set up in a vacant lot behind our fire station or at a rural, low traffic airport. Their helicopter was usually parked out in the open. I drove past one operation where a mechanic on a step ladder was working on the helicopter. I had to wonder how and where their heavy maintenance got done.

Other hospital based programs were not much better off than the gypsy air services. Our competitor to the south was based at a large and busy hospital in downtown San Antonio. I visited them once, mostly out of curiosity. Their crew was stuffed into a couple patient rooms on the top floor of the hospital. Their helicopter was parked outside on a rooftop pad. The crew quarters looked like what they were, a couple of single patient rooms separated by a bathroom. In one room there was enough room for a desk, a phone, a computer and a couple chairs. An area map hung on a nail hammered into the wall.

In the other room was a row of wall lockers, a vinyl covered sofa and a dilapidated easy chair. They were aimed at a television that was hanging from a mount in the ceiling. There were no kitchen facilities. I don't know where the crew slept. There was certainly no room for a bed that I saw. I considered that a serious fault with that air service. Fatigue is the bane of the Emergency Medical Services world. Fatigue in EMS is pervasive, chronic and continuous. The ability to snag a nap is vitally important to any EMS crew. Soldiers and EMS crews were the only people I ever saw who could sleep at a moment's notice. All of us who flew the line at Lifeline could sit down and drop off to sleep instantly. It may have been a developed skill. It may also have been a symptom of chronic fatigue. In those cases when we didn't particularly intend to take a nap we often slept like we were suffering from narcolepsy. One minute we would be alert and talking. The next we were snoring. That's not normal for most people. It was common for us at Lifeline.

In studying the phenomenon I found that shift workers traditionally suffer from sleep disorders. But EMS workers take those disorders to a new level. It was certainly our paramedics who suffered the most from chronic fatigue. Most people wake up in the morning and work during the day. They come home and sleep at night. That creates a normal "circadian rhythm." Our paramedics on the other hand had no circadian rhythms. Crew changes normally took place in the morning. But it was not uncommon for a new crew member to arrive and spell another any time of the day or night. The regular work cycle for paramedics at Lifeline was the same as it was on "the trucks," – what the medics calls ground ambulances. Paramedics worked a "twenty-four." That means the paramedic worked a shift that lasted twenty-four hours. During slack times they grabbed naps when they could. A number of ambulance stations were too busy even for those short naps. The ambulance crew at our hospital base was an example. They worked continuously. There the crew barely had time to eat, let alone take a nap.

Our paramedics divided their time between working ground ambulance shifts and working on the helicopter. Sometimes they worked "forty-eights." They worked twenty-four hours at a ground ambulance station, and twenty-four on the helicopter. I can't imagine how they did it. As if forty-eights weren't bad enough, a number of times I noted medics coming to work on the helicopter after working a "seventy-two!" Once a paramedic doing that showed up at Lifeline so goofy from lack of sleep I threw him out. "Go home!" I said. "Sleep for four days and then come back and see us." He resisted. But he had no business on the aircraft suffering so from fatigue. He finally acquiesced though knowing I was looking out for his safety and ours.

Sending the paramedic home wasn't a popular move so far as our management was concerned. They want people working the shifts they're assigned. But as I knew they would, the managers had a replacement for our worn out paramedic in less than an hour. Nobody is so valuable that they can't be replaced.

The nurses at Lifeline were the next most abused of regular sleep. They dealt with interrupted Circadian rhythms differently than the medics. As with paramedics, nurses mostly work twenty-four hour shifts. Paramedics worked one day and were off for one or two days. In a seven day period the last of the seven days alternated between being on and off every two weeks. Nurses worked two twenty-fours in seven days. That's less work per week when compared with the paramedics. But it's still eight more hours of work in a seven day week than most folks do. Most of working

America does forty hours of labor with weekend breaks. Nurses work forty-eight hours in the same period. The nurses on Lifeline worked a normal shift in the hospital. But Lifeline added one or two twelve hour shifts to their usual nursing load each week. No wonder our nurses were fatigued.

Last in the line of fatigue were our pilots. We worked a twelve hour day. Then we had twelve hours off before starting again. Because we worked a shift, we didn't live and sleep like the forty-hour workaday world. Ours was never a 'standard forty hour week' kind of life. Unlike our medical crews who worked endlessly, we pilots still had some semblance of circadian rhythms. They weren't the 'work-day/sleep-night' rhythms. Our rhythms danced to a Cuban beat: a sort of 'cha-cha-cha-step-step-step-cha-cha-cha, or day-day-day, off-off-off, night-night-night.'

A common EMS industry shift for pilots is "seven-twelves." That is, we worked seven days of twelve hour shifts. These were followed by seven days off. Then we'd return to fly seven nights followed by seven days off. Having a full seven days off in a row is enviable. I could get some stuff done around the house with seven days off. I could also get some serious family time. I made the Boy Scout meetings, football games and dinner dates pretty regularly during my seven off.

But during my seven on I was out of touch with everything. All I did was work and rest. I reported to work at either seven in the morning or seven in the evening. Normally, during the day shift I left for work before my family arose to start their day. I drove to work while the rest of Austin was scratching their heads and padding their way to the kitchen to start their coffee pots. I was often doing my preflight inspection on the helicopter as the sun broke the eastern horizon. I watched a lot of pretty sunrises over Austin from the top of a Bell 412. Day shifts were the best for me. About the time most of Austin was dressed, looking at their watches and heading toward their car to join the rush hour traffic to work, I was an hour at work already. Rush hour car crashes made for a busy part of my work day. I picked up a lot of those people who crashed their cars going to or from work. My commute was a little safer than those stuck in the rush hour glut. Early as I left for work there was no traffic on the roads.

Flying nights I was starting my work day as most people in Austin were just trying to get home. I left the house about the time most people were sitting down to dinner. On the way to work anyone left on the highway was heading the opposite direction. I pitied the people caught in those last clogged arteries of traffic on the other side of the expressway.

There were lots of positive aspects to working "twelves." But there were drawbacks. My family's life was divided by my seven day work shifts. Shifts started on Wednesday and ended on Wednesday. The seven day shifts also included working on whatever holidays fell on those working weeks. It amazed me how often I missed both Christmas and Thanksgiving on a seven and seven shift. Seven and seven also guaranteed that I worked half of the weekends on the calendar. A family does a lot of important things together on weekends. My family got every weekend off. I worked half of them.

Day shifts started at seven a.m. Since I left for work at six fifteen I missed my family's mornings. Getting the kids up and off to school was all on Linda. Unless I took time off, so were doctor's appointments, baseball practice and everything else a normal family with three kids does during a day. I was a part-time parent. "Lucky him," some might say. But I didn't feel so lucky looking in on my sleeping wife and kids before leaving for work. I just felt lonely.

At the end of my work day our kids were either in bed or soon to get there as I pulled into the driveway. I missed playing with them in the back yard, sharing the dinner making duties and even washing the dishes. I like to feed my family with my cooking. Call me odd but I even like washing dishes for the people I love. When I worked days though I ate alone. I came home to a plate of food covered with aluminum foil and placed lovingly in a warm oven for me. Getting up before dawn every day means going to bed before most of my neighbors. It also meant going to bed before my wife. As a teacher she had papers to grade and lesson plans to write. She did them while I slept.

When I worked the night shift I was again apart from my family most of the time they were home. I went to work shortly after they got home from school. If I was lucky I got home just before they left. If I had a late flight, a meeting or a traffic delay I just missed them altogether arriving to an empty house. A lot of my off days were spent at home by myself, too.

Off days were always welcome of course. But they were always affected by my weird Circadian rhythms. Remember that circadian rhythm with the Cuban beat? It never stopped just because I was off for seven days. When I started flying with Lifeline I found that I could get back into a normal sleep cycle during my seven off. But after a couple shifts I found myself wide awake at midnight, or wanting a nap during the day. I figured there must be a way that shift workers accommodate odd sleep cycles and live with people with normal ones. I have read about that.

Most of the advice focused on normalizing my life with diet and exercise. I tried improving my diet laying off of what I consumed with both hands at work. Having been a Marine I was no stranger to exercise. I especially loved to run. I took advantage of the days I was at home alone to do that. I also worked out with weights. But that only happened when I was off. I was on a fifty-percent diet and exercise improvement program. When the wife and kids were home those programs suffered, too.

Ultimately my EMS schedule ruled me. For the first time in my life I had trouble sleeping when I should. I would also wake up in the middle of the night ravenously hungry. If I gave in and made a meal I'd be up the rest of the night. If I ate a light dinner with my family because I wasn't hungry during their normal dinner time I'd eat another meal before retiring. That introduced me to another first in my life: indigestion. Jolly remained for me a living, breathing example of what could happen to me working EMS. Seeing him strain the seams of his flight suit gave me the willpower I needed to keep my weight under control. I carried my meals to work and left the snacks alone that were a terrible temptation for anxious, busy people like me. I also used the free weights at the ambulance station next door. Along with my fifty percent exercise program at home I kept my weight under control. But sleep was another matter. I never slept normally the whole time I flew for Lifeline.

Our seven and seven shift took another toll on the Lifeline pilots. Flying Lifeline One was the most challenging helicopter flying I had ever done. In order to do it proficiently and safely my skills were honed to a fine edge. Keeping them that way required that we had to use those skills frequently. Any given shift gave us plenty of opportunity. We referred to our level of capability in those skills as our level of "currency." Flying my shifts my currency at Lifeline was generally higher than it had ever been at any other flying job I had ever done. It had to be. There were too many hazards in the job to operate at less than our best. Takeoffs were from a small downtown helipad surrounded by obstructions. There was no place to land in the event of an engine failure on takeoff or similar immediate action emergency. All the hospitals we serviced were similar in this regard. There was no room for errors. Our weather minimums at Lifeline also gave us plenty of room to get into trouble in bad weather. I flew in weather that would ground airliners. If I could see the top of the capital building two blocks away I had good enough weather to launch.

Our scene landing sites were most often described as "unimproved." Wires, trees, moving traffic and traffic that ignored road blocks, soft or uneven landing surfaces, blowing dust and debris and wandering pedestrians were all common problems where we most commonly landed. We needed to be on our game to deal with these. Together we pilots came to the conclusion that in the short seven day breaks in our shifts we were losing the currency we needed to do the job at Lifeline. So we came to Jolly with a proposal. Arlen acted as our spokesman.

In a meeting we all called with Jolly, we proposed that we readjust our schedule. Instead of flying "sevens," we proposed we fly "fours." It sounded like a good idea to us. There was no pressure on Jolly. We were the ones who would have to live with it, not Jolly. We also said that if anybody found out that it wasn't working we could make adjustments. If it turned out to be a bad idea in the long run we could go back to sevens and regroup. There was nothing bad we could see in the plan. We all wanted to make it work. Consequently Jolly nixed the idea immediately. We should have seen it coming. We all knew that he was a tyrant. The longer he remained D.O. the worse he got. If an idea didn't come from him it wasn't a good idea. Fours weren't his idea.

So we kept flying sevens. Had Jolly debated the issue or convinced us our idea was untenable we probably would have returned to sevens. But because he bullied us, and because our currency remained an issue with us, animosity arose. It always does when managers won't even consider the worker's point of view. In this case our animosity had another valid reason to grow. We felt that the safe operation of our aircraft and the safety of our team was involved.

Because they were our friends and partners we let the crew know what was going on. Our proposal to fly fours made sense to them. A good EMS crew works together to face problems. Jolly's bone headedness was a problem. Since Jolly wouldn't listen to the pilots the crew knew he wouldn't listen to them, either. So the medics and nurses took the issue for action.

With Lifeline's odd chain of command the medics and the nurses had their own administration. So far as we pilots were concerned, Jolly was our boss. He made sure we knew it if there was any doubt on that score. He would not forget a pilot who went over his head to the county administrators. At that time there was nothing Jolly did that required us to do so. Not even the fours or sevens issue. But nothing kept the medics or nurses from going up their respective chains. Hospital, city EMS and county EMS supervisors talked. Addressing the fours or sevens issue was just a shared phone call on their level. And that's how our medical crews got the County to approve us working fours. By the time Jolly found out about it the issue was decided by his bosses.

Jolly knew he'd been had. We knew he would not forget it, that he saw the end-around as a slight to his authority. So he presented the change of schedule to us like it had been his idea all along. He just posted the schedule on the Quarters door. It was written just as we had suggested. The first couple of shifts of fours worked well. Its sole purpose was to help the pilots keep our edge in flying the helicopter. And that it did. I saw it at once in my own flying. After my first four day break was done, I saw it again. I was not only well rested, I was still on the top of my game in the cockpit. I saw it on the first call of the new shift. First flights after a break always seemed to be tough ones. My first call was responding to a car accident far out in the country at some county road intersection. We had little information about the patients or the landing site when we launched. Navigation information to get to the scene was nebulous. "Lifeline one, MVA (motor vehicle accident). Two county roads northeast of Austin out in the middle of nowhere..." Actually the dispatcher gave the road numbers. We were pretty good at knowing the numbers of the county roads and where they were. After that dispatch call we all looked at each other. As a crew we said to each other, "Where in the heck is that?"

To make matters more challenging the weather was already bad and slated to get worse. Low clouds kept us close to the terrain. Rain was already limiting visibility. Still we made it to the scene without too much hunting for the spot. I was as sharp running that call as I had been on my last one four days before. Then came the scene where there was only one spot to land. Getting in and out of it was a tight fit. It took all three of us working together to get the helicopter into a hole in the trees without knocking off the rotor tips or even turning them green with clipped leaves. The fours did it again.

When we got back to the hospital I talked over the call with my crew. We all agreed. The call was tough. The crew was the first to say it. We did it as though I had been doing calls like that all week. I had lost nearly none of my skills over my break. I was sold on "fours." So were the other pilots and for the same reasons. The issues with circadian rhythms were still there, but they were no worse than with sevens. The new schedule was accomplishing what we had hoped. We were coming back on shift ready to fly. That's all we wanted.

Jolly on the other hand, was suffering. He didn't talk to any of us for days. He just sat at his desk over at the hangar at the hangar and moped. We knew that was a bad sign. Jolly saw it as a loss of face. And Jolly didn't lose well. We knew something was hatching over at the airport. Jolly got even with us at the next staff meeting. As we pilots entered the room he handed us a new schedule. We came to called it, the "Jolly Modification."

He developed the idea on his own of course. He never worked cooperatively with anyone, pilots or medical crew members. I guess he thought that working as a group would let the enemy know his plans. As usual he instituted the change with his usual authoritarian lack of finesse. He even said as he handed the new schedule to us, "Read it and weep."

He started the meeting without preamble, and without donuts.

"You want fours?" he asked rhetorically. "Here's your fours."

He waved a copy of the schedule before him as though it were a battle flag. "You'll fly fours alright. From now on you'll fly two days, followed immediately by flying two nights."

Arlen raised his hand. Jolly ignored him. He saw his modification not so much as an improvement than as a counter attack. That was the kind of relationship that kept Jolly's at odds with the crews. It kept Lifeline in a constant state of stress, dissatisfaction and turmoil. If things were calm and working smoothly we just knew it was a brief hiatus. Jolly was thinking up something to make life difficult again. It must have been how he reminded himself that he was the boss.

When Arlen continued to get no acknowledgement from Jolly he finally lowered his hand. We other pilots just shut up, too. And then we executed the directive. We did it without comment or complaint. We didn't want to say anything really until we saw how the new schedule was going to work. Because we could not complain about what we didn't know we saw "the Jolly Mod" as an experiment. So we experimented. We got the results before the next crew meeting.

The Jolly Modification was a disaster. By the next crew meeting it was obvious. The pilots looked like so many zombies. Linda was alarmed by the black bags that had appeared under my eyes. The nurses picked up on it, too. Brenda, one of my favorites said the same thing Linda did. "You look like a new father, like one who stays up all night with a crying baby." Soon we all looked like that. When we came into the room for our next crew meeting the Jolly Mod was the eight hundred pound gorilla that came in with us. One of the nurses pointed it.

"What happened to our pilots? They look like the walking dead!"

Jolly nipped the debate in the bud. "If that's a way to have us discuss our schedule I'll tell you this right now. We're not discussing it. The schedule is new. We haven't even used it a month yet. The pilots said they wanted to experiment with it. So that's what we're doing. The schedule remains as it is."

The pilots knew it was pointless to start an argument with Jolly, especially where his ego was on full display in front of the crew. So we shut up. Jolly didn't make himself available for any discussion afterward, either. So that was that. We did another month of fours with the Jolly mod. It was a miserable time for me.

The first two days after we got the schedule were fine. I worked all day, stayed home all night. Then in order to start Jolly's two nights I stayed home all the following day. I was slept out. I got up with Linda and the kids. When they left I worked out. I did some outdoor chores hoping to tire myself out a bit. Then I tried to nap. It didn't happen. I was wide awake when the kids got home. And I was wide awake when the night shift started. I was dragging terribly when it ended, though. I went home and slept like I had partied all night. I woke up when Linda and the kids got home. Then I headed to work for my second night.

That night I was rested and made it through the shift fine. When I got home the following morning I started my four days off. I was willing to believe the Jolly Mod experiment might work. I wanted to sleep, but I knew if I did I wouldn't sleep that night. It was murder staying awake all day, but I managed. I was pretty droopy by dinnertime. I slept hard that night. I was pretty well back on my family's sleep schedule for the rest of my break and into the two next day shifts. Then I hit the night end of the Jolly Mod again. When it came to an end, I felt like I had jet lag. I felt that way a couple of days into the next off period.

The third shift the jet lag feeling got worse and lasted longer. I could see that our original fours schedule was far better than the Jolly Mod. By the fourth trip through it I was not a pleasant person to be around. I couldn't stay awake at work, and I couldn't sleep at home. I was as crabby as anyone who is sleep deprived. The bags showed up under my eyes. Jolly's veto of debate on the subject at the meeting just made it worse. Four times worse by the next meeting.

When we met again, Lifeline was a different operation. Morale was as low as I had seen it. If Jolly even noticed, he didn't say anything about it. He just ran the meeting with an iron hand as usual. When he got past the last action item on his list he made a mistake. He asked the rhetorical question, "Does anyone have anything else to bring up?" He expected the rhetorical answer. Silence. But instead he too late realized he had opened up both the floor and a tremendous can of worms. CJ, a skinny, mop-headed nurse with a gap between her front teeth shyly raised her hand.

Jolly looked surprised. He reminded me of the head of the orphanage in the Charles Dickens story "Oliver Twist," when the little boy Oliver asked for more porridge. His and Jolly's eyes bulged at the audacity. Jolly didn't want to give her the floor. But he really didn't have a reason not to, now.

"What?" Jolly challenged, as in "What do *you* want?"

CJ was an old Lifeline hand. She was frail looking, like she'd blow away in a high wind. But she was all gristle, took on the toughest calls, handled the meanest drunks and participated in rescues that would have earned her the Silver Star in a combat zone. She was not easily intimidated. Jolly wasn't going to bluff her into submission. She wasn't eloquent when she said her peace, but she made her point.

"Jolly, your pilots have become assholes. And it's your fault."

You could have heard a pin drop. Jolly was flummoxed. I almost burst a blood vessel stifling a laugh.

"This new schedule you came up with has turned them all into zombies. I won't say who, but I pinched one the other night to keep him from dozing off while he was flying."

I didn't flick an eyelash. It was me. She went on.

"The medical crews work crazy schedules. We're used to it. And if we fall asleep flying to a scene, who is the wiser? But that's not true of the pilots. They get no rest now. They're hard to live with. And they're losing their edge. We know what's going on. The pilots have been working your new schedule without saying anything to you or us. But the medical crews can see it. It's crazy. You're killing them. And if you don't change it you might just kill a couple of us, too. People were not made to work a shift like that, at least not for very long. I guarantee that if I was made to work that schedule, I'd quit."

CJ was right. We all knew it. My wife Linda would have agreed. She let me know that I was no fun to live with nowadays. I complained about everything. I couldn't sleep with the kids awake. They made too much noise. When they were home, Linda and the boys resorted to sneaking around the house so Dad wouldn't come out and holler. Linda knew that even when the kids weren't home I couldn't get into a deep sleep unless I fell into it in exhaustion. She urged me to go to Jolly and convince him his modification wasn't working. I knew Jolly would not listen to me or even all the pilots speaking as one. CJ's oratory came as a surprise to us. We found out later too, that it was not impromptu.

The medical crews knew we couldn't take another round of the Jolly Modification. They determined among themselves that something had to give. CJ's speech at the staff meeting was planned as their first assault on Jolly to get him to back off and let things get back to normal. Hotter heads wanted to call for his job. Wiser members of the crew knew that would draw a line the county managers might not be willing to cross. They convinced their fellows that CJ should do the talking to give Jolly the chance to address the problem in an open forum. If that didn't work, sterner measures would be used.

Sadly, the open forum didn't work. Jolly squashed the discussion before it could start.

"Maybe you ought to quit, CJ."

The room fell into the kind of silence that happens in a bar just before a brawl breaks out. Jolly saw it coming. He held up both hands as though stopping traffic.

"Hold it, hold it!" He scanned the room. "You might as well all hear this." Then he focused on CJ. "I don't care what you think." Then he looked around the room. "I don't care what any of you think. The schedule stands. If you don't like the schedule, you can all get another job."

Then Jolly dropped his hands to his hips. He looked around the room to catch the eyes of each of us. Nobody said anything. Personally, I figured there is no point transmitting if the other guy's receiver isn't on. I just kept my mouth shut. Maybe the rest of the crew thought something similar.

"You all better get this straight around here. I am the Director of Operations of Lifeline. I was picked for this job by the county commissioners. You didn't like the last director. I volunteered to take that position. I am here for the duration. And I will be the last man standing here when this operation is done. If you think otherwise, just let me know. If you go behind my back again I'll find out who did it and I will fire you. I don't care if you're a pilot, nurse or paramedic. You will be out the door and never work here again. In fact I'll blackball you so you never work on an EMS helicopter again. And I can do it!"

I am certain I winced. I half expected CJ to use the "A" word again. She didn't. Jolly stood a moment with his hands on his hips in a resounding silence. Then he adjourned the meeting, opened the door and left. The atmosphere poured out behind him like the hot blast of a furnace.

Probably before Jolly made it to the parking garage the crews did their end run on him again. The results were the same. The crew complaints went up the nurse and paramedic chains respectively. Soon after, the county management sided with the customers, those being the hospital administrators. The Jolly Mod schedule had to change back to straight fours. When his manager notified Jolly it is not enough to just say, "He was angry." He was instantly out of control. He vented his fury to his manager who had delivered the news to him.

Unlike Jolly, she was a reasonable person. She listened to him. She let him vent. Jolly never calmed down, though. So in order to help him get a rein on his anger she encouraged him to call the pilots in for one of our semi-regular "emergency meetings." Jolly thought that meant she was on his side. That move empowered Jolly. He called each of us personally and told us to come to the hospital meeting room the very next morning. His boss booked the meeting room for him. Again, her help there made him think he was in the driver's seat. Jolly could hardly wait to get us alone the next day.

Usually if a meeting was called and we were off shift, we'd come dressed casually. For this meeting however, Jolly ordered us to wear our flight suits. I'm not sure why Jolly did things like that. He always kept us guessing about how and why he made decisions. He didn't tell us the purpose of the meeting. He didn't need to.

All the pilots arrived early. We met in the parking garage in front of Quarters. When we were all there, we decided to head out together for the meeting room. We wanted to be seated when Jolly arrived. We walked through the hospital hallways and into the atrium lobby that led to the meeting room. From across the atrium we could all see that the door was propped open. We entered to find Jolly already there.

I was the first through the door. I was surprised to see Jolly's boss seated at the head table beside him. I had interviewed with her for my job. I liked her. She seemed a friendly and even tempered sort. She was a statuesque lady with auburn, almost red, shoulder-length hair. It was well-coiffed. She wore dark, horn rimmed glasses which looked good on her fair skin. Her dark green business suit went well with her hair and her green eyes. I couldn't help but notice with a quick glance that she was bouncing one of her patent leather black high heels on the ends of her toes. With her legs crossed and her skirt just above the knee those heels made her long legs look quite attractive. "*Classy*," I thought. "*... with the slightest hint of 'trampy' there, too.*" I felt a little smile coming on. I saw that she had clearly caught my glance at her legs. She grinned a little. I thought I caught a wink. "Good morning, Paul," she said with a pleasant grin and a knowing look. Then she shifted her eyes to the other pilots, greeting each of us by name as we walked in.

Jolly on the other hand did not greet us. Instead he stared holes through us. His arms were crossed over his chest so tightly I wondered if he might be having chest pain. He looked as usual like a homeless person. He wore his shabby and faded blue flight suit and dirty boots. He bounced one knee nervously. We took seats around the table and sat down. Jolly knit his brow. He stared across the table at us until we got settled. Then he stood up, walked over and closed the door.

We all knew things were going to get ugly. As soon as the door clicked closed, Jolly exploded. What he said and the way he addressed us was offensive from first to last. He took time to denigrate the medical crew, many of them by name. Both in delivery and content his harangue was almost manic. The words he chose became more embarrassingly crude as he continued. In the end, he blamed us pilots for "all this." I was surprised that I wasn't angry with him. I just thought him pathetic.

Because he began to repeat himself I could tell his rant was done. I glanced at his boss. She was staring at her hands which were crossed on the table before her. Then I looked at the other pilots. I think we were all embarrassed for Jolly's supervisor. When I thought he could lambaste us no more he went too far. "I can replace you all!" he told us. "I have a drawer full of resumes. All of them are pilots better than any of you."

His boss looked up at him. Jolly looked back at her for approbation. He didn't get it. Apparently she hadn't expected him to go that far, to threaten to fire us all. He would need her okay to do that. We could all see by her look that he wasn't getting it. Jolly had let the cat out of the bag, though. He tried to soften his last statement, back up some and leave himself an out. "I'm not sure I won't still do that," he said. His boss looked back down at her hands. It was an clever dynamic to control Jolly who had, up to then been out of control.

"If you are still employed by the end of the day, things are going to change around Lifeline. You can be certain of that."

Even at the peak of his tantrum I wasn't really concerned about my job. I had a house full of little boys. I had seen tantrums before. I knew that nothing came of them. I also knew that cooler heads would prevail. In this case, the cooler head was Jolly's boss. Both she and we pilots knew that the hospital, the city and the county were not going to let Jolly shut down the operation while he found a new pilot staff.

Jolly reached up with the back of his hand and wiped saliva that had gathered at the corners of his mouth. He was spent. The redheaded manager uncrossed her legs. She pushed out her chair, stood up and took over. She put out a calming hand toward Jolly.

"You can go now, Jolly," she said in an understanding voice. She moved her hand his direction and then pointed toward the door. "Go on," she said. "I want to talk to these men now."

Jolly looked confused.

"Go on. It's my turn." She flicked her fingers at him to shoo him out of the room.

Jolly nodded like a little boy told by someone's mother to go home to supper. Game time was over. He turned and slowly walked out of the room. We all followed him with our eyes until the door clicked closed. Through the narrow window in the door I watched Jolly disappear across the lobby of the hospital and through the atrium.

The room was quiet now. The manager was still looking at the door. I heard the air conditioning kick on. The word "pathetic," kept coming to mind. Then the manager took a step back toward her chair, thought twice and then turned toward us. She crossed her arms lightly across her ample bosom. She raised one toe balancing her foot on her attractive high heel. Facing us as though the last twenty minutes of abuse had never happened she said,

"Gentlemen, I understand that you are unhappy with your new schedule."

When we left the room we were back on "fours" as we knew the term: four days on, four off, four nights on, four off. The blinding fatigue we had suffered at the hands of Jolly's schedule modification quickly disappeared. At least our standard of weariness became manageable once again.

We were soon meeting our crews' high standards for us. Most important to me, there was no more barking or growling at my wife and kids, I again became the Dad and husband my family and I wanted me to be.

A lesson learned for the Jolly Mod was that I needed to warren all the rest I could get whenever I could. I became a master at cat naps. I also took advantage more often of Lifeline's one great tool for reducing crew fatigue the pilot's bedroom.

I need to make it clear that although the sleeping at Lifeline was well provided for, so was the method of waking us up. We were alerted to a call by "the pager." The system was based on amplifying the alarm signal of the digital pager the paramedic and nurse wore. When their pager wasn't clipped to their belt it was clipped into an amplifier setup on a desk near the door of Quarters. The amplifier was linked to a series of speakers in the ceiling of our crew quarters. One of those speakers was located in each bedroom directly above our beds. When the dispatch center needed us for a call, the tone of the pagers was increased to the level of pain. There was no volume adjustment to it. When it went off, its effect on deep sleep was akin to being dashed with a bucket of ice water while being simultaneously and suddenly blared at by a submarine dive alarm klaxon. There was no possibility that any living human could sleep through a call from the Austin EMS Dispatch center pager system.

After the beeping signal ended, the dispatchers verbally transmitted a message. Sometimes it was just an administrative message like, "Lifeline, call dispatch." Most often though the message was an EMS call. In that case we were given our dispatch message in the same format all the time. First, we were told the responding agency we were supporting. Then came the nature of the call and the address to which we were being dispatched. Then we were told the heading and distance we had to fly to reach the scene. A typical call sounded like this: "Lifeline One and Manchaca first responders, chest pain, 1235 Highland Drive, heading 232 degrees for fourteen point eight miles."

By the time the call was repeated we were most likely halfway up the stairs to the helicopter. When I was awake and that overhead alarm went off, adrenalin would pour into my system. It gave me speed like the wind. When it went off while I was in a deep sleep however, the experience was simply terrifying. Rising quickly from the lower bunk in the pitch dark pilot's bedroom often resulted in soundly smacking my head on the rails of the upper bunk. Rising quickly from the upper bunk I tended to launch myself into the air before I knew where I was. That resulted in landing in a crumpled heap next to the bed. I figured I could never really do myself too much harm with a skull fracture. There wasn't anything inside my bone head to damage, anyway. A broken leg was another matter. I might not fly for weeks. Consequently the lower bunk was usually my bed of choice.

After my first experience being awakened by the pager system from deep sleep I had trouble sleeping in the Quarters for a while. But fatigue eventually drove me to seek rest under the threat of the pager, anyway. I sincerely believe that if such a system is put in the funeral home in which I eventually lie, when it is set off I will most likely rise from my casket seeking a helicopter before I recall that I am dead.

Although the pager always got me out of bed, it didn't always sharpen my wits. More than once I found myself sitting in the helicopter before I was really awake. I had a justifiable concern that one day I would be so tired I would do something really stupid. I might fail to start one of the engines and burn the other one up attempting to takeoff. I might miss the fact that the aircraft was still tied down to the ground power cable and then attempt to takeoff. Both of those gaffes had already been accomplished by EMS crews. Both had resulted in destroyed equipment. On more than a few occasions they had resulted in fatal crashes. So especially late at night we backed each other up. We all walked around the helicopter looking for tie downs, open panels and leaks. During the call we acted as cheer leaders to keep each other alert. Usually it worked. But once it didn't.

Our shift had been brutal. We had a constant string of calls with no time between them to rest. It was hot. We were dehydrated. All three of us had worked long shifts already. We had just reached the Quarters door after a particularly strenuous call when the pager went off again. We looked at each other and hung our heads. We were just worn out. That's when the flight nurse threw the safety flag. A mantra in the EMS helicopter community goes, "Three to go unless one says no." That meant that any member of the crew could cancel a flight. There was supposed to be no fault or blame issued for cancelling a flight where safety was a concern. At least that's what our managers advertised.

In this case all three of us had concerns about taking another flight when we were so fatigued. It was just the nurse who expressed it first. She did not ask if we agreed with her. She didn't need to do that. She didn't want the burden of the decision to be shared. She just thought we had reached a point where we were going to hurt ourselves. So she took action.

"Guys," she said after calling the dispatcher to cancel the flight, "this is stupid. Taking another flight as tired as we are is dangerous. We're making mistakes already. I know I am, anyway. We don't need to make a bad one. We need to take a break."

The paramedic and I looked at each other and shrugged. "Okay," I said. "If that's how you see it, I guess we'll take a break." Because she had already called dispatch and took the aircraft out of service there was no point arguing, not that we would have. The die was cast. I hated missing a call and being out of service. But I knew the break would not be a long one. The new crew would be in to relieve us in a couple hours. Dispatch would phone the oncoming crew and tell them the situation. I already had the helicopter ready for another flight. My part was done. The medical crew went upstairs and double checked that their end of the business was ready for the oncoming crew. There was nothing more we could do. I went back to the bedroom. As I lay down I had the sneaking suspicion that this was not going to go well with the management. But I didn't worry about it too long. I was asleep in seconds.

That night she cancelled the flight turned out to be the last one that nurse ever flew with Lifeline. Jolly threw down the tyrant card and she was gone. I was surprised that it trumped her safety card. She was not just off Lifeline. Jolly pushed the issue and she was fired by the hospital. I would miss her. She was a good flight nurse. She stopped the flight for the right reason. She was already gone by then, but the next time I saw Jolly I took issue with what he had done to her.

"I thought any crew member could stop a flight they considered unsafe."

"It wasn't unsafe," Jolly said. "We all fly tired. We deal with it. She didn't. She's gone."

"This is going to have a bad effect on the whole crew, Jolly," I warned. "Nobody is going to stop a flight if they know they'll get fired. You just put a penny in the fuse box here. There's no way now to cancel a hazardous or even a dangerous flight unless you want to lose your job."

Jolly just shrugged his shoulders. "Maybe the crews should think more about what they're doing when they chicken out."

I didn't like the way this was escalating. It didn't bother Jolly a bit.

"It's a good thing it wasn't you that stopped that flight," Jolly added.

I ignored the threat. "If people think they have to fly whether a call is dangerous or not, they're going to quit."

Jolly smirked. "Maybe they should just go ahead and do that then. What has happened to this place?" He said it as if he was talking to someone who would agree with him. "You've all turned into a bunch of cowards."

That crack raised my hackles. If he wasn't such a cretin I would have taken it personally. In any case I was sure it was meant to rile me. It did. He faced me. As a sign of his arrogance he even stuck out his chin at me. He saw it as a sign he was in charge. I saw is as a perfect target. I subconsciously balled up my fists. I think he noticed. I suppressed my desire to punch his lights out. He refrained from calling me or my colleagues cowards again. I think he sensed that would be unwise of him. Instead he said, "She's gone, Stone. That's the end of it." Then he turned away from me, opened the door and left Quarters like he had somewhere else to go.

Jolly's assumption that the nurse's departure was "the end of it," was an incorrect supposition. I saw it as a point somewhere between his assumption of the job as D.O. and his last day in that position. The way he was running Lifeline I suspected he was a lot closer to the latter point than the former. Jolly was a thug and a bully. I knew I could deal with him. Bullies are cowards. If they think you'll stand up to them they'll buckle every time. What concerned me more is that I was losing respect for the management of Lifeline above Jolly. All three arms kept Jolly in charge. They knew he was a bully and yet they kept him on as D.O. That was a lesson I learned at this juncture of my career with Lifeline. To management, money was the most important issue. Jolly kept the aircraft flying. When it flew, it made money. If it made money, Jolly had a job. Nothing else mattered. They'd let Jolly beat things back into line for them if that is what it took to fly.

When the nurse got fired it was also not "the end it" because the crews were not happy. There were many long and interesting conversations shared in Quarters between calls as a result. Over the intervening shifts I heard spooled out the history of Jolly backstabbing and lying his way to the top of Lifeline. Interestingly, one of the more senior nurses told me how Jolly had gotten rid of my friend Tony Rosso.

Buying the Four-Twelve was Tony's idea. He sold the concept to the County Commissioners who provided a wonderful asset to the citizens of

Austin as well as Travis and surrounding counties. Tony and the Commissioners sold it to the hospital because we could carry four patients in their money machine. Unless the conditions were just right, the LongRanger could only carry one. When Lifeline bought the Four-Twelve, Jolly was the chief pilot and trainer. He reported to Anthony Rosso as D.O. The pilots all went to school at Bell Helicopter for initial training as part of the purchase package on the aircraft. But the training of the pilots in flying Lifeline's profile fell to Jolly. At the time, all the pilots had as much time in a Four-Twelve as Jolly. But Jolly acted as though he had invented the machine. Besides harassing the line pilots as he probably had Army flight students, he treated the helicopter as his personal hotrod. He trained the pilots in maneuvers he made up. Some of them the manufacturer most certainly would have frowned upon. Other's Bell probably would have cancelled any warranty on the aircraft for doing. Some of his made-up maneuvers were as hazardous as my engine failure in the dead man's curve.

The pilots to a man were disturbed that Jolly was putting their lives and the helicopter in jeopardy. They each told him so. Jolly ignored their growing list of concerns. With no redress the pilots went to Anthony. Anthony Rosso was a very experienced and professional helicopter pilot. Jolly was a cowboy. There are many ways that aviation managers handle cowboys. Like the gentleman and professional he was, Anthony used a gentlemanly approach to try to get Jolly in line. In that, he made the mistake of assuming that Jolly would be both reasonable and reasonably intelligent and accept Anthony's efforts to get him to train the line pilots as Bell suggested. Anthony thought he could address what the pilot's had told him about Jolly's shenanigans without getting the pilots involved. Anthony got in the books to show Jolly why he needed to fly the Four-Twelve differently than he was doing. Anthony was skilled in larger helicopters than Jolly had ever flown. Anthony made his case in the cockpit by flying profiles with Jolly that Jolly had never seen before.

He showed Jolly by example of skillful flying the kind of training Jolly should be doing with the line pilots. After training flights he conducted with Jolly, Anthony referenced training material, operating manuals and charts provided by Bell Helicopter. He explained with manufacturer's specifications why Jolly had to teach the pilots how to use the helicopter within its limitations. He assumed in doing so that Jolly would act professionally and tailor his training to meet Anthony's outline.

In assuming Jolly would act like a professional, Anthony was grossly mistaken. Because Anthony had addressed the pilots' issues without letting Jolly know, Jolly didn't turn on the pilots. He turned on Anthony. He would have satisfaction for what he saw as a slight by Anthony for teaching him how to fly the Bell Four-Twelve. And he would do it by taking Anthony's job as D.O. Jolly was manipulative and without a conscience. Behind Anthony's back he took advantage of the crew. He spread falsehoods among them. Ironically, he used the same system he reviled when it had worked so effectively against him later. He relied on the nurses and medics to carry his lies about Anthony through their own management chains. He was sure they would reach Anthony's bosses that way.

Jolly told the crews that Anthony was out of his league now that Lifeline had a much larger aircraft. He said that Anthony's experience in the corporate world had made him too careful and conservative. He had never been an EMS pilot. He really didn't know what he was doing in an EMS operation. Jolly pointed out that Anthony spent all his time in the office, isolated from the crews. That made him an elitist. Anthony's flying was done in books, while real pilots like himself flew the aircraft. Jolly said he could show the other pilots and the medical crews how flights were supposed to be accomplished in a Four-Twelve by flying with them. In brief, Jolly convinced the crews that he was on their side. Anthony on the other hand, didn't care about them and was inexperienced and not fit to run an air ambulance service. Most despicable of Jolly's lies, he inferred that Anthony, who earned medals for valor while flying in combat, had lost his nerve. Jolly had to go behind Anthony's back to get away with such a charge. Gentleman though he was, Anthony would have fired Jolly after beating him to a pulp.

But Anthony was a gentleman. He made the mistake of trusting Jolly. Jolly put the crews up to getting rid of Anthony and that is exactly what happened. The triumvirate of hospital, Austin EMS and Travis County commissioners just waited for the opportunity to fire him. Jolly gave them the opening. He continued to operate the aircraft in a reckless manner. Anthony's patience worn thin, he grounded Jolly. In doing however, he also grounded the Four-Twelve until he could train the pilots himself to properly operate it. While Anthony trained the line pilots he had Jolly fill in for them on their shift in the LongRanger. Jolly was working with the crews regularly now. It gave him the chance to push his agenda with them.

Jolly's didn't really throw the trump card that got Anthony fired, though. Anthony did that when he grounded his boss's new nine million dollar investment. Then the local newspaper got wind that the county's new helicopter was sitting unutilized in the hangar. The newspaper editor, no friend of the Country Commissioners, blasted the commissioner for mismanaging an asset the county probably didn't need in the first place. Loss of face to a politician is far more toxic to them than the loss the taxpayers' money. Loss of face equates to loss of votes. And loss of votes requires immediate action. A meeting between Anthony and his bosses at the county was called. The conversation was one way. Anthony Rosso walked out of the Travis County administration building that morning without a job. Jolly was put in his place.

I joined Lifeline during that nexus. In the month my training was done, I thought I saw the real Jolly Pearson. It took a few weeks flying the line to realize he was far more complex, far more vicious than I first supposed. I knew he was a bully. He had a tremendous ego. He led through brute force. I missed it that he was a wily and manipulative liar, too. I had even been a victim of his manipulative side when I caved to it the first day I flew with him. He coerced me to fly inside the Dead Man's Curve, something there was no need to do that day. Now that I was becoming more of a veteran on the Lifeline pilot staff I knew that he was both dangerous and unpredictable. These traits can spell disaster in an aircraft cockpit, even when two pilots occupy it.

Jolly's bosses were either unaware, unconcerned or both regarding Jolly's transgressions. They wanted Jolly to run the program because he convinced his new bosses that he would do anything they wanted. They wanted to make money. That meant keeping the Four Twelve flying. He kept the aircraft flying, no matter what. In firing the nurse, Jolly protected the hospital's income stream. The commissioners knew that there would be no more such excursions by the crews. The most difficult thing for me to accept wasn't that the nurse was sacrificed on the altar of safety. It is that she was sacrificed on the altar of money.

In flying EMS it took some time for me to adjust to the living arrangements. Quarters were co-ed. I came from a family of five boys. Until I married Linda, my mother was the only woman I had ever lived with in close proximity. Living and working in close quarters with women besides my wife took some getting used to. It wasn't just the bathroom and sleeping arrangements that gave me pause. I had heard stories of EMS stations and air ambulance services in particular where debauchery and cheating on spouses was the order of the day. During my tenure at Lifeline, several marriages ended because of it. Knowing this, friends have asked me if it ever bothered Linda that I was sleeping in the same quarters with other women.

It worried me at first that Linda would become jealous. The better I came to know my female co-workers, the more information Linda garnered about them. They all had stories I thought Linda would become concerned about. I tried, but couldn't hide that some of the ladies were pretty attractive, too.

Later, when several of those women were more like sisters than colleagues, they told me that Linda never had anything to worry about. They knew I was taken. We have been exclusively each other's mate since the time we first met. We have been blessed to have complete and mutual trust and confidence in our love. The ladies at Lifeline picked up on that.

Linda being who she is, it wasn't long before she knew the women I worked with better than I did. It was not uncommon for our crews to bring their families to Quarters sometimes. Linda took advantage of those times to invite the ladies of Lifeline to our house for dinner. The dinners included families. Together, Linda and I came to know and bond with the families who loved the ladies I worked with. Then came invitations to Linda's famous, "high teas." Linda Stone's soirees' included good company, good canapes, some form of alcohol, no men and hours of 'girl talk.' It was during those events that the ladies I worked with came to love Linda. Several of these women are like family to this day. Those women were Linda's insurance that she need never fear for her husband's chastity so long as he flew for Lifeline. I believe if Linda hadn't killed me for cheating, they would have.

In our co-ed Quarters we had two bathrooms, one for the ladies and one for the gents. We respected each other's space...usually, but not always. As a result the men got lessons occasionally on how the toilet seat worked. Arlen was also much less respectful of which bathroom was for the ladies. He was working with Mary one day when he got a life altering lesson on toilet seat positioning.

Mary was hands down the toughest of our very tough nurses. On the day in question she came out of the hallway into the living room. She was wiping her hands on a paper towel.

"Arlen." Mary was not in a good mood. Arlen was stretched out on the couch, arms crossed over his chest watching a football game on the television. He ignored Mary. She went over and stood between him and the TV.

"Arlen." She tossed the balled up paper towel across the kitchen and into the wastebasket. A neat three pointer. Arlen raised an eyebrow.

"Did you pee in the ladies room?"

Arlen grunted.

"Because if you did you left the toilet seat up."

Another grunt. Then he said, "I thought you wanted us to put the seat up."

"Before you pee, you Neanderthal. Yes, raise the seat. I don't want you peeing on the seat I have to sit on. And let me mention, even though I had to put the seat down for you I still had to wipe off the toilet bowl before I could sit down. How do you do that? Pee on the seat while it's up, I mean?"

Arlen leaned to one side to see who had just intercepted a pass.

"That was gross, Arlen. I sat in your pee before I knew you'd peed on the seat."

Arlen was missing his game. He waved his hand for Mary to step aside. "Okay, Mary. I'll raise the seat next time."

Mary was not ready to give up the instructional session yet. "You weren't even listening, Arlen. Raise before you pee. Lower after you pee. Clean it off if you pee on it. 'Get it?"

"Got it, Mary." He looked directly at her trying not to eye the T.V.

"You've said that before. Maybe you should just stay out of the ladies room."

She stepped out of Arlen's line of sight. Arlen raised a fist at the football game. "Yes! He scores!"

"I'm telling you Arlen, I better never sit on a wet toilet seat again thanks to you!"

Arlen knew it was a parting shot.

"Ok." He said. Arlen knew better than to crack wise. She wouldn't think he was cute. And the football game was almost over. He'd surely miss it if he made a smart remark.

Later on in the day not much had changed around Quarters. There were no calls. Arlen was still on the couch watching another sporting event. From around the corner and down the hallway came a shriek.

"ARLEN!"

Arlen smiled and reached down to the floor beside him. He picked up the can of lemonade he was drinking. He smiled to himself and took a sip. He knew he'd only have to wait a minute.

"You!" The bathroom door opened. Mary stomped up the hall. She didn't wait to enter the living room before she started lambasting Arlen. He was going to get it now. "You ANIMAL! You didn't just sprinkle my seat this time! And I SAT in it! You are such a pig, I..."

She rounded the corner. Arlen was holding up his can of lemonade over his head so she could see it.

Mary screamed. She realized she'd been had. Arlen had deposited a shot of lemonade on the toilet seat in the ladies room.

Smiling broadly he said, "Hey, was the seat down or not?" And that's what caused the tussle to break out.

Mary lunged at him. "You bastard!" Mary grabbed his nearly empty can and dumped it on him.

"No wonder it was sticky! Mary landed on Arlen's belly with both knees. She laughed and slapping him with her open palms. Arlen was a foot taller and a hundred pounds heavier than Mary. He caught most of the blows or fended them off with his hands. She dodged around his hands and arms when she could. Then she started on him with her elbows. They were both laughing crazily. Arlen finally quit defending himself. He was paralyzed with laughter. After Mary got done with him, Arlen took a shower and changed his flight suit.

We had showers in each bathroom, too. They were used more than you might think. Our flight suits were dark blue. On hot summer days we soaked them in sweat. Even when the weather was cool, after back to back calls I would sweat so hard I couldn't even stand the way I smelled. A shower came in handy. On those days I sometimes changed my socks, underwear and flight suit several times a day. I also showered and changed when I spilled fuel on myself pulling the fuel nozzle out of the tank port. Jet fuel is a fancy name for kerosene. Kerosene doesn't evaporate like gasoline does. If it gets on you or your clothing you smell like kerosene until you change your clothes and wash up. Kerosene also puts chemical burn blisters on you if it stays in contact with your skin. That was another reason why I used the shower at Lifeline and kept several changes of flight uniforms in my locker all the time.

We also got splashed pretty often with body fluids. Blood and vomit were the most common ones. Even without getting splashed, I noticed I often reeked of whatever was happening in the medical cabin. Burns victims were the worst. Imagine being shut in a closet with a freshly burned steak. You smell it. You can even taste it. Now imagine the steak is well done and weighs one or two hundred pounds. The cabin of our helicopter, especially the LongRanger was not much larger than a closet. After a burn victim transport my flight suit would reek of burned flesh. I never put a flight suit smelling of burn victim in my car. Instead I washed it several times in the washer at the ambulance station next door to Lifeline's Quarters. My general guidance on when to change flight suits after a call was simple. If I had to breathe through my mouth during the call it was likely we were going out of service for a shower and flight suit change.

Sleeping in Quarters also posed a logistical challenge we had to get used to. We respected each other's right to privacy. At the same time we slept together like brothers and sisters. We only had two bedrooms. With a three person crew, when all three crew members wanted some sack time somebody was going to get a bunk mate, usually of the opposite gender.

Sometimes it was me. Most often the nurse and paramedic shared a room. I'm not sure why the pilots usually got a room to themselves. Maybe we snored. But I still woke from a nap sometimes with one of my crew mates in the other bunk.

Their gender meant nothing to me, even though we didn't sleep in our flight suits. Sleeping in a flight suit is not just uncomfortable. Our flight suits carried whatever germs lived in our helicopters. We didn't want to take those to bed with us. So we never even sat on a bed in a flight suit, let alone laid on one. Same thing with our boots. We walked through some terrible stuff. Body fluids, pathogens, fuel and battery acid and other hazardous materials from vehicle accidents resided on our boots. Nobody ever walked barefooted in Quarters. If we shed our boots we all scuffed around in slippers or sandals. Those never went home with us, either. They ended their lives in the garbage can at Lifeline.

We most often went to bed one at a time. One reason was that it allowed us each the privacy of a bedroom to shed our flight suit. If we weren't wearing a pair of shorts underneath our flight suit, that was the time to get some on. After the lights went out we were all wearing a t-shirt, shorts and socks. Nobody wanted to expose or be exposed to bare skin when the klaxon went off. More than once a crew member got to the pad in their sleeping clothes before they realized they forgot to jump into their flight suit. Never mind exposing your naked self to your crew mates. It would really be embarrassing to arrive at the helicopter in your birthday suit.

We all mastered the art of dressing in seconds in a dark bedroom. We were good at it. But sometimes getting dressed in a flight suit in the dark was like wresting the Hydra. So we installed lights near our beds that came on if we so much as touched them. Even with the light on, getting into a flight suit and boots still posed a challenge we had to meet. Boots were a particular conundrum. We all had to wear boots. They had to be black for uniformity. (Even though we were living in the heart of

Texas nobody wore cowboy boots). Our boots had to provide protection from the broken glass and torn metal from car accidents. They also had to provide ankle support to help us handle rough terrain. We didn't want to turn an ankle as we carried stretchers and medical bags down into a roadside ditch or across a dry stream bed or farmer's field.

I liked wearing the kind of boots I wore in the Marines, the lace up kind. As an officer candidate I learned to get out of bed, dress and get my boots laced in three minutes. In EMS that is too long. If I was going to take a nap I used what I called my "sleep boots." They were the kind I could just stick my feet into and go. No laces. When I undressed to sleep, I unzipped my flight suit and rolled it down over my sleep boots. Then my flight suit lay on the floor around my boots looking rather like a fire fighter's boots and turnout gear. You've probably seen how they do it. They leave their firefighting suit standing next to the truck ready for a fire alarm to sound. They just jump in their boots, pull up their trousers and jump on the truck.

When the pager rolled me out of bed I did more or less the same thing. My feet hit the boots. The flight suit came up over both shoulders. Heading up the hallway I was zipping up the suit. I practiced with and without light until I could do it all in seconds. I took some pride in how fast I could be ready for a call. I was rarely beaten to the pad by the crew. Often I had the aircraft started before they even showed up at the top of the stairs all sleepy eyed and still waking up.

A normal start, run-up and systems check on the twin-engine Bell Four-Twelve is complicated. It takes an experienced crew of two pilots between ten and fifteen minutes to properly complete. Before I started flying as a line pilot in EMS I could not have imagined stepping through all those procedures – especially solo -- in less time. I certainly would not have attempted such procedures without a checklist. But in the interest of speeding up the takeoffs at Lifeline and with the blessing of our FAA inspector we modified those procedures.

When we got to work the pilots did all the systems checks. We checked fuel pumps, cross-feed valves, radios and electrical and hydraulic systems. We did everything necessary to get the helicopter ready to fly. We took our time and did it by the checklist. When we were done, all we had to do was start the machine and go. At the beginning of my training period I practiced starting the helicopter using the checklist. When I first joined Lifeline I spent literally hours practicing the start procedure. I used the checklist until my hands moved around the cockpit with the confidence and skill of a concert pianist. Before long my hands moving from switches to throttles to starter and back looked like they were playing Chopin's "Minute Waltz." We did things differently than other commercial users of the Bell Four-Twelve. But we did everything required by the manufacturer's guidelines, FAA regulations and common sense. We did it safely. We just did all that faster than I ever had before.

I knew I was fast. But I wanted to know exactly how fast I was. I found out one night when I actually timed myself. I was in bed in my shorts, socks and t-shirt, sleeping the moment the pager went off. I hit the light. "Start the clock!" I said. I then hit the start button on the stopwatch on my wrist. I leapt from the bed directly into my boots. I pulled the flight suit zipper up as I passed through the bedroom door. I threw open the door of Quarters and mounted the stairs to the helipad two at a time. Once there, I trotted over to the helipad and made a quick lap around the aircraft. That cleared the helicopter of any umbilical except the Auxiliary Power Unit (the APU) plug. The jogging also cleared my head of the last of the cobwebs of sleep.

Turning on the APU I hauled myself into the cockpit. Before my butt was in the seat, I reached overhead and turned on the battery and inverter switches: two each. Those powered up the lights and the gauges. As they whirred into life I buckled my seatbelt and shoulder harness. My eyes scanned the gauges as I buckled in.

Electrical voltage: check.

I flipped on the switches that turn on the fuel pumps. Then I hit the switch that opens the fuel valve to feed jet fuel into one engine.

Fuel pressure: check.

Tripping the starter switch on the collective I allowed my eyes to dance to the turbine speed gauge. The turbine fan in the engine whirred to life.

Engine oil pressure: check.

At twelve percent turbine speed I rolled the throttle open. Fuel flowed into the combustion chamber and the engine lit off. My eyes bounced to the several oil pressure and hydraulic pressure gauges and landed on the turbine temperature gauge. It climbed through five hundred then six hundred degrees and stabilized. Out of the corner of my eye I saw the blades begin to turn. That was the signal to strap on my helmet. By the time my helmet chin strap was snapped the rotors were turning at a fast idle. I turned off the starter switch to the operating engine and flipped on the generator. Starting the second engine was a repeat of what it took to start the first. As engine number two wound up I pulled on my flight gloves.

That's when I whispered the prayer. It was a special one. I knew who I was working for. I knew the lives of myself and many of his children would soon be in my hands. *"Lord,"* I'd say, *"put me on like a glove. Guide my heart, my head and my hands."* I never failed to say the prayer. I think it was the part of my checklist that kept me from failing to do the other important things I needed to do to keep the flight safe. Regardless of where and what I flew I have started out every flight with that prayer ever since.

That night with the clock still running, the crew appeared. One unplugged the APU and pushed it out of the way. The other boarded as I turned off the number two engine starter switch. With the flip of another switch the number two generator came on line. As I wound the throttles fully open I glanced at my watch. Stop the clock: three and a half minutes had elapsed since I had been on my back in bed starting the stop watch. That is fast by anyone's measure.

But you don't get points in flying for being too fast and making mistakes. You don't takeoff being almost ready. I always took an important few seconds to make a last visual sweep of the cockpit. Most important I took one more look at the rotor RPM:

100 percent. Check.

Caution lights: all extinguished.

Engine and transmission temperature and pressure gauges: in the green.

Fuel gauge: showing adequate fuel for the flight.

"Are we ready, crew?"

By then one medical crew member sat next to me in the copilot seat, strapped in with helmet on and visor down. "Ready in front."

The other crew member faced aft into the medical cabin: "Ready in back."

I smartly raised the collective. Lifeline One rose slowly to a two foot hover. After one more glance at the rotor RPM I pushed forward on the cyclic. Keeping the nose straight with the pedals I pulled up until the six tons of aircraft and crew jumped like a deer over the lip of the helipad and dived into the darkness down Red River Boulevard.

The paramedic stepped on his radio transmit button. "Dispatch, Lifeline One. We're airborne."

People might say that medical emergencies come at random intervals. I would challenge that precept. If I had just rested my bottom on the toilet, warmed my dinner, poured a fresh cup of coffee or arrived a few minutes late to start my preflight inspection *that* is when the call would come. If on the other hand, I was standing next to the aircraft with the crew ready to go, all of us fed, rested and prepared for anything, we could have stood like that all day and no calls would have come.

Similarly, randomness should rule. Trauma calls like car accidents would most likely happen when the weather is bad. I understand that.

Factors like rain on the windshield, slippery roads and people who are challenged by driving create a higher chance of a car accident occurring. But I found that medical emergencies like strokes and heart attacks also happen more frequently when the weather is bad. That is one reason I got so much experience flying in bad weather. Calls come in most often when the weather gets bad.

A police officer was the first person to tell me that emergency service work gets busy when the moon is full, on paydays and on Fridays. I thought he was jesting. Then I saw that the ER staff had a calendar posted on their bulletin board. Marked in yellow were full moons, government paydays and Fridays. If all three fell on the same day, the block on the calendar for that day was colored in red highlighter. The squares on the calendar for dates in the past had tick marks on them, too. When I asked the charge nurse why they were marked she told me each tick mark represented a patient admitted to the ER. She and the tick marks confirmed what the cop had told me. I recognized the bulk of the tick marks were on squares marked as "payday." They were the same days when I got my paychecks from the National Guard. I asked the charge nurse, "Why are these dates marked as "paydays?" People get paid all the time."

She looked at me with narrowed eyes. "Those are the days the welfare checks arrive. Pray they don't fall on a full moon. Paydays are bad enough as they are."

Keeping this in mind I did some investigation of my own. The paramedics on our aircraft and on the city ambulances called full moon nights, "meeting nights." That is when "membership meetings at the gun and knife club" occur. I never stopped flying when a full moon fell on a payday *and* a Friday. It wasn't long before I marked those days on my own calendar, too.

Jolly hated flying at night. He would fly day shifts without grousing about it too much. If we had a doctor or dentist appointment, if we were legitimately sick or injured then flying for a line pilot during the day was okay by Jolly. But he never flew a night shift unless one of the pilots called in sick at the last minute. He always tried to find another pilot to take a missing pilot's shift at night. When he had notice that he was going to take over for a pilot, like when one of the pilots took vacation, he did the day shifts. The missing pilot's opposite shifted over and took all the nights. When my partner went on a long vacation I flew two weeks of nights opposite Jolly.

We all knew it was payback to stick Jolly with flying on New Year's Eve. We did it three years running before he caught on. Whoever got the New Year's Eve shift called in sick at the last minute. Jolly had to cover it. New Year's Eve was always the busiest night of the year for Lifeline. We – or in this case Jolly - flew all night picking up drunk drivers and the people they injured. The fourth year he got wise. He knew we were going to stick him with flying New Years, so he scheduled the chief pilot to filling in if somebody got sick again on New Year's Eve. Then the duty pilot and the chief pilot both called in sick. Jolly had to fly. He was fuming. His threats fell on deaf ears at Quarters. He complained to the county manager. We knew that would do him no good. She rather enjoyed it when we banded together to put it to Jolly.

My medical crews were always concerned with my health. I knew they liked me and were concerned about me. I understood that their cause for concern went beyond just our friendship. The crew knew that I was the only one of us who knew how to fly. If something went wrong with me on the way to a scene, Lifeline One would become a scene of its own. Put another way, if I was the first to arrive at Lifeline One's crash site, the paramedic and nurse knew that they would be numbers two and three respectively. Whenever there was something physically wrong with me they'd spot it. If I had worked out too hard and sore muscles slowed me down a little, if I limped from a blister I got playing soccer with my kids, or if I rubbed my forehead like I had a headache they'd pick up on it. If I asked for an aspirin I got twenty questions about my physical well-being. Sometimes they'd even get out the thermometer and blood pressure cuff. They didn't just express sympathy about my headaches. They'd check me for symptoms of a stroke or neurological deficit. Being a helicopter pilot as well as a former Marine I naturally had to plead guilty to the latter all the time. They didn't see the humor in it. Sometimes the wily ones while pre-flight checking their equipment would ask to test their equipment on me. I knew what they were doing. I usually went along.

I got a kick out of holding my breath while they checked my oxygen saturation. They called the procedure, 'checking O2 sats.' They would clip a battery powered device to a finger and watch a meter tell how much oxygen was in my blood. As I got more and more hypoxic holding my breath the numbers on the O2 sat monitor would drop until it looked like I was about dead. Watching their face as the sats dropped was usually enough to get me laughing and breathing again. Sometimes their concerns for my health would get tedious though. When the medics would start asking me how I was feeling today, I knew where the questions were headed. So I always answered, "Terrific!" or "Better than I have ever felt in my life!" That's when they knew I had their number.

Crew members who didn't know any better were happy to learn that my good health was monitored by FAA mandated annual flight physicals. They thought a flight physical must have been akin to the physicals the Mercury astronauts endured. Those early astronauts got everything checked up to and including a sperm count. I didn't tell them that my FAA flight physicals were each so cursory that I doubt the doctors would have noticed if I had no pulse at all. When I took my annual FAA physical one year, I had been suffering from chronic fatigue for an extended period. My heart started skipping beats. It felt like a flutter in my chest. It didn't hurt. It just fluttered a little. I took my pulse. I could feel it: beat…beat…skip...beat. It had happened before. The first time it did that I took my concerns to an ER doc with whom I had become friends.

"It's nothing to worry about," he assured me. "Emergency services people quite often get cardiac arrhythmia like yours. It comes with fatigue. Rest up and it will go away."

I took his advice. I took a week off. I slept at normal times, exercised, got rested and sure enough the skipped beats went away. When I got the heart flutter just before my flight physical though, I thought I'd have some fun with it. I arrived at the doctor's office after my last night shift. I was tired. Sure enough my heart was fluttering away. My pulse was anything but regular. I knew four days off would settle it down again. Based on my previous flight physicals I didn't expect anyone to catch it.

After I finished filling out the FAA form for my physical I was ushered into the exam room. An attractive young lady in scrubs stepped into the room and got the basics out of the way: weight, height, blood pressure and pulse. *This is going to be interesting*, I thought. She took my blood pressure. She listened for a pulse but missed the skips.

"Low side of normal," she said. "No problem."

Then she picked up my wrist and looked at her watch. She had been palpating the artery in my wrist for a few seconds when I felt the flutter. Her brow wrinkled a little. I could see her start over with the timing and counting my pulse. The flutter came back again. I saw the wrinkled brow again and hid my grin. The third time it happened she dropped my wrist and put her hand on her hip.

"Okay, what's your pulse?"

I couldn't hide the smile. "Sixty," I said. She smiled back at me. She didn't mention the skipping beat she'd felt. She just wrote it down "60" on the clipboard that was holding my medical exam form. So much for the report to the flight surgeon, "Patient suffers cardiac arrhythmia." In my defense, though, I told the doctor I had it. He was a healthy looking, white haired gentleman who always wore a sport jacket over an open collared golf shirt. No white coat for him. We knew each other. He told me that he owned and flew his own airplane. He always talked about that while he examined me. After a minute or two of small talk about his latest flying adventure he picked up the clipboard with my FAA form clipped on it. As he read it he asked without looking up, "So how's your health?"

I answered, "Well, except for the chronic fatigue, poor diet, lack of exercise and cardiac arrhythmia I'm a healthy specimen." I was totally truthful. A doctor could not have explained my medical condition better. He just grunted. He didn't even look up at the comment. When he finally did look up though, he just said, "Okay! Open your mouth and let's see the throat."

Then he had me do some coordination exercises. He had me unzip my flight suit, take off my t-shirt and did a quick physical exam. In fifteen minutes with the doctor I paid the lady at the front and was folding up my second class FAA medical and putting it in my wallet. The exam was over for another year. *If my medics only knew*, I thought to myself. I got in the car and headed home for some sleep.

6 THE NATURE OF THE CALL

I have heard a hundred people who know better say, "Our pilots never know the nature of the call until the decision is made to fly or not." I guess they all have their reason for saying that. When I heard a couple of rookie nurses say it during a tour of our helicopter and facilities I realized they needed to know the truth. After that they could lie if they wanted. So after the tour was over I tracked them down. I said that telling people that I didn't know the nature of the call was baloney. I always knew the details at the same time the rest of the crew did. I was present when we were dispatched. We all heard everything dispatch knew about the call and the patients. The pager would go off followed by the dispatcher's voice. "Lifeline One, pediatric cardiac arrest. Mother reports seven year old female." Yes, I knew when it was a kid and I knew when it was bad. I was one third of the crew. Just like the other two thirds I did what I had to do regardless of the nature of the call. I couldn't let my emotions take over. That's one of the most common ways EMS helicopter crews get killed.

Every call we did had different risk factors to consider before we decided to fly. We made the decision together whether or not to launch. For safety's sake we all *had* to know what we were going into. We came to know the city as well as we knew our own neighborhood. We knew the demographics of the different sections of the city. We knew what kinds of calls were riskiest to us. All shift we paid attention to what was happening in the city. Listening to the dispatcher we watched message traffic as scenes escalated. We paid attention to the radio traffic. Reports of more crashed cars, more shots fired or more victims discovered alerted us that we could expect to fly.

I also heard it spread widely in the helicopter EMS community that, "The pilot doesn't know the nature of the call until he decides whether or not to take it." I can sum up the truth of that statement with one word: Baloney. I always knew the nature of the call. I had to know. Otherwise I could not assess the risk or otherwise plan the flight. I had to know the condition of the landing zone. I had to plan the flight to accommodate the number and weight of the patients I might carry. I had to know whether or not a shooter was still present at a gunshot wound call. I had to know if it was a pediatric call. First responders often get upset, make mistakes and improperly set up or improperly secure landing zones when a child is involved. Even so, I heard people from the hospital nurses and administrators to our medical director say that the pilot made the determination to fly based on weather alone. I know they knew better. The pilot always knows the nature of the call.

7 KEEP YOUR FLY ZIPPED UP

Acting impulsively causes aircraft accidents. I have known that for a long time. Impulsive acts performed in an aircraft that seem like a fun idea at the time always look stupid in retrospect. Take for example the pilot at a neighboring squadron when I was a Marine pilot. He believed that doing a snap roll in the helicopter he was flying would be a fun thing to do. Any helicopter pilot with even a little experience knows that you don't roll a helicopter. Trying it will most likely result in shearing the rotor from the mast that joins it to the helicopter. If the mast survives, the unloaded rotor blades will more than likely make contact with the structural members of the helicopter. The first blade to strike ordinarily shears off the tail or the top of the cockpit. Then the unbalanced rotor system shakes the remaining components apart from each other. Down you come in an aluminum shower. Under their breath at your funeral all your flying buddies will say, "that was stupid."

In the subject pilot's case the impulse arose from his knowledge of the H-53 "Sea Stallion." The H-53 was a very unique aircraft. It had astounding amounts of power and a unique rotor system. The combination of these assets allowed it to do things no helicopter had been able to do before. Its manufacturer Sikorsky wanted to demonstrate what this combination of power and maneuverability could provide. So during experimental flight tests the H-53 performed a series of loops and rolls. These are aerobatic maneuvers. Helicopters of the day could not do aerobatics without being destroyed. But no helicopter in America had the immense power and a rotor system like the H-53. Before the maneuvers were attempted the Sikorsky test pilots discussed the program with the engineers who designed the aircraft. Together the pilots and engineers carefully planned each maneuver. Then the pilots did it in stages until they were sure they could complete the maneuver safely.

Once the factory pilots had performed their loops and rolls for the camera they were never to be done again. The aircraft operating manual had a bold print warning, a prohibition from performing aerobatic maneuvers. But impulse won out on the day in question. Adding to the impulse was the fact that this was to be the last flight of this pilot before his discharge from the Marines. *What can they do to me if I am getting out of the Marines?* He thought. Better, he should have thought, *What can I do to myself by trying this?* But that's the thing about impulsiveness. You don't think about what you are going to do. You just do it. In this case, "just doing it" didn't come out well for him.

When the impulse took over the crew was returning from a job at Camp Pendleton about sixty miles to the south. The H-53 was about ten miles southeast of the airfield in Santa Ana. They had just crossed the coastline at thirty-five hundred feet. Below them were a series of low, rolling grass covered hills. The incident pilot was flying. Without notifying his copilot of his intentions he executed the maneuver. A properly performed snap roll requires the pilot to start by raising the nose. Otherwise the aircraft will pitch down abruptly as the roll begins. Without pulling back on the cyclic the pilot simply snapped it smartly to one side of the cockpit. Then he held it there. As the helicopter responded with a swift roll toward the inverted, a struggle ensued. The other pilot grabbed the cyclic and pushed it in the other direction. As the aircraft continued toward the inverted neither pilot pulled back on the cyclic to load the rotor. This would have created the same force of gravity on the aircraft in which it normally operates. With no normal forces of gravity on the helicopter the crew chief back in the cabin became airborne on his tether. He floated toward the open window. Just as he got a death grip on the window frame his shortened tether stopped his travel altogether.

The zero gravity environment of inverted flight also caused the oil in the engines and gearboxes to cease flowing. The gearbox between one of the two engines and the main transmission was first to suffer a failure. Without lubrication and turning at thousands of revolutions per minute the gearbox exploded. That caused the affected engine to over speed and then fail altogether. Hearing the explosion of the gearbox, seeing the lights and gauges that indicated an engine failure and feeling the negative g loading, at least one of the pilots finally pulled back on the cyclic. This probably kept the rotor blades from chopping the aircraft to ribbons. Now the aircraft was inverted but pitching downward straight toward the earth. With gravity restored the crew chief suddenly fell up to the floor.

Both pilots now on the controls simultaneously decided to keep pulling back on the cyclic. Both stopped rolling the aircraft. Neither pilot was sure that they would complete the half loop necessary to pull out of the dive before impact. Fortunately the descent stopped as the helicopter pulled out of the loop with no room to spare. They started to climb again on their momentum built up in the dive and on the power of the remaining engine. Now they had a dead engine, an exploded gearbox and an airframe grossly overstressed by the wild maneuvers they had barely survived. Certainly they all must have wondered if it the Sea Stallion would even hold together for the short flight back to Santa Ana. There was no place else to land with just one engine, though. So Santa Ana is where they ended up going.

They declared an emergency and fire trucks rolled. The H-53 landed on its wheels like an airplane and rolled the length of the short runway. After they landed they were followed to parking by the fire trucks. I was told that the fire fighters had to break up a fight that was taking place in the cockpit between the pilots. This very near miss was all because a pilot gave into impulse.

I can't speak for other pilots. But I can attest to the fact that I too have been tempted to give into impulse in an aircraft. Most of those were ego related. I would call "showing off." I still have those impulsive spells. I can feel them coming on. I have learned to apply strategies to offset them. When the impulse to do something stupid and childish in an aircraft comes upon me, I recognize that if I wait just thirty seconds the impulse will often pass. I also try to imagine having my wife and kids or my boss onboard with me. I ask myself, *Would I do what I am now contemplating with them in the back?* A subset of this strategy is to ask myself what the contemplated act would look like in tomorrow's newspaper. Stupid acts look like the stupid acts they really are when they are printed in the newspaper.

Giving in to a mid-life crisis event also takes its share of pilots' lives. Midlife crisis is an ego related dysfunction where mature adults act like children. Acting irresponsibly in that case is a form of denial about the inevitability of getting older. Ironically, many pilots who make bad decisions at these times do not grow older at all. They make decisions they would never have made were their egos strong and intact. And then they kill themselves. No more birthdays.

Birthdays are hard on egos. Midlife crisis often appears at birthdays ending in a zero (30, 40, 50) although they can happen at any age. As a Marine squadron aviation safety officer I was formally trained to recognize and prevent ego centric accidents. It became my job to stop a pilot who had the potential to let their egos do the flying. I was told to look for the man whose wife, girlfriend and mortgage were all a month late. I thought that was just a humorous way of explaining the likely candidate. Then I attended the memorial service for a friend whose life – before it ended abruptly in a helicopter – fit that description almost exactly. More often I saw an out-of-control ego cause otherwise stable family men to do any or all of the following: buy a red sports car, divorce the love of his youth, marry a twenty-six year old stripper, take up spelunking, parachute jumping, scuba diving or any other dangerous sport that came into vogue. Weak egos create a huge market for penis enlargers, hair growth tonics and hair dyes, exercise equipment, vitamins and drugs that enhance sex, performance and pleasure (usually in that order).

Sometimes the first onset of a pilot ego disorder results in a fatality. At other times death in an accident is avoided by a near miss, like the snap rolling H-53 for example. They are stopped when some concerned friend or colleague reports its likelihood. Sometimes the pilot in question gets a grip on himself before things go terribly wrong. These revert to acting in a mature manner. Unfortunately though, pilots in midlife crisis don't generally stop before they lose everything important in their lives. These include their spouse and family, job and career as a pilot. Survival of an ego episode does not guarantee evasion of subsequent mid-life crisis events, either. Some people just never learn. I learned however. I was slipping into a mid-life crisis. I was approached by friends and got a grip on myself. I learned how to handle my own mid-life issues. More often I learned to avoid ego related mishaps through the experience of others. The examples were many and obvious. I like to think that my counsel prevented a few accidents. I thought I was pretty good at spotting their onset. But then I joined Lifeline and worked with Pete Reynolds.

Much of my early training with Lifeline was conducted like the ride along program. The pilot on duty flew and I watched. I flew with every one of the five pilots on the line. They were all day flights at first. I was introduced to just about every kind of operation Lifeline flew. When I began to feel comfortable enough with that experience, I was scheduled to fly with the pilots on the night shift. I was particularly happy that my first night shift in training would be spent with Pete.

Pete and I had history. We had known each other since I joined the Texas National Guard five years before. Pete was about ten years older than me. Both his hair and mustache were snow white. He was ten years older than me but looked more like twenty. Pete was in good shape though, a marathoner. He was so slender as to look emaciated. He was probably the only one of Lifeline's pilots who ate a salad for lunch every day and never snacked on the fattening goodies we always had in Quarters. I knew Pete's wife. She was often at Quarters visiting her husband. Like Pete I had met her years before. I liked her as much as I liked Pete. Together they were happy, buoyant and charming, a regular pair of lovebirds. They had been married for ten years or so. They exhibited every indication that they were in love and devoted to one another. I thought Pete's marriage and my own had a lot in common.

When my first night shift came I got to work early. By the time Pete arrived on the pad I had already conducted the pre-flight inspection of the helicopter and hung my helmet over the left seat. Pete was a veteran. He'd been with Lifeline since it started. He was enthusiastic and good at his job. But he was far beyond the "new guy" enthusiasm I had. He walked up the stairs from Quarters right on time with his helmet in hand. He joined me on the pad, shook my hand and walked around the bird. He didn't open any panels in deference to me, I thought. But I gave it a good looking over so it made sense to me. When he was done with his walk around he smiled through his long whiskers. "Well Paul, if you'll certify that all the big parts are firmly attached, I guess there's nothing left for me to do." I confirmed that and we walked downstairs to Quarters. We checked the weather together. Then we went over events from the day shift as well as the aircraft status with the crew. Afterward we sat down and had a cup of coffee with the crew. It was the textbook beginning to a Lifeline shift.

The sun set with no call interrupting a slow evening of filtering through the newspaper and watching T.V. Eventually the nurse got bored and went into the office to finish a project she had been engaged in on the computer. Pete took the move as a cue. He looked at his watch. Then he stood up and headed for the hallway. I thought maybe he was taking a bathroom break but I heard the pilots' bedroom door open and then close. I thought it a little odd that he didn't say he was going to take a nap. He didn't say anything at all. I looked at Karen our paramedic. "Is Pete hitting the sack early?" I asked.

"Maybe so," she replied. She had been staring at the T.V. but she said that in such a way that she left a door of doubt standing open. She snapped a look at me out of the corner of her eyes, and then went back to watching T.V.

Karen was a savvy, streetwise paramedic. She had been on my interview committee. After I joined Lifeline and met her on a shift she told me that the vote to hire me had been unanimous. I got her meaning. She liked me. I had worked a couple shifts with her already. She wasn't shy. In fact, before this shift with Pete came around, she shared her life story with me. I felt I was coming to know her pretty well. When she talked about working on an ambulance on the street she sounded like a tough, veteran cop. She had been an Austin paramedic for a long time. Her career, and more particularly her personal life had been hard on her. She had seen and treated probably every kind of trauma and disease a human living in urban America could suffer. She had seen the darkest side of people there. But her home life had been tough for many of the same reasons we were treating our patients. Alcohol, drugs and abuse were all parts of the picture of her life.

She told me on the first shift I worked with her that she had *four* broken marriages behind her. She had a child from each one. Her ex-husbands had all been drug or alcohol addicted men who beat her and her children. Each was now a deadbeat Dad. They left Karen and her kids without support of any kind. I felt sympathy for her trying to raise four kids alone on a paramedic's pay. I tried to ignore her phone calls but there wasn't much privacy in Quarters. I heard and watched how she parented with phone calls to her kids during our shifts. Apparently the older ones took care of the younger ones. Karen was a skilled negotiator and mediator during those calls. I supposed that she had much practice acting as a mom by remote control while she worked on the ambulances.

For her, twelve hours on Lifeline must have been easy by comparison to working twenty-fours or more on the trucks. I tried to visualize why she kept winding up married to the same kind of men. I didn't realize at the time that I was sitting right in the middle of one reason her life had been so difficult and unstable. I would come to find out personally that life and death jobs like the ones in the emergency services are hard on people. The traumatic stress of calls and the long and odd shifts disrupt what most people consider a stable lifestyle. Even though the family separation was less at Lifeline we went to all the tough calls. We saw the most brutal trauma. We dealt most often with terminal illness, not just the more minor calls ambulances get. For us death, sudden or otherwise was often a daily part of our job. Nobody who lives a life exposed to that comes away untouched. Karen's life must have been brutalized by it.

Pete didn't come back from the bedroom. I didn't give Karen's signal much more consideration. I just went back to watching the television with her. About the time Karen made her last phone call to her kids for the night I got restless. I stood up and walked over to the EMS computer. I watched the lines of messages scroll past on the screen. They came from the dispatch center, ambulances and stations in the city. Sometimes the lines scrolled steadily past. Not so tonight. There weren't many ambulances dispatched. Those that were made transfers from nursing homes or responded to minor complaints. It was a quiet night all over Austin.

I was a little disappointed to see that the city and its EMS system were taking a break. I wanted to fly. I scrolled the screen until the messages disappeared. That's when I heard the tapping a pace or two away from me. I looked up from the screen and tried to place it when it happened again. It sounded like someone tapping a penny lightly on the crew Quarters door. I wasn't even sure I was actually hearing it. I looked at Karen. She had put the phone in its cradle. She sat back on the couch with her legs up, ankles crossed on the coffee table. She caught my look and nodded toward the door. "Are you gonna' answer that?" she asked.

She had that look on her face again. Her eyes were squinted a little. They seemed to be telling me that she had expected someone to come calling. Being and feeling every bit the rookie I was I nodded and said, "Keep your seat." Karen's eyes slid across her narrowed lids toward the door as I reached for the door knob. She knew something was coming that I most certainly did not.

The moment the door opened I was greeted by a wisp of sweet perfume. I found myself inhaling it deeply as I pulled the door full open. Then I held my breath. Standing there was a woman. She was a stunningly beautiful young woman. She was petite, maybe five feet tall barefooted, which made her about five foot five in the heels she was wearing. Her legs went pretty well up from there before they reached the hemline of a sheer black skirt. The skirt was split for an enticing distance up one very shapely thigh. Her skin was like cream. Mounds of it rose through an ample parting in her blouse, which was tied at her wasp-like waistline. Her lips and every nail on her fingers and toes was painted blood red. Her long and curly auburn hair was swept across the top of her head and tied high on one side. Long soft lashes and careful makeup gave her brown eyes the look of those of a baby doe. Those warm brown eyes looked up from under her ample eyelashes. Her red lips parted slightly.

I am quite sure my mouth fell open. I thought for a moment of stallions and bulls and elk in rut. I felt something rise in me that would itself have made a guttural, animal sound had it escaped. I stood there way too long holding the door. I realized I was staring and saying nothing until at last I asked, "Are you lost?"

She tossed her head back and smiled at me. I saw two rows of perfect teeth. I could tell by the expression on her face that at least *she* knew exactly where she was. She also knew why she was there. She said as she shook her head slowly, "No, I don't think I'm lost." Then she bit the corner of her lower lip and tried to look past me. It felt like a bolt of energy passed by as she most certainly saw but seemingly ignored Karen. Then she looked back at me. "Where's Pete?" she said blinking.

I thought I had regained control of my lower jaw, but lost it again. I mumbled. "Uh, uh…I think he's napping, but let me go see."

The pensive look on her face changed to a sardonic smile, as though she knew right where to go. She stepped in the door and pushed up close to me, looking up into my eyes. Her perfume swept around me. Then she placed one of her very long, red and highly polished fingernails into the middle of my chest. She never took her eyes off mine. She pushed lightly. I think I stepped back but I might have just floated out of her way.

"I bet I can find him," she said. She turned unerringly down the hall toward the bedrooms. As she did so I could not take my eyes off of her. Her hips swayed with a slow rhythm of a boat rocking gently on the open ocean. She reached the end of the hall and without turning around, opened the door to the pilots' bedroom. She slipped inside. The door closed behind her. I believe I heard it lock.

I stood for a moment still holding the door open. I stared down the empty hallway. When I came out of my trance I let the door close and turned scratching my head. I looked inquisitively at Karen to find her now reclined on the couch. She was propped up on an elbow and had drawn up one knee. She held a pose I'd seen before. She looked like a flight suit clad woman in a picture I once saw in a western. In the movie the woman was nude. The picture of the nude hung over a bar. Cowboys gathered below it and drank whiskey. Like the girl in the picture, Karen's eyes were half closed as though experiencing sexual ecstasy. She was running her tongue lightly over her upper lip. She didn't say a word. In my current state of mind I knew exactly what Karen was saying.

I put my hands on my hips. "Naaaaaw…" I said. I refused to believe what she was telling me. Pete had been my friend and flying companion for years now. I knew him. I knew his wife. I refused to believe that in this most important way I had been so off base. But Karen slowly nodded in the affirmative. Then she made a circle with the thumb and forefinger of one hand. Still looking at me she placed the index finger of the other hand through the hole. She drew it slowly back and forth.

"I refuse to believe it!" I shook my head and pointed my thumb toward the pilot's bedroom. "Not him!"

She nodded again. "Oh yeah. That's Charlene. She's married to an Austin cop." Karen said without modifying her body language.

I turned to look down the hall as if I could see through walls. Still confused I made my way back to the lounge chair. "Here at work?" I asked as I sat down.

She sat up and nodded again. "Yep…and elsewhere too."

"But his wife…" I let whatever I was going to say trail off. In my mind I could see Susan, Pete's wife. She was sweet and pretty, obviously in love. She had a cute dash of freckles across her nose, a musical laugh. I loved the way her eyes sparkled when she looked at her husband. I suddenly felt a wave of sadness. I could not imagine why Pete would cheat on her. I wondered what she would look like when she found out. I wondered what she looked like when she cried.

I spent the evening thinking about another friend I had made in the Marines. He got himself a girlfriend and trashed his marriage. Then he killed himself doing something stupid in a helicopter. All his friends were at his memorial service. All his friends had known he was living for his ego. Everyone was saying, "I wish I had done something to prevent this." I was one of them. I resolved not to let that happen again to anyone I knew if I could change things for the better. I realized during the night that the promise I made to myself applied to this situation with Pete. I thought about talking to Jolly about what was going on. But I suddenly realized that if Karen knew, Jolly already knew. I stayed on the couch awake long after Karen and the nurse went to bed. I thought it fortunate that we did not have any calls that night. I didn't know how I would remain on a professional bearing with the guy I would be flying with.

An hour or so before shift change I heard a bedroom door open down the hall. A moment later I watched the beautiful woman appear out of the dark hallway and open the door. Her hair was down on her shoulders now. She held her heels in one hand. She just slithered out the door without looking around. In the parking garage a moment later I heard a car start up and leave. Then a few minutes later Pete walked out. He either ignored me or just didn't turn to see if anyone was in the room. When I heard another car start I jumped up and looked out the door. I stuck my head out just in time to see Pete also drive out of the parking garage. I knew he wasn't coming back.

I looked at my watch. It was forty minutes before shift change. If a call came in now we were in trouble. I had not been cleared to fly trips alone yet. Regardless of how it went for Pete, making my first EMS flight as pilot in command this way would put *my* judgment in question. I resolved to deal with that when the pager went off. I went upstairs and moved my helmet to the captain's side of the cockpit. I gathered up Pete's helmet, gloves and clipboard and took them all back downstairs. I walked into the bedroom to put the equipment in his locker. The smell of perfume lingered there. Pete hadn't even folded the sheets he had shared with her. I stood there for a few moments hurt, angry and confused. Then I heard the front door open again. It was the pilot for the day shift arriving a little early. I was relieved.

I finished my training and never flew with Pete again. After my flight with the FAA check pilot I was put on the schedule as the full-time pilot following Pete's regular shift. Based on my experience with people like Pete I could almost have scripted out what was going to happen. It happened quickly. Within my first month flying the line his professionalism as a pilot and his attention to detail dropped sharply. Then it totally disappeared.

It started with the way we relieved each other. After a shift the off-going pilot usually walked upstairs with the on-coming pilot to swap out flight gear. It gave us time to discuss the condition of the aircraft. We also discussed local flight information or company business that the on-coming pilot would want to know about. When I arrived after Pete's shift though he was often already gone. If not he would soon get in his car and leave without saying a word to me.

More often than not he didn't even bother to remove his flight gear from the aircraft. He left that for me to do. He wasn't just too lazy to remove his flight gear. The crew told me that on a couple occasions after I started flying, a call had come in just before I arrived. Pete had already taken his flight gear down to his locker. He had to rush in from the parking lot, grab it and race upstairs. It had delayed response to a couple calls. So now, rather than stay and wait to be relieved like he should, he had evidently decided to just leave his equipment in the aircraft. It didn't seem to bother him that someone else had to take it down to his locker for him.

Pete's performance continued to deteriorate. I began to notice things he missed or just decided not to do on his aircraft inspections. He started making errors in the logbook entries. Everybody makes the occasional error in math or misses a box on a form. But Pete started making a lot of those errors. Soon he was failing to even update the aircraft logbook at all. Sometimes he didn't even sign the book accepting responsibility for the aircraft during his shift.

After bringing up things to him that he forgot to do it became plain that he didn't care about his omissions. Pete had been my friend. I already had experience with midlife crisis and dealing with friends suffering from it. I had a couple of heart to heart talks with him when he stayed long enough for me to do so. The last time I tried it was through the window as he started the car. He responded to my plea as a friend by putting the car in reverse and backing away from me. Without a word he drove away.

Those efforts to talk to him were difficult for me. I was still stunned and offended by Pete's infidelity. I felt so sorry for his sweet wife. In the weeks after his liaison in Quarters I lost confidence in myself so far as judging Pete's character was concerned. He showed no remorse and no desire to change. His poor performance on the helicopter then became my focal point with him. Mr. Nice guy went away. I took the hard route with him. I cut him no slack when I found things out of line. I pointed them out. He shrugged them off. Then I resorted to threats of getting the management involved. But I realized that management already knew. Everybody on Lifeline already knew how badly Pete's performance diminished.

I figured that out when I was sitting in the cockpit one day after my preflight. I was looking through the logbook and grumbling over several incidences of Pete's inattention. The paramedic who was sitting behind me in the cabin heard me grousing to myself. He tapped me on the shoulder. He said that he was glad I looked over the aircraft carefully. He said Pete never did that at all anymore.

I thought the last straw had come when I started coming in after him to find the aircraft filthy. Where we worked, landing in open fields and dusty landing zones the aircraft and particularly the windshields got dirty fast. Pete quit taking the time to clean the bugs off the windscreens, something I did sometimes after every landing. He stopped washing the helicopter altogether even though the pilot was supposed to wash it every day. He left that job for me or the mechanics. When I called him on it as I was coming off a night shift he said, "That's a job for the night shift."

Then I arrived one morning for the day shift and found the aircraft hadn't been washed. He had already left. So I talked to him about it when he came in for the night shift. I was coming downstairs and he headed up.

"That's a job for the day shift," he said. He tried to squeeze past me to take his helmet up to the pad. I blocked his path.

"Well, if it's dirty when I come back tonight we're going to take it up with Jolly. We'll let him figure out which shift *you're* going to wash the aircraft."

As I let him pass I said, "...and you better clean the windscreen. I'm tired of coming in here and making things right for you." He stopped on the stairwell, turned and stared daggers at me. Then we parted.

The next day I passed Pete as I came in the door. He was headed for his car. He said nothing to me. Once again there would be no turnover briefing. I went upstairs and found the aircraft a mess. I flipped on the batteries and checked the fuel gauges. The fuel level was too low to fly a trip. I ran around the aircraft and grabbed the fuel hose. While I was hauling it over to put fuel onboard the paramedic informed me we were just about out of oxygen, too. That's when the pager went off. We had to delay the launch while I serviced the aircraft. We had to delay patient care for fifteen minutes because of Pete. I resolved to tell Jolly what was going on. Then I changed my mind when the takeoff I made that day almost killed us.

I was trained at Lifeline to get off the helipad and head out on a trip expeditiously. One reason we could do that was that all the pilots did things the same way. We left all the switches and power settings right where they would need to be to get off the pad and on the way to the scene quickly. One of those settings had to do with rotor RPM. We left it set so that as soon as the throttles were fully open the rotor RPM would be at one hundred percent: flying speed. After the delay caused by Pete leaving the aircraft without fuel and oxygen I raced to get the aircraft started and off the pad. The medical crew was already seated, helmets on and waiting for me to get going. I was plenty mad by the time I strapped into my seat. I started the aircraft, further distracted because I was looking through the filthy windscreen. I was in a hurry now. That is a good way to make mistakes, but I hurried anyway. I rolled the throttles up and asked the crew, "Everybody ready?"

The paramedic answered from the cabin by clicking his helmet cord transmit button and letting Dispatch know, "Lifeline One is off the hospital, delayed." I knew he would be on the phone to Dispatch when we got back with an explanation for our delay. I also knew that nobody would tell the Dispatcher, "Pete left us without fuel…again." Or. "Pete left us without oxygen…again." Jolly would hear about the delay from dispatch right after they got the paramedic's call, too. Then he would call me.

My nurse, a big guy we called Ronbo sat in the copilot's seat. I liked Ronbo. He never got worked up about anything. He reached over to the hand I had on the collective and gave it a pat.

"Easy does it, Paul. We'll get there soon enough." I looked at him. He winked at me and put his hand back in his lap. Then he looked forward and said, "Okay. I'm ready now, Paul."

His calming presence was just what I needed. I regained my composure a bit and lifted the collective. The helicopter rose into a hover. Thanks to Ronbo I took an extra moment to check the engine gauges carefully one more time before pushing the cyclic forward. That was what saved our lives. That extra second in a hover allowed the rotor RPM to bleed off. The rotor RPM needle drifted down out of the green arc that indicated flying speed. As the needle settled into the yellow arc on the rotor RPM gauge the aircraft followed it. The Four-Twelve settled back on the helipad. I knew immediately what had happened. Pete had intentionally set the rotor RPM at less than flying speed. Sitting on the pad before takeoff the RPM was where it should have been. But when I raised the collective to demand power the rotor slowed to the setting where Pete had left it.

The landing we made was smooth enough. But Ronbo looked at me, calm still in his face but concern in his eyes. The low rotor RPM audio warning blared in our headsets.

"What just happened?" Ronbo asked in a calm voice.

I knew just what had happened. "I'll tell you later, Ron," I replied.

I instinctively hit the rotor "RPM increase" switch on the collective with my thumb. The rotor speed roared back to one hundred percent. My initial surprise and embarrassment quickly changed to anger as we thundered off the pad and climbed out over Austin. I was certain that Pete had set me up to have that happen on takeoff. I thought about it after we were on our way. I realized what would have happened if I had been quick to push the cyclic forward. The helicopter would have cleared the helipad about the time the rotor stopped flying. A rotor RPM decrease like that would have caused us to settle toward the street below. Settling on takeoff most probably would have caused me to knock the tail rotor off on the edge of the helideck. In that case we would have wound up in the street below in a cloud of flaming jet fuel.

I stayed focused on my job during the flight but I was furious. Pete had been listening to Dispatch on a flight before I arrived. He heard ambulances dispatched to a call that would probably need us eventually. He intentionally left the aircraft unprepared for the flight he was pretty sure would come in about the time he left. He set things up so I would be in a hurry. He counted on me to be in a rush when I took off. He knew I wouldn't catch the rotor RPM decrease until it was too late. Pete's plan didn't succeed because Ronbo slowed me down.

After we returned from the call I wondered if Pete had stopped a block or so away to see if his plan had worked. It would have been a spectacular way to murder me and my crew. I seethed at the thought of him watching us spin uncontrolled into Red River Boulevard. I wondered how he would have felt driving home after seeing us killed. Just as I knew would happen, the paramedic called Dispatch about our late response. Jolly didn't call me about it, though. I was glad. It left me the latitude to take care of that business myself at the end of my shift when Pete showed up the next morning.

When the shift was done I was not surprised when everyone had been relieved to go home but me. My crew left. Pete's crew went upstairs. I stepped into the garage and waited. That's where I was when Pete arrived. It was okay with me that he was late to work as usual. The aircraft was clean and fully serviced. My helmet was still up there. I was still ready to take any call. I anticipated taking at least the first call of Pete's shift. After that I would go home and Jolly would fill in. Pete would be in the ER – as a patient.

When Pete's car raced up the parking ramp nobody else was in the garage but me. I walked toward his car as he parked on the back row. He swung into a slot between two cars. His front bumper was against the concrete block wall of the garage. He stepped out of his car and quickly closed the door. Locking it he looked up and saw me. He appeared surprised. I was standing between the two cars, blocking his way to quarters. My arms were crossed. My legs spread out shoulder width apart. I left no room for him to pass. I think he was going to try and push past anyhow. He realized that would not have been a good idea. I was six inches taller than he was. I outweighed him by fifty pounds, at least. I was not that long out of the Marines and my level of fitness showed it. It was clear that at this moment those issues were about to make a difference to him.

"What's wrong?" He said as though he couldn't imagine.

"You left the aircraft empty and filthy again."

"I was in a hurry."

"You also left the rotor RPM at minimum."

His eyes looked away. "No, I didn't."

Rotor RPM is an innocuous little detail. We never adjust it between shifts. It stays the same for all of us. My comment about it should have surprised him unless he had moved it on purpose. Because my mentioning it didn't surprise him, I was absolutely certain he had done it on purpose. I was also certain he had set up the whole incident to cause us to crash. I was standing six feet away from a man who had tried to murder me.

"You set me up to be in too big a hurry to see the RPM was set on the bottom, Pete. You set me up to lose the rotor RPM on takeoff."

He smirked. "The rotor RPM is supposed to be set to minimum on landing," Pete said. "Read the book."

"Read the book, Pete? When did you start doing that? You bastard. You set me up to crash that helicopter. You set me up to kill myself and my crew."

Pete looked past me. He swiveled his head looking for a way past me. He didn't want to find out where this conversation was going. I waited for him to say something, to deny what he did. But he didn't deny it. Instead, knowing he was trapped he looked at me defiantly and said, "You make a mistake, Stone it's on you. Now get out of my way."

I dropped my hands. In one smooth motion I took a quick step in his direction, swung my hand up from beneath his line of sight and grabbed his scrawny neck. I moved so quickly he never saw it coming. He dropped his car keys and reached back to steady himself. I pushed him straight back several steps. I grabbed his flight suit at the chest with my other hand and rammed his shoulders against the cinder block wall. He reached out to push me away but my arms were longer. His hands flailed at me. Then I pushed him up the wall by his throat. The toes of his boots came off the pavement. He tried to say something. It came out as a squawk as I closed my hand on his windpipe. He reached up with both hands and grabbed the wrist of the hand holding his neck. He couldn't move my hand. His eyes bulged with panic. Veins stood out in his face and forehead. His skin went from bright red to a shade of blue. He wasn't going to breathe again until I let him. Neither of us was sure at that moment whether that was ever going to happen.

"I never had anybody try to kill me before. Now it's your turn, Pete. How does it feel?"

Just before he passed out I relaxed my hand on his windpipe and let his feet reach the ground. He drew a huge breath of air. I held him there against the wall as his face changed from blue back to red. As he came back to himself he struggled a little. I gave his windpipe another quick squeeze, then let go of it. He stopped struggling. I let him breathe. He was on his feet now but firmly pinned to the wall.

"You've sunk low, Pete. I should mop up this garage with your skinny ass before I finish choking you out." I let him wonder if I would. Then I abruptly let him go. I backed up a step.

"Last warning, asshole," I growled. "The helicopter better be ready to fly or I'm going to finish what I just started."

He struggled to regain his composure. He stretched his neck and pushed his hair back it place. Then he stepped forward as though to push past me. I turned into him and gave him a knee to the thigh. He folded and went down on his hands and knees. I kicked his keys under the car. As I backed away he looked up at me with hate in his eyes.

I left him on the ground, turned and walked away to go upstairs and get my helmet.

The next shift Pete's wife showed up at quarters and caught him cheating. She left him right there and later divorced him, I heard. The next week Jolly fired Pete Reynolds. I hadn't said anything to Jolly to cause it. Apparently I didn't have to offer him my observations. My concerns were evidently shared by the crew. Their complaints made it to Lifeline's managers who had Jolly pull the trigger. I hated seeing what Pete had done to himself. A good man went down hard to a gross lack of character, impulsiveness and pride. It was the same play I had seen acted out when I was in the Marines. Pilots there ruined their marriages, their careers and even lost their lives to the same faults. Most of those people I carried to the ER got there by doing the same stupid things for years before I met them. They smoked for forty years and got heart disease or lung cancer. They drank too much until a drunk driving accident or organ failure got them a ride on Lifeline. They overdosed on drugs. They suffered from sexually transmitted disease like hepatitis and HIV that sooner or later would kill them. Every time I saw the same act replayed with different players I wanted to cry out, "Don't you ever learn?"

Lifeline brought me to the sad conclusion that generally, people don't learn. They don't learn from other people's mistakes. Most don't even learn from their own. We human beings make the same stupid blunders that generations of us have made back to the dawn of time. Good people of promise give away every blessing they possess for almost nothing. It was always the same. King Solomon and his son King David in the Bible both gave away even their favored positions with God that even armies arrayed against them couldn't take away. They were immensely wealthy. They had more of everything good in life than any one man could want. And they gave it away for sex.

As far back as you want to go, everybody makes the same mistakes I saw played out as an air ambulance pilot. I resolved to give the condition of these people to the one who made them. I came to the conclusion that everybody's life is their own. It's unique. When He gave it to us God gave us the great gift of a free will. He offers us his guidance. He even wrote it down for us in the form of the Bible. We can take that advice or leave it. We choose how our life goes. We don't have to choose to follow the tortured paths of our predecessors. Those who do often flew with us on Lifeline. Except for Pete. He never flew on Lifeline again.

8 FIRST SHIFTS

Shortly after he hired me Jolly wandered into Quarters. I was still in training. I was waiting for a call with Bob, the duty pilot. With a pedigree that included three tours in flying in Vietnam and hair more gray than otherwise, Bob was our senior pilot. Bob and Jolly knew good helicopter pilots do not always make good EMS pilots. Both had seen more than a few pilots hang it up after their first experience washing blood out of a helicopter with a bucket. Bob was indifferent about how I would react. Jolly not so much. He didn't care about me one way or the other. He cared about how my suddenly quitting would affect him. It took time to recruit me, hire me and train me. He didn't want to find that he had wasted his time.

He arrived at Quarters unannounced. When Jolly opened the door he wanted to know how his investment in me was going. He stepped into the middle of the room because that was where he commanded the most attention. Bob was sitting in the Barko lounger watching TV. Because the lounger was the chair our most senior pilot preferred the crew called it, "the pilot's chair." They never challenged us for it. Bob made it ours.

I was sitting on the couch when Jolly walked in. The newspaper was open in my lap. I looked up from it. Bob's eyes never moved from the

TV. Jolly made sure he wasn't blocking Bob's line of sight. Bob knew the visit had nothing to do with him. Jolly was just nervous about *the new guy*. Jolly didn't even say good morning to either of us. He just leaned toward me and asked, "So, you think you can handle this?" I gave him a half smile. I wondered how he could ask that question let alone start a conversation with it. It was particularly odd after the ride-along, all the interviews and interactions I had to date with the crew. I had seen a lot of calls during the training I had already done. So to answer his question I nodded. Once.

"There's a lot of blood and gore on this job ya' know."

I looked for an article to scan in the newspaper and nodded again.

"Lots of dying and crying going on at the scene."

He evidently expected me to react. To say something. But he saw he'd lost me to the newspaper. I said nothing.

"Are you up to that?"

I nodded my head slightly. "Sure, Jolly." I looked up from the paper. He must have seen the questioning look in my eyes. *What does he expect me to say? How do I know if I'm up to it? I've never flown air ambulances. Except at funeral homes, I've never even see a dead person.* But I wasn't going to go all soft and say, "Geez Jolly, I don't know. I don't know if I can handle blood and gore. I don't know if I can handle traumatic deaths, children drowning, and families slaughtered on the highway."

Even if I waxed philosophical, there was no way I'd do it with Jolly. If he thought I would he picked a bad stage for the show. I'd keep my own counsel sitting here in the quarters with Bob. That Jolly would think I might do otherwise reestablished what I knew about the man. Quarters, Lifeline and life in general was better without Jolly in it. Bob and I wished he would leave from the moment he opened the door. But there he stood waiting for me to say more.

"Dead people? Blood and guts, Jolly? I guess we'll see," I replied.

Then he shrugged, probably thinking the same thing: we'll see.

As he turned to leave I glanced over at Bob. Neither Bob nor his eyes had moved. But he was grinning.

When the door close behind Jolly I asked, "How'd I do?"

"Fine," said Bob.

"'Seems like a long way to drive from the hangar just to ask if I had the sauce for this job," I replied.

"When he gets jumpy he has to come over here and bug us. He'll stop doing it after a while. You'll get a few bad calls under your belt and he'll leave you alone. You'll see."

And I did see. On several calls I got that experience flying with Jolly. Dealing with Jolly was the most difficult part of the call. He really didn't care about anyone but himself. He didn't concern himself with a patient bleeding to death. He only worried that their splashed blood might expose him to some blood borne pathogen. He hated blood.

He didn't care about the woeful moaning of a terribly burned person. He just hated the smell of burned bodies. He hated the smell of blood and vomit. They were equally unpleasant to him. He said they distracted him from his flying.

On one flight with him we were carrying a couple of badly injured children. I was flying. Jolly had nothing to do but sit and observe. As we took off from the auto accident scene the kids cried and occasionally shrieked as our crew treated them. I could tell that they were in unimaginable pain. Finally, as we neared the hospital, Jolly could stand it no more. He keyed the intercom as though the children would hear him. In his irritating high pitched voice he said, "shuuuuuuut uuuuuup!" He rolled his eyes at me. Their crying was such a bother to him. He shook his head. "I hate kids." I looked for some sign of mercy in him.

"Don't you have kids, Jolly?" I asked in a conversational tone.

"Yeah, but the placenta was the better part of them. I should have insisted on an abortion."

There was no mercy in this man: no grace, empathy, sympathy, kindness or understanding. So far as I could tell Jolly loved no one. He was married to a woman other than the mother of his children. He never broached the circumstances of his divorce with anyone, least of all me. On those rare occasions when he spoke of his current wife he could well have been talking about a roommate. He called his two sons, "the abortions." The only thing I could detect that he did love had nothing to do with people. They were flying, being in charge of Lifeline and his ridiculously over-sized pickup truck. The only hobby I knew he had was selling some kind of specialized motor oil to other people who liked trucks like his. I never bought any of it.

As for flying, it's a skill most people can learn. Some people are better at it than others. Jolly was very good at it, at least the physical skill it required. Giving credit where it is due, Jolly might have been the best manipulator of helicopter flight controls I ever met. Certainly he thought so; he thought he was a better pilot than anybody he flew with. But his personality made him a risky pilot with whom to fly. I always thought that he was likely to get himself into a corner one day out of which neither he nor anyone with him could fly. Starting with the low RPM recovery I did with him during my interview I kept on my toes watching Jolly when I flew with him.

During my training he continued to have me fly at the far edge of both my abilities and his. We landed in impossibly small zones. We flew at the absolute base of our weather limits. He carried less fuel than was prudent, but always just enough. I rarely flew an entire flight with both engines running at operating RPM. He simulated failure of at least one engine on me regularly by rolling the throttle to idle.

One day he even rolled both throttles back to idle. The Four-Twelve has the glide ratio of a greased safe when that happens. Descending fast with no engine power was bad enough. But Jolly pulled that little trick on me as we were crossing the middle of Lake Travis, Austin's water reservoir. We had one way out if the engines stayed at idle or failed. There was a rocky little island, little more than a short length of beach out there in the middle of the lake. It was not much larger than the helicopter. It was passing behind us on my side as Jolly set the throttles to idle. I lowered the collective and I went there. On the way down he held the throttles closed against my efforts to open them back up. As I maneuvered I finally said, "Jolly, let go of the damned throttles." He did. I rolled them up just in time to recover from the autorotation. We came to a four foot high hover smack over the middle of the island.

I didn't say another word to Jolly on the flight back to the hospital. He knew I was hopping mad so he didn't push the issue by inducing any more emergencies. He hadn't left us an out. If anything went wrong, landing on that island was the only option. That autorotation could have played very differently. We could have wrecked the helicopter. We and the crew could have drowned. But Jolly knew he was so good that he didn't believe it could happen. And that was the major risk involved in flying with Jolly. No credit to him and despite the risk he was willing to assume, Jolly's egocentric instruction did me good. The absolute requirement to remain on my game around Jolly really made me a more skilled helicopter pilot than I had ever been. I got much better at assessing risk and unintentionally flying myself into a situation I couldn't handle. So far at least when Jolly put me in a tight corner my increasing skills got me out of it. So far.

Jolly liked being in charge, but I think he missed flying the line. He liked to fly. And he like where Lifeline took him. Death and dismemberment fascinated him. There is no other job like flying an air ambulance helicopter which combines these two unlikely fascinations under the same common umbrella. I watched Jolly at scenes during my training. Where I gravitated toward the living victims at a medical call or accident scene, Jolly did the opposite. He purposely sought out the dead. After a patient expired he hung back to look at them. A dead man lying in his living room after a heart attack was much more interesting to him than efforts to revive him. He was particularly interested in trauma scenes. He walked through the room where a suicide victim had just blown out his brains. He sought out the ejected passengers furthest from rollover accidents as they were least likely to have survived. After they were discovered dead, the responders usually covered them with a tarp. Jolly always unabashedly lifted the tarp to look at the dead. Besides the dead, live patients with gruesome and disfiguring wounds interested him, but only if they were unconscious. He would not abide their flailing blood on him or disturbing him with their screaming.

He knew his barbaric fascination with gore was odious to the experienced helicopter crews. That's why he liked to drag over new guys like me to see the dead. Toward the end of my training, while I was being observed by Jolly, we landed at the scene of a single vehicle accident. A pickup truck had departed the roadway at high speed. The truck rolled. There were two passengers. One was already dead. That's all we knew when we launched from the hospital. We landed near the rolled up truck. It lay upside down on the shoulder at a wide curve in a lonely ranch road. A half-dozen emergency response vehicles were there at the scene. As I shut down the helicopter and hung up my helmet on the hook behind my seat I was impressed with an eerie calm about the place. I came to find that calm was present at many fatality scenes.

Jolly and I stepped into the dry grass beside the road. It whistled in the breeze as we walked through it toward the accident. The grass crackled as we crushed it beneath our boots. In the distance puffy clouds scooted low above the dry hills. Blotches of olive green live oak trees splashed the hillsides. The two teenage boys who had been inside the truck were not wearing seatbelts. Driving too fast around the curve, the truck rolled. Both were ejected through their respective windows.

One of the boys landed in the grass on one side of the road. He was still alive when we landed. All the attention of the first responders at the scene were focused on saving his life. A yellow tarp was hung on a fence on the other side of the road. I knew and Jolly knew that the other boy was lying dead under that tarp. Jolly waved me over to explore the body with him. I went. As we got closer I could see the boy's boot sticking out from beneath the tarp. His body evidently lay under the barbed wire fence.

Jolly got to the tarp first. Without any respect for the dead person who we knew lay below it he pulled the tarp completely off the body. I was astonished. When Jolly began to chuckle I was sickened. Then he looked up at me and signaled me to hurry, as though the boy would perhaps get up and run off before I could get there. As I drew closer I could see the body clearly. It was that of a young man, perhaps sixteen or seventeen. His long sleeved western style shirt was partly tucked into a pair of blue jeans. His clothes and boots were covered with dust. There was no blood visible, no gore that gave away what killed him. He lay flat on his back, hands crossed on his chest. I suppose some responder there before us had laid them in repose like that. Drawing closer I saw the boy's eyes were half open. Then in disbelief I saw that above his eyebrows there was nothing. The top of his head was entirely gone. I knew at once what had happened. In falling through the fence the taut wire had cut his cranium. It was removed as cleanly as though done by a great egg slicer.

Jolly was staring at the wound seemingly fascinated by the sight. I stood there in disbelief, in shock. I was deeply shaken. But then I realized that this was exactly the reaction Jolly would look for me to exhibit. It would show a weakness in me. I knew he would take advantage of it. My only defense from it would be to regain control of myself. It was only because Jolly had started looking on the other side of the fence for something that I put the tarp back over the dead boy. Then I joined Jolly. I took charge of myself by asking him what he was looking for.

"I wonder where his brain went?"

In a moment of defensive brilliance I replied, "'Same place as yours, Jolly."

He appeared not to hear me. Then when he realized what I said Jolly snapped his head around and gave me a quizzical look. "Wha…? What did you say?"

I pointed to the hillside in front of me. "It's lost out there somewhere."

He blinked at me absently trying to understand what I had just told him. Meanwhile I turned and started a slow walk back to the helicopter. I glanced down at the tarp as I passed. I prayed for the boy in the dusty boots and for his family. From behind me Jolly started chuckling.

"That's a good one, Stone!" Jolly had caught on. I walked away. "That's good! His brain is out there."

I could not bring myself to look back until I had climbed into the pilot's seat. "God, rest his poor young soul," I whispered.

I watched Jolly walk toward the crowd that was packaging the other young man for transport to the helicopter. When the group carrying the backboard got closer the paramedic turned toward me, raised his hand above his head and made a whirling motion. Before he and the crew reached the helicopter the rotors were roaring and I was ready to fly away from this place.

I was almost done with training. I did the flying and communicating now while the regulars took it easy in the left seat. I knew what I was doing by now. Jolly had been flying with me for the past several days. After the rollover with the decapitated boy the flights I flew with him were much more routine. So the day Jolly took a break and turned me over to another line pilot he missed an opportunity to test me. He was at his office in the hangar. He had his feet up on his desk. He was leaning back in his worn out leather desk chair reading a motorcycle magazine. There was a handheld EMS dispatch radio in a charger on his desk. It was turned down to low volume. But his ears instinctively prick up when he heard, "Lifeline One and Elgin first responders, MVA. US 290. Mile marker to follow."

He dropped his feet and reached for the radio. He whirled the volume knob so he could hear it better. He heard us call dispatch as we were leaving the hospital. Then he heard the Medic unit – the ground ambulance that called us - report dead children in one of the cars.

"Damn, that one might do it," Jolly mumbled to himself. "Dead kids are always a sure way to break down the sissies."

He was sure I was hiding a weakness for other human beings that he had long ago killed and buried. Jolly set the magazine on his desk and picked up his truck keys. He climbed into his over-sized diesel pickup truck for the trip to the hospital. He was comfortably ensconced in Quarters by the time I got back to the hospital. He knew better than to stand by the pad and wait for me. The helicopter always kicked up dust even on what looked like a pristine, white helipad. That dust contained germs. Jolly pictured vomit and blood the crews had washed out of the cabin. In his mind he saw its dried crust powdering him, carrying its poisons into his lungs. The thought sickened him. He hated being exposed to these sick people and all the bacteria they brought with them. Once he had confidentially told his wife, "This job would be okay if it were not for all the sick people I have to deal with." She had laughed long and loudly, not knowing he was serious. He had gone along with it as though it had been one of his very rare jokes. But actually being serious about hating to work with sick people, her reaction had embarrassed him. He thought it okay that the director of an air ambulance service didn't like people, especially those who needed his ambulance's service. He also thought his employees didn't know he hated working with sick people. He was wrong. Even Lifeline's newest pilot knew better than that.

The helicopter roared into downtown and came to a hover over the hospital helipad. Jolly stayed in the parking garage away from the germs and the sick people. He knew we'd landed when the rotors changing pitch. He stood at the foot of the stairwell to the helipad listening for me to roll the engines to idle. When he knew there would be no more dust blowing around to infect him, he climbed the stairs. Topping the stairway he saw the medical crew close the helicopter's rear door on the far side and walk toward the hospital. There was no patient with them. The regular pilot with me stepped out of the left side of the cockpit. He turned toward the tail of the helicopter and started looking the aircraft over. I was still in the pilot's seat. My helmet hung on the hook behind my head. I had my door swung open. I had snatched my ball cap from beneath the seat and pulled its brim down low over my eyes. My sunglasses sat on the end of my nose. Jolly could see that I was filling out the maintenance logbook in my lap.

My fingers worked automatically now, filling out squares on the helicopter's maintenance logbook form. My mind was still back on the highway near Elgin, Texas. There a young woman still sat pinned in a tangle of torn metal that a few minutes before had been a minivan. After I landed I could see from the cockpit that she was dead. I didn't know she had two little girls in the van with her. They had been struck broadside at high speed by a loaded dump truck. I missed the radio call about the dead children. All the crew had told me was that we were going to a "T-bone collision." I was learning the language.

The mother pulled up to a stop sign on Highway 290 to cross its four lanes. In the last ten seconds of her life she had been looking at the two lanes she was heading for rather than the two she was crossing. She pulled out looking right. The truck hit the van squarely from the left. The terrific impact caused a dozen injuries to her body that would have killed her before the car stopped moving.

My copilot took off his helmet and said, "I'll just stay here." So I got out of the aircraft and walked toward the scene. We had landed on the highway where the truck's skid marks started. I passed within hearing distance of the driver as he told the State Trooper that he didn't even have time to hit the brakes before he hit the van. Irregular grooves were gouged out of the asphalt leading to where the truck finally stopped. The remains of the van were splashed over all four lanes of the highway. The remaining bulk of the van lay on the left shoulder of the road in front of the dump truck. The whole scene glittered with little diamonds of broken safety glass. Every window in the van was missing. I imagined them exploding into sparking powder as the truck smashed into the van.

My crew had joined emergency workers clustered around the driver's side of the van. Trying to stay out of their way, I walked around the back of the truck and approached from the back of the van. Through the van's empty back window frames debris and twisted metal appeared to be piled up inside. I walked up and looked in. The bottom of the rear bench seat was folded up like a wallet against the back of the seat. Among the torn seats, torn metal and twisted plastic was the sleeping face of a little girl. She appeared in sharp contrast to the chaos of the shattered van. A tangled ball of hair framed her face. Behind it were blood and gore, blood soaked cotton rags and little human appendages. I couldn't tell which ones were arms and which were legs. I closed my eyes and turned my head away. But the image was still there. They remained burned into my retinas like the image a photo flash leaves after you close your eyes. I feared it would remain burned into my mind for as long as I lived.

I did not need to wait for a medical assessment now. I wondered why the medics on the scene had not cancelled us. Perhaps they thought the truck driver had been injured and needed us. I walked back to the helicopter as though it was just a routine call. I remained in control of my emotions as I waited for my crew. I chatted with my chaperon, the other Lifeline pilot. I was busying myself with readying the medical cabin for takeoff when the crew returned. After the engines were running I asked the crew if they were ready for takeoff. They each said, "Yes." There was no elaboration. There was no banter on the way back to the hospital.

I was now functioning by recently developed muscle memory. I landed at the hospital and shut down the engines. My copilot and the crew walked away. I donned my hat. I set my sunglasses. I filled out the aircraft maintenance logbook. I was unaware Jolly was there until he stepped to the pilot's door and asked, "How'd it go?"

I didn't look at him. I just kept writing. "Three DRT," I said.

'DRT' or "Dead Right There," was an example of the EMS jargon I was learning. It was part of the lexicon of black humor we used to deal with the tragedy of sudden death. Had it been anyone at Lifeline other than Jolly standing there I would have used the proper acronym for what I found at that scene. "Three DOS," for Dead On Scene. Had anyone made it to the hospital before being declared dead by a doctor they would have been DOA or "Dead On Arrival."

When I got home that night, Linda would ask the question we all ask our spouses. "How was your day?" I was an air ambulance pilot now. From now on that simple question's answer would always be a pregnant one. The question would have an edge of concern, full of the knowledge that death had probably passed close by me. I had already learned how to answer that question now without detail. There was no use ruining my homecoming with the tragedy I often saw. So today I would say, "I did a bad car accident on 290." If Linda left the door open for me to say more, I would shake my head and say, "Three people died." I would never elaborate. If she pushed me I would avoid her eyes, claim I would tell her later or tell her I wasn't ready to tell her yet. Usually she would let it rest and hug me.

I never told her about the kids. I hated seeing children die worse than anything. Except for perhaps Jolly, we all did. And the little girl? She still scars my heart. I gave nothing away to Jolly. I kept my own counsel. I kept the wound covered. He knew it. We both knew I was building a skill I would need to do the job. He thought it was detachment. I never told anyone that I cried for that little girl all the way home.

I did a training flight with Arlen as my copilot. It was my first "DOS" call. The call came in as an "unconscious man." That cryptic description of the event and the address was all the Dispatcher told us. The ambulance at the scene called in over the EMS dispatch channel as we were about midway to the scene to say that C.P.R. (Cardio-Pulmonary Resuscitation) was in progress.

I did one quick orbit over the scene to slow down and to look at the landing zone. It was right in the middle of a neighborhood full of pretty new single family houses. I decided to put the helicopter down in a four-way intersection a block from the emergency vehicles. They filled a cul-de-sac. Landing right in the middle of the neighborhood concerned me because each yard bordering my landing spot had a high wooden privacy fence around it. When the rotor blast hit them they usually wobbled and rippled along their length. Sometimes sections of them broke off or blew down. I watched to see if that happened. Shards of wood passing through the rotors would be bad for us and the surrounding observers. But none of the pickets got airborne so I lowered the collective and shutdown the engines. That's one good landing for Lifeline One.

Stephanie, the nurse and James, the paramedic, removed their helmets as I rolled the engines to idle. They jumped out with their bags and walked to the nose of the aircraft where I could see them. Both showed me the "thumbs up" asking if it was clear to leave. I returned it and they ducked under the rotor. They walked up the street and disappeared into the cul-de-sac. Arlen didn't say anything. He just watched me shut down the helicopter. He followed me on the walk around. As we finished he said, "Let's go see what's happening, shall we?"

I followed him in the direction our crew had gone. In front of the house was a police car and fire truck. Last to arrive had been one of our Austin EMS ambulances. The emergency lights on all the vehicles were on. I could hear the emergency radio blaring in stereo over the external speaker in the ambulance as well as on the handheld radio I carried. The rear doors of the ambulance stood wide open. I noted that the wheeled stretcher was still inside. I knew I might be called on to go get it when it was time to move the patient.

The police officer and a couple of fire fighters I saw through the open front door were lined up in the living room behind a couch. They were all watching our crew. Fire fighters and the ambulance crew were assisting them. The patient was a man who looked to be in his forties or fifties. He lay supine on the living room carpet. The man was bare-chested, in a short, blue silk robe, red and white striped boxer shorts and tan leather slippers. He certainly had not been expecting guests.

His robe was open exposing his chest. It was covered with red and white EKG wires clipped to round, gummed sensors stuck to his skin. A burley looking ambulance paramedic was pushing mightily on the patient's chest, compressing his heart to keep his blood flowing. I figured the CPR must have been working. The patient's skin had a healthy pink tone. The paramedic was sweating heavily from the effort. I determined that CPR wasn't as easy to do as it looked on T.V.

Meanwhile, our paramedic was completing an intubation, placing a plastic ET (Endo-Tracheal) tube into the patient's throat to open his airway. When it was done he placed a blue, football shaped "ambu bag" on the end of the ET tube. Then he began squeezing air down the tube, breathing for the patient. Two fire fighters had started an IV (Intravenous) line on the man. One fire fighter held a clear plastic bag of normal saline solution that would carry heart medicines into the man's veins. He adjusted the drip rate as the other handed Stephanie medications from her medicine box. She drew up a hypodermic syringe from a bottle she had in her hand. She loudly read the name of the medicine from the bottle. Then she said how much she was using. She withdrew the needle from the bottle and pushed it into a joint in the IV tubing that went into the patient's arm. I hadn't yet seen these drugs used on an unconscious patient, but I figured they and the CPR would do the trick.

"Go guys!" I said out loud. Nobody appeared to notice, not even Arlen. The CPR and the administration of drugs progressed without much change from the patient. He was still pink, still getting air. Time was passing. I was wondering why were weren't loading the patient. I watched while James and subsequently three fire fighters wore themselves out, one after the other, doing CPR. I began to wonder if they were ever going to call for me to get the stretcher so we could fly him to the hospital. That's when Stephanie called over one of the fire fighters. He had been standing behind the couch with a clip board. He handed her his clipboard. She stood up with it and walked into the kitchen. My attention was split between her and the work that was being done on the patient. She made a phone call on the patient's phone. I heard her ask for somebody and then wait. A moment later she identified herself.

"This is Stephanie Lusco. I'm the flight nurse on Lifeline One at the scene of a forty-six year old male. He was found unconscious by his wife upon returning home from work. Patient was found in a chair in the living room. He had been down for an unknown length of time. Wife denied the patient has a cardiac history. Medic Fourteen arrived and noted the patient was pulseless and pale, apnic and cyanotic. They started CPR."

I had been asking the crew questions all through my training when I didn't understand what they were saying or doing. "Pulseless, pale, apneic and cyanotic," meant the patient had no pulse, was pasty white, not breathing. Cyan means blue. So evidently the patient had not been breathing for a while because his lips and nail beds had turned blue. He was "cyanotic." She went on listing the things I had seen them do for the patient. Then she referred to the clipboard and started reading the names and doses of the medications she had used. She noted the time she had administered (she said "pushed") each drug through the IV port. I felt like we had been there an hour, but she had the drugs onboard within five minutes of arrival. I realized I had lost track of time. Then she paused. "That's correct, negative pulse times four." That meant they stopped CPR four times and took the patient's pulse with no result. I didn't know at the time but she was saying that the patient was dead. She paused again. "Is there anything else you want us to do?" Stephanie listened and then she hung up the phone. She wrote something on the clipboard. "Sixteen fourteen, people," she said.

I didn't understand what that meant. I was picking up on the police and ambulance "ten codes." I had already been teased by our medics because I said "roger" on the radio instead of "10-4." "Roger" is the pilot word. "Ten-Four" is the EMS code for "I understood the last radio transmission." I already knew I was "10-8" if I did something right. But I didn't understand what 16-14 meant. It was clear that everybody else in the room did, though. The latest in the series of sweaty fire fighters immediately quit doing CPR. I could tell he was grateful as he wiped the sweat from his brow. The fire fighter squeezing the ambu bag stopped doing that too. Then he detached it from the ET tube and laid it on the floor beside the patient's head. Everybody else started gathering up the pile of debris that had accumulated in opening medications, tubing and bags of IV fluid. The fire fighter with the IV bag bent over and laid it on the patient's chest. The show was over.

Behind the couch everybody turned toward the door. Since I was the last one in the room I was expected to be the first one out the door but I didn't move. The patient was still pink. I thought maybe I had seen him breathing. Arlen gave me a push. Then he stepped past me, took my elbow and moved out of the door with me in tow.

"Let's go," he said.

I must have looked at him in surprise.

"Let's go, it's over!" he said again. He pulled me a little more firmly now. I stepped out the door and into the yard. I looked back into the house to see the patient as the cop and fire fighters stepped out behind me.

"But…what happened? He looked like he was doing okay!"

I was talking to myself. Arlen had let go of my elbow and was already approaching the curb setting a businesslike pace across the cul-de-sac back to the helicopter.

"Hey!" I said as I stepped out quickly to catch up. "That man looked like he was breathing!" I jogged across the yard and caught up with Arlen. "He was pink as a rosebud! He didn't look dead to me! Why did they stop? Why aren't we taking him to the hospital?"

"I'll tell you later," Arlen said without looking at me.

When we got back to the helicopter, old habits took over. I walked around the aircraft automatically looking for leaks, open cowlings and anything that could obstruct our takeoff. I walked around the tail and looked up and down the street. A cop car had blocked traffic several houses away. Some of the neighbors had gathered there. Nobody was near enough to the helicopter to be at risk from our rotor blast when we left. I noted that the wind was calm and which way I would turn after we got some altitude. I looked for wires, telephone poles and radio towers. Then I climbed in the right side of the cockpit and buckled my seatbelt.

As I did so I could plainly see the last image I had of the man lying on the floor. His eyes were closed. His skin was pink. I could see his striped boxer shorts and those goofy looking leather slippers on his feet. He looked like he was going to get up and close the door behind us. He might be embarrassed to be dressed like that and for all the excitement he had caused. Except for the plastic tube, which protruded several inches out of his mouth, he looked like a healthy, middle-aged man who had laid down on the living room floor for a nap.

"Start it," I heard someone tell him. I wondered who was telling the man that, and why. "Start it!" I heard again. This time I got a poke in the shoulder. I was suddenly back in the cockpit, looking at Arlen. He was staring at me with a perplexed look on his face.

"He's dead, Paul! There was nothing else we could do! It's time to start the helicopter, man!" He leaned over to my side of the cockpit, reached up to the overhead switch panel and smartly snapped the two battery switches on. That got me going. I reached up and snapped on the two inverter switches. I heard the gyros spool up. The ship was coming to life. I automatically reached down to the collective with both hands and set the throttles for start. My hands flew nimbly now turning on the fuel pumps, opening the start valve. I leaned forward, looked all around.

"Clear and ready on one!" I shouted.

Only Arlen knew what I was saying. Nobody else would have. I had not said that phrase since I last used it in the H-53. It meant I was ready to start the number one engine. To Arlen and me it meant I had checked to see I was clear to start. He knew it was a good old habit. He let the Navy lingo pass. I hit the starter switch and the turbine whined. As the engine sucked in great gulps of air I opened the throttle to mix it with a spray of fuel. Behind me igniter plugs snapped rhythmically and the 'woof' of the fuel-air mixture lighting off in the engine's combustion chamber sent the sweet smell of jet exhaust into the air. The blades began to move.

When we got back to the hospital Arlen left the explanations to the medical crew. He stood nearby watching me as I put the pieces together. James did most of the talking at first, with Stephanie occasionally reaching into the medical kit to do the 'show-and-tell' part. They went through the call step-by-step. Stephanie reached into a flap in the side of her medical bag and withdrew a wrapper containing an ET tube. It was at least a foot long. I had not realized so much of it went down the patient's throat. As James kept talking, she held up a curved, stainless steel blade and a knurled metal handle I had seen in a doctor's office before. The nurse called it a "Mac," short for a MacIntosh blade. She assembled the two parts and showed me how it was used to insert the tube through the man's larynx and into his trachea. "His windpipe," she explained using a term I was sure to understand. Then as the paramedic went on she pulled out a plastic wrapped ambu bag showing me the hose I hadn't noticed that had been connected to their oxygen bottle. They weren't just breathing for the patient; they were pumping his lungs full of pure oxygen. Then the nurse took out the cardiac meds one by one. She and James explained how each one worked.

"But none of them worked for the man in the living room."

The medic knew I was still not straight on why we gave up. "Paul," he said. "You have to keep this in mind. The patient was probably dead before his wife got home. He was certainly dead when we got there. His wife found him in the living room in front of the T.V when she came home from work. He could have died hours before she got there. He probably just died in that chair from a sudden heart attack. One minute it's 'The Hollywood Squares,' on T.V. and the next... poof, he's gone. It's probably not so bad a way to go."

"So why did everybody go to all the heroic efforts then, James? That CPR wore out three fire fighters."

The medic turned to the nurse who gave him a knowing smile. "That's why God made firefighters," James said.

Stephanie continued. "When someone dials 911, Paul, the Dispatcher has protocols to follow. They're like scripts. When a person is found unconscious dispatch has to believe they're still alive. She coaches the caller on how to do CPR until the first medically trained responder arrives. Once they get there, by law we have to keep making the effort until a doctor tells us the patient is dead."

"So what doctor told you he was dead?"

"I'll take you into the ER and introduce you to him if you like."

"He was right here?"

"Yep," she said. "That's who I was talking to on the phone. He was here at the ER. We keep a record at the scene of all the medical protocols and drugs we use. The doctor just wants to hear that we followed the protocols the medical director gives us. We are actually working under our medical director's license using those meds. Otherwise we couldn't use them."

"So what was that code you used to stop everybody from working on him anymore? What was it, 16-14?"

Stephanie, James and even Arlen smiled at that. "That's from the doctor, Paul. That was the patient's time of death!" said Stephanie.

James told me something I would hear hundreds of times in my new career. "You're not dead until a doctor says you're dead."

"Unless you lose your head," Arlen alliterated.

"Or you're shot to death instead," James responded straight-faced.

"Or slipped off while in bed," Arlen continued. They were enjoying themselves.

Stephanie rolled her eyes and gave the guys a "cut" sign across her throat. "Okay, poets. Enough!"

"I get it, I get it." I smiled for the first time since the call. "Thanks for answering all these questions."

"We could tell it bugged you," James replied.

"Don't worry. I went through the same thing. It's part of the process," Arlen noted.

I turned to Stephanie.

"I've got one more question, Steph. I thought I heard you say on the phone the patient didn't have a heart history? What was that all about?"

"You were paying attention!" she replied. She looked at Arlen. "That's good." She squinted at him. "Most pilots don't."

I picked up her signal, but Arlen seemed not to notice. I was looking at the patient as a person, a husband, a man that James, Stephanie and I wanted to see live a while longer. Arlen was completely detached throughout the call. He was being offered the same opportunities I was to participate, and he passed them all up. Stephanie knew – as I was beginning to suspect all the other nurses did as well – that Arlen just didn't care about the patients, or the nurses for that matter. I wondered for the first time what he really *did* care about on this job.

Stephanie had more to tell me. She knew I was hungry to learn. "The doctor would want to know if the patient had a history of heart disease, but frankly, heart history doesn't mean much. You'll probably be surprised to find that most of the people you'll respond to who just drop dead from a heart attack had no heart history at all. One minute you're sitting there…" Stephanie started to say.

"And the next minute your wondering who the distinguished looking dude is in the white robe and the wings standing there by the pearly gate," James finished for her. "And you'll see lots more calls like this one too, Paul. We've all been there and we've all got the t-shirt."

I got a sheepish grin. "That would be *some* t-shirt! 'I'VE BEEN TO A HEART ATTACK,' Do you think they sell them in the hospital gift shop?"

Stephanie and James looked at each other, then at me. "Naaaaa." They both shook their heads at me while Arlen looked at his fingernails. I could see that he was the only one of us who wasn't enjoying the chat about what we really do for a living. For me at least, flying was only part of the program.

It was dark now. Mercury lights brightly illuminated us and the helicopter. I stayed on the pad as the crew restocked their medical kits. Then I walked down stairs. Arlen had been in Quarters a while. He handed me a can of soda as I stepped in and let the door swing closed behind me. He took a swig of his own Dr. Pepper.

"I know that call was hard on you. I had to let you see it for yourself. It's part of the job that is so different and so hard for us to figure out. You and I have been flying helicopters for years. We're good at it and these medical crews trust us. It took a while for me to reciprocate, but I've gotten to the point where I just trust that the crews know their jobs as well as I know mine. After I saw something I didn't understand I waited until the call was over and asked them to explain it. I've gotten to the point that I just don't ask them anything anymore." He put his soda down on the table. "I can already see I'm probably different from you in one respect. I am not really interested in the medical side of things. Flying is my job. It's a big enough job for me. It takes all my time and attention to do it right. You like this medical stuff. That's okay, but I recommend that you keep the medical side of the job separate from the flying side of what you do. It will be easier for you if you do."

Perhaps it was wise advice. I resolved to follow it, and I did. For a little while.

The D.O. writes the schedule for the new guys. He started me off on the night shift. I'd fly seven nights, get a week off and then fly seven days. If I had been in Jolly's shoes, I would have started a new pilot off on days. I looked at my night assignment as Jolly's vote of confidence in me thus proving my naivety. In retrospect it was probably just the luck of the draw. I got nights. When I showed up at Quarters for the first night shift I failed to notice that my medic and nurse were the same crew I had on my ride along before I was hired at Lifeline. Both were the strongest and most senior of the medical crews. I didn't know that they had been tasked by Jolly with watching out for the new pilot on his first shift. I was so new I just thought I had gotten lucky to get such a great crew. What did I know?

I especially liked Mary, who always called herself "the nurse du jour, monsieur." She was petite and precocious. Her flight suit was the smallest size the company made. It still had lots of room for her inside. When I first met her I wondered if they made flight boots in child sizes. I may have been a new guy but I knew something about working with women. And I knew these women of Lifeline in particular well enough not inquire about ladies clothing sizes, even if they're combat boots.

Her bleached blonde hair had grown out some since I first met her. It was almost collar length cut short and uneven, like she'd cut it herself with a pair of round-nosed scissors. During our first meeting I had barely talked to her. But now that I was part of the team I found her very outgoing. She had bright eyes, a button nose sprinkled liberally with freckles and a dazzling smile that she was quick to flash at the slightest provocation. Small as she was, she was actually as tough as one of her little boots. She could curse like a Navy Chief and tell raunchy, dirty jokes that made me blush. She loved to make me blush. She knew I was a little more intimidated by her than were the rest of the pilots, probably because I had only worked with her a few times and had not figured her out yet.

On this my first solo shift we were gathering our flight gear for the walk upstairs when Mary called me a pig. I found out later that she called all the pilots her "pigs." It was actually a pet name for us. But I took umbrage. I thought she was inferring that I failed to respect her as a person. I thought she believed that as a women I considered her my lesser. "I'm not a pig!" I complained. "I treat my wife as my equal. Just ask her!"

She loved it. She had gotten to me. She didn't bat an eye when she said, "You really believe that. I know you pilot types, '...a whore in the bedroom.' That's what you think of us, isn't it? Be honest! I bet if you ask your wife that's what she'll tell you too if she's honest."

"I'm honest," I replied. "So is she." I was getting miffed.

Mary refused to be swayed. "I am too, Paul. You are a pig. Sorry."

"Hold on a minute," I complained. "I believe women can do any job a man can do."

"So let's see you give birth!" Karl our "paramedic du jour" pitched in.

"Okay, Karl. So they can do things men can't do. But hey, whose side are you on, anyway?" Chauvinist or not I had relied on the other male in the room to support me. But he was having fun taking Mary's side.

"See, Paul? You men are all pigs! Even Karl knows it so he won't support you."

I pouted.

"Now don't get insulted, sweetie." She folded her bottom lip like she was talking to a moping little boy. "It's not your fault. Even though pilots most especially are pigs, I think *you* are a very *nice* one, Paul."

I kept pouting. I didn't let on I knew she was teasing... sort of.

We all went upstairs together and the banter between my medical crew continued as we all checked our respective areas on the helicopter. We completed our work as the sun went down. Then Karl walked over to the loading dock to visit with an ambulance crew that was restocking their truck from the hospital stores. Mary and I closed the doors on the helicopter and walked down the stairs together.

We entered the Quarters and settled on the couch. She was at one end. I was on the other end. She drew her legs up in front of her making herself look even smaller and younger.

All the while she gave me pointers on how to be less swine-like, more caring and more concerned for the well-being of the nurses, particularly her. Finally the conversation lulled. I turned on the T.V. After a while I was lost in its mindlessness. I thought Mary was too until I began to get the feeling someone was looking at me. I turned and sure enough, Mary was staring over her knees at me like an owl. She didn't try to avert her eyes. She made it plain that she was staring at me and that she had been doing so for some time. It unsettled me. "What? What are you looking at?" I asked defensively.

She looked directly into my eyes. Then she nodded like she had just discovered something certain. "You're scared," she said. It wasn't a question. It was just a comment to confirm what she already knew.

I was taken aback. My brow wrinkled. "I'm not scared! What makes you think I'm scared?"

She didn't say anything. She knew I was considering what she had said.

Was I scared? No, there was nothing about the job I couldn't handle. I'd done about every scenario during training I would ever get by myself. I had practiced emergency procedures with Arlen and Jolly who had only caught me off guard a few times. I did things to keep the helicopter flying I hadn't seen before. I even auto rotated to that little island in the middle of Lake Travis. I was ready for anything now. In fact, I was probably as good a helicopter pilot as I had ever been.

"Well?" Mary asked. "I made you think about it. So what are you scared of?"

I thought I'd disappoint her when I shook my head confidently. "Nope, I'm not scared of anything," and I was sure of it. But then I got a little flutter inside. I was sure she saw it. She leaned toward me, narrowed her eyes and inhaled through her nose as though to smell fear. "Just tell me one thing. Are you afraid of the flying?"

My answer was immediate and positive, calm and absolute, without a shred of doubt.

"No. I'm not scared of flying: not here, not ever."

"Okay." She paused. "I believe that." Then she looked at me up and down as though confirming her observation. "Good. That's good! I was a little worried you were afraid of doing this job." She straightened her legs and stretched out a little. Even with her legs extended I had plenty of room before she'd have reached me with her little boots. She wasn't done with me though. "I know what it is, now. You're just scared of the dying."

I wasn't expecting that. I'm sure I looked confused. That was apparently right where she wanted me. I was evaluating the mission of Lifeline now, a part of the mission she wanted me to look at full in the face. "Isn't everybody scared of dying?" I asked.

"Well," she smiled, "put that way the answer to the question is certainly, 'No,' not everybody is afraid of dying. But that's not what I am talking about. What I mean is that you're afraid to see someone else die. Am I right?"

I turned my eyes away and thought about that. Then I looked back at her. "Yes. I guess I didn't know I was exuding fear about that. But I suppose you're right. This is all new to me, the whole Lifeline thing. I mean, before I started working here I never saw anyone actually die.

"Hmmmm." That sounded like her affirmation. I haven't been to a shrink, but I hear that's what psychiatrists do. They affirm and let you talk. She let me go on.

"I guess you figure it's being there when people die that is getting to me, huh?"

She said nothing.

"I know I feel helpless about it sometimes. Worry a little that maybe I'm not shaking it off like I should. Do you know what I'm trying to say about that helplessness?"

"Sure, I know what you mean." She stood up and moved closer to me. Then she sat down on the edge of the couch next to me. She half turned toward me. Then she surprised me a little. She slung her bent knee up over mine. She took one of my hands in both of hers and held it. She was very comfortable with doing it. It was very affectionate how she did it. More sisterly than sexual. The unusual physical frankness of it put me at ease. She wanted to set the tone that would carry on through the many sometimes traumatic shifts we would work together. Her little hands were soft and warm around my comparatively big hand. She looked into my eyes.

"It shows that you're a caring man, Paul. I can see it. And I know that this part of our job is hard for you. But we'll work through it. Too many people like you try to carry the burden of other peoples' pain all by themselves." She looked down as if to gather her thoughts. Then she fixed her gaze on me again. "I'm going to tell you something *important*, so listen to me closely."

She shook my hand back and forth to emphasize the word, "important." "There are two times in our lives when we can actually see the door to eternity crack open. In that brief instant when it does, we can see what is on the other side. We can see eternity. Do you know what I'm talking about?"

I wasn't sure I did, and she could see that. She backed up.

"There *is* something waiting on the other side of death you know." Her eyebrows rose as though a question had been asked. Then she asked it. "Do you believe that?"

I was with her so far. "Yes," I said. "I believe on faith that there is something waiting for us after death." My faith was not yet as strong as it would become during the days and weeks that followed. But that much I knew. In my heart I believed that death was not the end.

"Good. Good. That's a start." She put my hand down on her knee and crossed her hands on top of it. "Those times I just told you about...the ones when you can see through the crack in the door, when you can see eternity, do you know when they occur?"

I shook my head.

"They only happen when someone is born, and when someone dies."

She gave me a moment to think about that. She sensed I was skeptical. "You may not see it during every birth or at every death. In fact you won't see it on *most* occasions, or at least I don't. But when you see it for the first time, you'll know *exactly* what you're looking at. It's instinctive. I can't explain it exactly. But when it happens it doesn't need explaining anymore. After the first time you see it you'll look for it every time because it's beautiful! And the beauty of it will help you carry the burden you're trying to shoulder all by yourself right now."

Now she lost me. "Wait a minute, Mary. I don't get it. You're saying death is beautiful?"

She rolled her eyes. "No, dummy! I'm saying that sometimes when people die you'll *see* something beautiful. I can't explain what it is. You'll have to experience it for yourself. But when you see it you'll look for it from then on. You won't be able to get enough of it. And I'll tell you something else. You won't be afraid of *the dying* anymore. In fact you won't even be afraid of your *own* death anymore." She sat up now and put her feet back flat on the floor. Still half facing me she took a deep breath and let it out. "This is going to sound odd to you now, but death really is quite beautiful. It's what I live for in this job."

"You live for death?"

She smiled again. "No, I live for what I see sometimes when somebody dies." She knew she wasn't getting through. She bit her lower lip, then said, "I know that sounds strange to you now. You apparently haven't seen it yet. But watch. You'll see it here if you look for it. You'll recognize it when it happens. But you have to believe in it. You already believe that there is life beyond death. If you're not open to that you'll certainly miss a beautiful experience."

She wrinkled her nose a little. "Apparently you're different from the other pilots here. Being true pigs they turn their back on anything supernatural."

"It's supernatural?"

"Well Paul, nothing is supernatural. We humans just don't sense things that are as natural as breathing sometimes. We don't perceive mostly because we don't believe. But yes, if you believe you will see things on this job that other people would certainly call supernatural."

I turned my head away. She knew I was thinking about something in particular she had said. Then I turned back toward her. She looked ready to listen.

"You said it happens at birth too, right?"

"Yes. I did. Sometimes. But you won't see that here."

"Yeah, I know. We don't do babies. But I think I *have* seen what you're talking about."

Her eyes brightened. She looked hopeful.

"I was there when my twins were born. I was so elated. I was uplifted in a way I had never felt before. I could see why some people have big families if only to feel that rush. Watching my twin boys being born I felt like something spiritual had happened. And you're right, it was beautiful in a way I can never explain."

She listened patiently.

"Then when my third son was born, I was in Korea in the Marines. He was born in California. He was born two weeks early. I could not have known that eight thousand miles away on the other side of the date line my wife was giving birth. But at 7:30 on a cold March morning in Korea I knew to the minute when it happened. I was so sure my son had been born that I wrote down the time and date on my map. 'My baby was born when I was here.' Accounting for the thirteen hour time difference and the crossing of the International Date Line, the time on his birth certificate differs by two minutes from the time I wrote on that map."

She smiled and clapped me on the hand. "That's it!" she said. "That's exactly what I'm talking about! That's the same sort of miracle you'll see here. When you see it you'll be able to walk and work among the dead, the dying and those we can help. You'll see. You're going to love this job."

9 SHOT IN THE HEART

Driving past the hospital I always looked up to see which helicopter was on the helipad. The Four-Twelve was having some maintenance done. Today the LongRanger was waiting for me up there. I mumbled under my breath about getting stuck with the runt. I had been spoiled flying the Four-Twelve. It had size, power and all the pilot toys for doing any job we were called on to perform. Flying the Four-Twelve was like driving a Lincoln Town car. The LongRanger by comparison was like driving an economy class rental car. It was small and cramped. We could only carry two patients. If we did they were stacked like lunchmeat on top of one another. Their feet and lower legs reached into the cockpit beside me. Regardless of whether I carried one patient or two, the total couldn't be over three hundred and fifty pounds. I had to burn down fuel just to carry that much.

I tried to be positive as I pulled into the hospital garage. The LongRanger would do the job in most cases. On most of our calls we to transported a single patient. The LongRanger did one patient just fine. The LongRanger was also the better helicopter when the zone was really tight. I could put it down in about as much space as it would take to park a city bus. Once I landed in a spot like that it took all the power the engine could produce to take off again. But with all the power applied it always came back out of the spots where I landed it. Still, it wasn't a Four-Twelve. It just wasn't as roomy. It wasn't as powerful. And when its single engine quit it didn't have that second engine the Four-Twelve had to keep flying or land back safely.

I resolved to stay positive. This morning was cool with the promise of a warm day to follow. The sky was clear and blue. The first call came in long after we had finished our morning coffee. When it came in I knew the address. It was the home of a frequent flier. We had made several flights already for this lung cancer patient. He was losing the battle. Lung cancer is an ugly way to go. Watching a loved one suffocating to death over months, weeks, days and finally hours is difficult for a family. This particular man's family often called 911 when they couldn't take the dying process any longer. We couldn't do much more than turn up the oxygen or increase the meds to relieve the pain a little.

The patient lived out in the country southeast of Austin. Beside his house was a large, grassy field. I landed the helicopter there and the crew headed for the house. Then I shut down the engine. While the rotors coasted to a stop I stepped out. I was walking around the aircraft checking for leaks when the back door of the house opened. The medical crew came out carrying their bags. I knew the meaning. The patient's end had finally come. It was sad but I felt relieved for him and for his family.

In such a situation the ground ambulance crew takes over. So do the first responders. They stay around until the mortuary sends a van for the deceased. The helicopter crew had already called for a declaration of death. There was no reason for us to stay on scene any longer. It was time to get back in service. So I untied the blades and prepared to leave. While I did so the nurse strapped in the medical bags. The paramedic called Dispatch.

"Lifeline One, stage," they said over our handheld radio.

We looked at each other with wonder. Usually when a patient died Dispatch put us back in service immediately. If we had the fuel we needed we could run a call from where we were. Most often though, we went back to the hospital to refuel for the next call. Sometimes however we "staged," which meant we waited where we were. Dispatch staged EMS units when something was happening nearby that might require us. If we were close to a developing incident we could respond faster if we went there from wherever we staged. It was done all the time with ground units. Staging was rare with the helicopter. This was one of those rare times. So "stage" is what we were going to do.

Rather than stay by the helicopter out in the growing warmth of the field, we walked over to the ambulance. It was parked in the late patient's driveway. It was running. Ambulance, police and fire crews never shut off the engine at a call. In this case it was important because the air conditioning in the ambulance was running too. We climbed in the back. The ambulance crew came out to stow their empty gurney and medical bags. They were surprised to see us when they opened the doors.

"What are you guys still doing here?" the driver queried. "We thought you were probably sleeping back at the hospital by now."

"We're staging," our paramedic replied. Then he raised the handheld to his lips. He keyed the mike. "Lifeline One."

"Lifeline One, stage," came the monotone reply.

"See?"

"What's up?" the ambulance driver asked him.

"I don't know," our paramedic replied. "But I think I'll find out." He excused himself and stepped away from the helicopter to use the phone in the house. When he came back he said, "I don't know what's going on. There aren't any calls pending: no action, no need for a helicopter. They just want us to stage." He shrugged.

I opened a cooler in the front of the ambulance and passed out bottles of water for everyone. We all watched the fire fighters come out, jump on their truck and pull away. A couple of first responders got in their cars and did the same. I heard the fire fighters on our radio clearing the call with Dispatch. They were going back into service. We, on the other hand, still waited.

After a while a big Navy blue Suburban arrived. It backed into the driveway beside us. Its windows were tinted almost black. An older gentleman with a few wisps of hair on his pate stepped out of the passenger side. He wore a dark suit and light blue tie. His long, dour face and deep set eyes never turned toward us. Instead they turned back toward his seat in the car. He reached inside and grabbed something. Meanwhile, the driver, another guy in a suit stepped out and walked to the back of the Suburban. He was stocky with broad shoulders and brush cut blond hair. He opened the double doors and drew out a gurney similar to the one in the ambulance. It was covered by a muted green velvet blanket. Through a window in the ambulance I could see the older guy walk across the yard toward the front door. He carried a folder in one hand and a pair of rubber gloves in the other.

"Undertaker," my paramedic mumbled.

"Indubitably," I replied.

The other guy dragged the gurney behind him and stopped a few paces from the front door. The velvet cover was loosely fitted to the gurney. There was plenty of room under it to mask the shape of the body that would soon lay beneath it. I wondered to myself why people who were dead were suddenly so distasteful to our culture. They had been the center of attention one minute. Then they died and nobody wanted to talk about them anymore. Just the same I joined the others in the ambulance trying unsuccessfully not to stare.

About the time the undertaker stepped back outside, Dispatch called.

"Lifeline One, return to base."

And that we did. Three minutes later we were climbing away from a call I would have forgotten about had a miracle not occurred. As I got above the trees I could clearly see the cityscape of Austin in the distance. I aimed the helicopter for the cleft that represented South Congress Street. It cut straight north toward the capital building. The red granite dome stood next to Breckenridge hospital, our destination. As I drew closer I would drift a degree or two off of South Congress and head directly for the hospital.

Meanwhile, up there several miles ahead of us on South Congress a situation was developing. A twenty-three year old man was standing on a corner where South Congress crossed Ben White Boulevard. It was a busy intersection controlled by traffic lights with four lanes of traffic on each road. The young man stood on the corner of a vacant lot there. It was filled with trash, brush and small trees. Where he stood was a patch of bald dirt large enough to accommodate the young man's pickup truck and box trailer. On the side of the trailer was taped a poster that said in large letters, "Top dollar paid for your old blue jeans."

It was Saturday. He was there every Saturday working this business he had started buying and selling used blue jeans. Wearing worn out jeans was a fashion trend that was sure to be short lived. But while people were wearing them he was selling them. He bought them from passers-by at this vacant corner. Then he and his family washed and folded them. The young man then sold them to high end clothing stores in town. The stores then sold them as "pre-washed jeans" for several times more than the price they paid the young man. He too turned a tidy profit having sold them for considerably more than he paid for them. Business was brisk this now very warm Saturday morning. As we flew toward him a car pulled up at the curb. The passenger window was down. The young man leaned down and struck up a conversation with the driver.

Just before the rattle of our helicopters rotors could be heard there at that corner the young man suddenly stood up. His gesticulations at the man parked in the car were noticed across the street. There, a man at a bus stop saw the man in the car point at the gesticulating young blue jeans buyer. The man at the bus stop then heard a loud pop. He knew at once that the young man across the street from him had been shot in the chest. It was unmistakable. A bright red column of blood immediately spouted from the wound. As the car with the gunman sped away, the man at the bus stop stepped over to a pay phone. He dialed 911.

I noticed the intersection ahead where I would begin my right drift: South Congress and Ben White Boulevard. Then the EMS dispatcher called. "Lifeline One, divert. GSW (gunshot wound). Ben White and South Congress."

I pulled back on the cyclic and lowered the collective. *Whoa, Old Paint!* I said to myself. The helicopter slowed reluctantly. I keyed the intercom switch on my cyclic and said, "We're almost over top of that intersection, guys. I'm going to circle right and see if I can find a place to land." The nurse relayed my intentions to Dispatch over the radio.

As we descended I lined up the intersection to pass on my right so we could all look down. We saw exactly what the man across the street from him had seen. A young man on the street corner looked down incredulously at a hole in his shirt that was spouting blood from his heart. As we watched he sat down hard on the curb. Cars drove by him as he sat there dying.

We all scanned the area for someplace to land. The vacant lot behind him was unsuitable. There were too many trees, brush and lots of trash. Even so I turned the helicopter smartly to the right to complete a circle that would point me down South Congress toward downtown. By the time I got lined up on final approach I would either have a landing zone or I would not.

Unknown to the crew of Lifeline One, as I began my circle to land the 911 dispatcher called a police car. It was crossing the interstate headed west on Ben White. I rolled out on final and setup an approach to land in front of the man with the hole in his heart. The cop car was a block away. Traffic was still passing the gunshot victim. I pulled up on the collective to slow the forward speed. There was still no place to land. I was about to rock the nose forward and start gaining altitude again when the cop car came to a stop in the intersection. It blocked traffic completely. I followed the last car through the intersection and did a no-hover landing in front of the young man on the curb.

I noted the wires I had landed between. They had passed close on both sides of my rotor disk. I knew that this place would have been too small for the Four-Twelve to land. As I lowered the collective the crew bailed out. I kept the aircraft at full throttle and watched. My crew worked fast. Each placed a hand under the man's arms. Then they just snatched the young man off the curb. The paramedic looked at the bullet wound. Then to my amazement he just plugged his big index finger into it. The bleeding stopped abruptly. Then they all piled into the back of the helicopter. They didn't even plug in their helmets. Somehow they closed the door. Then they just shouted at me above the noise, "Go! Go! Go!"

So I went. I pulled up hard on the collective. The torque gauge registered its limit. The helicopter jumped off the ground and rocketed straight up. The moment we were above the wires and poles I pushed the LongRanger over on its nose. The rotors clawed the air. The little machine gained speed quickly. Without my crew plugged in I had to work the medical radios for them.

"Dispatch, this is Lifeline One pilot."

"Go ahead, Lifeline," the Dispatcher replied, sounding bored.

"I've got my crew in the back with a GSW patient. He has a hole in his chest. They're busy. I'm a minute out of Brackenridge. We need a lot of help on the pad right now."

"Received, Lifeline," was the calm response.

The flight to the hospital took only seconds, not minutes. I barely got to a high enough altitude to cross the city before I began descending again. I saw the helipad in the distance. People in scrubs were pouring out of the double doors of Crash. A couple of them pushed a big metal gurney. I swung out over the park across the street from the hospital and came skidding into the helipad like a baseball player sliding into home plate. We hot-unloaded, that is, we unloaded the patient while the rotors were still turning at full speed. It is a risky procedure, especially with the low rotor clearance of the LongRanger. But the ER crew was very experienced at it. They all stayed bent low at the waist to avoid the rotor blades that whirled just above them. In a moment the young man was off the helicopter and on the gurney. The flight crew kept their helmets on. The paramedic still had his finger in the hole in the young patient's chest.

The whole gaggle of scrubs and flight suits rushed past me. The crowd surrounding the gurney was through the ER doors long before I could get the engine shut down. Once the rotors stopped I stepped out and walked around the helicopter. The cabin door was held open by a strap made for the purpose. Inside the cabin it looked like a slaughter house. Blood was everywhere. Usually a flight like that left a lot of medical litter to clean up. There would be empty or half full I.V. bags, medical tubing and tape, EKG strips, sheets, medicine vials and syringe covers and so on. But oddly there was nothing back there. All the medical bags were still strapped in like we were ready to go flying. But they were all sprayed liberally with blood. It would take the crew some time to clean up their equipment. But that would come later. I opened the cabin windows and swung the door closed. Then I tied down the rotor blades.

After I refueled the helicopter my job was done. So I wandered into the ER. When I got into Crash the young man and my crew were nowhere to be found. A nurse told me they were back in Surgery. I thought that odd. I had never seen our crew go directly past the ER into Surgery before. So I left the ER the way I had come. When I reached the double doors to the helipad I called Dispatch on my handheld radio.

"Hold Lifeline One out of service."

"Received, Lifeline," the dispatcher replied.

I took a look at the helicopter as I headed toward the stairwell down to quarters. The bulbous windows of the aircraft seemed to look back at me. Its chin bubble seemed to form an ironic smile. I squinted into the sunlight glaring off the windshields. It formed bright eyeballs of sunshine in each dark blue windscreen. I thought again how fortunate we were to be in the smaller helicopter instead of the Four-twelve. Even though the patient might be dead now at least in the LongRanger he had a chance. We landed right next to him. Then I thought about the timing of the call. It was impossibly coincidental in so many facets.

There was no explainable reason that we had been there at just the right moment. Had we arrived a minute earlier or a minute later he might just have died there where he had been shot. Had we not responded to the tragedy of a family losing a loved one to cancer we would have been back at the hospital instead of overhead south Austin. Or we might have been on another call on the other side of the county. In either case we would have been too far away to respond as we did. I wondered why we had staged at the scene of the dead cancer patient. Why had we staged for exactly as long as we did? We were never told. Then there was the cop car that blocked traffic at exactly the right moment. Had it been two blocks past the scene as I rolled in to land, the patient would have bled to death as I circled above him.

I went back to Quarters thinking about all these things and waited for my crew. It was past lunch time before they came back. The story they told me just added to the unbelievable nature of our call. From their perspective, neither the nurse nor the paramedic had ever run a call like the one we just completed. Our paramedic said it was just a reflex reaction that he stuck his finger into the bullet hole. Doing that was in none of their medical protocols.

"It just seemed like the right thing to do at the time," he said. I thought about what the Medical Director of Lifeline would say about that reason for not following established protocols.

The nurse and the paramedic had never just thrown themselves in the helicopter with a patient. Even when we were in a hurry they carefully strapped the patient in first. In this case while lying on the floor with the patient they weren't even strapped in themselves. Neither crew member had ever failed to plug in their helmet on a call before. Neither had failed to give a medical report to Crash while inbound to the hospital. But in doing those things, they stopped an otherwise fatal chest wound from bleeding out. Their unconventional medical decisions had shortened the time from injury to surgery to an impossibly few minutes. Without their split second decisions, that young man would most certainly have been dead even before we got him to the hospital.

Another impossible stroke of good fortune was that a cardiologist and his team was preparing to do open heart surgery on a patient when the GSW call came in. Their patient was waiting in pre-op for a heart bypass when we landed at Brackenridge. The cardiologist was unaware of what was happening in Crash. He was just suddenly presented in the surgical suite with our patient and a gaggle of excited ER nurses and our flight crew pushing a man with a bullet hole in his heart. My crew and the ER Crash team never even stopped in the ER. They pushed the gurney straight through Crash and into the surgical suite.

The nurse and paramedic told me that the scene in the surgical theater was utter chaos. The cardiologist shouted above the din. "What in the blue blazes is going on here?"

Our paramedic gave the surgeon his report. Before he was done, surgical nurses had cut the patient's shirt free of the wound. They bathed his chest and our paramedic's gloves and arms in Betadine solution. When the surgeon saw the paramedic's finger in the hole he said, "Don't move that finger, son! Keep it right where it is!" The anesthesiologist knocked out the patient and intubated him while the cardiologist cracked his chest. As he exposed the man's heart he saw that the paramedic's finger was stuck like a cork in the man's aorta.

"I had my index finger right smack in the bullet hole," said the paramedic. "The doc told me to remove my finger on the count of three. As I did, the surgeon clamped the aorta."

While the cardiologist was suturing the man's wounded heart he glanced up over his mask at our still helmeted paramedic.

"Son," he said, "Today you folks were working for a higher power."

I believe truer words were never spoken. This whole call had God's hand in every stroke of it. I wonder if anyone else on the call saw that. Certainly I couldn't miss it.

Some days later I heard that our patient walked out of the hospital. I never heard from him or about him again. I don't know if the shooter was prosecuted or even caught. As a crew we moved on. We didn't talk about that call again. That was common, though. We never kept a call on our mind. We couldn't. The burden of doing so was too great. But for me, this call was a waterline. It was an event I could not forget or deny. I had seen a miracle, or rather a series of them. There was no other explanation about how all the pieces fell together so perfectly to save that young man's life. It brought home that I was regularly seeing miracles, too. Instead of shaking them off, now I was beginning to anticipate them. In doing so I even expected and prepared for miraculous events to occur that would change the outcome of a call. The weather would clear just in the locality I was flying. We would be diverted from a routine call to one that needed us overhead immediately. More often than not, those calls came in just as I was approaching or passing the scene of the call to which we had been diverted.

I came to firmly believe that no matter how insignificant it may appear, everything happens for a reason. People live, people die. But the results either way happen for a reason. Sometimes I was shown the reason later. But mostly the next call blotted out the answer. I have far more questions about our patients' outcomes than answers. But I came to believe in sight and not just by faith that God has his hand in every event in our lives. I had less of a need to see how things turned out for our patients as I came to understand more clearly that God had their well-being in His hands.

I don't feel guilty that it took me so long to come to that realization. Myopia is the normal human condition. From our narrow point of view in time, space and distance, we humans rarely see the whole picture. We are temporal beings. We don't often see events or other humans around us as connected by God's will with one another. On those rare occasions when we do see those connections, we who are bold in our faith call those event's "miracles." More often though, we human beings are quick to write them off as luck or fate. We ignore altogether the intercession of God in our lives.

That day in south Austin was staged for every person that participated in the event. It was one of probably thousands of opportunities all of us have gotten or will get in our lives to acknowledge the intercession of God. It was but one opportunity to accept Him. I believe that it was only one of thousands of events God staged, an unmistakable series of miracles for me to see. Finally, I saw them. Each one and then all of them together opened my eyes. It was one of the phenomena of the supernatural that my nurse friend Mary was trying to have me anticipate and recognize when I started flying with Lifeline. From that day on just as Mary said, I regularly saw miracles occur. They were all events that would require impossible odds to occur naturally, like winning back to back lotteries in a few days, or flipping a coin hundreds of time and always landing on heads.

What I saw regularly at Lifeline were supernatural events. But I found out that supernatural events happen every day. As Mary said I would, I came to live for those events to occur.

10 CRASH

When I told people in town I worked at Brackenridge hospital they would say, "That's nice, what do you do there?" Then I'd say, "I fly a helicopter for Lifeline Air Ambulance." Most would confess they'd never heard of us. As much as we got around, that surprised me. We stopped traffic all over town. We had our name painted on the bottom and sides of the helicopter. Sometimes as I took off over long lines of stopped cars the drivers sent special hand signals to me. I thought *they* at least would remember Lifeline, even if unkindly. Whenever I landed in neighborhoods and intersections we were an impromptu airshow. And it's not like we were stuck in a hangar hiding from the public, either. Every day people driving past the hospital could see the helicopter. It was parked up above them on the ER parking garage. Lots of people stared at it as they drove past. The helicopter was even lighted up like a billboard at night. Still, most people I met didn't know the city even had an air ambulance.

Plenty of people knew about Brackenridge Hospital, though. It had been a part of Austin since the late nineteenth century. Nothing of the old hospital remained. But its reputation from then until I worked there was the same. People with some connection to the medical profession especially perked up when I said "Brackenridge."

"Brackenridge is not a Trauma Center," they would say. "Brackenridge is 'Trauma Central.'" It was true. "Brack" always got the bad calls. Car accidents, poisonings, industrial accidents, gunshots, knifings, falls, multiple patient calls, multi-system trauma, and multiple casualty incidents - you name it. "Brack" got it.

One night I landed on the helipad to find a line of ambulances parked in front of Crash. They were all lined up in the circle drive with their rear doors open and their engines running. A couple of EMTs wandered among them. We had just brought in a medical patient from an outlying city on a hospital transfer flight. I had a feeling based on the traffic there ahead of him that our patient would be waiting a while to move from the ER to the treatment floor. As my troops headed through the door with the patient I refueled for the next flight. When I finally followed my crew into Crash, every trauma room was full. By the swarm of activity in the hallways I knew that the trauma rooms each had a critical patient in there. In each I could see and hear a trauma team working busily and noisily to save their lives. It sounded like a riot. I bumped into a nurse I knew who was part of one of the trauma teams.

Before she rushed past I said, "Busy!" quite unnecessarily. She stopped, turned a look toward the four rooms and looked back at me, nodding.

"What's going on here tonight?"

She pointed at one room after the other. "Gunshot, gunshot, knife, gunshot. The knife and gun club has been busy." Then she scooted off into the crowd to do whatever she was doing for her team.

As I suspected, our patient had been shuffled into one of the rooms in a hallway off of the trauma hall. That's where the medicine patients are placed. The sliding glass door to our patient's room was closed to keep out the noise. My crew was in there with the man we had transported. I stuck my head in to find out what was up. From the answer, I knew we'd be out of service for a while. So I decided to let my nosiness get the better of me. Instead of shuffling back to Quarters, I decided to stay in Crash and watch the trauma circus.

I had no sooner gotten to the nurses station before a physician came through a curtain in front of Trauma Room four. He threw back the curtain with force. It stayed open. Looking over his shoulder I saw a tough looking young black man sitting up on the examination table. He wore no shirt. He was covered with tattoos. They blended with his dark skin in such a way that none of them were legible. They just looked like shades of black on black. I failed to notice the bullet holes in him. Instead I was drawn to his wide grin. Most of his teeth appeared to be capped with gold. In his ear I could see what appeared to be a large diamond. It had to be a rhinestone. I'd never seen a rhinestone, let alone a diamond that big.

The doctor was very angry. I knew this because he called his patient a "bastard." Calm and collected doctors don't do that. Specifically, he looked toward the nurses' station and me and said, "That bastard called me a chump! A chump! I'm in there trying to save his life and he's calling me that!" Since the patient was grinning, I suspected he didn't mind being called a bastard. If he knew his life was in jeopardy he didn't appear to care. The doctor looked frazzled. It was clear that he needed a moment to collect himself. When he had done so, he waded back through the fray in the hallway. I had to admire him when he re-entered the trauma room. The patient was still grinning his golden grin. Then a tech pulled the curtain closed.

A nurse who had been in Trauma Four was chatting with the charge nurse. She said the patient in there had at least two nine millimeter gunshot wounds. She also said that the patient had given the doctor a hard time as he did his examination. He was playing tough guy with the doctor. He did indeed call the doctor a "chump." He said he made more money in one night selling drugs than the doctor made in a month. As the doctor looked for more bullet holes the man with the golden teeth said, "A man gotta' be a chump to be a doctor. Workin' this hard for no money. You doctors is all chumps." That's when the doctor exploded.

The trauma circus went on. I walked down the hall past "Trauma Three." In the room beside the mouthy drug dealer lay a dirty, sweaty and heavily bruised white man. He had a prominent shiner on one eye. It was big and blue. If he was still alive by morning I figured he wouldn't be looking out of that eye for a while. His hair was thin and heavily shot with gray, as was his beard. Both were mixed with dirt and dry grass, as though he had been rolling around in both. He looked to be in his seventies. Clearly, life had not been kind to him, especially recently. He had several bullet holes in his torso. I spotted them by the little trickles of blood that ran down his chest and side. Otherwise the skin on his chest and arms bore several wide and apparently both old and newer scars. He was naked but for his underwear. Despite the fact that a half dozen scrub clad people were simultaneously working on him he was loudly shouting curses and epithets. I gathered that they were aimed at the man in the next trauma room. I was just guessing, but willing to bet that the guy in Trauma Two had delivered the black eye at least. He'd probably done the shooting as well.

The target of Trauma Three's sobriquets lay on the exam table in Trauma Two shouting back. His muddy work boots lay on the floor. A nurse was busily removing his blue jeans with a set of shears made for the purpose. He looked to be in his fifties. His hair was long and black. Along with the rest of his exposed body it glistened with sweat and smeared blood. Across his forearms and shoulders were deep wounds. The flesh at these wound sites was laid open as though someone had been trying to fillet him. I could see the white dermis, yellow fat and the red flesh of muscle within the wounds. I couldn't understand why they weren't pouring blood. I moved on.

Since first arriving in Crash the last trauma room had grown quiet. The bright exam light had been turned off. Except for the dead person on the exam table the room was empty. He had apparently succumbed to the gunshot he received before his trip to Brackenridge. The body on the exam table was covered with a green sheet like those used in surgical suites. Above his face the sheet tented above what I knew was an ET tube. It was common to leave it there after a patient died. During the autopsy the folks in the morgue could then attest to its proper placement before the deceased had shuffled off his moral coil. I knew the body would be there for a while. In Crash, dead people were of the lowest priority. Until some tech could break free to remove the body to the hospital morgue, he and the hospital waste on the floor around him would remain where they were.

That was not a typical night at Brackenridge Hospital, but it happened on my watch from time to time. It was the kind of night that made Brack's reputation. It was always a magnet for patients with potentially fatal illness or injury. Even though I was new to Austin, I already knew that about Brack. I had known it since I was just a little boy. That was when I saw pictures of Brackenridge Crash in action. Most of the country saw the same pictures, too. They were published in Life magazine. In 1966 a sniper firing from the University of Texas clock tower randomly shot dozens of innocent people. His shots ranged across the campus and the streets of downtown Austin in what was called, "the first mass casualty assault in American history." Whether or not it was, the mass murder shocked America. Through the eyes of Life photographers America saw Brackenridge Crash which received and treated the sniper's victims.

Seeing those pictures was the first time I realized that hospitals don't just birth babies. It was also the first time I heard the term, "trauma center" used. The pictures in the magazine were black and white. They were in some cases blurred images suggesting the speed and controlled chaos with which the trauma teams worked. Triage sorted arriving patients, separating the dead from those who might yet live. The seriously injured received a classification and the concerted actions of a dedicated team. It was called a "trauma stat." "Stat" meant fast. Stat mean "first priority." Trauma stats called for fast and efficient execution of treatment protocols. It is not melodramatic to say the "trauma stats" I saw often snatched people out of the jaws of death. Trauma Room One that night was the example of a Trauma Stat that was unsuccessful. Memories I have of times like that at Brackenridge stay with me. They are preserved in a cluster. Those memories mostly blur together like the black and white pictures I saw in that 'Life' magazine. Some of the images in my mind's eye are in color. But always the images seem blurred, full of shock and chaos.

Most Lifeline pilots were happy to remain ignorant about what happened in the cabin. There wasn't much a pilot had to know. We were trained in avoiding airborne and blood borne pathogens. Anybody in the helicopter was exposed to those. They were carried in the air and bodily fluids of our patients. Exposure to HIV, hepatitis, tuberculosis, even influenza were risks we took in carrying sick people in the closed cabin of our aircraft. We got shots to lessen the likelihood of contracting some of them. We wore masks sometimes as protection against others. They were probably slightly better to have than nothing. We were stuck with the airborne stuff, but the pilots learned ways to avoid blood and body fluid. The most popular method was to walk away from the mess after the flight and leave it to our medical crew to clean up. That was not always popular with the crew, but they understood the reason the pilots shied away from the spooge (body fluids).

I was different. I usually helped the crew clean up. They taught me how to avoid the hazards like dropped needles or splashing spooge or bleach in my face. I often wore a smock and a plastic mask for the splashes. I always wore rubber gloves. The medics left me to doing the big stuff like washing the cabin and sides of the helicopter with a hose. I picked up the big items like expended IV and ambu bags. I saw it as my contribution to the medical end of our business. I never minded helping the crew. In fact, it fascinated me. I liked being involved and learning about the diseases and mechanisms of injury that got our patients a ride on Lifeline. In truth, learning about the physiology of sickness and injury was probably selfish of me. I found that knowing about the medical problems of my passengers helped me deal better with their outcome – good or bad. I cared about the patients. I wanted to know whether or not they got well. The other pilots surely cared for their patients they carried. They just didn't want to know much about them. It may have been part of their coping mechanism. They would rather just as soon forget about one call and go on to another.

Since I was interested in the medical part of what we did, I followed the patients inside. Sometimes I kept touch with them and their families for days or weeks. Noting my interest, my crew and the people in the ER were happy to educate me. I got to know the whole regular ER staff and most of the doctors. The docs included a full range of specialists. Besides trauma surgeons, they included dentists and oral surgeons, eye specialists, ear, nose and throat docs, plastic surgeons, orthopedists, radiologists and doctors who treat every system, organ and organ group. When they saw my interest they often took time to explain what they were doing. Because it was all so new to me I was fascinated. I was especially captivated by the neurologists.

It was fortunate for me that Brackenridge Hospital was a "Level One" Trauma Center. That means that besides all the other specialist that were always there, Brack had a full-time neurologist – a brain surgeon - always immediately available. We brought in lots of work for them. I saw all kinds of brain injury cases. I thought the bulk of them would be from car accidents. I thought that was all brain surgeons did in Crash was fix heads broken in cars. But trauma was only one kind of brain injury we transported and they treated. Stroke victims probably constituted as large a group of brain injury patients as the ones we brought in from trauma.

I learned that there are different kinds of strokes. To my layman's view, hemorrhagic strokes looked easy to diagnose and hard to treat. They were called "brain bleeds." When a neurologist suspected that blood was leaking inside a skull, radiologists got involved. They would inject a radioactive dye into the patient's blood. Where the blood was leaking the dye left a dark patch on an x-ray. Neophyte that I was, I could see even the small leaks.

Trauma causing a brain bleed came from some sharp blow. Hitting a dashboard, an assault with a blunt object or a fall from a ladder could do it. The cranium didn't need to break, either, to get it bleeding. The brain could bruise from bouncing against the inside of the skull. That's a brain concussion. Concussions can ring your bell or kill you. It was up to the neurologist to quickly decide which was more likely and treat it properly.

Brain bleeds could also take place from a leaking aneurysm. Aneurysms are thin spots in the blood vessel walls that can swell like a balloon. Sometimes they leak. Sometimes they rupture. Caught in time, they could often be repaired. Those that couldn't be repaired burst quickly and painlessly. We didn't transport people whose brain aneurysms ruptured because we didn't fly dead people. I always thought that an easy way to go.

The strokes that came in from a 911 call usually presented the classic signs. The patient would have facial droop, weakness in the limbs on one side and difficulty speaking. These strokes were usually either high blood pressure related leaks or ischemic strokes. High blood pressure caused brain bleeds. Ischemic strokes didn't leak blood. They were also called "brain attacks" because the mechanism of them was the same as a heart attack. A clot would block an artery or vein within the brain. No blood flowing beyond the clot would cause tissue to die. The longer it took for the patient to reach treatment, the more brain tissue would die. Those were the kind of strokes where Lifeline could make a difference. We trimmed minutes off their transport and saved a lot of brain matter by doing it.

Hemorrhagic strokes needed rapid chemical or surgical intervention to stop the bleeding. Ischemic strokes needed tPA. I never heard it called by its name, "tissue plasminogen activator." But I knew it worked like drain cleaner. It ate away the clot and restored blood flow to the affected area of the brain. Another kind of stroke where tPA was administered was for "Transient Ischemic Attacks" or TIAs. Little clots in the brain would move and stick, move and stick. The result presented a patient who was with you one minute and gone to their own little mental place the next. I told my wife about TIAs once. She responded that I must have had lots of them. "No honey," I replied. "I just have my 'wife filter' working. Sometimes when you talk I drift off to my own happy place and miss what you're saying." She threatened me with a hemorrhagic event.

The first stroke patient I transported was a transfer from a little hospital west of Austin. I noticed as we loaded him that he appeared to be sleeping peacefully. Occasionally though, he would yawn widely. I asked the crew why he was yawning so much.

"That's what we do when we don't have enough oxygen in our brain," the nurse told me. "This man's stroke is blocking the blood from getting to his brain. The brain is sensing it needs more oxygen."

Any raw blood leaking into the skull kills brain tissue. It also increases pressure inside the skull. I saw neurologists install what looked like a pressure relief valve in people's skulls. These were used like the valve on a tire to measure the amount of pressure in the skull. As an injured brain would swell pressure would increase. Too much pressure in there and in short order the patient would die. I always wondered why the neurologists didn't remove a section of skull to let the brain swell. Maybe I should be a brain surgeon. I hear they're doing that now.

I learned something about the practice of medicine every day I flew sick people. Because I worked out of Brackenridge I learned more than I would have in a less critical medical environment. I saw the most critical cases come into Brackenridge. After a while, I came to see these terrible, life changing or life ending events as part of my normal day. Consequently, I lost empathy for people who came to the emergency room for anything less than a life threatening emergency. Then I met the fakers and attention getters. There were many of them. They were very clever. They knew just what to say to the 9-1-1 dispatcher to get a ride to the hospital. Many of them were drug dependent and poor. The used the EMS system to supply their drug habits and support their terrible life choices. They even knew how to get transported by Lifeline. The more of those types I carried, the less I liked them.

I felt the same way about people who walked into the ER under their own power. If a patient arrived on a gurney, or even in a wheel chair I gave them the benefit of the doubt. But pedestrians who weren't broken, bleeding profusely or suffering from an obvious stroke or crushing chest pain got the jaundiced eye from me. In some cases those pedestrians were just clogging up the system for people who really needed care.

I knew Austin. It has its own character. Part of that character includes a type not seen in say, West Texas. There a cowboy has to lose a limb or break a major bone before he sees a doctor, let alone goes to an emergency room. In Austin however, there are a good number of sissies. I looked at them as "the latte' crowd." No cowboy worth his salt would ever order, let alone drink a latte'. Coffee, black – yes. But not latte'. Not so in Austin. In fact there were many I met or saw in Austin who would consider being served a cold latte' an emergency in itself. An emergency calls for immediate action. If you think of getting a cold latte as an emergency, chances are you'd fit in Austin. When these "cold latte'" characters walked into our ER, I was piqued. They never seemed to have anything wrong with them that couldn't be treated by two aspirin and a nap. Watching them come and take up the time reserved for life threatening emergencies irked me. The nurses and doctors who treated them were almost always compassionate, sympathetic, patient and professional.

They were also diplomatic, something I could never be if I was a triage nurse. But the triage nurses would never give a patient the impression that the latte types' emergency didn't merit their attention. When I saw these wimps arrive at the triage desk and check in I played out a fantasy. In my fantasy, I worked in triage. In my fantasy, I was the ultimate authority in charge of who was treated. Some sissy my age and gender would show up whining about a broken finger. I would say, "Put on your big-boy pants and get out of my emergency room. Go home and tape your broken finger to a Popsicle stick, Mr. Volleyball Player. If it hurts, ice it down and take an aspirin. The sign on the driveway says 'Emergency Room.' Get out of here before I demonstrate on you what that word "emergency" means!"

A latte' type complaining about a rash would get the demonstration. In my fantasy, I would simply grab him by the collar, drag him outside and throw him off the helipad. The two story fall into the street below would probably qualify him for emergency room treatment. Then, I could then shout down, "Okay, now you qualify. I'll send an ambulance. You must have missed the sign out front here. This is a trauma center. Your rash, headache or virus doesn't qualify for service here. Your broken femur and battered head is trauma. We'll come get you now."

But all I could really do for the sissies was shake my head and walk on while they clogged the system. Because of them, people with a real medical emergency sometimes died waiting for treatment. I saw it. People in obvious distress were mixed in the waiting room with no real reason for them to be in the ER at all. The fakers made the most noise. Perhaps that was why they were seen first. I once saw a stoic old lady sitting in the ER. I came back over an hour later and she was still there. The next time I came by she was gone. I asked the triage nurse what happened to her. She said the old lady had suddenly drawn their attention by dying of a heart attack. That changed me permanently so far as my tolerance for people who stole medical care from those who needed it. I could forgive the triage nurses for missing really sick people sometimes. They saw so many whiney cold latte' types.

I never saw anyone arrive at the ER and look confused about where to go to see a doctor. They all went through the big glass doors under the "Emergency Room" sign and stepped up to the triage desk. While some people with a headache and fever arrived in wheelchairs, I saw people walk in who were having a stroke or a heart attack. People with a bump on the head or a gunshot wound to the head would walk into the ER with their head wrapped in a bloody towel. Sorting out the serious from not so serious patients was the job of the triage nurse they met.

The busiest part of the emergency room after triage was referred to as "Treatment." This was where the less serious patients went. Treatment took care of the headaches, flu symptoms, minor cuts that needed stiches and broken wrists that needed a cast. Treatment cases were most always released after the treatment was done. Odd ones stayed overnight, but not often. These were referred to as, "treated and released." Most of those people who came into Treatment never knew about the other side of the ER – Crash. That's where we worked. Crash was for the really serious stuff. Crash could work multiple trauma stats simultaneously and the patients in treatment would never know it was happening. Lots of people went from Crash to surgery. Lots of others went from Crash to the morgue. If Treatment patients had to wait it was often because the whole ER staff was called to work a trauma stat in Crash. There were just so many people available to staff the ER. Crash was life and death. Crash always got first priority.

The EMS entrance to Crash was probably not even noticed by people heading for the emergency room. The "EMS Only" sign above our entrance to Crash was so innocuous most people probably never noticed it. If they did try to enter the double doors we used they would find them secured by a numbered keypad. The keypads to all the hospital ambulance entrances I visited always included the numbers

"9-1-1." At Brack, the double doors opened into a long, wide and well-lit hallway. Here, backboards and gurneys lined the walls. The backboards were painted with the initials of the ambulance service that owned them. "TCEMS" (Travis County EMS) was a popular one, for example. After the patient was moved off the board, the board was moved to the hallway. EMS services that dropped off a patient on one backboard went to this row against the wall to replace the one they left the patient upon.

The boards stood on end in a long row. They looked a row of coffin lids. Often they were still covered with adhesive tape, dried blood and sometimes tissue and hair from the trauma victims who had come into Crash strapped and taped to them. It was up to the backboard's owners to take the bloody boards outside to the wash rack and clean them up. When I had time to kill, I cleaned backboards for them. I figured it helped the ambulance crews and volunteers to get back into service faster. They seemed pleased when they could just grab a clean backboard and leave. Occasionally I'd see a few boards from the ambulance service in my little home town west of Austin. I'd clean them, leave one in the hallway and throw the rest in the back of my pickup. On the way home I'd drop them off at the ambulance station.

In the hallway along with the backboards were a line of stainless steel hospital gurneys. Ambulance crews had their own gurneys. But they'd grab one of the big stainless steel ones when they had more patients on-board than ambulance gurneys. We didn't have a gurney on the helicopter so we used the steel gurneys exclusively. The pilots were not supposed to help load or unload patients. If we strained our back at the scene, the helicopter, crew and patient would be stuck. But on occasion I helped the crew unload the patient at the hospital. Mostly I'd just get a gurney and hold it in place while the crew slid the patient onto it. Nobody strained their back then. But I only did that when there were no Crash personnel available to help.

The crew would wheel the patient off the helipad and through the double doors to Crash. Once past the row of backboards at the end of the hallway there was a second set of sliding glass doors. They were electrically opened by slapping a metal plate on the wall while approaching the doors. Behind those doors were the heart of Crash – the treatment rooms.

Medical emergencies we looked at were categorized as either "medicine" or "trauma." At Lifeline, "medicine" patients didn't suffer from a sprain or generalized pain. In Lifeline's arena, "medicine" was a heart attack, a rupturing aneurysm, a stroke, overdose or other poisoning. Often I saw medicine patients survive against impossible odds. They did so mostly because they were treated within minutes of the life threatening event. Saving time: that's what the helicopter was for. Rapid and professional treatment, that's what the medicine rooms in Crash were for.

Plenty of medicine calls we ran were life and death. But the most critical medicine cases never seemed to generate the kind of action that the arrival of serious trauma case caused. Serious trauma would be a thoroughly broken body, known as "multi-system trauma". A crushed chest, a crushed skull, severed or amputated limbs, knife or gunshot wounds all qualified as the kind of serious trauma we transported. Trauma always got people worked up. Arriving at the scene seeing first responders running was a sign. First responders are supposed to offer an example of calm. A running first responder meant something bad was happening. A pediatric case most often garnered a serious response at the scene. Cardiac arrests, CPR in progress, multi-car accidents and electrocutions all seemed to raise the bar on how serious the situation was. I also found that if there was safety glass in a wound, it probably qualified as our kind of serious trauma. If the patient was alive after any of these injuries they got a ride to Crash with Lifeline. And when we got there, they went to a trauma room there.

The main hallway in Crash was lined with trauma rooms. There were five of them. The first four were for adults. The fifth room was designed and stocked for children. It was paid for by golfer Tom Kite, a local celebrity whose name was on a plaque that hung outside the room. The children's trauma room could be almost instantly warmed to a hundred and thirty degrees Fahrenheit. Children in shock often become hypothermic. A cold core temperature can be fatal, especially to little kids. Part of Tom Kite's largess bought a heater that worked in that room with the speed and probably about as many BTUs as Lifeline One's turbine engines.

The adult trauma rooms were open bays separated from each other by opaque glass dividers. Each one was similarly well stocked to handle any traumatic injury that Brack saw. They were likewise kept clean as a surgical theater because they often became just that. I saw plenty of surgery done in them. Although each could be closed off by sliding glass doors, usually their sliding doors remained open. A privacy curtain could be pulled across the doorway, but I didn't see them used very often.

Crash as a whole was kept very cold. I was told it was because germs don't do well in the cold. That cold temperature was often uncomfortable on the patients though. Patients in Crash were almost always relieved of all their clothes. The patient took them off or the Crash team cut them off. Patients usually lay naked, covered only by a thin sheet or hospital gown. Lying on a backboard or cold metal examination table, it wasn't long before their teeth were chattering. For these people there was the blanket warmer. I spent a lot of time fetching warm blankets for cold patients. When the nurses didn't have the time, I loved wrapping some chilly person with warm blankets. Sometimes I'd bundle them with four or five of the cotton blankets fresh out of the warmer. It often made me a popular guy with a chilly patient and with the nurses who could go on with something I could not do.

The long hallway with the trauma rooms ended at the nurses' station. Then it turned ninety degrees into a shorter hallway. Four more glass enclosed rooms opened onto this hallway. They were the "medicine" rooms. We rolled heart attack and stroke patients in there. Unlike the trauma rooms, the medicine rooms were sparsely equipped. We rolled in the steel gurney and moved the patient into a hospital bed. The crew worked with a Crash nurse to hook them to a heart monitor and oxygen and hang their bags of medications. After the crew made their report to the attending physician their job there was done. They'd grab a couple of armloads of medical supplies to restock and head back to the helicopter.

All the rooms and hallways in Crash were done up in the same light green tile walls. On the floors was seamless linoleum. Paint on the walls and cracks in floor tile trap germs. The tile walls and one-piece linoleum floor in Crash shed blood. The single piece linoleum was also curved at the base and ran a few inches up the wall. It acted as a catch basin for spilled fluids. A big brass floor drain allowed the fluids to drain out of the room. Out of them came the powerful scent of antiseptic floor cleaner. The hospital was big on keeping things clean. That was never truer than in Crash - except when it got really busy. Most often though, Crash smelled more like a hospital than the rest of the hospital. I came to look forward to that smell when I slapped the plate that opened the hallway doors. It usually overpowered the smell of gasoline, oil and diesel fuel, burned flesh, vomit, blood, feces and urine that came in with the patients. Yes, I much preferred the smell of hospital disinfectant.

An x-ray viewer was mounted across the hall from each trauma room. I got pretty good at being able to tell what was happening in each room just by glancing at the x-rays as I passed. At first, X-ray film looked to me like so many shadowy black and white images. But because I showed interest in what happened in Crash, x-ray techs, radiologists, nurses and my flight crew all took time to teach me how to read them. The most obvious images showed the stark outlines of broken or shattered bones, shards of metal or medical hardware like a pace maker or metal hip joint. Sometimes I saw the business end of various kinds of ammunition among the shadows of an appendage or torso. Because they were made of lead, bullets and shotgun pellets showed up in bright silhouette.

After I learned what to look for, I could tell what was going on inside soft tissue, too. Once I learned what normal x-rays looked like, I could pick out abnormalities. I could tell when organs were displaced. Sometimes I could see compressed lungs or organs in the belly displaced by blood. I could see a heart struggling to beat inside a chest cavity filled with blood, or air or organs intruding through a ruptured diaphragm. I could see the cloudy image of cancer or serious internal bleeding. I saw small and large blank air cavities in parts of the body where no air belonged. I was told those conditions were known respectively as a pneumothorax or hemothorax. A "pneumo" was an invasion of the body by air. A ruptured lung or punctured chest wall could cause these. A "hemo" was caused by crushed organs or ruptured blood vessels leaking into the body cavity. When I heard my crew report that we were inbound with a "hemo-pneumo," I knew what was happening to the patient. After I got my helicopter ready for the next flight I got to see how the doctors treated all these injuries. Often a surgeon working in a trauma room would cut an incision between the patient's ribs. Then he would insert a chest tube. It was a thick rubber surgical tube attached to a vacuum system. The vacuum drained air and blood from inside the chest wall. Lungs work in a vacuum. When the vacuum is compromised, lungs collapse. When lungs collapse some quick action is required or the patient dies. One of those actions was inserting a chest tube.

I didn't see it done often, especially in the ER where a doctor can install a chest tube. But on the helicopter my crew sometimes used chest "darts." In order to restore the vacuum in the chest, the darts were inserted between the ribs and through the chest wall. The darts were long, large gauge hollow needles with a balloon valve on the end. The valve allowed blood and air to pass out of the chest. Then they closed flat and sealed to keep from admitting air back in. I saw darts inserted that spurted blood. At first I was taken aback by seeing that. But then I saw relief on a patient's face. Suddenly, the blood in their chest that was crushing their lungs was emptied to allow them to draw an increasingly deeper breath.

Occasionally, I saw really unusual x-rays. Early one Sunday morning for example, I followed my crew as they pushed a medicine patient into Crash. A set of x-rays snapped up on a reader in front of one of the trauma rooms had drawn a small crowd. They were pointing to something and nodding knowingly at one another. The patient represented by the X-ray was reclined on an examination table only a few feet away. He was facing away from the crowd at the x-ray reader. The group was saying nothing out loud. I stopped to look. It was indeed a most unusual set of x-rays. It showed the patient's belly. In the middle of the x-ray was the stark outline of a long, steel, police-style flashlight. I realized that it had not been laid on the patient's belly and then x-rayed. Rather, it completely filled the area normally occupied by the patient's colon. How it got there was open to speculation. That speculation was silent but rampant in that little clutch of Crash and EMS personnel standing before the x-ray.

In my time at Lifeline I found that such incidents were not uncommon. I saw x-rays of colons bearing some amazing things. The patients always denied knowing how these things got up there. Besides the police flashlight, X-rays I actually saw revealed: a Coke bottle, light bulbs of various sizes, a comb, a hair brush and a large cucumber. I even saw one set of x-rays showing a pair of gerbils contained within the patient's lower digestive tract. One of those little fellows managed to climb much farther into the patient's large intestine than the other. I thought the gerbil incident was the most interesting. Those little animal skeletons inside the guy's belly looked so out of place. I asked how the doctor was so sure in diagnosing the species of rodent he was looking at on the x-ray with me. All I could make out after all was a pair of little skeletons visible in the X-ray.

"What you see here is called, 'gerbiling,' in the community that practices it. I've seen it a number of times. It's a fad, I suppose. The individual sets a gerbil loose in his intestines and lets it wander around in there."

I must have appeared as astonished as I felt. "Well doc," I replied. "I don't even want to know how they get in there."

"No, Paul," he replied. "You wouldn't want to know. But look here. Once they get in there they are full of surprises. I guess that's why people do it. You'll see here that one of them has made it almost the full length of this patient's large intestine. Unless they suffocate like these two apparently have, I'm told they eventually find their way out."

"The same way they got in, I hope."

"We would hope so." The doctor grinned, but tried to maintain some decorum as he pointed out the gerbil farthest up the patient's colon. "This little fellow apparently got lost."

"Good thing," I replied. "Otherwise this guy might have found out what a live gerbil tastes like."

The trauma rooms were lined by stainless steel and glass cabinets standing along the green tiled walls. They were stocked with larger quantities of the same medical equipment our nurse and paramedic carried in their medical bags. These included large stocks of plastic bags of IV fluid and surgical implements otherwise found in the surgical theaters behind the emergency room.

A stainless steel examining table stood bolted to the floor in the center of the room. An ER tech told me that morticians used tables like these where embalming was done. They could apparently hold a significant volume of spilled blood and fluids. A drain at one end allowed the fluid to be collected into catch basins or plastic bags. I saw the tables at Brackenridge drain more fluid from a person than I thought a body could hold.

Above the examining table was an exceptionally bright adjustable light. The light was focused with a parabolic mirror a couple feet in diameter. When the light was on, it emitted a distinctive bright orange glow. The exam light shone from any trauma room was so bright that it illuminated the hallway from end to end.

When things were quiet in Crash there was usually a janitor or ER tech mopping the place. This was a continuous, tedious and dirty job that never ended. Someone was always mopping the emergency room. Especially after a trauma stat concluded, the rooms looked like abandoned battlefields. Medical debris was scattered across the floor. Bloody bandages, pieces of clothing, and splatters of blood and body fluids covered the floor around the exam table. Rolling stainless steel trays were piled with used surgical instruments and 'Sharps," (things that cut, poke or stick, like scalpels and hypodermic needles). After the patient was moved out of the room though, the cleaning crew really got busy. When more trauma was inbound the cleaning crew sometimes looked like a medical version of an Indianapolis pit crew. One tech literally ran around the room filling red plastic bags with the piles of medical waste. Another swabbed counters and trays. Yet another was mopping and spraying disinfectant -- all this to get the room ready for the next patient.

The nurses who worked in Crash had already worked in every specialty area of a hospital. They worked in burn units, dialysis clinics, Intensive Care Units (ICUs), Cardiac Care Units (CCU) Neo-natal ICUs (NICUs, pronounced "Nick-You"), the ER triage desk and treatment area and on all the patient floors from pediatrics to geriatrics. They worked on people in preparation for surgery. They worked within the surgical suite. They worked in recovery and out the door in discharge. They wheeled patients in from their car on gurneys and in wheel chairs, from their cars, from ambulances and from my helicopter. They cared for patients with every medical problem, disease and traumatic injury I would ever see. I considered the ER nurses the "A" team. Our flight nurses were drawn from this cadre.

Nurses came in as wide a variety of specialties as the doctors. There were Registered Nurses (RNs), Licensed Vocational Nurses (LVNs), Nurse Practitioners and Certified Registered Nurse Anesthetists (CRNAs). Once I realized the wide varieties of specialties they had, I no longer asked if nurse was an RN. I asked their specialty. They were justifiably proud of their academic achievements, their training and qualifications. Like college professors, they liked having their degrees and special qualifications listed after their names. They reminded me of Boy Scouts with their sash covered with merit badges. They appreciated it when I recognized them for the hard work. They maintained their specialty by taking continuing education and arduous testing. This was done at great personal expense. They often had to think and act quickly. They had to know their jobs well. They were understandably perfectionists. No excuse was accepted if they didn't do things right one hundred percent of the time. And they expected no less of the people they worked with. They all hated to lose -- a life or an argument.

The Emergency Room Technicians (ER techs) did some of the hardest and most thankless jobs in Crash. They were to Crash what Grunts (infantry riflemen) were to the Marines. They did the heavy lifting and the dirty work. Important as they were they got the lowest pay, the least notice and were the least appreciated of the Crash crew. In those rare times when there were no techs available I realized that Crash couldn't run without them. When the deck of Crash was cleared for action for an inbound rush of trauma it was the techs that did the deck clearing. On the helipad, when I landed there were usually six people lifting the patient from the aircraft to the gurney. A couple of the lifters were always techs. Once the gurney was moved into the trauma room it was often just two techs moving the patient and the backboard from the gurney to the examining table. Before the patient left Crash, techs had probably lifted them for x-rays and CAT scans from the gurneys to exam tables and back a half dozen times. When patients bled, or voided their bowels or bladders or threw up it was the ER tech standing by to do the cleanup. When the patient died the techs loaded the body bag, shuffled the corpse to the morgue and cleaned and prepared the trauma room for the next patient. They also stocked the trauma rooms, assisted in the acute care and Treatment areas, ran errands, tracked down staff, called the cops and generally did anything that anyone in Crash couldn't or didn't want to do.

I found that regardless of the harassment they sometime received or fatigue they suffered, emergency room technicians always did their jobs well and faithfully. They all seemed to maintain an attitude of service and a willing spirit. Busy as they were, I often saw the techs take the time to do for others. They would reach out a hand to comfort a patient. They'd stop what they were doing to meet a patient's need or request. I even saw them take a moment to offer a sensitive word of sympathy to patients or their families. Lots of others working the ER could well have learned things about maintaining a positive, caring attitude toward people by observing the ER techs. They may not have had the degree or the social stature of others who worked Crash, but that never mattered to them. I always suspected that some of those humble people were actually the angels it is said wander among us unrecognized.

Besides the medical professionals in the ER, I found that cops too helped to populate Crash. I have seen city police officers, county sheriff's deputies, homicide detectives, state troopers, federal marshals, constables, F.B.I., D.E.A. and even U.S. Secret Service agents in Crash at one time or another. The hospital hired moonlighting cops for security. They hung out most of the time in a little bulletproof glass booth near the triage desk. Since they were moonlighters the police agencies represented in the booth were a mixed bag. Most often Austin PD and Travis County deputies were in there. But we had a fair number of state troopers and cops from outlying towns and counties in the security box, too. It was a little office faced in bullet proof glass that offered direct observation to the doors of the ER. Everybody entering got the visual once over by at least one of the policemen on duty. They made a surprising number of arrests of wanted individuals' right there in the ER lobby.

The hospital decided to put police in the ER after the murders that took place in Crash one night. Some years before I joined Lifeline an ambulance crew brought in a patient from a drug deal gone bad. The patient had been shot. While he was being treated in Crash, the man who shot him showed up at the ER. He walked right past the triage nurse carrying a pump shotgun. She called the police. Before they could respond the gunman walked into Crash like he knew right where he was going. He found his intended victim being treated by a doctor and nurse. He opened up with the shotgun and killed all three. Shortly thereafter a policeman arrived and killed him. So now there's a plaque in one of the trauma rooms at Brackenridge with the name of the doctor and nurse who were killed that night emblazoned on it. The hospital didn't want to make any more plaques like that. So Brackenridge has their own police officers in the ER.

Our hospital cops did a lot more than protect the people in the ER. Among their duties was to run a "wants and warrants" check on everybody who showed up at the ER. I recall several occasions when they walked into Crash and quietly chained a patient to their gurney. If the patient was conscious the cops informed the patient that they were under arrest. If not, when they woke up they found the shackle on their ankle attached to the gurney. One patient I brought in had already had a really bad day. When his name was reported to the hospital police that bad day got even worse.

Hard as it might be to believe, the patient was drunk when he jumped into the Colorado River for a swim. He was floating some distance from the dock near the lakeside bar where he had spent most of the day. He floated far enough out in the river that he was run over by a boat driven by another drunk. The swimmer almost got out of the way in time, but the boat's propeller clipped his ankle. As we got him loaded on the helicopter I could see that the propeller had almost shearing off his foot just above the ankle joint. When I came back to the ER to see how he was doing I found the patient had a shackle on his good ankle. He evidently had an old warrant out for his arrest. It was a bad day for him.

The cops in the bulletproof booth dealt with the riff raff so neither the Lifeline crew or the hospital staff had to do so. Bums were constantly coming in saying they were sick. Some were, and they were treated. But most were just looking for a place to spend a cold night indoors and maybe get a free meal. I can't blame them. But once triage or an examination determined they were fakers the police showed them the door. I heard shouting once in a while from them but never saw any of them leave in a police car in handcuffs.

Working on the helipad or while in Crash I saw quite a number of the Austin PD officers handling patients. Most were suspects needing treatment before they went to jail. They arrived in cruisers. The officers usually led their charges through treatment for triage. Sometimes though, the police brought a banged up suspect directly into Crash. These usually came through the EMS door in a wheelchair or on a gurney. The cops did a pretty good job of triage with these patients. They were pretty beat up looking.

Once I saw an officer quietly sitting in Crash looking like a patient himself. His uniform was badly torn. It was scuffed with grass stain and mud. He had made an effort to neaten himself up some by tucking in his shirt. But he had numerous bruises, contusions and scratches that needed attention. I thought he was definitely "out of service for repair." When he rose and walked into one of the treatment rooms I thought it was his turn. But when he parted the curtain, on the treatment table lay a guy looking considerably worse than the cop. I leaned inside the room and over the cop's shoulder.

"Anybody you know?" I asked him. He turned, saw my flight suit and smiled.

"We haven't been formally introduced, but I brought him here shortly after we met."

The doctor treating the battered subject saw the cops cuts and bruises. "Officer, let's get you seen to." He nodded to a nurse. The police officer raised his hand.

"No, thanks ma'am. Let's get this guy fixed up so I can take him to jail. Then I'll come back."

That was not uncommon. I often saw officers ignore their own injuries while making sure the patient they had brought in was treated first. I was in and out of the ER all night. I never saw the officer come back for treatment. That was pretty common, too.

Getting a beating from a police officer was not as common a cause of a suspect's injuries as I would have thought. People under their arrest arrived with knots on their heads, or bruised elbows and knees that could have come from police batons. But in the patient's explanation of their injuries they usually had nothing to do with the coop. Even with no officer present they professed to have been beaten up in an altercation, a robbery or a domestic dispute. By arresting them the police officer had in most cases rescued them, often from themselves. Whether they got one or not, I don't doubt many of these patients deserved a working over. Some of them generally still deserved one by the way I saw them act in the ER. Many were sloppy drunk or high. They were abusive and mouthy when they arrived and remained so with the ER staff. When they became too much for the ER staff to handle, it was always a cop handy who subdued them. The more mouth they gave the doctors, the quicker the shackles appeared. Often they then ended up in "isolation.' This was a steel walled room with a big, thick window through which they could be observed. I saw more than one ill-mannered patient in there shackled wrist and ankle. Even locked in isolation, spread-eagle on a metal hospital gurney they often still spewed vitriol. Some who got to spend time in isolation were spitters. Beside shackles, spitting at the ER staff got the miscreant a surgical mask to wear during their hospital stay as well as assault and battery charges.

Lifeline picked up its fair share of aggressive drunks. By the time they were onboard the helicopter they were appropriately restrained. For this we had "spider straps." These were long Velcro straps sewn in the shape of a star. The center of the star was placed on the patient's chest. Then the Velcro straps were fastened through the handles of the backboard in such a way that the patient was completely immobilized. We could have turned the backboard upside down and the patient would have stayed securely stuck to the backboard. The Lifeline crews used two sets of spider straps on some drunks. They could make all the noise they wanted, but they weren't going to swing at us, or even move much more than their fingers.

I loved working with the Texas Department of Public Safety, our State Troopers. They looked good in their pressed, gray uniforms and Stetson hats. They were always completely professional in manner. And they were tough as nails. There was never a doubt who was in charge with a Texas Trooper at the scene. Troopers mostly patrolled the highways outside of the city. I saw them a lot at motor vehicle accidents (MVA) on the rural county roads and state highways.

My crew and I were sent one night to an MVA on a state highway not far from my hometown. The patients turned out to be a man and woman about my age. Everything about them pointed to lives wasted making bad decisions. The latest one ended with them wrecking their car in a ditch and busting up their faces. Both were profoundly drunk, loud and profane. Neither of them were wearing a seatbelt in the crash. Consequently, both of them hit the windshield so hard with their faces that they made a bloody, star-shaped impressions in it. The man had evidently been driving. His mouth was full of blood but without any visible teeth. One of the volunteers told me he left them stuck in the steering wheel. The impact also opened the skin on his face to the jawbone. The woman's upper lip was split up to her nose. She lisped bloody profanity as we pulled her gurney toward the far side of the helicopter.

I happily noted that they were both double spider strapped to backboards. Bloody and belligerent, the man in particular really started shooting off his mouth as we pulled his gurney toward the aircraft. He struggled unsuccessfully against the spider straps. When we pulled his gurney under the rotor blades of the helicopter he began to shout.

"I ain't ridin' in no helicopter! I rode in too many of them helicopters in Vee-et NAM! Them things is dangerous. I ain't ridin' in no helicopter, and you can't make me!"

And drunk driving isn't dangerous? I thought to myself.

I had a pretty long career in the military service of the United States. Many of my friends had served in Vietnam. It didn't take me long to identify the likelihood that someone was a veteran, let alone a combat vet. I had also been around Lifeline long enough to make a few observations about drunk drivers, too. In the case of this self-declared Vietnam veteran I was willing to believe he had probably indeed served time – in prison. I thought the chances that he served in Vietnam about as likely as his girlfriend having held the title of Miss America.

As the crew and the volunteers prepared to lift his backboard onto the helicopter the drunken man really started giving the medical crew a hard time about riding in the helicopter. I was standing on one side of the gurney. A Texas Trooper was standing on the other side. He happened to be stationed in my hometown. I knew this because he was also a friend of mine from church. We didn't mention that at this juncture. Instead the trooper leaned across the drunk and winked at me. Then he said for the benefit of the drunk, "Mister Pilot, we're going to give this gentleman a choice." Then he looked down at the drunk. "He can go with you on the helicopter, or he can go with me."

The drunk changed his tune so fast I had to step back and stifle a laugh.

"Oh! Oh! My back!" he cried out suddenly. "It's really hurtin!' I think I need to go straight to the hospital on that helicopter."

My flight nurse smiled at the trooper. She had to get her dig in. "What about Vietnam?" she asked.

"What about it?" the drunk stammered through his recent spate of back pain. "Let's get goin'. I need to see a doctor!"

I have always liked and respected Texas Troopers but especially since working with them at Lifeline. They were the last to get flustered at anything we ran across in our travels. At a scene I could count on them to get things under control. When I saw them in Crash they were all business. Troopers more than most other police agencies showed up after every DWI related accident I worked with them. Other police agencies weren't so conscientious. One of our nurses did a study on the drunken driving suspects we flew in. She found that if a drunk driver arrived at the ER by helicopter they were rarely charged with DWI. I was astonished by that. But I doubt that was true when a Texas Trooper was investigating a drunk driver accident. They always looked like they had a personal investment in collecting the blood samples that would be used in court. They had a special focus as they stood watching the ER staff draw the blood. They would personally testify later in court to the results of those samples. I was especially gratified when I saw them in Crash after I flew in a drunk who killed people. I felt as though perhaps justice might be served. Without that kind of diligence we may have helped some of those people literally get away with murder. Unless there was a trooper waiting for us, I suppose in some cases that is just what we did.

11 "PRIDE GOES BEFORE DESTRUCTION..."

Although most of the docs I saw working Crash were princes, there were plenty of them who were not. Emperors, perhaps but not princes. I think the egotistical doctors got that way because nobody challenged them. That was because in a hospital environment, those who did usually put their jobs on the line. The hospital almost always sided with the doctor, or so I was told by our flight nurses.

The doctors with the mammoth egos were not hard to spot. I saw my first one early in my career with Lifeline. I was standing outside a trauma room during a trauma stat. The doctor was the last one to arrive in the room I was watching. He entered and literally pushed the staff out of his way. Then he began to yell at them. He yelled at the charge nurse in the room for not giving him the information he needed before he asked. He bullied the technicians and nurses in the room, too. Then he started demanding things he needed to treat the patient. Fortunately, most of what was needed to prepare the patient for treatment had already been done. I heard no positive words for the people in the room who had been doing his job for him before he arrived.

I pitied the people subjected to him. But that doctor was so ill-mannered that I felt embarrassed for him, too. I leaned over for some guidance from the social worker who was standing next to me in the hallway.

"Am I just new at this," I asked, "or is that doctor a jerk?"

She smiled and asked if I knew the difference between God and a doctor.

"No," I said dutifully.

"God doesn't think he's a doctor," she replied.

I only saw a few doctors who were as rude and inconsiderate as that one. In a couple of cases I think their bluster was a way to hide their insecurity. Medicine is called a practice, after all. Some doctors probably just needed a lot more of it. I know that some doctors we encountered were not as good as our crews. That light bulb went on for me when we landed at a small county hospital one night to pick up a trauma patient.

Two teenage boys decided to jump their motorcycles over a couple of steep piles of packed dirt. They did it simultaneously but in opposite directions. The plan was for the two motorcycles to pass each other in flight. The accident happened when during the jump they hit each other in midair - head on. I don't know what happened with one of the boys. He wasn't in the ER when we arrived. But our patient was a mess. His entire face below his eye sockets looked like bloody hamburger.

The EMTs have a mantra for remembering the priorities for saving someone's life. The acronym is 'ABC,' which stands for "Airway, Breathing, and Circulation." An injured patient's airway must be open and protected first or they are going to die quickly. This poor boy's airway was obstructed by the mass of bloody injured tissue, shattered mandible (Jaw), teeth and crushed facial bones. When we walked into the little ER a doctor was standing next to the boy with his back to us. It was clear that no one had yet done anything to open his airway. I could hear that the boy was breathing, but he was having a very difficult time of it. It must have been like trying to breathe through a blood soaked towel.

The doctor on duty in this little ER clearly wasn't up to the task of caring for him. The doctor was holding an ET tube. He was poking at the mass of destroyed tissue in the boy's face but he wasn't getting the job done. We speculated later that he must have been a podiatrist or dermatologist or something. The boy was fortunate to have Dennis our paramedic on duty that night. He was especially skilled at establishing airways. Dennis put down his medical equipment bag and watched the doctor take a couple ineffective stabs at the boy's face with the plastic ET tube. He stepped up close to the doctor and said quietly, "Doctor? If you'll turn that ET tube around and insert the other end it will probably be easier to intubate this patient."

I thought Dennis was being diplomatic under the circumstances. I doubt that the doctor felt the same way. But he didn't say anything. He didn't even turn around. He just handed the ET tube to Dennis and walked out of the ER. As the doctor disappeared, Dennis grabbed a Macintosh blade from a steel tray next to the exam table. He snapped the metal spoon shaped device to the lighted handle used to expose the opening of the trachea for intubation. He worked it into the damaged tissue until he found the opening that used to be the boy's mouth. A moment later Dennis had the ET tube properly placed in the boy's trachea. I heard a deep sigh as air began flowing through the ET tube into the boy's lungs. I was glad the doctor wasn't too proud to give Dennis the ET tube and leave.

Pride wasn't limited to the doctors we met. I was fortunate that I saw it looking back at me before it killed me. I got into flying air ambulances because I wanted to use my talents and skills to save lives. I had yet to find out how arrogant that objective was. I had to learn that I had no more to do with saving a life than I did with losing one. Early on, after we flew a patient with a good outcome I felt like a god. I became addicted to the feeling. The power of life and death was in my hands. I got an increasing confidence in myself and my abilities as a pilot. I believed I was better than I really was. That attitude was clearly false pride. In the EMS pilot community that is called, "The White Knight Syndrome.

It manifests itself in a number of ways. One sure symptom of the syndrome is when the pilot calls the job as "a mission." Military pilots use the term. They keep using it when they get out of the military. That is a manifestation of the White Knight syndrome. Military pilots fly combat missions. On these the survival of the pilot and crew is worth risking to accomplish the objective. A civilian pilot does not fly a "mission." They fly a job. If the job can't be done safely we aren't expected to sacrifice our lives as a soldier on "a mission" might.

Air ambulance pilots have to learn that many calls are not even critical. A fellow EMS pilot told me he almost killed himself and his crew picking up a patient who – it turned out - only had a broken collar bone. I asked him why he took the flight or picked up the patient when the risk was so high. He said one word in reply: "Pride." He was too proud to turn it down and too proud to quit once he started. He had lived and learned the lesson. I nodded. I understood, too.

But when I got the job at Lifeline, I didn't understand. I had to learn. I had good instructors.

EMS flying programs rely of the compliance of the crew from start to finish of any flight. If anyone on the crew believes that the flight should not be made or should be terminated, the flight is cancelled. Mike, one of my excellent paramedics knew that better than me. He had a t-shirt that he sometimes wore beneath his flight suit. On the front were printed the words, "It's your emergency, not mine." I was working with Mike one day when we got a call. The weather was at our minimums but was predicted to get worse. Even so, I made the move to head for the helicopter. When I realized Mike wasn't following me toward the door I turned to see why. He had his flight suit zipped down. He was holding the flight suit open for me to see his t-shirt. He looked at me like I didn't know any better.

"Paul, it is dumb to try to fly in this weather."

That's all he had to say. I knew the old adage in aviation: "If you kill yourself flying on a bad weather day you'll be buried on a beautiful one." The message in that adage and on Mike's t-shirt was the same. Wait. No flight is imperative. Weather is bound to change. If you don't know for certain you can fly safely, don't fly at all.

Mike also had me keep in mind that the patients had mostly gotten themselves into the condition that had required an EMS response. He pointed them out with the single word question, "See?" Call after call he would turn to me and say it. He would say it at the hospital when we dropped the patient, or at the scene taking them to the aircraft. "See?" Lifelong smokers, chronic alcoholics, drug users, drunk drivers and most of the other patients who caused us to fly to their aid, always "See?" He also said that chances were that even if we pulled them out of the pot they'd be back in it as soon as they were discharged from the hospital. These were patients I met on our "frequent flyer" program.

Even for the innocent patient who got injured or sick through no fault of their own, an aircraft accident certainly wouldn't change the patient's outcome for the better. "The White Knight Syndrome" still sings its siren song to me sometimes. But I know her. I know what to call her. She goes before destruction. Her name is "pride."

I don't remember the circumstances that led to my catharsis. I only remember that the patient was critically injured. On the flight to the hospital the patient seemed to rally. I could hear it in the positive observations the crew reported to the hospital about the guy I was flying there. The flight crew was hopeful. When I told them the hospital was in sight they reported that the patient was still doing well. Crash told us the patient was going right into surgery. They were waiting on the pad. When I shut down the engines it looked to me we had saved another life. I was elated.

The Crash crew, our flight nurse and paramedic all ran across the pad with the gurney. I got out and slid the stretcher back into the helicopter thinking about what was happening. When I headed into Crash expecting good results there were no patients in the place. Then I saw my crew appear in the hallway coming from surgery. They carried their helmets in one hand. As they drew near I asked for the prognosis.

"He's dead," the paramedic said as he passed me by.

Game over. Back to work. The crew headed for the medical supply cabinet. I looked around me. I was alone. I felt like a ghost. Nobody even noticed me as I left. When I got back to the pad I climbed up in the cockpit and sat in the pilot seat, deflated. The lights surrounding the helipad cast an orange glow in the cockpit. I looked over the instruments and switches. No life in them, needles on zero, systems inert.

The crew opened the cabin door and got to work. I smelled alcohol wipes, heard the zippers of medical bags and the clunk of storage cabinet doors as the crew worked. I stepped back out of the cockpit and walked downstairs silently reviewing the flight. I went over the actions I had taken minute by minute. I wondered what I could have done to save that man's life. I had probably flown higher than necessary. That added time to the transport. I didn't pay as much attention to demanding all the power I could get from the engines. I might have been able to get the helicopter going a few knots faster. Perhaps those few knots *could* have made a difference in the patient's outcome. On many calls I knew the outcome was a forgone conclusion. But on this call I felt as though I made a difference.

Taking responsibility for a save was easy. But now I was looking at the flip side of that coin. Taking responsibility for a man's death was the biggest burden I'd ever carried. I knew that there would be other calls like this, too. I wondered how I would handle them. How would it affect my decision making, how I did my job, how I slept – or didn't sleep. There was no one with whom I could share this burden, this grief. I was trying to handle something bigger than I was.

And then I suddenly remembered God. I always called on Him when I was in trouble. Thinking back it seemed to be the only time I ever did call on Him. Stuck in a dead end again, it occurred to me I was like those people I had met in my life who always said 'please' but never said 'thank you.' So I took a minute to bow my head and say, "Thanks, God." It seemed at once an odd thing to say, and at the same time the right thing to say. It must have been the prayer God needed to hear. I sought nothing. I expected nothing. I just called up to say "thanks." The moment I did I felt an answer to that call well up in my heart.

That man's life was not in yours to give or take. That is not yours to decide. I am the giver and taker of life.

I suddenly realized that I had been playing God. I heard myself in retrospect. I had come to refer to our calls as "saving lives." They started in jest, but I began to believe what I was saying. I began to think that I was literally "saving lives." But with that comes the question about taking credit for the deaths. That would also be my responsibility. No man is up to that.

That was a night when I made a most important transition. It started with the death of a man I never met. I never really even saw him. But God used his death to change me. I learned to ascribe the work I did each day to God's purpose, and not my own. The role I played in the life or death of our patients was important only because God made it so. Later, when I heard someone say, "You're a hero," or "You're the one who saved his life," there was no longer any temptation to take the credit. Neither did I take the blame. I pointed out to whoever was talking to me that they were talking to the wrong man. I was quick to say, "I don't save lives. I don't take them either. I just work for The One who does."

12 BAD CALL

We were in Quarters. A couple of hours into the night shift a call came in. "Lifeline One, two car MVA..." It was near the interstate on the south end of the city. Three minutes later we were airborne and heading south down the interstate at five hundred feet. As soon as we were clear of the hospital I checked in with Austin Approach Control to tell them where we were going. They didn't sound busy but the medical dispatch radio surely did. I heard the on-scene commander ask how far out we were. That's usually a bad sign for the patients involved. He also informed dispatch that one of the two cars involved in the accident was on fire.

Great, Burned people, I thought. I pulled down the window so I wouldn't forget to do it after we loaded the burn victims.

A mile or so out, I could see the brilliant orange flames in the distance. I figured it must be a gas truck. The flames were thirty feet high. I did a quick orbit so we could all see the scene. Below us the scene was brightly lighted by a burning car. It was totally involved. In discussing options with the crew I accidently hit the radio trigger instead of the intercom switch.

"Well, we won't be transporting any burn patients tonight. Anybody in that car is toast!"

Austin Approach was quick to respond. "Sounds like you have a bad one out there, Lifeline One."

I paused a moment realizing what I had done. I didn't want to follow up one irresponsible radio transmission to Approach with another one. I keyed the mike again.

"Affirmative, Austin. We'll be on the ground at this location. I'll call you coming out."

The controller was very professional and understood the situation.

"Roger, Lifeline. No problem. I don't see how you guys do that job. Be careful. We'll talk to you on the way back to the hospital."

The crew and I agreed on a landing spot uphill from the burning car. Thanks to the column of flames and smoke I had all the light and the wind reference I needed to land. I landed upwind of the fire and downwind of a large fire truck blocking traffic. I did a nice no-hover landing and excused the crew to unsaddle while I shut down the helicopter. By the time I got out of the cockpit my crew was already talking to a fire fighter about the scene. I stepped up and caught the tail end of the plan. I was gratified to hear that no one was in the burning car. The youngster driving it had been going downhill way too fast. He lost control at the top of the hill and spun out. His car drifted sideways into another car heading uphill. When they made contact the rear end came off the spinning car and the fuel tank burst into flames. The driver abandoned the vehicle as it slid to a halt. The fire fighter talking to my crew pointed him out. I could see him sitting on a curb in the distance watching his car burn.

"He's okay. You're here for the other driver," said the fire fighter. He pointed to a cheap four-door sedan resting upside down uphill and across the road from the burning car. It was surrounded by fire fighters, hoses and rescue equipment. I could hear the familiar sound of the little generator running that powered the "Jaws of Life" the fire crew was using to tear open the cab of the inverted car.

"The driver is still in there. We're trying to pry him out. But he's hurt. We're not sure how badly."

Our paramedic excused himself and headed for the tail boom of the helicopter. The nurse and I followed a pace behind. "Munchkin" was a little round paramedic I had always liked. But I would come to admire him this night for the rest of my life. When I opened the storage compartment in the tail of the helicopter, Munchkin reached in and pulled out two sets of bunker gear and threw them on the ground. He took the smaller set. I had rarely seen them out of their storage spot on the helicopter, let alone put to use. But the crew had them on in a jiffy. As he popped on his fireman's helmet and shouldered one of their medical bags Munchkin said, "I'm going to see what I can do." I stood by the helicopter until the nurse got her bunker gear on, too. Then we both grabbed medical bags and headed toward the inverted car.

By the time we got to the car, Munchkin was already inside. He lay on his back with his legs sticking out of the driver's side window, the toes of his boots pointing up. Meanwhile the fire fighters continued prying at the car with the "Jaws" to free the driver. It was both brave and foolish of Munchkin to slide inside that car. I wasn't sure it was even braced to keep it from collapsing on him. I saw a fire fighter standing by with a charged hose. It looked like he had wet the car down. But Munchkin laid in a pool of liquid that could have been contained with fuel or battery acid. If he had even considered these things he never told me. So far as he was concerned there was an injured person in that car. He just slid inside and went to work.

Inside he found a man trapped behind the wheel. He was hanging by his seat belt. Munchkin could see that his scalp had largely been torn loose. He was conscious and talking rationally but he was bleeding profusely. I stayed back with the fire fighter with the charged hose while our nurse walked up to the driver's side window and promptly sat down Indian-style in the road next to Munchkin's feet. She began to dig into her medical bag and pass in those things Munchkin called for. First came a stiff-neck collar, then large gauze compresses and tape. While Munchkin worked she rigged IV bags to tubing. These she passed in through the window, one ready-to-use IV and then another. At the nurses request I went back to the helicopter and brought back our short spine board. It was like half a back board rigged with short spider straps. Munchkin would strap the driver's torso into it to protect his spine as he drew him out of the car.

Munchkin performed all this care for the driver while lying on his back in his bunker gear. When the IVs and spine board were in place he called for some help from the fire fighters. Several of them crawled through the windows to help lower the patient to the inverted car's ceiling. Then they cut the patient's seat belt. The Jaws never did cut through the car before Munchkin and the fire crew had the patient out where we could move him to the helicopter.

Munchkin had him packaged like a Christmas present. His bandages, IV's and his torso harness were all in place. He, the nurse and the fire crew put the patient on a full sized backboard and we transported him to the hospital. On the way back north over the interstate, approach control didn't ask for details about the toasted people and I didn't offer any. After we landed at Brack I followed the driver into Crash. I kept track of him after he went through surgery. I met his family that night and a couple of days later when the man ended up in a room in the hospital. Close as he came to death, his family was most concerned that I would tell him that his Chevy Nova was a total loss. I kept my own counsel on that. I guess everybody has their priorities.

Not long after the call, Munchkin and I were on the day shift. We were both sitting on the couch when a guy from Austin EMS showed up in Quarters to give me a booster for the Hepatitis B shot series I was taking. He sat on the coffee table in front of the couch and opened up his tackle box. As he drew up the hypodermic with the vaccine I noticed

Munchkin grow pale. His lower lip began to quiver. I thought he was joking. Then the EMS guy stuck me in the shoulder with the needle. Munchkin passed out cold.

The EMS guy had some smelling salts in his tackle box. When we popped it under his nose, Munchkin came right back from "lala land."

"What the heck just happened to you," I asked Munchkin.

He sat up and looked at me, still a little pale. "I hate shots." He said.

"What?" I was incredulous. "Didn't I see you starting IVs upside down in a wrecked car on a guy bleeding like a stuck hog?

"Oh, that," Munchkin said. "That's different. I didn't know that guy."

13 THE BOX IN THE SLEEVE

At the beginning and end of every shift the medical crews passed each other a little plastic box. It was the kind smokers used to keep a pack of cigarettes dry. The crew was very careful with that box. Losing it or any of its contents would probably end their careers. The little box fit neatly into the sleeve pocket of a flight suit. I once saw an incident where a paramedic forget to pass the box to his relief. He drove all the way home before he noticed. He got back into his car and drove all the way back to work. The box was that important. It contained vials and ampoules of several powerful drugs. Among them were the pain killers Morphine and its cousin Dilaudid. Using those drugs on a sick patient was serious business. Normally only a licensed physician could do that. Even though medical crews had protocols and the medical director's dispensation to use it, the crews still knew that their careers were on the line every time they cracked an ampoule. They even had to account for what they didn't use. I often signed a witness statement that I had seen the nurse or medic "waste" some. They drew up the unused amount in a syringe and showed me how much was in the syringe. Then they sprayed the drug into the grass at the scene or down a sink in Quarters. They recorded the amount on the form I cosigned with them.

The medical crew made plenty of medical decisions on their own. But when they had to open the little box they almost always contacted the doctor on duty in Crash. They wanted a doctor's concurrence in using those drugs. They didn't always get it. Mary was the first nurse I saw who was denied its use. It happened the day we picked up an old farmer at his home east of town. When we reached him he was sitting on the wide porch of a little farm house. Idling in the front yard was an Austin ambulance. Idling behind the house was a piece of farm machinery. Except for the little front yard and the recently mowed corn field I landed in, the house was surrounded by head high corn. I found out from the ambulance crew that the machine behind the house was a corn picker. The old gentleman had caught his hand in its mechanism somehow.

The man sat in a rusty metal chair with the ambulance paramedics standing on both sides of him. His hand was wrapped in a bloody white towel. He seemed very stoic. He didn't make a sound. It wasn't that hot but I noticed that he was sweating profusely. "Diaphoresis," I heard it called. People having heart attacks sweat like that. I wondered if he might be suffering a heart attack. Then as Mary unwrapped his hand to examine the injury I realized why he was sweating. He was in intense pain. With all the nerves in our fingers hand injuries are especially painful. This one surely must have been as painful as they get. The farmer's fingers were knotted together in a bloody mass. I could see shards of white bone protruding from the twisted lump of bloody tissue that had been his fingers. A wave of nausea came over me but quickly passed.

I looked at the old gentleman's face. He was so brave. He didn't even whimper. He just sat quietly, sweating. Terrible as the injury was, it was the only one he suffered. He hadn't hit his head. He wasn't having a stroke or heart attack. Nothing but the pain could be altering his mental state. I saw no reason he shouldn't have morphine for a wound like that. I knew of its use on the battlefield. There a twenty-two year old Navy Hospital Corpsman could stick a wounded Marine with a morphine syrette from his first aid kit and get the job done. The relief for even the most painful wounds was instant. So I wondered what took Mary so long to reach for the plastic box in her sleeve. As we took the man to the aircraft on a stretcher she made a call to Crash on her handheld radio. A doctor at the Brack ER listened as she rattled off her report on the radio. She noted academically that she was about to administer the dose of morphine as directed in her protocols.

"Hold off on the morphine, Lifeline. You'll be here in a few minutes. We'll re-evaluate using it when you get here."

Mary instantly stopped. She stepped away from the stretcher and turned her back to us. As we continued toward the helicopter she stood her ground about using the morphine. I could hear her tone of voice. Apparently she tried diplomatically to couch her observation to make the doctor comfortable with letting her administer the morphine. But I could hear that the doctor was having none of it. Still, Mary wouldn't let the issue rest.

Finally as I climbed into the cockpit and strapped into my seatbelt I heard the doctor over the radio. He said with finality in his voice, "Just transport the patient, Lifeline!"

That trip of just a few miles at a hundred and twenty knots seemed to take all morning long. We could all see the pain in the poor farmer's face. We knew that it could have been easily relieved long before we arrived at the hospital. Over the intercom I could feel and hear Mary's anxiety for him. She seemed directly connected to the patient.

Mary was wearing her helmet. The farmer wasn't wearing a headset. He was sitting up on the stretcher. He just continued to look straight ahead, still pouring sweat. Mary spoke into the intercom as though the old man could hear her.

"You're such a brave, brave man," I heard her say.

She was so plaintive. "You poor, brave man. I'm so sorry. You poor man." She repeated this over and over all the way to the hospital until we landed.

I got the helicopter refueled quickly while Mary and the patient disappeared into Crash. By the time she got there she was beside herself. She could hardly give her report to the charge nurse. Down the hallway and seemingly unconcerned was the doctor. He still stood near the radio on which he had denied the patient morphine. By the time I got into Crash, Mary had not spoken to him yet. He appeared to be reviewing a chart on a clipboard. I could tell that Mary couldn't even look at him. I think he knew it. There was certainly an atmosphere of tension there.

Diminutive though she was I knew at that moment she could have quickly killed that doctor with her bare hands. Instead she busied herself caring for the patient, taking over some of the duties of the ER nurses. Finally the doctor ambled down the hall, clearly in no hurry to step into the trauma room. He stepped up to the exam table opposite Mary and unwrapped the towel. He slowly and carefully examined the man's mangled hand. Then he looked around the room at no one in particular and casually ordered morphine for the man. Mary already had the syringe drawn up. She showed the charge nurse the dose she had drawn up. It happened to be exactly what the doctor ordered.

Mary pushed the drug into the farmer's IV herself. The relief in the man's face was almost immediate. He slumped back on the table and sighed deeply. Mary reached out and stroked his forehead.

"Better?" she asked. For the first time the old man looked at Mary. He smiled a little and nodded. She smiled back at him.

The doctor stepped out of the room and walked back toward the nurses' station. Mary gently patted the old gentleman's shoulder and said, "I'll be right back."

Then she turned and walked down the hallway. She quickly caught up with the doctor. I heard her sweetly ask him if he might step down the hallway a bit so she could talk to him for a moment. The doctor looked a little anxious but complied. I knew what was coming. I did not envy that doctor.

It should be said here that nurses' careers don't usually survive chewing out a doctor. I wasn't sure that Mary's would. But I knew that she was about to take that chance. From a distance her face and body language gave no hint of what I knew was happening. She kept a benign looking smile on her face. She kept her weight cocked back on one leg and crossed her arms. Her body language said nothing threatening. But I could see she had murder in her eyes. She must have said something particularly egregious because the doctor stepped back half a pace. His arms fell to his side and his mouth fell open. Whatever she said must have made her point. She was finished whatever she had to say without losing that smile. But just before she stepped past the astonished doctor she blinked her eyes at him in an exaggerated manner. Then she marched back toward me.

In what I supposed to be a gentlemanly gesture of apology the doctor followed her, a step or two behind.

"Of course I agree with you..."

She didn't look at him.

"Under the circumstance it would have been perfectly appropriate to use."

Mary stopped, turned toward him and said sweetly, "So why did you stop me?"

She was now barely in control. Her face reddened. She stared daggers at the doctor again. The air hung heavy between them as she put her hands on her hips, waiting for a reply.

He stammered, then said, "You know you don't have to call me to use morphine if you think it's appropriate. I thought you were asking me if you should use it."

She looked at me. Her smiled disappeared and her face darkened like an approaching storm. She growled and turned back toward the doctor.

"Well doctor," she said. "You can bet your sweet ass I'll never do *that* again!"

And so far as I know, she didn't. I never saw her hesitate to reach into her sleeve and pull out that plastic box when she thought it was called for. Word got around, too. The paramedics still called for concurrence in using the box, but I rarely saw the nurses do so. They just reached for it as they did any other tool in their kit.

When Mary left Lifeline she went on to train as a Certified Registered Nurse Anesthetist (CRNA). Now she's in the full-time business of managing people's pain. I think it's just the place for her.

I think the scariest drug in the little box was one called Adenocard. When it is administered it quickly and effectively stops the human heart. The first day I saw it used we responded to a cardiac call. I landed in a field where a man with a heart problem had been repairing a wire fence. I shut down the aircraft while the medical crew put the man on oxygen and a heart monitor. When I walked over to him he was sitting on a blanket on the ground surrounded by volunteers and the ambulance crew. The patient was diaphoretic (sweaty), pale and short of breath. All those symptoms are classic signs of a heart attack. I glanced at the heart monitor. His heart rate was over two hundred beats per minute. That was faster than I had ever seen a heartbeat. The paramedic engaged the man in conversation. He asked all the standard questions about the patient's medical history, medications, food and water intake and so forth. One of the first responders recorded the man's answers on a clipboard.

Kris our nurse, apparently already knew what was going on with the patient. She was a few paces away with her back to the patient. She was down on one knee looking through her medical kit. The kit was really just a large fishing tackle box. It was exactly the kind you can buy at any sporting goods store. Instead of fishing lures though, it was well stocked with medical supplies. She picked up a small syringe, put on a small gauge needle and then reached for the little plastic box in her sleeve pocket, the one with her career inside. I knew something important was happening. I squatted down near her and asked, "Heart attack?"

"Nope. He's real tachy," (meaning tachycardic – his heart was beating too fast.) I knew that. "He's going into a-fib," (meaning atrial fibrillation. That's a state where the heart just quivers rather than beats. Blood stops moving and the patient starts dying.)

"What are you going to do for this patient, Kris?" I asked.

She took the vile of Adenocard out and put the box back in her sleeve. She held it up close to read the vile and check the expiration date. Just before she filled the little syringe she looked at me and said in a matter-of-fact manner, "I'm going to stop this man's heart."

I wasn't sure I'd heard her right. I always thought nurses and paramedics were supposed to keep people's hearts pumping, not stop them. She turned away from me and paid close attention to the syringe, narrowing her eyes as she tapped the last little bubble out of the syringe.

"There isn't any time to take him back to the hospital. He'd probably code (his heart would stop beating) on the helicopter. So we're going to take care of this right here." She used a stage whisper to say, "So I'm going to stop his heart. Then we're going to shock him back into a sinus rhythm." She shifted her eyes toward the patient. "This is a little scary."

"I guess so!" I whispered. "Stopping someone's heart would be a little scary for me too, especially if the 'somebody' getting the juice was me."

"No," she responded. "What's scary is that I've never administered this stuff before. I saw it done in the ER but there was a doctor there. Here at the scene…"

My eyes must have grown pretty large because she smiled at me when I said, "Yep, that's scary alright!"

She put on her game face, stood up and stepped over to the patient. "Okay, sir. I'm going to give you some medicine now that will get that heart rate slowed down."

Boy, that's no kidding -- all the way to zero! I thought.

She uncapped the needle and pushed it into the IV tubing beneath the bag of saline solution one of the volunteers was holding. Then she pushed the plunger. The medicine was clear, but I could imagine it running down the IV into the man's arm. "You're going to feel a little strange for a minute," Kris said nonchalantly.

I watched the heart monitor. *I reckon! He's about to feel dead!* The man's heart rate dropped dramatically and then abruptly went flat. I was impressed that the drug was so fast acting.

"Boy, I feel bad!" the man said.

I grunted under my breath, *"Yep. That's called dying."* And I thought it odd that a man technically dead was saying anything at all. He really was clinically dead, too. He had no heart rhythm at all. There was a steady tone from the heart monitor where the rapid blipping sound had been a moment before. The patient sat there quietly for a few seconds. Even with his heart stilled he was still with us. He looked like he was trying to figure out what was wrong. Then his eyes and head rolled back.

Dead.

Several sets of hands caught him and laid the man back on the blanket. His shirt was already unbuttoned but the volunteers opened his shirt wide. Our flight paramedic already had the defibrillator charged and ready. He grabbed paddles and rubbed them together. That spread the lubricant that would insure electrical contact with the man's chest. Then he placed the paddles on the patient's rib cage and shouted, "Clear!"

We all stood back. Nobody wanted to share the jolt that would go through the man's body and into the ground beneath him. The paramedic checked everybody was clear. Then he pushed the button on one of the paddles. The sound of the jolt made an audible thump and threw the man's chest up off the ground. One shot. When he came back to rest, the heart monitor recorded the flash of energy. Then two irregular beats appeared followed by a flat line. But a moment later the line jerked abruptly before settling down to record a normal sinus rhythm, eighty beats a minute.

"Just like it's supposed to," I said out loud. I looked over at Kris.

She crinkled her nose at me and said, "Nothing to it!"

14 BLOOD

Dealing with the wide variety of human suffering was the most obvious difference between any other flying job and flying an air ambulance helicopter. I thought that I was pretty well seasoned to it after almost a year seeing the trauma. The carnage didn't bother me. Any anxiety it initially caused me quickly went away. I thought I had forgotten about it. Then came the dreams. They would come in my deep sleep. Other times I would pop awake from a doze. I would waken happy to find that what had invaded even my light sleep was just a phantom version of what I had seen perhaps months ago.

I thought I had been dealing with what I saw in a healthy manner. But quite suddenly, along with the dreams I developed a sudden aversion to the sight of blood. It started one night at the scene of a head-on collision. I landed and shutdown in the grass beside the highway. I could see my medical crew packaging up a patient for transport. I could see the bloody bandages on the patient's head. As I stood by the helicopter I caught myself saying out load, "Oh no, this is one I'm going to remember." I walked back around the nose of Lifeline One and pulled myself up into the cockpit. I knew what I was doing. I was hiding.

I stayed there until the patient was loaded on the other side of the helicopter. I climbed down and did my usual walk around the helicopter to make sure we were clear for takeoff. I remember consciously averting my eyes from the passenger. I knew I'd see blood. And so it began. I decided that I would do all I could to avoid looking at blood. It was a fool's errand. There was no avoiding it. The job put the injured and their injuries right in my face every shift, sometimes many times a day.

I tried various strategies for blinding myself to bloody wounds. I tried to turn my head away. Other times I focused at a distance to blur the image. Sometimes I just closed my eyes; but sometimes there was no avoiding it. I would have to look. Those times were bad, but seeing the wounds was not the worst of it. The real bad times were when I got surprised. I would be unprepared for something tragic displayed before me in vivid detail. *I'm going to see that one again,* I'd think. And I did. In my dreams.

Eventually, they began to appear in my conscious mind like a glimpse at a snapshot. I would be reading the newspaper in Quarters or watching the traffic go by the helipad and I'd get a flash of something I had seen. The man I watched kneeling in his driveway suddenly shoot himself in the head; the pedestrian run over by a train; a person who fell in a ditch at a building site skewered on concrete reinforcing rods; or a car accident with gross traumatic injuries and fatalities. They would flash into my consciousness as well as my unconscious. Fearing the sight of blood was a subset of all that.

Seeing deep puncture wounds or dramatic lacerations in particular made me suddenly weak and sick at my stomach. Sometimes my lower back and flanks would spasm involuntarily when I saw them. I would find myself standing at a scene grinding my teeth, or holding my breath. I didn't believe that I exhibited obvious manifestations of my discomfort. I certainly never fainted. But now I understood firsthand how people could pass out at sights that should have been routine for me by now.

I worried that the medical crews would notice my sudden fear of blood. But they always appeared too busy to notice. I thought it was a subtle enough change that they might just think my fading away from the blood made me more like the other pilots. I was helping less at the scenes. I spent less time standing near their patients. As always, I walked around the aircraft before takeoff, but I tried to save the side they loaded the patient for last. I insured the doors were closed, but I let the medical crew close their cabin doors. I always did what my job required to keep us all safe. But I became increasingly less involved in the medical end of our business. Who would notice that now I serviced the aircraft and went straight to the quarters? That's what the other pilots did. Like the other pilots at Lifeline, I avoided visits to Crash altogether.

During the shift I spent more time in the pilot's bedroom. Back there I could sit in a lounge chair watching TV or reading books. Sometimes instead I'd stretch out in one of the bunks and hope that sleep would come. I thought that I did a good job hiding my growing fear of exposure to injured people. But I was wrong. The medical crews knew me by then. I could *not* have known that they too had all been through anxiety similar to mine in their careers. They knew I was too proud to ask for help, just as they had been. So without telling me, they made plans to help me. I didn't know that, so I didn't see it coming the night they put their plan in place.

We brought a patient into Crash from the scene of a Motor Vehicle Accident (MVA). The patient was "unrestrained." Read, "No seatbelt." His head went through his windshield. In such a case, whether or not the patient lives, that particular mechanism of injury always creates major scalp lacerations. Scalp injuries are particularly bloody. In this case, the medics on the scene reported to us over the radio that the patient's scalp had been peeled back from above his eyebrows to behind his ears. In my current anxious state over seeing bloody wounds I planned a way to avoid seeing another bloody injury like that.

At the scene I looked on from a distance. The patient was unconscious. The stretcher was set to keep him in the sitting position. I could see that the medical people had wrapped the patient's head in gauze. One wide band wrapped around his forehead. His black hair protruded like a carrot top from the gauze wrap. Another wide band of gauze was wrapped beneath his chin. I was glad to see that there was no blood on the bandages. Before we took off I made no effort to help the crew. I just readied the helicopter. I pulled the stretcher out on the side opposite my seat. I figured they would use the stretcher already pulled out. My tactic worked. I never saw a thing. When we landed I stayed in the helicopter until the patient was well on his way to Crash. Then I disembarked and walked around the back of the helicopter to reach the fuel hose. Once the helicopter was fueled I planned to go right back to Quarters and wait for the next call. But that was not to be.

As I serviced the aircraft with jet fuel, over by the doors to Crash I noticed one of my favorite ER doctors. He noticed me, too. I waved a hand and he responded in kind. He kept watching me as I finished getting the helicopter ready for the next call. He appeared to be waiting for me. The first time I met him I liked him. He was different than any doctor I had met to date. The first time I took any particular notice of him I didn't know it was him at first.

I was at the nurses' station when I looked down the hall. In one of the medicine rooms I saw a couple of Chinese people. They were standing by what was apparently their young daughter's bed. They were looking across the room at someone I couldn't see. Being nosey I walked down the hall to see who they were listening to. As I drew closer to the door, I could see the child and her parents were very intent. I could hear a man's voice and I was close enough to hear what was being said. But I couldn't understand it because it was apparently in Chinese. This surprised me as I didn't think we had any Chinese speakers on staff in the ER. I took the liberty to walk past the door to see who it was. And there stood the doctor now waiting for me to finish refueling my helicopter.

He was a big guy. He looked rather like a Viking. He was at least six and a half feet tall. He had broad shoulders, a deep chest and ropy muscles in his arms and neck. He couldn't have had half a percent of body fat on him. His light skin, high cheekbones and the shape of his eyes all looked Nordic as did his corn flower blue eyes and his collar-length white blonde hair. Even just passing by listening to him speak Chinese I could tell he had allot of presence about him. Even in a large crowd a guy like him would be hard to miss.

After that time I heard him speaking Chinese, I paid attention to him. It was impressive to watch him work with the patients and staff in the ER. He brought with him contagious confidence and calm. In trauma rooms where things were particularly hectic he smiled allot. Big as he was he moved easily and nimbly among the busy staff. He never raised his voice. He treated the staff like friends and spoke to them with consideration and respect. I was certain he always knew what he was doing. I think his crew and mine believed that, too.

One night Lifeline brought several patients into Crash during his shift. In between flights I watched him work. Even when it got very late and the rest of the Crash crew looked fatigued, he looked fresh, healthy and fit. That weary night he passed me as he left a trauma room. He came to a sudden halt, tuned and smiled at me. I smiled back as he put out one big powerful hand. He offered a strong handshake and his first name – "Call me, Rich." I always did after that.

I really got to know Rich one night while we were both taking a break outside of Crash. I told him about the eavesdropping I had done the first night I saw him.

"How did you come to speak Chinese?"

He didn't appear surprised that I knew that. He just said, "I learned Mandarin at the Defense Language Institute in Monterey, California."

I knew about Monterey. I knew why the military sent people there. Most of them were there to learn how to be spies. I told Rich earlier that I had been in the military, but he did not reciprocate. Telling me he'd learned Mandarin at Monterey he was sending me a signal, sharing a trust. I knew then that he had been a soldier of a different cut than most of us. I bet that he was a good one. But I played along.

"You were in the service?"

"Yeah," he replied offhandedly. "I was a medic in Special Forces."

The Army calls their most elite fighting unit, 'Special Forces.' They also go by the name "Green Berets" for the distinctive headgear they wear. Similarly, the Navy has their 'SEALs.' The Marine Corps has 'Force Recon(naissance).' All three organizations are indeed "special." They are specially selected from among many quality warfighters of their branch. They are then specially armed and specially trained to fight in the toughest spots in America's wars. But they also fight in America's many 'secret wars' about which most of us remain blissfully unaware. They arrive in hostile environments like spirits, often in the night. They collect information and often leave behind dead enemies and not uncommonly, significant destruction behind them.

"I thought I heard you speaking Spanish in the ER one night, too." I told him. "Do you speak Spanish?"

"Si!" he replied. "I also speak Dari, Urdu, Farsi and passable Russian when I have to."

"Dari?" I asked. "And Urdu? I've never heard of them."

"They're Persian languages. Dari and Urdu is what most Afghans speak. Farsi is used along the Afghan border with Iran. I served there. I picked up the Russian because I was in Afghanistan when the Russians were there. I figured it would be good to know how to speak some Russian. I'm not very good at it though."

"Russian? You were in Afghanistan with the Russians."

"Well, not exactly *with* the Russians. More like *against* them. But if they caught me I was ready." He rattled off something in what sounded like Russian.

"What was that?" I asked. I was still trying to grasp that he had been an American soldier fighting Russians when we weren't at war with them.

He laughed. "Excuse me sir, is this the train to Moscow?"

"Useful. I bet you used that all the time in Afghanistan."

"Not in Afghanistan. But I probably could have really used Russian if they put me in Scandinavia or Eastern Europe. That's where I asked to go. My family is Norwegian."

I told him he reminded me of a Viking.

"The Army thought so, too," he said through a laugh. "That's why they taught me all the Spanish and South Asian languages. Typical of the Army they sent me, a Norwegian to Central America, Central Asia and Korea where I would stick out like a sore thumb."

I chuckled and repeated the old Groucho Marks line, "Military intelligence..." I began

"...is a contradiction of terms," he continued. "I know. I'm a living example."

"Fighting in Afghanistan against the Russians? Isn't that still a secret?" I asked.

"Yeah, so don't tell anybody I told you."

"And where were you were in Central America?"

He laughed again as he delivered another old line I had used myself. "I'd have to kill you if I told you that." He was enjoying himself. "Actually, I wouldn't have to kill you because I really don't know exactly where we *were* in Central America. We were given maps at the mission briefing. They had all the topography for where we were going. They just didn't have any names on the maps. We jumped in by parachute at night, or we were dropped off by helicopter and never got a good look at where we were exactly."

"What about your time in Korea? I've been there. Where were you? I was mostly in the south, near Pusan?"

"I was in the north," he replied cagily.

"Near Seoul?"

"North Korea," he replied.

"Isn't that…"

"Yeah, I guess that's secret too. I won't kill you if you promise you won't tell anybody I told you that, either."

That was Rich: I came to call him "Doctor Viking," or just "Doctor V." He was always full of surprises. I admired him. I loved his wit. And like the other Special Forces people I have met in my time I came to find that he was completely unflappable, calm and methodical in any emergency. I knew that his keel ran deep. He treated the patients like family and the staff with equal respect and compassion. In the quiet times I often heard the Crash crew speak with a hushed awe about him. He worked fast and effectively, made decisions and issued doctor's orders without hesitation and without changing his mind. And he always addressed the staff with decisiveness and calm. I found out in time that he intentionally kept his emotions in check and his voice at a low volume, even when it was noisy in the trauma room. He said that using a low volume made it hard for the Crash crew to hear his orders. That's why if it was too noisy in the trauma room he made a point of talking softly. Everyone's voice volume dropped a notch in order to hear him. With the decrease in volume in the room there was a concomitant drop in the anxiety level. That positively affected the crew, not to mention the patient.

So there he was on the night I arrived with the scalped driver, my good friend Dr. V. He stayed where he was near the entrance to Crash watching me until I was done refueling. He called to me as I rolled up the fuel hose.

"Come here. I want you to see something."

When Dr. V saw I was coming he punched in the combination for the doors to Crash and walked inside. By the time I got there he was about ten paces ahead of me. He kept that interval walking through the inner doors to Crash as well. When I got to the hallway in front of the trauma rooms I smelled the blood. I stopped in mid-step and started to get a sick feeling in the pit of my stomach. But now Dr. V was standing in the doorway to Trauma Room Three, arms crossed and waiting for me. I walked toward him breathing through my mouth. As I got close he reached out and put his sinewy hand on my shoulder. Then he ushered me into the brightly lighted area next to the exam table. There was nobody else in there but Dr. V, the patient I had brought him and me. The doc pointed to the deep sink that was across the room behind the patient. "Come over here with me and wash up. I need you to help me."

I looked over my shoulder and out the door. My crew was at the nurse's station, heads down and filling out reports. They paid no attention to me. I turned back toward the exam table and looked at the patient. The exam table had been brought up so that the patient was in a semi-reclined, sitting position. The bright exam light above him had been turned off to one side so it didn't shine directly on him. The room was bright anyway with the orange glow added by the exam light making the room appear rather warm and pleasant. The man's shirt had been removed. He was a bare-chested and dark skinned. A green sheet covered him from about the nipples down past his feet. But his arms were outside the sheet and hung limply at his sides. His head lolled a little to one side. He appeared to be sleeping. Over his mouth and nose was a non-rebreather mask. He was breathing pure oxygen regularly and easily. An IV of what I suspected was normal saline dripped with slow regularity beside him and down into the IV port in his arm. I knew it was the port the doctor used to administer the medication that had him sitting so peacefully on the exam table. The bandages I saw at the scene were still wrapped around his head. They made me think of the American Revolutionary soldier in the painting "The Spirit of '76," or from the color bearer in Stephen Crain's novel, The Red Badge of

Courage. A little blood stain had soaked through the thick winding of gauze on the patient's forehead. His black hair looked wet and sticky, poking out of the top of the bandage wrap like the top of a pineapple. I thought, *Hey! This patient doesn't look so bad.*

Dr. V gave me a push toward the back of the room where there was a large steel sink. "Get with it! Wash! Roll up your sleeves and wash well. Use lots of soap and real hot water. I'll tell you when to stop."

Like him I grabbed a small brush and dug at my nail beds and the backs of my knuckles to remove whatever was on my hands, including the top layer of skin. I watched and mimicked how thoroughly he washed. When he was done he pointed to my arm and said, "'missed a spot." I kept scrubbing while Dr. V turned and walked over to the patient. In a minute he said, "You're done. Now dry off and put on some gloves." I did. Then I turned around.

The doc had removed the bandages from the patient. He had readjusted the exam light to point right at the top of the patient's head. I closed my eyes involuntarily. The doc didn't seem to notice. He just said, "I want to show you something. Look here." When I opened one eye again he was pointing to a spot in the margin of the patient's hair above his forehead. The patient's hairline was crusted with dried blood. It seemed to sparkle as though he had diamond dust in his hair. There was a little seep of blood beginning to trickle under the sparkles and down his cheek. I opened the other eye.

"Does that bother you?" he asked pointing to the droplet of blood.

"No, doc. Blood doesn't bother me."

"Hmmm," he replied still looking attentively at the patient's hairline. Then he reached out and wrapped his hand over the patient's scalp and unceremoniously rolled it back from his skull. The pelt of hair looked rather like a wet, black toupee that was attached at the back of the patient's head. The patient didn't flinch. I did. I felt that cramp in my buttocks I had become familiar with. I stopped breathing. My vision narrowed. I knew I was about to pass out. I put a gloved hand in front of my eyes.

"Look at this," the doc said.

I moved my hand a little and looked. "Ooooo, that's going to leave a mark, doc!"

Dr. V laughed. "C'mon," he said as though I were being a baby about this. "He's out. He can't feel it. Look!"

I opened a little space between two fingers and looked out of one eye. Then I closed my fingers. The doc laughed.

"C'mon, look at this. You're never gonna' get used to it if you don't understand what's going on here."

I dropped my hand and opened my eyes, grimacing and biting my lower lip involuntarily. I felt my shanks spasm. I felt the pain I thought the patient must surely feel. The doc still had the man's scalp laid over his hand. He rolled it back and forth over the bare skull. It appeared Dr. V was trying to fit it back on somehow. As he rolled it back the bottom of the scalp looked like the inside of a bloody rabbit's pelt. Now I could see what had been sparkling in his hair. It was glass. The hair as well as the inside of his scalp was salted with tiny cubes of it. The top of the man's skull was too. It looked like little squares of rock salt bathed in bright red blood. Then the doc pointed to something in the bloody wetness on the man's skull.

"Thank goodness for safety glass," he said, "or this man would really have been cut up!" My knees got a little weak. The poor man on the table looked cut up enough for me.

"We've got to get this glass out of here," said the doc.

I noticed he said "we." I suspected he meant "we" like the President of the United States uses the word -- the "royal 'we'", the third person "we," the "we" that means "I" as in "*I* have to get the glass off his skull and out of his hair." But then he pointed to several bags of saline IV solution and tubing kits lying on a tray nearby.

"Spike one of those and help me out here?"

Spiking an IV bag meant preparing a bag of IV solution for use by connecting the tubing to the bag. One of the paramedics had taught me how to do it one day after I finished my preflight inspection. It wasn't a normal pilot function. I wondered how the doc knew I could do that. But I let it pass. I grabbed a bag of saline and opened an IV kit. It contained the tubing with a spiked end that I inserted into a port in the bag. I let the salt water flow down the tubing and dribble out on the floor a little before clamping it off. The doc saw it was ready for use.

"Now squirt that tube where I point. We're going to wash out this glass." It didn't appear that he cared that I was a pilot, not a nurse or ER tech. He wanted me to help. So I pointed the IV tube with one hand where the doc pointed and squeezed the IV bag with the other hand. I squirted saline solution where he pointed. The doc caught the runoff in a little kidney shaped steel bowl pressed against the patient's skull. We started washing with the inside of the pelt -- his scalp. The saline flowed down across the top of the patient's exposed skull. I emptied the bag and set it down on the tray. Then I took the bowl and emptied the blood and glass into the sink for the doc. I handed it back to him and spiked another bag. We repeated the process more times than I counted. But every time I turned around to spike another bag, there were still three of them sitting there on the cart waiting for me and the empty one was gone.

I didn't even see who it was that kept bringing them in. I'm not sure how long I was there in that room, but I noticed after I had been there a while that the time seemed to go quickly. My radio squawked a couple times during the process, but things on the street had slowed down. Lifeline got no calls. So I kept working with Dr. V. I looked over my shoulder once to see where my crew was. I was surprised to find them both standing in the entrance to the trauma room with their arms crossed, smiling at me. Then they left. They went back to work, and I went back to work with Dr. V.

We washed all the glass out from under the man's scalp, off of his skull and from around the margin of his wound. By then I had come to inspecting the detail in the top of his skull. I came to see it in its detail. I could see the joints between the plates of his cranium. It was more fascinating than the time I first saw those plates on a skeleton in biology class in high school. I was a little awed that I was gazing at living bone. Under that bone I knew was a living brain of a sentient man. I thought, *His spirit, his life lies just a couple millimeters below that bone.* The drugs in him were keeping him calm and his pain beyond his feeling. This thought calmed me. I was surprised that I felt the wonder of his life, of what we were doing to preserve it. My small part as I squirted warm saline solution and washed the glass and blood away made me feel useful and warm inside. I didn't feel his pain anymore. I just felt good as I did my little job and washed the glass out wherever I saw it.

We finally cleaned off his skull and the underside of his scalp to the doctor's satisfaction. Dr. V put the man's scalp back in place. Soaked as it was with water it sounded like a wet mop slopping down on a floor as he replaced it. He shifted it around to match it up to the torn margins of the wound. It took a three more bags of saline to wash out the man's hair. The doc gave the man a very gentle shampoo with antibiotic liquid soap. I collected the glass and blood this time as it ran out of his hair. I dumped it and the soap down the sink.

When the man was cleaned up, the doc talked me through a search of the steel cabinets in the trauma room. I went through them and found sutures for him that were appropriate for sewing the man's scalp back together. He needed several sizes and types of suture. He told me to look for catgut. I looked at him incredulous.

"Yeah, it's really made from pussy cats. I use catgut inside the wound because the body will absorb the stitches we can't reach. They don't have to be pulled out like these others I'll use at the margin of the wound." The patient slept on while Dr. V worked with a small curved needle and forceps stitching up the man's scalp. A nurse came in with a stack of green surgical towels. "Was that you bringing us all the saline?" I asked her.

"No," she smiled broadly. "That was your crew."

I finally realized why I was in that room. My crew had conspired with the Viking to re-introduce me to why I pursued this job. By concentrating on the outcome I could find the freedom to help the patient without immediately concerning myself with their injuries. As he worked, Dr. V didn't even look up from what he was doing. He just kept sewing as he told me about how he went from becoming an Army medic to an ER physician. It was a story of incredible effort and dedication. When he finished his job he put down his forceps. They made a clink on the metal tray. He looked up at me. "I bet you'd make a good doctor. Have you ever thought about doing that?"

I didn't say anything for a moment. I was shocked to recognize that he was sincere. Then I was both flattered and embarrassed. But I thought about his question. He didn't rush me. He just dabbed at the new line of stitches with gauze. I thought for a second about the long and difficult road Dr. V had walked to get from Army medic to Emergency Room physician. I knew at once that I didn't have the intelligence, discipline or especially the dedication to become a doctor. But I knew something else about myself as well. Something I didn't know when he called me into that trauma room.

"Doc, I was beginning to think I wasn't cut out for any of this anymore. You knew that, didn't you?"

He squinted as he examined his stitches in the man's head.

"Your crew likes you, Paul. They think you're a great pilot. Unless you decide to pursue medicine, we all think you're right where you need to be. You have the heart for this."

I bit my lip. I felt more relieved than I had in weeks. Dr. V smiled and looked up at me. He put his hand under the sleeping patient's chin, presenting him to me like a trophy.

"Well, I'm done. What do you think?" He turned the patient's head one way and then the other, like a sculptor admiring his work. I admired the cleaned wound, the neat stitches.

"Nice job, doc! That might not even leave a scar after all."

He agreed and then called gently for a nurse. "You should never fear things you don't understand. Just learn more about them until the fear goes away."

He let the man's head fall gently back on the exam table. Then he lowered the table so the man was reclined. When the nurse arrived, Dr. V gave her orders to salve and bandage the wound and continue treatment with IV antibacterial and pain medications. It sounded more like a request for a favor from a friend rather than doctor's orders. He turned and pointed to me, "And, please let him help." Then the Viking stepped into the hall as the nurse smiled first at him, then at me. She pointed toward a cabinet where I could find rolls of gauze. I saw Dr. V filling out the man's chart at the nurse's station where my crew had been standing just after I arrived. When the patient was bandaged I turned again to ask him how he thought the patient looked, but Dr. V and my fear had both vanished.

15 BEDLAM

I had the night shift. My radio sat in my lap, the volume turned down low. Things were quiet from where I sat in the Crew Quarters. But out on the streets of Austin things were hopping. EMS calls were out all over the city. I knew it was about to get busy upstairs. *No surprise*, I thought. *The moon is full and its pay day.*

I took my radio and pager, left the crew watching T.V. and walked upstairs to see what I could see. Topping the stairs I heard the rumble of diesel engines. A line of ambulances already stood on the loading dock empty, engines running. I walked over to the entrance to Crash and punched the code into the keypad. As the double doors slid open I noticed that all the gurneys that usually lined the walls were gone, another sign of a busy time for Crash. I walked up the hallway and slapped the plate that opened the final set of doors. A wave of smells other than antiseptic and a cacophony of excited voices and screams of pain met me like an oncoming wave. I stepped into bedlam.

Every sound, every voice rebounded off the green tile walls, amplifying the indistinguishable dissonance where everyone was heard and no one was understood. Every trauma room was full. Every examination light was on. The hallway outside all of the trauma rooms was alive with moving people. They wore scrubs of every description, white coats, EMS and police uniforms and now one flight suit.

Beyond the nurses' station, there was a full house tonight. A constant flow of people passed in and out of each room as well as the nurses' station and the hallway leading to Radiology and Surgery. People were shouting and jostling each other without apology as they went. Above the crowd in one room I saw the top of the portable x-ray machine poking up above the mass of medical people. It looked like a shiny black periscope. I followed it down to the wrinkled brow of one tall, gangly and overworked x-ray technician whose head appeared above the milling crowd from time to time.

"Excuse me!" the x-ray tech kept shouting. He was yelling it loudly enough for me to hear and understand him above the fray, but nobody in the room appeared to pay him any attention.

I caught the eye of a nurse I knew as she passed me.

"Help or get out," she said in no uncertain terms.

I pressed myself against the wall to let her pass and resolved to find something that needed doing.

"Yes, ma'am" I said to her as she disappeared around a corner.

She knew me, knew I'd help somewhere. I had done it plenty of times before, especially when things were as busy as tonight.

Passing each trauma room I glanced at the x-rays that were clipped up on the viewers. It was the easiest way for me to determine what was happening in the trauma rooms. "The Austin Gun Club" was busy tonight, I could tell. I knew that the gang bangers had recently shifted from automatic pistols to shotguns. I guess it was a fad. We'd had a lot of shotgun wounds showing up in the last weeks. Shotguns will kill you. But for some reason the bangers had decided to use bird shot recently instead of something more lethal like buckshot. The smaller the number, the bigger the shot. Buckshot was designated "0" or "00" and contained six or eight ball bearing sized pellets. Bird shot shells contained perhaps a hundred tiny lead pellets. Because they rapidly spread out when they were fired they had limited range. So unless the gunfight was close up birdshot just punched tiny and generally non-lethal holes in their target.

The first two x-rays on Trauma Room One's reader showed lots of stark little dots of bird shot scattered throughout the ghostly body mass and organs of that patient. By the pattern, I guessed it was a belly shot at twenty yards or so. Each pellet did its damage which might or might not be substantial. Bones stopped most of them. But a pellet puncturing an artery or organ would require surgery to fix.

Trauma Room Two contained what I might call with no pun intended, "a bull's eye." The two x-rays showed a frontal and side view of a man's head. Both x-rays were speckled with tiny, bright dots of bird shot. This guy had apparently taken two charges of shot full in the face. Number eight lead bird shot was distributed all over his head. I doubted that any had actually penetrated his skull. But sadly, a large cluster of pellets had come to a stop in the back of his eye sockets.

I glanced into the trauma room. The patient was sitting up facing me. He was both conscious and irate. His face was covered with what looked like dozens of little needle-pricks. They all leaked blood. The vitreous humor that had formerly filled his eyeballs was running down his face like tears. I knew he was blind for life now but he was still acting the part of the tough gangster with the ER staff. As he felt them pass by he called them ugly things in Spanish. He slapped them away sometimes as they tended to his wounds. Then a Latino ER tech stepped up to the gangster and leaned into his ear. He muttered something in Spanish and the gangster quit fighting the people tending to him. I'd have paid a dollar to know what the tech said to him.

On the counter in front of the nurse's station the EMS crews diligently bent shoulder to shoulder over clip boards and filled out their paperwork. On the other side of the counter a focused social worker sat at a telephone with a stack of wallets in front of her. She was trying to figure out who the patients were that I had just passed. Because most of them were criminals and/or in the country illegally, the gangsters kept their identities to themselves. Most of them had police records so they didn't answer questions or carry identification. The thick wads of money, condoms and pictures in their wallets didn't tell the social worker anything about them. She didn't care about their police records. But getting information about their medical history was literally a matter of life or death for them. Diseases, drug allergies, and medication they used - both legal and illegal - all played into the treatment program the doctors prescribed. Pressing on with medical treatment at the risk of giving an allergic patient a lethal dose of a medicine, or overdosing a patient who already had narcotics in his system was an unacceptable risk. The doctors wouldn't take it. So the social worker had to work fast or all they'd get was the most rudimentary of lifesaving medical care and nothing more.

The harried efforts of the social worker was only one facet of what made Crash look like bedlam. But I had come to realize that Crash was to emergency medical treatment what the trading floor is to the New York Stock Exchange. The overall picture of both places is often one of chaos. People yell back and forth. Scurrying players each focus on their individual tasks. They bump into one another getting from point to point. But despite what they look like, both the stock exchange and Crash are quite well orchestrated enterprises. It took me a while to sort out what went on in Crash because so much happens simultaneously. Dozens of tests and medical interventions take place on behalf of multiple, often critical patients. To get an idea of what was happening I started to watch and concentrate on the actions of one staff member at a time.

Sometimes a single individual did a single task. Blood, urine, vital signs and blood gasses were taken simultaneously, but each action was performed by a different individual. Other times everybody in a group worked as a team to accomplish a job. For example, x-rays were taken by a team of people. Techs lifted and moved patients on their backboards.

Two techs lifted the patient's backboard while an x-ray tech placed the x-ray film underneath. Then the x-ray tech called out a warning, "x-ray," and the whole trauma room team stood clear while the x-ray was taken. When that happened it reminded me of a school of sardines dodging a shark. After the x-ray was done they all returned unperturbed to what they were doing.

The overall direction of the medical efforts on each patient was done by the attending physician. But in each trauma room the work each doctor, specialist, nurse or tech accomplished was always under the close scrutiny of the charge nurse. The charge nurse kept detailed records of each action. Their records were referred to in order to document treatment. The record helped doctors seeing the patient later determine the treatment regimen used. Often too, those records ended up as evidence in both criminal and civil courts.

I flew in many people suffering multi-system trauma. For each injury they suffered, for each damage system in their body the Brack ER had specialists on staff. There was always a trauma surgeon attending the patient. That one doctor often did the whole job, as when Dr. V sewed on the patient's scalp with me helping. But if a heart or aorta was involved a thoracic surgeon might lend the trauma doc a hand. Nerve damage, particularly injuries involving the brain or spinal cord drew in the services of a neurosurgeon. For any difficult intubation or to prep a patient for surgery, an anesthesiologist showed up. Orthopedists performed surgery to reconstruct broken and shattered bones or to amputate hopelessly damaged limbs. When I told my medical crew I wanted to observe surgery one day they warned me away from orthopedic surgery. They called the ortho docs, "the butchers with hand tools." Their surgical tools come from hardware stores. Electric saws, drills and even hammers are used along with carpentry hardware like bolts, screws and threaded lengths of stainless steel. Ortho surgery is ugly, they said.

Other specialists appeared sometimes, like ocular bone specialists for people whose faces, eyes or eye sockets were smashed. An ophthalmologists would certainly take charge of the treatment of the banger with the eyeballs full of birdshot. Dentists and oral surgeons showed up to reconstruct broken faces, mandibles and teeth. All kinds of patients were visited by radiologists. Doctors treating patients with traumatic injuries including broken bones and internal bleeding, people with cancer, heart disease and strokes all relied on the services of radiologists.

Because I liked helping, just about all these specialists gave me carte blanche to ask questions when they weren't busy. The radiologists in particular let me follow them into their warrens and watch what they did, how they did it and ask questions. They had a number of impressive machines and technical tools at their disposal. Some were quite large, like the CAT scan machines, PET Scans, and even the venerable and irreplaceable old x-ray machines. I saw my first fluoroscope there, too. I thought they were obsolete until I saw a radiologist save a man's life using one.

I flew this particular patient in from a high-speed, head on car wreck. Even though I didn't see a drop of blood I knew he was bleeding to death. In Crash nobody could figure out why. I not only flew him to the hospital, I pushed his gurney into radiology where I got a look at my first fluoroscope. A radiologist talked me through what he was doing as he injected radioactive dye into the patient's arm and put him in front of a fluoroscope. Almost immediately, even I could see the leaking artery. A fluoroscope showed the dye-filled blood leaking into the man's chest in real time. It looked like ink dropped into a pool of water as the dye and blood spread into his chest cavity. The leak was coming from a punctured subclavian artery which runs under each collar bone. The shoulder harness in his car had probably broken his collar bone during the impact of the crash. The man went right to surgery where the artery was repaired. The man survived.

The radiologists used similar methods to see contusions and other damage to soft tissue and organs that would have been impossible to detect without surgery. They were especially good at spotting problems in the brain: concussions, strokes and other kinds of brain bleeds. They were also expert at spotting hairline fractures in bone that even the orthopedists might miss. They were like sleuths at detecting the presence of foreign objects like glass, plastic and other compounds that wound up in wounds from explosions or car accidents. These items don't reflect x-ray. They're often impossible to spot even by visually searching an open wound, too. But the radiologist spotted that junk. They never told me how. I think it was probably magic.

The night the banger came in with a face full of bird shot I got a lesson from a radiologist on tracking projectiles. I found out that bullets don't generally create what is called a "through and through" wound – in one side and straight out the other. Even when they do, fragments of the bullet often break off the projectile and do damage off the line of the bullet's travel. Bullets generally expand and slow down when they strike a body. When they do they can take unpredictable tracks. I saw a man shot on the chest who baffled those looking for where the bullet ended up. A radiologist found it lodged inside the man's pelvis. It hadn't hit bone or anything other than soft tissues and organs, but it tracked ninety degrees down from its original path after it hit the man.

With a gunshot wound a radiologist had to track the path of every piece of shot. I watched him do it for a while on the banger with the shotgun wound in the face. While I watched he showed me that each tiny projectile or fragment thereof leaves traces of lead. These tiny traces could be picked up by the imagery the radiologist took. He followed every fragment or piece of bird shot from impact to where the shot came to a stop. By the time he was done he had multiple images with traces he had drawn showing in three dimensions where each pellet had traveled.

Surgeons could uses these maps to determine what work had to be done to repair the damage and retrieve the projectile.

Many pellets had hit bone in various parts of his skull and traveled around its contours within the flesh. A pellet that hit his forehead for example, could follow the curve of his cranium and end up in the back of his neck. Some of the pellets hit nerves and pierced critical blood vessels. This patient had to have surgery to patch bird shot holes in the arteries in his neck.

When I started my observations of each member of Crash in action I was ghoulishly drawn first to the technician or nurse who drew blood gasses. They used the longest hypodermic needle I had ever seen. It is no exaggeration to say that the large bore needle they used to draw blood was at least three inches long. It was screwed into the end of a syringe that looked like something a vet would use to administer a large bolus of antibiotics into a horse or cow's rump. When the cap was pulled off the hypodermic needle, the nurse preparing to use it kept it elevated above their shoulder. They didn't want to stick anyone but the patient. With the other hand, gloved fingers would feel around in the patient's naked groin area. Seeing that immense syringe poised for immediate use, I generally didn't even notice the patent's gender during the search they made for a pulse from the femoral artery.

When the pulse was located the needle was carefully placed on the spot and unceremoniously inserted to its full length. The goal was to strike the femoral artery. A direct hit would cause the syringe to quickly fill up with blood. With a miss, out came the needle for another try. Sometimes the nurse got the artery on the first stab. Usually it took a couple tries. Once I counted six attempts before the last try hit the artery and started filling the syringe. The procedure looked like it would hurt enough to get the patient's attention. Oddly however, the patients rarely even seemed to notice there was three inches of needle stuck in their groin. There was usually a lot happening on the other end of their body to distract them, though. And many patients were unconscious, semi-conscious or on drugs that kept them blissfully unaware of the assault their body, too.

I asked a nurse the purpose of the procedure.

"The doctor needs to know if the oxygen content of the blood reaching the femoral artery is the same as that of the blood close to the heart. If the oxygen count is significantly lower in the lower body, the patient might have a blockage or leak somewhere between the heart and the groin. The patient might have a ruptured aorta or iliac artery, for example."

I nodded like a kid watching card tricks at a carnival. I didn't know an aorta from an eyeball at that time. I went on to learn some more about human anatomy. In this effort, Brenda, one of our flight nurses helped me a great deal. She gave me a brand new medical dictionary. She called it a birthday present. Later she came into Quarters on a shift and gave me an armload of books on emergency medicine. I think she was gratified to see I actually read them rather than just looked at the pictures of the female anatomy like most pilots would. She said that I asked intelligent questions about what I learned, too. Damon, my favorite flight paramedic, was also proud of me for wanting to learn more about the medical end of the job. He taught EMT courses, so the information I got from him was tailored to a neophyte like me. He reviewed the high school biology I had forgotten. But then he went on to teach me about each system in the human body and how it works. I began to understand not only what the Crash crew was doing, but why they were doing it.

Most important, I gained a new appreciation for the miracle that is the human body. I came to feel empathy for those patients whose bodies were broken or sick or failing. I counted my blessings that all my systems worked as advertised. I felt sympathy toward those patients who suffered the loss of function of some part of such a beautifully designed system. I was saddened to see the ruin caused by dependency on drugs and alcohol.

I came to understand how important the body was to our attitude toward life. In tune, it was a miraculously functioning vessel for a unique and precious soul. In learning medicine I came to see how Crash and Lifeline worked together. Lifeline got the lifesaving treatment's started that Crash pitched in and passed to the surgeons, specialists and specialty branches our ours and other hospitals. As a pilot and crew member I better understood just where I fell into the well-designed matrix of care that hopefully led a patient from trauma and sickness to fully restored health.

Nothing I did in the ER was critical. Flying was my priority. But I liked helping out the patients in ways that took the load off the ER staff. Across the board patients in the ER were very often cold, cramped and thirsty. Most of these discomforts came from the trauma and shock they suffered from whatever got them their trip to Brackenridge. The patients were cold because of shock, but also because their clothes were usually cut off of them when they got to Crash. When I saw cold patients I didn't have to get permission to give them a blanket out of the ER's blanket warmer.

Not so with thirst and cramps. Thirst comes from shock and blood loss. It's the reason wounded soldiers on a battlefield cry so plaintively for water. Personally, I never heard it on a battlefield myself, but I know what that plea sounds like. I heard it a lot in the ER. I learned why it is generally not a good idea to give an injured person water. One problem with doing so is aspiration. That happens when someone breathes vomit into their lungs. Laying strapped to a backboard doesn't allow a patient to void the vomit. They can drown in it outright, or they can get the fluid in their lungs and contract pneumonia from it. Water can cause an internally injured patient to vomit. The water can also cause further damage to already injured internal organs. Whenever I'd hear plaintive cries for water I would check with the nurses. Sometimes I could give them a sip of water. Sometimes I could only wet their lips with a wash cloth or give them a little crushed ice. I hated it when I couldn't give them anything. Listening to those pleas for something to drink was almost as hard on me as it was on them.

Strapped to a backboard or laying on a cold steel table would be uncomfortable for anyone. Add an injury and the discomfort of lying still and flat on your back could be intense. I learned on one call though that attempting to relieve a patient's discomfort could injure or kill them. I got the lesson responding to an MVA at a rest stop on the interstate. A drunk driving a pickup truck at highway speed had run into the back of an eighteen wheeler trailer parked at the truck stop. The drunk thought the rest stop was his exit. When I landed next to the wreck the fire crews were using the Jaws to pry the driver out from behind the steering wheel. I thought it a fool's errand until I walked over to the wreck. The pickup was flattened against the trailer from the headlights to the back of the door frame. I saw no room for anyone in the pickup cab to live. But then I heard the driver inside asking the fire fighters to hurry up and get him out.

When they pried the flattened steering wheel from his chest a flattened beer can he had been holding fell into his lap. We got him spider strapped on a backboard and on his way to the hospital in the helicopter. The whole way the patient complained of back pain and begged our nurse and paramedic to loosen the straps and shift him a little to alleviate it. They were deaf to his cries. The thoracic surgeon who repaired his severed aorta later told me that if we had moved him an inch in any direction he would have died immediately. Lesson learned: don't move a patient or massage a cramped muscle without permission.

Don't get me wrong. I often asked for and received permission to put a pillow or wound up sheet under a leg or back, a pillow under a head. I straightened a cramped limb or massaged a muscle spasm on many occasions. I just asked permission of the doctors or nurses first. One day I passed an exam room where an old man was having a heart attack. He was laying on an exam table complaining of muscle spasms in his back. Back pain is a common complaint and symptom with a heart attack. I figured the heart attack was causing the pain. Still, I asked the cardiologist treating him if I could help the old man out with a back massage. "Sure," he said. So I reached under the man's back with my fist and used a knuckle to loosen what felt like a knotted muscle along his spine. It worked! The old man turned his head and looked at me with a big smile on his face.

"Thanks, son," he said. "That's all I needed."

I'm happy to say he was treated for the heart issue and later discharged home.

I got a lot more work to do when the Crash crew realized I wasn't afraid of blood and vomit. After they trained me what to wear to avoid the bacteria it carried, I moved and often helped them clean up quite a number of bloody patients. There I'd be in a smock, mask and gloves wiping blood and windshield glass off of a patient right alongside the nurses.

When there was nothing else for me to do I sometimes helped the techs clean up the trauma rooms. After cleaning a particularly messy room an ER tech dubbed me "the spooge master." I had to ask Steve, one of our flight nurses what "spooge" was.

"Spooge, my man, be the ultimate funk," he replied. Steve was a great flight nurse and I loved him. He was a little, skinny guy. His salt and pepper hair was cut short. He wore round wire framed glasses, and a Van Gogh beard. He actually looked a little like Vincent himself, I thought.

"Clarify, 'ultimate funk' if you please, Nurse Steve."

He explained like the intellectual medical practitioner I knew he was. "'Spooge' is any gross or disgusting fluid, or combination of fluids emitted from a human body." Now that he was talking like an educated nurse, I nodded, understanding. But he wasn't done. He went into more detail about the color, odor and hazard of various varieties of spooge. He went into far more detail than necessary. In doing so I detected he was making an effort to gross me out. So I told him a joke I learned in the Marines that made my drill instructor sick at his stomach. The punch line included something about a drunk eating a viscous form of sputum from the surface of the bar in order to win a bet with the bartender. It not only confirmed my complete understanding of the concept of spooge, but grossed out Steve as well. He gagged. And my medical terminology dictionary grew by one important word. That's one way I learned the medical end of our business: from friends, one word at a time.

The pilots were supposed to wash the helicopter every day. When calls got bloody, though it got washed more often than that. The other pilots never cleaned up blood, whether it was inside or outside of the aircraft.

One evening I arrived for shift change just as the helicopter was landing. I arrived on the pad in time to see Skip climbing out of the Four-Twelve. He was a respected and a long-time pilot with Lifeline and I liked him. It was clear at first glance at the helicopter that he had just returned from a bad scene call. Two patients were hot-unloaded before he shut down the engines.

From where I stood I could tell that the patients had both been bleeding profusely. The Four-Twelve was bad about leaking blood. When blood pooled on the medical cabin floor it leaked out of the seals on the bottom of the sliding cabin doors. Then it blew back under the belly and around the tail boom of the helicopter. As I stood at the top of the stairs looking at the bloody helicopter, Skip turned to see what I was looking at. It looked gruesome.

I walked past Skip and over to the fuel pit where the water hose was also stored. I was preparing to wash off the tail when Skip stepped around the nose of the aircraft. I guess he thought I was about to refuel the aircraft. When he saw me with the water hose in my hand instead of the fuel hose though, he started giving me grief about doing the medical crew's job.

"Why do you do that? Get with the program, Paul! If it bleeds or breathes it's none of our business. We're pilots, not medics." I ignored him as I ignored the other pilots when they gave me grief for doing something they left to the medical crew. Before I could get started on the wash down, Skip and I heard a shriek emanate from the ambulance dock behind us. I turned just in time to see a lady getting out of the passenger side of a car collapse on the dock. Fortunately she fell into the arms of a man who was opening the door for her. His face appeared grief-stricken as he looked back toward me. Then I noted he wasn't looking at me. He was looking at the helicopter. He lowered the lady into a sitting position on the sidewalk. As he squatted down next to her he kept his eyes locked on the helicopter.

The lady, wracked with sobs was soon joined by the man who hugged her to his chest. I knew who they were. They were parents of at least one of the boys whose blood now covered our helicopter. I found out later that both of the bleeding boys were their sons. They got to the hospital just after their sons were unloaded and brought into Crash, but just in time to see their sons' blood sprayed down the side and tail of Lifeline One.

A couple of people in scrubs came out of the ER and helped the man and his wife to their feet and into the ER. I turned and looked at Skip. He watched the ER doors for what seemed like a long time. Then he looked at me, the tail boom of the helicopter, then back at me. I knew what Skip was thinking. I handed him the hose. I washed the helicopter with a long handled brush while he washed off the soap and blood with a hose.

During the next crew meeting, Skip asked to have the floor for a minute. He told the pilots and the medical crews from his point of view what happened on the pad that day. When he was done I saw tears in his eyes. The room was silent. Everyone focused on Skip.

"I will never forget the sound of that boy's mother breaking down there on the loading dock. I will not forget the look on his father's face. Never. I know none of you ever want hear something like that either."

He looked down the table at me and gave me a sad smile.

"I know we've given Paul a hard time about doing the crew's job for them -- washing the blood off the helicopter, I mean. We've been calling him 'Nurse Stone' and such, saying he's more medical crew than pilot."

His smile and a little ripple of laughter broke the tension. His face brightened a little.

"And he may be working on a nursing degree for all we know…"

More laughter.

"But in this case, I think he may be right. The informal policy we have had about pilots not washing off the blood ought to change. In fact, it already *has* changed for me. I never want to hear something like that again. I never want to do something like that again…to anyone."

Skip sat down. Jolly looked around for comment. I thought he might overrule Skip. We all knew of his paranoia about germs. We all knew that is was Jolly who as a line pilot first fought to keep the pilots from helping the crew clean up body fluids. Jolly made it clear he couldn't care less about the patients or their family. I could tell that he wanted to stand his ground on that issue about cleaning up the helicopter with the crew. But since he no longer flew the line, he didn't feel the threat personally. He was the D.O. If he flew a bloody flight he could still stick the crew with the cleanup. So he decided to let Skip have his say. He let the line pilots do as they wished.

I stepped out of the way of the paramedics and Crash team as they rolled through the code protected double doors and rushed past me in the hallway. They were headed for the trauma rooms. An ambulance had just brought in the patient, a black teenager. As he passed, I saw a pained expression, a non-rebreather mask and that his chest was bare and covered in blood. When I caught up with them in Crash they were sliding his backboard onto the exam table in Trauma Room Two. An ER tech pushed the gurney out of the room and back toward the entrance hallway. I looked past the tech. I thought the patient looked to be probably sixteen to eighteen years old. Except for the bullet hole I could now see in the middle of his chest, he looked like a normal, handsome and healthy kid. That's what I was thinking too: *Normal, healthy, handsome and shot*. He was not saying anything, not even, "it hurts," like many gunshot victims do.

I noticed that among the pack of people in scrubs was an overweight black man in a blue nylon windbreaker. I didn't see him arrive, but I couldn't help but notice him now. On the back of his windbreaker was printed in yellow letters the word, "HOMICIDE." Everybody knew why he was there. With the Crash crew working all around him I knew there was no room for that cop in that room. They were all working hard to keep the kid alive. The homicide cop saw that too, so he slipped out of the room and stood next to me in the hallway. He was wearing a white shirt and tie under his windbreaker. His collar was open, his tie loose. Rivulets of sweat ran down his face and neck staining his shirt. He held a clipboard in one hand. He had a limp looking handkerchief in the other. I thought for a moment he would wipe his face, but he didn't. He just stared at the patient on the examination table.

The boy's face and upper body was now lying brightly illuminated under the examination light. A nurse was asking him questions about his name and medical history. I didn't hear any response. Other scrub clad people went about the tasks they routinely employed to save the life of a gunshot victim: cutting off clothing, starting IVs. The cop edged forward. He tried to slip back into the room behind the Charge Nurse. She put one hand in the middle of his chest and made it clear he'd get his turn as soon as they got the patient stable. The cop backed off, but I could tell he thought his time to interrogate the patient was quickly passing him by, probably forever. When he stood beside me again he was pensive. He finally wiped his face.

"What happened?" I asked.

The cop didn't look away from the patient. He just said, "He was flirting with the wrong girl is all it was. Her boyfriend just walked up and capped him. Bang, just like that. The shooter is a gang banger, a drug dealer, a real tough thug. We've got him in custody. If this kid dies he's going to be a tough thug in prison for the rest of his life."

He moved one way and another to keep an eye on the young man as people swarmed around him. "But we won't get his assailant for sure unless I can get the victim to identify the shooter before he dies."

I noticed he thought the young man's death a foregone conclusion.

"Don't you think he might live to point to the guy that shot him in a court of law?"

The cop turned to me with a look of incredulity on his face that seemed to say, *Are you stupid?* "He's been shot twice in the chest at point blank range with a .357 magnum. What do you think his chances are of making it to court?"

The question was clearly rhetorical, so I just shrugged. I hoped the cop was wrong.

A shout from the patient turned my attention away from the detective. It was the first sound I heard him make since he arrived. It energized the detective to head back into the room. This time he dodged to the opposite side of the exam table from where the charge nurse was standing. He elbowed his way into the crowd, leaned over the boy and put his face up close to him. If he was conscious and saw anything, the cop probably looked like a silhouette surrounded by bright light.

"Who shot you, Rodney?" he shouted.

I looked over at the charge nurse and saw her face redden.

"Who shot you? Just say the name."

The charge nurse stepped into the hallway, a determined look in her face. Then she rushed past me as she hailed a gray haired man wearing scrubs. He was standing at the nurses' station. He walked toward the charge nurse and met her a few steps away from me. The two conferred briefly. Then both turned and the man and the nurse passed me and headed into the room on the opposite side of the table from the cop.

"Who shot you, Rodney?" The cop kept saying.

Apparently the patient wasn't saying. Meanwhile, the gray haired gentleman in the scrubs stepped through the crowd in the trauma room and walked up to the head of the exam table. I think he excused himself because the cop looked up and stepped back half a pace. Then the gray haired man took off the boy's oxygen mask and said, "Open your mouth, son." Then in one smooth move the gray haired man reached up with something in each hand and placed an ET tube down the boy's throat. A nurse attached an ambu bag to the tube and began breathing for the boy. The crowd around the table parted briefly, and the gray haired man left the room.

The charge nurse and cop exchanged glances. His witness had just been silenced, and he knew it. He just shrugged and came out of the room a few steps behind the man in the scrubs. He was shaking his head. He looked at me as he passed, utterly frustrated.

"Anesthesiologist," I said to him. The cop nodded at me.

"A good one, I bet." Then he walked past me and back down the hall the way we had come in. I followed him out of Crash. He went his way and I went mine.

About an hour later I came back to see how the patient was doing. It was as though he had never been there. The trauma room in which he had been was empty, clean and ready for the next patient. I saw no one who had been working on him anywhere in crash. I never found out whether or not young Rodney even survived.

16 BRENDA

In Texas, and specifically where we worked in Austin, most people consider eating something between recreation and sport. In Texas, and specifically where I worked, taking a bite of something on someone else's plate was not just "okay." It was expected. A person who offered you a sample of the peach cobbler, pecan pie or broccoli rice casserole on their plate was breaking bread with you. It would be considered a slight to turn that down.

Sheryl was one of our paramedics. She was pencil thin but always on a diet. She was one of those chronically skinny people who always complained about being fat. She knew the eating etiquette of Texans and particularly the crews at Lifeline. Sheryl however, always turned down those invitations for, "a bite of something really good." Instead of taking the offered bite she might respond, "How can you eat that?" or "That is way too fattening for me!" Either comment inferred that the person offering the bite was not only being snubbed, but that they were fat, far fatter than Sheryl. That didn't make her the most popular paramedic on our staff. What particularly bugged me about Sheryl turning down food was what usually happened when the person left the room after Sheryl had turned down her offered taste. In the absence of the person who offered it,

Sheryl would sneak the bite anyway. She did that several times as I sat at the table with her. I think everyone knew she did it. When she did it she would always crinkle her nose at anyone present and say, "Aren't I bad?"

I never answered her. I thought she was not so much bad as rude and possibly condescending. I thought she was probably borderline anorexic, too. But I kept my own counsel. I thought I was the only one bothered by her irritating habit until one day when Brenda our nurse, was working with Sheryl and me. It had been a busy morning. We had missed breakfast because of an early call. After that call we immediately flew a hospital transfer. We didn't get a break until it was way past lunchtime. We were all famished by that time. When we landed at the pad we all hustled down to Quarters to grab something to eat before the next call came in.

Each of us had brought something from home. We grabbed our food from the fridge and sat down together at the table in Quarters to eat it. Brenda had a killer Chef salad. It had the works on it and a special salad dressing that she had bought at one of the specialty grocery stores that are part of the Austin scene. She asked us if we'd like to taste it. Of course, I took a sample. It was really good, and I thanked her for it. Sheryl as usual, begged off saying it would ruin her diet. Then she added something that Brenda and I both took to mean that Brenda was getting a little hippy.

"Maybe you should cut back on the dressing a little bit, Brenda," she said.

Brenda didn't even appear to have heard her. I knew better than to react to Sheryl, and I knew better than to think Brenda hadn't heard her, too.

A few minutes later when we had all just about finished our lunch, Brenda's cell phone rang. She picked up her plate and walked over to the kitchen. She set the plate down next to the sink and kept eating as she conducted her cell phone conversation. In a minute, she came back to the table, still talking on the cell phone. She put her plate back down and stepped out into the parking garage to finish what she had to say to the caller.

Brenda's salad sat there, the unique dressing now well worked into it now. I knew what was going to happen. Sheryl couldn't resist. She reached across the table and scooped up a big forkful of Laurie's salad. She quickly jammed a wad of it into her mouth. She looked like a starving person allowed just one bite of something delectable before they died. She took a look at me and crinkled her nose as usual. He mouth was too full of salad to say what I knew was coming. She tried to swallow the salad but suddenly began to choke.

I thought she couldn't say how bad she was because her mouth was so full of salad. But then suddenly her face changed into a look of panic or pain, or possibly both. She lunged from the table knocking her chair a kilter as she ran for the hallway. She was gagging. I thought she would vomit her food on the floor as the bathroom door slammed shut.

A few seconds later Brenda came in from the garage. She stuck her cell phone in her flight suit pocket, picked up her plate. She walked over to garbage can and scraped the salad into it. Then she rinsed off the plate and stacked it to dry. Turning toward me she picked up a red bottle of nuclear Cajun hot sauce that was on the counter. She shook it at me with an evil look in her eye.

"So Paul, how'd the skinny bitch like my Tabasco Chef salad?"

17 LAURIE

I had been on the line a while. I had seen medical crew members come and go. When Laurie was selected by the interview committee to be our next flight nurse I didn't think she was going to make it. Before she applied for the job I had seen her working in the ER and in Crash. I suppose she just did her job because nothing about her work there caught my eye. I certainly noticed her, though. She kept her hair cut boy-short, and regularly changed it from one un-natural color to another. One week it was maroon, the next orange. The longest hair on her head was always heavily loaded with mousse and spiked. She wore a dozen small earrings or plain bead studs in her ears. Unless you could call a black plastic sports watch jewelry, she wore no jewelry at all. She was short and stocky with a figure that was round and pudgy enough that it could have been either male or female. If she had curves, her baggy scrubs and perhaps a little extra weight around her middle erased them. She had plain features on a wide, square face that pointed to ancestors of east European or possibly White Russian heritage. People would probably have noticed her pretty, dark blue eyes had she used a little makeup or shaped her thick, black eyebrows. Other nurses wore tennis shoes or Birkenstocks. Laurie wore sturdy looking leather work shoes or military style boots. She was about as un-feminine looking as they come. Long after she started flying for Lifeline and we had become good friends she was surprised when I told her I had first thought she was a lesbian. By the time I told her, I knew she was not one. She was not offended or defensive when I told her, just entertained by my supposition.

I never worked with a flight nurse who was a natural at it. I worked rookies who never figured it out. They didn't last long. And I worked with rookies who became terrific flight nurses and aircrew members. Laurie was one of these. As a rookie she got a rocky start. When she joined us all her medical experience had been inside hospitals. She had no pre-hospital experience at all, which means she never worked on the street in an ambulance. In the hospital though, she had done just about everything that a nurse could do treating really sick people. She went from neonatal intensive care to Crash, and she worked from student nurse through charge nurse positions. Early in her career she had been a traveling nurse. Besides being well-travelled, she had experience in lots of different hospital settings. She worked in everything from little country clinics to busy, big-city Level One trauma centers. Brackenridge probably fit somewhere in the middle of where she had worked in the past. I watched her work in Crash. She was good. People respected her. When she applied to work for Lifeline I was ready to welcome her.

She found out that working on an air ambulance helicopter was very different from anything she had done before. First, it was an ambulance. She'd never worked on one before. It was also an ambulance that went to some of the most hectic and disorganized scenes that dispatch could find for us. The paramedics were quick to complain about working with her. She had a hard time at first working in the confines of the aircraft. Then she had to deal with working in a machine that moved in every axis, pitch, roll and yaw. We also traveled fast. We got in, got the passenger and got out of the landing zone generally in less time than she used in the past to check her patients into the ER. Treatment onboard had to be equally fast. Our flights generally took less than a half hour from scene to Crash. So, one of her first challenges was learning to operate quickly and confidently. I couldn't help her with that.

The paramedics also complained that she was weak. It was true. She couldn't hold up her end of the backboard or carry heavy medical bags very far without great effort. I had to give her credit though, and so did the paramedics. On her own accord she went on a diet and joined a gym. Her focus on both skinny and stronger showed. Before long she was lifting, carrying and getting around the scene stride for stride with any other medical crew member.

A crew member on Lifeline has to be able to "aviate, navigate and communicate." Some don't get past the "aviate" part. I wondered if Laurie would. When she sat up front with me the first time, she was clearly frightened. She had never flown in a helicopter before, let alone run an emergency call from the front seat of one. Just flying in a helicopter is sometimes akin to riding on a thrill ride. The pilots at Lifeline were not shy about handling the helicopter aggressively, either. We weren't cowboys. We just did what we had to in order to get to and from the scene quickly and safely. The call didn't start until we landed. We didn't waste time getting the aircraft on the ground. New crew members either got used to that kind of flying or they quit. Somehow I knew she wasn't a quitter.

She and I both knew she was out of her element in the "navigate" part, too. Our paramedics didn't have problems with this. They had all driven ambulances all over the area. They knew where we were going as soon as they heard the volunteers we would be working with. Sometimes they even knew the street addresses we were visiting. Laurie on the other hand, was a Yankee. She hadn't spent much time south of the Mason-Dixon Line, let alone in Austin. I had taught lots of fledgling pilots how to get oriented and navigate. I knew I could help Laurie get oriented, too. At least, I hoped so.

Communication was another challenge. Even as an experienced commercial pilot, on my first ride-along I was overwhelmed listening to four busy radios simultaneously. I told Laurie that she had challenges as big as an elephant before her. But she smiled when I said we were going to work on those challenges together just like you eat an elephant.

"One bite at a time," she replied.

She proved to be a real fast learner. Her strong suit was her nursing skills. They were excellent. Once she arrived on scene she was often ahead of the paramedic in figuring out the treatment plan and executing that. That translated to being able to do it in the confined and moving space of the helicopter. She was also strong at reading people. She had tremendous empathy for our patients and their families. She was intuitive and wise. At the scene, particularly the scene of medical calls, she was able to put difficult concepts in simple terms. She could bring patients and their care-givers to a quick realization of the situation they were in. Most important, she gained people's confidence in her ability and desire to help them. In this, she was always the best of all the medical crews I worked with. She applied those skills to working with her colleagues, too. As a consequence, she made friends fast among the pilots and crew. Because of who she was we all worked a little extra with Laurie to get her up to speed. We wanted a quality person like her to succeed.

She quickly got her bearings at Lifeline. In fact she was imperturbable, even at major disasters. She just stepped off the helicopter, took charge, and took care of the patients. I became confident that if there was anyone who could get a patient to Crash alive, it would be Laurie. I think the paramedics came to agree with my assessment. Soon they were paying deference to her assessments and her judgments. But she was willing to listen as well. She listened and took action when anyone had something to offer that would make her better at her job.

She came to me to learn to fly. She didn't come to any of the other pilots. She told me that she wanted to help the pilots and be as much of an asset in the cockpit as she could. I asked her if she was willing to start with the basics.

"That's the only place to start," she assured me.

So we started with opening the door.

I knew that the sudden alarm of our pager flustered her. When the pager went off she had trouble even opening the door to Quarters, let alone the door to the helicopter. So we started our training in Quarters repeatedly practicing each step of the beginning of a call. We even ran up and down the stairs until we were both tired and winded. In doing so, I saw the tenacity in Laurie that inspired me not only then, but later. She never quit. She worked tenaciously at everything she did until she had conquered her fears.

Once, as I came up the stairs to the helipad, I saw her climbing in and out of the helicopter. I stopped at the top of the stairs and watched for some time. She apparently didn't notice me there as she opened and closed the sliding door, followed by the cockpit door. The paramedics and I soon saw the result of her practice. She often became the first of us to be seated and strapped in for takeoff. When we complimented her on how good she was getting at the job, she just grinned sheepishly.

But she wasn't done getting better at what she did. Laurie insisted I familiarize her with some of my duties as well. She followed me around the helicopter when I did my preflight inspection. She asked enough questions that I decided to just show her how all the systems on the aircraft worked. She was not just willing, I could tell by her questions that she was putting all the pieces together. When I showed her the complex electrical systems and how they worked I focused on how her medical equipment tied into the aircraft. She followed up by telling me which generator and which electrical bus provided the power to that equipment. I was stunned.

I showed her how to service the oxygen system. She got so good so fast that I let her service it while I was doing something else to get the helicopter ready for the next call.

She even helped me washing the helicopter. I gave her corresponding help cleaning the medical cabin. One morning when we finished washing the helicopter I opened the pilot side door and said, "Get in."

She did. I climbed in the passenger side of the cockpit and familiarized her with the helicopter from my perspective. I not only showed her what all the switches and gauges did, I had her manipulate the switches and handle the controls. I pointed out the complex series of circuit breakers and how they were organized. She knew the electrical system so well already that she understood the function and organization of the circuit breakers as well. As far as I was concerned, we were done with the basics.

Now we're going to get into what we do here at Lifeline to run a call. I plugged in the external power cart and put her in the left seat. Meanwhile I sat at the flight controls, right where I'd be for a call. We donned our helmets and I played the part of all the agencies with which we would communicate. Having flown in the back during most calls she was familiar enough with the radio calls to know what to say and who to talk to. But she didn't know how to operate the radios or the pin switches that allowed her to listen to and talk on just the radio she wanted. We used the intercom where I played the pilot or the controlling agency we spoke with. But she had to flip the right switches or change the right radio to the proper channel to get me to respond. We did this every day of our shift until she was as good at using the radios and at running a call as any pilot or crew member at Lifeline.

Navigation in Central Texas was the next challenge. She could get lost in the parking garage. But Laurie was a shopper. When I asked her what she knew about getting around Austin she replied, "I can get you to any shopping mall in the city."

I wasn't a shopper, but if getting to shopping malls was what she did, that was where we would start learning to navigate by air to get somewhere. First we did map exercises in Quarters where she figured the magnetic headings from the hospital to every shopping mall in town. It was a great start. We built on that to figure a heading to each volunteer EMS and Fire agency sector in Austin and Travis country. We expanded our exercise to include small clinics and hospitals we serviced in surrounding counties. Soon we were using a real estate map book to figure headings to specific addresses. Laurie caught on fast. We practiced with using the maps and map book in the cockpit. She learned not only how to navigate, but how to remain organized in a moving helicopter while she did so.

Even after years of working with her though, she still reverted to her old basics. She was the only crew member I had that would give me a street address, a heading and distance and then follow up with, "It's about a mile north of Barton Creek Mall."

"Roger," I'd reply.

When I came to Lifeline, that's how navigation was done. But soon after I came aboard technology made a giant leap so far as navigation was concerned. The county bought us brand new Global Positioning Systems (GPS). The GPS systems on the Lifeline helicopters were complex. Our pilots took some time to get them figured out. Although we didn't expect the crews to learn how to use them, Laurie would have none of that. She wanted to know how the GPS worked and how she could put in positions so I wouldn't have to be distracted from my flying duties to do so.

She wanted to know all I could tell her. I drew lots of pictures explaining the Global Positioning Systems and how they worked. I explained the concept of latitude and longitude and how it fit our navigation. We plugged in the auxiliary power cart and spent many hours sitting in the cockpit operating the GPS. We plugged in coordinates until we could do it in seconds. We also set up the memory features of the GPS box. We loaded and made a guide that showed many of the common destinations we went to. The guide contained waypoints for distant hospitals, clinics, towns and major highway intersections so crews didn't waste time putting in long strings of latitude and longitude coordinates.

We even delved into the more arcane functions of the GPS. In doing so I learned some things while trying to explain to Laurie what I thought I knew. She grinned when I learned something and said, "Well, how about that! I didn't know this GPS would do that." That's when it was my turn to blush. When she was satisfied she understood the system she asked me to let her use it to see how good she was. Her setting up the GPS quickened our response times. Soon I found her as good as any pilot I could have flown with in getting us to the scenes. Laurie and I even set up a friendly competition. When we started off on calls, sometimes we raced to see if she could enter the latitude and longitude coordinates of the scene before I took off. She got so good at it she usually told me the heading and distance to the scene before I was light on the skids. Soon it was no competition at all. She could beat me every time.

Laurie was a team player. That's why she challenged the status quo. Those two statements seem in opposition to one another. But a team player makes sure that the whole team plays by the rules. That is certainly something Laurie did. She earned a reputation as a person who did things by the book. She saw that the bar was set where it was supposed to be. Then she made sure we all reached it. When we let our standards slip, she called us on it. She even held my feet to the fire a few times. As a result I tightened up my own standards. I maintained the professional polish I would not have had without working with Laurie. Laurie had that effect on all of us. She was good for Lifeline.

Laurie looked for new ways to do old tasks. Often in doing so, she improved the system. But sometimes she screwed things up, too. That's the price of boldly challenging "the way it has always been done." Her bold attitude in doing old things new ways got her in some trouble once when we got a call on a "man down." The man in question was down at a construction site of an industrial building. The building site was well out in the hills on the west side of Austin. The patient turned out to be a very big guy who also happened to be obese. He was supervising the pouring of a great slab of concrete.

When we landed at the site a medic unit was already on the scene. They had started CPR. The patient was on his back with his arms and legs splayed out as though he had fallen straight backwards and hit the ground in that position. The people standing around him wore rubber boots covered with wet cement. Their clothes and faces were covered with lime and cement dust. They gathered around and watched, but didn't offer to help. They may have been concerned for his health. But I bet they were also concerned that the man with their day's pay in his pocket just had a heart attack.

This call was one of the rare occasions I saw at Lifeline in which CPR actually worked. The man had no pulse when the ambulance got there. He had a pulse back when we arrived. It was weak and thready, though. That posed a conundrum. He needed advanced medical care quickly. That made the helicopter the best choice for transport. But if his heart stopped again *en route* the cramped quarters in the helicopter would make CPR much less effective. After some conversations with a cardiologist at Brackenridge and with her partner, Laurie decided to fly the guy. With the help of the concerned concrete workers we loaded him up and I took off.

We weren't in the air very long before Laurie and the paramedic were reporting to the hospital that the patient's condition had again deteriorated. We were still twenty minutes from the hospital when the man's heart stopped again. Usually in a situation like this the crew starts and continues CPR. I would fly to the hospital and land. The crew and hospital ER team would offload the patient. CPR would continue while the flight nurse, the flight paramedic and the Crash crew wheeled the patient into Crash. At that point a doctor would stop CPR, make a short examination of what was usually a dead person and make the call official. A patient is not dead until a doctor says so. That's why Lifeline never carried a dead patient. Physiologically they may well have died. But since the doctor hadn't declared their time of death while they were on the helicopter, we never carried dead people.

But that's not what happened this day. Laurie was in charge. We were in the LongRanger. That big man with the bad heart barely fit in there. There just was not enough room to do CPR. So Laurie decided they might as well pronounce the man dead. The paramedic knew Laurie did things differently so he went along with her call. When she asked for the pronouncement over the radio I could tell that the doctor in Crash thought it a little odd. But after a few questions about the patient's condition and what had been done for him, he too agreed with Laurie.

"Okay, Lifeline. The time (of death) is twelve seventeen."

Laurie got her wish. The guy in my helicopter was dead. Laurie seemed pretty proud of herself. Maybe she thought that we had set a precedent that would result in putting us back in service faster in the future. I think we were all a little worried though when we landed at the hospital and nobody came out from Crash to greet us. There was no gurney, no Crash team. Laurie was the first to realize what was happening. We had a dead man onboard. Dead people go to the coroner's office to be stashed in a cooler in the city morgue. Since this man was already declared dead no hospital would have anything to do with him. This dead guys was ours, or more specific, Laurie's.

I rolled the throttle to idle to let the engine cool before shutdown. I was glad I was just a pilot and not the nurse on this flight.

"You have two minutes to come up with a plan before I shut down the engine, Laurie." She acknowledged my warning and called Dispatch on the EMS radio. Sounding very confident she said, "Lifeline needs a coroner's truck to respond to the hospital helipad."

"Received, Lifeline One. Standby."

We stood by. I looked at the clock; a minute to go before I shutoff the engine. Curious ambulance crews began to appear along the loading dock. That drew people in the emergency room to see what was going on. They lined the tall windows of the ER. Time marched by. I let the engine run a while longer.

"What do you want me to do. Laurie?"

"Well we can't shut down!" she pouted. "Look at all those people!

Then Dispatch called. "Lifeline One, the Coroner said to tell you they would be by in an hour."

I almost heard Laurie's jaw hit the floor.

"Received," she said, sounding both unhappy and confused.

"Well, girl," I said. "You're going to have to execute some kind of plan because I'm shutting this thing down."

I rolled the throttle closed. I let the rotor coast down rather than use the rotor brake while Laurie came up with a plan. When the rotor finally stopped I took off my helmet. I stepped out to tie the rotor down. I could see in the cabin that Laurie and the paramedic were arguing about how to deal with the dead man. It was kind of embarrassing standing between the helicopter and the hospital watching all those people watching us.

I opened Laurie's door. She stepped out and looked into a bag that contained the man's personal effects. She held it out for me to look into. The bag was full of twenty dollar bills. It looked like the loot from a bank robbery.

"Holy crap," I said. "That's a wad of money! Where'd you get it?"

Laurie pointed at the dead man.

"'Must have been to pay his day labor," I speculated. "So what are we going to do with all that," I nodded toward the corpse, "...not to mention him?"

Her brow wrinkled. But then a realization struck her. She would yet persevere.

"Paul, go get us a gurney," she said.

I did. When I brought it back to the pad she and the paramedic had the dead man covered up with a sheet, his face exposed. He looked like he was sleeping. If they had covered his face he'd have looked dead to the peanut gallery on the loading dock. Fortunately, Good Samaritans from the ground ambulance crews volunteered to help lift this big guy out of the helicopter. He weighed a ton. I looked at Laurie and nodded toward the deceased.

"Dead weight," I said. She grimaced.

Together we rolled the gurney up to the doors at Crash. One of the street paramedics punched in the code for us.

"'You guys flying dead people now?" he asked.

Damn the radio traffic, I thought.

We said nothing as we glided the gurney past the smirking ambulance paramedic. When she slapped the door plate and we entered Crash with the body, nobody in there said anything to us. Like the people on the loading dock they just stared. Some had their arms crossed. The paramedic and I kept pushing the gurney and Laurie kept steering. I had no idea where we were going.

Laurie guided us as we pushed our charge right through Crash and into the hallway on the other side. The sign on the wall pointing to the right said, "To Surgery." But we turned left. We came to a stop at an elevator I didn't know was there until now. I had never been down this hallway before. Laurie pushed the "down" button.

The doors opened on a big, stainless steel cargo elevator. We pushed in the gurney and together with the dead guy, we rode silently down to the hospital basement. That's the day I first visited the hospital morgue.

Laurie knew the people who ran it. They were Laurie's old pals. They took the dead man. The part of the event that took the longest was counting out the money. We got the morgue tech to sign for it, as well as the rest of the man's personal effects. The bundle came to well over three thousand dollars. I wondered how all the concrete workers were going to settle up. Laurie didn't go into details with the morgue crew about the money or why the flight crew was delivering its first dead patient directly to them. She just told the man at the morgue that the coroner would be along soon to pick up the stiff in question. Then we left.

Heading back out through Crash, Laurie grabbed her radio off her belt and in a very authoritative tone of voice, keyed it so the Crash crew could hear.

"Lifeline One to Dispatch. Place Lifeline One back in service."

"Received, Lifeline," the Dispatcher's replied in her standard, disinterested tone.

Laurie stopped at the nurses' station, ignored the charge nurse and picked up the phone. She called the Coroner.

"Lifeline One has dropped one dead male for you at the hospital morgue. He has personal effects signed for there by the attendant." She told the Coroner's assistant the name of the deceased, and the name of the morgue technician who had the money. "You can pick up my receipt for his effects at our Quarters at the hospital when you get the body. What's your name?" She jotted it down on the clipboard on the patient run sheet, right next to the patient's time of death. When she hung up the phone she looked up at the paramedic and then me.

"Where are we eating lunch?" she asked.

Laurie and I had dropped of the patient and completed a call. We were standing in Crash awaiting the next call from Dispatch when a couple of ambulance crews arrived. They each had a conscious, bloody, loud, combative and intoxicated patient restrained on their gurneys. The charge nurse directed each patient into adjoining trauma rooms. They shouted profanities at each other as the paramedics gave their reports to the charge nurse.

By the time they got to the ER their shirts had been cut off by the medics on the ambulances to expose their bleeding wounds. Besides the bullet holes, they bore many other outward signs of years of bad decisions. I saw needle tracks and their healed abscesses, livid scars not long healed as well as washed out looking prison tattoos. Their faces too showed years of hard living and bad mistakes. Here in Crash their very lives were in jeopardy, yet they blasphemed and badmouthed the only people who stood between them and the Grim Reaper. My empathy switch moved quickly into the OFF position for these two good-for-nothings. I began to think they would have been a lot less trouble for everybody if they had both just been better marksmen.

Laurie and I backed away from the trauma rooms and watched the action from the nurses' station. A doctor walked into Crash behind us and approached the first trauma room. A path opened among the people working on the patient. As the doctor stepped into the room he told the patient to shut up. I chuckled. I hadn't seen that done before. It seemed to me like just the right thing to say to the mouthy drunk on the exam patient. I looked at Laurie. Apparently I was wrong. She blanched, her mouth open in shock. Apparently telling a patient to shut up was not a normal protocol of treatment.

He made no secret that he was displeased with the crew in the trauma room. He dressed them down for failing to finish cutting off the patient's pants.

"I'd like to examine this patient TONIGHT, people!"

Then he left them and walked over to the other trauma room. He shouted at the patient and belittled that crew as well. Then he put on a pair of rubber gloves. Stepping up to the patient he looked at him closely from head to foot. The patient remained quiet. He watched the doctor just as closely. Then the doctor stuck his index finger into a bullet hole in the man's side. I winced. The patient shouted out in pain. The doctor ignored him. He continued his exam by exploring each bullet hole, poking his finger into each hole in the same manner. He ignored the patient's pain and the epithets that accompanied it. When he cursed, the doctor repeated his command for the patient to shut up. He pried open the knife wounds on the patient's arms, bloodying his gloves in the process.

Under her breath Laurie said, "I can't believe this man!" It was clear to me she was talking about the doctor. But we had seen nothing yet. The doctor concluded his exam of second patient and walked back into the room containing the first. His pants had been removed by then. A nurse had begun to clean the man with gauze sponges and antiseptic soap.

The doctor snarled at her. "Get out of my way."

Then, without changing his gloves he probed each bullet and knife wound in that patient just as he had the first. He stuck his bloody fingers into each injury.

I looked at Laurie's shocked face and asked the obvious question. "Isn't he supposed to change his gloves before sticking his fingers into another patient?"

As I spoke, the doctor transferred the microbes from the blood of the first man into the body of the second man. By the needle tracks I saw in the first guy's arms, I knew he was an IV drug user, a likely candidate AIDs or hepatitis. Laurie's jaw clamped shut. She reddened so she looked like she was about to explode. But the doctor wasn't done. Again, without changing gloves, he walked back into the other room without changing gloves and effectively ensured that both patients were cross contaminated with the other's blood borne pathogens.

"Did that doctor just do that on purpose, Laurie?" I suspected that the doctor must have done that on purpose. There was no other explanation, not even blind stupidity. Maybe he really wanted to kill them both, just slower than they tried to kill each other.

Laurie was beside herself. In a clear voice the whole ER staff could clearly hear Laurie said, "I can't believe this!" The doctor turned around. She walked toward him pointing at him.

"You'll be hearing about this, doctor!" she said. The doctor just looked at her blankly for a moment, shrugged, turned his back on her and continued with his work. Laurie left Crash like she was on fire. Not wanting to walk through the storm she may have started I took the back way out through the ER lobby. By the time I reached the helipad she was probably already in the office in Quarters.

We fielded a call before she could finish her objective. Yet still before the end of our shift she gave me a report she wanted me to read. It was a very professionally written document describing in detail what we had seen in the ER that morning. It was void of emotion but highly and justifiably damning of the doctor. I offered her the same advice I had gotten from a commanding officer I admired in a past life when I had to write a similarly condemning document.

"You might want to soften some of those adjectives a little bit Laurie. I'd also suggest you sit on this for a day or two. Let the emotion bleed out of you. Then rewrite it. It will help clear your judgment and allow you to re-examine your decision."

She did nothing of the sort. That report as written was submitted to the hospital's director of trauma services before Laurie went home that evening. I don't know where else it went, but I am quite sure that it raised quite a ruckus. I'm also not sure of everything that happened to the doctor. But a couple of months later Laurie shared a letter with me that she had received from the dangerous doctor. It had a cover letter attached written on the letterhead of a law firm. I skipped past it and read the doctor's carefully worded formal apology. Although it was on his letterhead, I was sure it had been written under the close scrutiny of the lawyers who sent it with their cover on it. Had I been that doctor I would not have wanted to write that letter for fear it would one day appear in court. I bet the doctor had nightmares about Laurie reading it to a jury as he sat at the defendant's table. She could have been called on anytime to do so by any patient or attorney who thought the doctor had stepped out of line. I thought he should lose his license to practice medicine. Knowing that his letter was in Laurie's hands must have been a heavy punishment from his perspective.

17 PASSING HEROES

The ambulance was parked in front of a residence on a country road southwest of Austin. The ground paramedic knew before he attached the leads of the EKG to the old man's chest that he was having a heart attack. Even before the first tombstone shaped blip on the monochrome EKG screen had finished filing by, he knew that this attack would probably be fatal. If the old man was to survive at all, the medic knew the ambulance outside couldn't get him to the hospital fast enough. So he keyed the radio mike on his epaulette and said, "Medic Four. We need Lifeline."

The pager in Quarters went off with its ear splitting tones about the same time a sheriff's car and fire truck got to the home of the sick old man. Their flashing lights made the zone easy for me to spot. I circled and descended, landing in a field beside the house. Although we usually stayed and stabilized cardiac patients I knew we wouldn't be here long. The patient report I heard on the way told us all that we would have to know to move this patient immediately. We would do what we could for him *en route*. By the time I got the aircraft shut down and stepped into the living room of the patient's house, our flight nurse Brenda and flight paramedic Damon had the patient sitting up on our stretcher. They were lifting it up to put on the ambulance crew's wheeled gurney for the trip to the aircraft. Standing behind him I could see the patient's white hair. As I stepped past Damon the old man looked up at me. He appeared relaxed. He didn't look like he was in pain. Rather, he seemed to enjoy the attention he was getting.

His face was deeply lined and the color of leather. His shirt was open. Among the EKG leads and white hair on his chest I saw a mass of old scar tissue. The scars formed circular patterns stretching from his shoulder, across his torso to his beltline. I wondered what could have caused them.

Tony saw the question in the old man's eyes when he spotted me standing there. "Mr. Salem, this is Paul, our pilot. He is the one I was telling you about being in the Marines."

When the old gentleman smiled at me his face and eyes lit up. He stuck out his hand past Damon. I took it. He had a strong grip.

"Where'd you serve?" he asked. "Vietnam?"

I shook my head. "Missed it." I replied.

He chuckled. "You didn't miss a thing, son."

I figured him to be my father's age at least. That made him probably too old for Vietnam. Maybe he had served in Korea though. "Where'd you serve, sir?" I asked.

"I was a Ranger. Two combat jumps, my first and my last." He chuckled. "Both into Italy."

World War II: I knew the Army Rangers had jumped into Normandy but I didn't know they jumped in Italy as well. "Why was that your last combat jump?"

He chuckled. "A Kraut got me before I got very far."

With a crooked old finger he drew a line across his body over the line of circular scars from his shoulder to his hip. "He had a machine pistol. 'Shot me fifteen times from here to here. He just stitched me. Like that, 'rat a tat tat.'"

I'm sure I looked surprised. "Holy cow!" I said as the medics moved the stretcher through the front door. "What were you doing that you got in a fix like that?"

I saw the old man's eyes go cloudy. I wasn't sure he heard the question as the wheeled stretcher bumped across the front yard. He was quiet so long that I wondered for a second if he was dying. We pulled the stretcher up to the helicopter when he said, "We were clearing houses in a little village. We knew the Germans were in the village because we had been taking sniper fire getting there. We lost a couple of our guys along the way. They were good guys, too. Friends. We'd been together since the beginning."

The medics removed the straps between the helicopter stretcher and the wheeled ambulance gurney. I watched the old man as Brenda made preparations for him in the helicopter. I wondered if he had told anyone else his story. It dawned on me that nowadays many similar stories were going to the grave unspoken by heroes like this old warrior.

He looked at me and went on. "So we were all pretty mad. We wanted to get those guys who shot our friends. I guess I wasn't as careful as I should have been." He paused again, remembering. Damon, my paramedic pushed the old man on our stretcher into the helicopter. He handed Brenda the heart monitor and joined me as I listened to the old gentleman.

"We rushed this two story farm house. My buddies were firing at it, keeping a Kraut sniper busy upstairs. Meanwhile I circled the house expecting to get the drop on the guy upstairs. I didn't count on him having a buddy downstairs. I just kicked in the door and stepped into a hallway. That's when a Kraut with a Schmeisser machine pistol stepped into the other end of the hallway and let me have it. With that little Schmeisser of his he moved faster than I could with my big M-1 rifle."

In my mind I could see the two young soldiers suddenly paces apart in the narrow hallway. Two startled kids, both fixed on shooting first. Time must have stood still as the muzzle of the German's weapon began flashing and spitting bullets. I could almost see the bullets slamming into this old man, the young soldier. The impacts rising across his body with the recoil. Hip to shoulder. Left to right. Fifteen hits. I wondered how this man had survived. I looked at the man on the stretcher. His jaw was clenched now. I knew he was in pain and wondered whether it was from his heart or the memory of German bullets.

"What did you do?" I asked.

He looked at me seriously and the pain left him. His eyes flashed. "Well, I killed that son of a bitch! What do you think I did?"

That was when I noticed that the fire fighters and the volunteers standing nearby had been listening to the old man. We all looked at each other and as one burst out laughing. The patient looked around at us, apparently entertained that his comment had caught us off guard. As I slid the medical cabin door closed I was still laughing. I wiped my eyes as I climbed in the cockpit.

When we got to the hospital I was out of the cockpit as soon as the blades stopped. I helped scoot the old man's stretcher onto a gurney.

"That's quite a story you told back there, sir! But I have to know. How did you make it after you were shot?"

He winked. "I almost didn't. I spent the rest of the war in hospitals." He looked around at the interior of the aircraft as the crew placed the monitor and oxygen bottle on the gurney with him. Then he looked toward the ER.

"I hate hospitals," he said.

I flew with a different crew every shift. Living and dealing with tough situations together over weeks and months and years we all came to know each other like family. Each of us had our favorite crew members. Paramedic Damon and I really liked being assigned together. He was half my age. No one in his family had even served in the military so I was an anomaly to him. Damon was actually a registered nurse as well as a paramedic. He was as strong in math and science, particularly biology. That is particularly important in understanding the physiology of the sick and injured people we carried. He did much to teach me that science.

On the other hand, I taught him history. I pointed out to him that quite a number of the people we were transporting were veterans of World War II. They were quickly dying off. They were national treasures, so far as I was concerned. For me it was an honor to serve them. He knew I liked talking to them. Damon got interested in them, too.

Together we made many calls out to a community we jokingly called, "Cardiac Island." It was an upscale community on Lake Travis, west of Austin. The people who lived there were mostly old folks and so were predisposed to suffer cardiac events and strokes. When they called 911 they were often pretty sick. It was a long drive for an ambulance, so we got called to do a lot of their transports. One morning we were paged out there to a call that was pretty typical. An elderly man was suffering chest pain. I didn't get to talk to him before Damon and the nurse loaded him up. But Damon talked to him a good deal.

After I took off and we were cruising back toward Austin I looked over my shoulder to check on the crew. I saw that Damon had put a headset on the old gentleman. He must have isolated the intercom because I couldn't hear what they were saying. Damon appeared to be thoroughly engrossed in what the old man was telling him.

As we approached Austin and I began to descend, Damon came up on the intercom again.

"Ready to land back here, Paul!. And hey, you've got to meet this gentleman! He flew B-24s during World War II. He said he flew on the Polesky Raid."

That turned my head. "You mean, PLO-esti, muchacho. P-L-O-E-S-T-I: It's in Romania,"

"You've heard about it, huh?"

"Yeah," I replied. I'd read whole books about that raid. It was one of the greatest and most heroic bomber raids of that war.

"You'll have to tell me about it later," Damon said. He already knew I would. Later I would tell him that the raids on the German oil refineries at Ploesti, Romania helped stop the German war machine. Those raids flown at very low level slaughtered the American bombers and their crews. The refineries were possibly the most protected bombing target in Europe. This man we carried had literally helped win the war. Little as he knew about the history of that conflict, Damon knew he was in the presence of a hero. I was proud that Damon took the time to listen to his story.

"You should hear what it was like in his B-24, Paul. He ought to write a book!"

Yes indeed, I thought. We often met these veterans on what would be the final day of their lives. I felt like they were leaving us a personal legacy with their final stories about those days of their youth when they helped save the world. Many of those we carried were aware they were probably going to die soon. I think for that reason they often spoke openly with us if they could.

I lined up the Four-Twelve on final approach to the hospital. The capitol dome floated past the window. I glanced back over my shoulder again. The old pilot sitting up on the stretcher watched it pass the big window beside him. I wondered what his mind's eye was seeing, what he was thinking. As I passed over the edge of the helipad I kicked the rudder pedals to swing the tail and align it with the pad. I set the aircraft down. It rocked and settled on its skids. I rolled the throttles to idle. As the engines cooled and the Crash team pushed their gurney up the ramp to the pad I heard a shout from behind me. It was our patient.

I turned. The old gentleman on the stretcher had his hand to his mouth shouting something. I pointed to my helmet and shutoff the engines. As the rotors coasted I took off my helmet and hung it up. "Yes sir, I can hear you now."

"Hey, Captain!" he shouted as I reached for the rotor brake. "Nice ride." He gave me a 'thumbs up.'

I pulled the brake and the whine of it stopped the rotors with a jerk. As I pushed the brake handle back in place he added, "But that landing was a little rough, wasn't it?"

I belly laughed as I turned back to face him from my seat. "Hey, don't get picky with me. You probably haven't been flying in this end of an airplane since the Ploesti Raid! Who are you to criticize?"

He laughed too. "That's a good one, captain!" He gave me another thumbs up. I could see a young man looking out of the open cockpit window of a B-24, the same smile on his face. He was laughing still as they swung his stretcher out and put him on the gurney for his ride into Crash.

18 LOVE HAS NO COLOR

Somebody sent me a photo. It was probably taken in a trauma room. If not, then it was certainly snapped in some ER Crash unit somewhere. The scene is like the one I saw of Brackenridge Crash in action during the University of Texas sniper incident. The shapes of the characters in the picture all had the fuzzy, slightly out of focus look of pictures taken of fast action. In the picture, a Crash crew is in the middle of trying to save a man's life.

This picture in particular moved me. It pointed out to me how the faces I had seen in Crash reflected unconditional love. It took me years of seeing it before I recognized it as such. In the case of this picture, the patient was a white racist. He was stretched out on a gurney wearing the white robes of a member of the Ku Klux Klan. His robes had been cut open, exposing bloody gunshot wounds. The Klansman had been shot full of holes. He was bleeding profusely. The people attending him were undoubtedly working with great focus. It made no difference that he was in Klan robes. Neither did it seem to matter that all those attending him were black. To them their patient was just a desperately injured human being. He was in pain. They were using their best efforts, for without those the man would surely die. The looks on their faces said that they weren't going to just let that happen.

I brought many people from tragic circumstances to similar teams at the hospital trauma center. Many of the patients I carried had gotten themselves into the situation they were in by making bad decisions. Some had done so for years. Often we had seen and saved some of them from similar situations before, only to see them go back to the same lives, the same mistakes. Other people we treated had irresponsibly and selfishly done things that should have earned our ire. Drunken drivers were flown away from the scene of the crash where we left behind people they had killed. In a just world it would be the drunk who was killed. Yet the crew of Lifeline One and the crew in the Brack ER only focused on the care and treatment of this patient, no matter who they were. We set aside anger, judgment, bias, race, personal beliefs and our own past history. Just like the black people in the blurred picture treating the Klansman. Working on Lifeline showed me, love has no color.

19 THE PILOT WHO CARES

People, who are not on the hospital staff or functioning in some official capacity don't often get back into Crash when patients are being treated there. It's a rarified environment. In the long run, I think it is better not to know how the wizardry is done. It would scare the pants off the average citizen.

Because I know what to expect, I fear that one day I will arrive there after a car crash both conscious and alert. Strapped to a backboard, I will know that a large number of people are going to lay hands and a variety of metal implements upon me. I know when and how these will cause me exceptional amounts of pain. I especially wish I didn't know about the treatment to expect if I arrive with a broken femur or two.

On the way to a car wreck I heard the medics on scene say that our patient's injuries included, "bilateral femur fractures." When I landed in the gas station parking lot near the crash scene, I looked through the windscreen at the stretcher that held our patient. The patient's feet lay flat on the backboard pointing in opposite directions. The femur bone is the longest and strongest bone in the body. It reaches from the hip to the knee. The muscles that surround it are the longest and strongest voluntary muscles we have. They allow us to stand erect, give us balance and provide our locomotion. Solid, dense and inflexible, the femur can support thirty times the weight of an adult. It takes a real blow to break it.

Muscles attached to the femur orient our feet to point the direction we are facing. When we lay on our backs the muscles surrounding our femurs point our toes straight up. When both femurs are broken, the patient's feet lie on the backboard pointing ninety degrees from their normal direction. I could see that this patient's feet lay flat on the backboard pointing in opposite directions. *Yes*, I thought as the medical crew slid the man's backboard out of the ambulance. *Both femurs are broken.*

Breaking a femur is life threatening. When the femur bone shatters, the excruciating pain of the injury alone causes shock. Shock is a failure of the circulatory system, a critical medical emergency. The patient's pulse gets weak, they hyperventilate, become cold, clammy and sometimes combative. Then they die. But there is another threat in breaking a femur. Located alongside these bones are the femoral arteries. They provide blood directly from the heart to the lower extremities. When the femur breaks, a sharp piece of bone can cut the femoral artery. In such a case the body's entire blood volume can drain into the injured leg and the patient would bleed to death without shedding a drop of blood.

By the time we got him loaded, the ambulance and flight crews had placed a Hare Traction Splint on each of the patient's legs. This metal device works like the rack, a torture device of the Middle Ages. Like a rack that stretched its victims, the Hare Traction Splint stretches a broken leg. Its purpose is to stabilize the break. By pulling down on the patient's foot, the splint keeps their thigh muscles from contracting and moving the shattered bone.

The man we were transporting this night survived the flight to the hospital. Once the patient got to Crash, x-rays were taken with the splints in place. An Orthopedic surgeon examined the x-rays. Then he called on two members of the Crash team to start cranking away on the first splint. A strap around the patient's ankle was pulled tight against the other end of the splint anchored in the patient's groin area. As the leg stretched, shards of shattered bone within the broken leg moved back toward their normal alignment.

I often heard patients cry out in pain in the ER. But I never heard the kind of shrieking that took place every time Crash started cranking on a traction splint. Brave-looking, burley men would shriek like little girls. They would beg the trauma team to stop cranking on the splint. It was hard for me to hear, let alone watch. When I saw a traction splint on a patient, I usually left Crash and found something that needed doing on the helicopter. One day however, an ortho doc I liked saw me leaving the ER. He knew why I was leaving, stopped me with a word and then convinced me to stay.

"Watch and listen! That screaming is a good sign."

The cranking on the traction splint began. The screaming started. I cringed.

"Just listen now. The screaming will stop all of a sudden."

Sure enough, about the time I thought I couldn't stand anymore of the shrieking and begging to stop the pain, the patient stopped screaming. It happened just as the doctor had said it would. I thought maybe the patient had passed out, but he hadn't. I looked at the surgeon as though he had predicted a miracle.

"See?" he asked with a smile on his face. "When the bones align again, the patient is instantly out of pain! That's when the screaming stops and I know the job is done. Pretty cool, huh?"

Before I could answer, he nodded at the nurses and they started cranking on the other splint. The screaming and begging started again. I gritted my teeth and said a prayer that the man's pain would stop quickly. And it did. The doctor held a hand up to his ear as though listening for distant music.

"Yikes!" I said to the doctor. "At least I knew what to expect this time. But remind me not to break my femur."

He chuckled and shook his head. "You pilot's kill me!'

He walked into the trauma room and ordered more x-rays. When they were done he put them up on an x-ray viewer near the nurse's station to look them over. Several other doctors gathered around. The ortho doc saw me watching from a distance and waved me over. He put his hand on my shoulder and shuffled me closer to the x-rays.

"Look at this!' he said. He pushed his arm past his colleagues and pointed out to me how badly shattered and out of place the bones were in the first shots. Then he showed me the shots taken after the screaming stopped. They were all in alignment. But the bones were really crushed, broken into many smaller pieces.

"How in the world can you fix that mess?" I asked him.

"Bad as that is, you'd be amazed to see that the body will bind those pieces together and repair even this massive bone damage."

Another physician who was in the group looking at the x-rays chimed in. I don't know what his specialty was, although I had seen him in the ER before.

"I've seen patients completely recover from injuries much worse than these."

The doctors standing around me all took turns explaining to me what they would do in surgery and over the course of the man's recovery to get him back on his legs again. I was fascinated and touched that this group of doctors all took time to bring me, a lowly pilot, in among them to explain their work to me.

I noted that there was no dark spot on the x-ray around the bone as I had seen in other such injuries. It looked like a dark cloud on the x-ray when internal bleeding was present. Without really thinking I blurted out, "It doesn't look like it got an artery. That's fortunate."

The doctors looked at each other, then me. One pointed out that it was an astute observation. I knew he was sincere. But I instantly thought how ludicrous that must have sounded, me making an observation like that to them. The doctors gave me no indication that I was either out of line or off the mark, though. Instead, they told me how they would treat the patient if the artery had indeed been cut. One doctor started the sentence and another finishing it for him. They were an amazing team. They all thought the patient's treatment through as a group. It reminded me of a well-run cockpit with pilots flying in heavy weather.

Despite their graciousness though, I felt suddenly self-conscious. I also felt as though I was being watched. That's when I noticed a charge nurse and two of her colleagues. The charge that night was a lady about my age with curly blonde hair and a big smile. Beside her was a more matronly looking lady. She had probably been working in hospitals longer than I had been alive. A young, petite red-head in print scrubs was with them. They were smiling at each other and then looking at me.

When the explanations to me devolved into a collegial discussion between the doctors, I excused myself. Hoping to make it out of Crash without having to talk to the nurses, I attempted to angle past them. But they were standing between me and the way out. The charge nurse knew me well. We were friends. She was the one who overtly blocked my path as I tried to scoot past them. Trapped, I admitted to the three of them that I must have looked pretty stupid standing in the middle of all those surgeons talking about trauma injuries. I blushed and tried to explain my way past them.

"The docs were kindly explaining what they were doing for that patient we brought in with the broken femurs," I said. I spread my hands to offset my embarrassment. "What could I do?" I asked.

But they weren't letting me get away with that. The charge nurse said, "That's the first time we've seen any *one* of that group do that. They usually don't give us the time of day. We've decided you're something nobody sees around here."

"How's that?" I asked.

The red-head in the print scrubs giggled. "You fit here with everybody, even the doctors! And you're a pilot!" she bubbled, as though she thought that maybe I needed that point emphasized.

But then the older nurse added, "We thought that maybe it was *because* you're a pilot, and not somebody who routinely works in a hospital that the doctors took you aside like that.'

The charge nurse continued. "But we've concluded that *everybody* feels comfortable about having you around. I know all you pilot-types. We usually don't even see the other pilots for more than a few minutes when you guys bring someone here."

"No," the little red-head was quick to agree. "The other pilots don't come in here. They sure don't show any interest in what goes on in here. Either they don't care what happens, or they don't want to know what happens to the patients. But they sure don't stick around like you do." She wrinkled her brow and looked up as if the answer might be suspended above her.

"That's how we realized you're different."

"You care," said the charge nurse. "That's the difference."

"That's it!" said the younger one. "You've got a nickname, ya' know?"

My face told her I didn't know. She smiled broadly. "You're the pilot who cares!"

"The other pilots care too!" I quickly pointed out. "They just do it differently. I think mostly they don't like being around the blood and screaming. They don't like the medical end of what goes on. We're pilots. We fly. You can't blame us, or at least them for that."

The nurses looked at each other again. The matronly nurse noted, "That's true. But you're not afraid to help in here, either. You put up with all the ugly stuff the others don't like because you really want to know how the patient is doing. You care enough to see them through this part of it. I bet you follow some of them to the floor, don't you?"

"I know you do!" the charge nurse quickly added. "I've heard the nurses on the floors ask who the guy in the flight suit was who visited the patients so often. It's pretty clear that you're interested in more than flying."

I couldn't argue. I couldn't really say anything. I blushed. The ladies saw I was embarrassed. I think they rather enjoyed my embarrassment. I made another move toward the door. This time they stepped aside to let me by. The matronly nurse patted me on the back as I passed.

"You could do worse than being known as a man who cares about people."

The red-head stepped up and followed me for a few steps before saying in a stage whisper, "Ya' know any unmarried guys out there like you?" I turned and smiled at her. She winked and then shooed me away.

I felt a little awkward as I headed down the hall for the entrance to Crash. I didn't even notice the little guy in the uniform of the street paramedic as I passed him by. He had been listening to the nurses' talk about me for the last ten minutes. He had seen the deference the doctors had paid to me, too. I could not have known that in passing him in the hallway of Crash that day I had crossed a line. My job at Lifeline would become harder as a result.

As the little paramedic watched the doors of Crash close behind me he resolved to find out just who in the devil I thought I was.

GLOSSARY OF TERMS

7700 – The pilot's radar transponder code meaning "I require emergency assistance."

Abeam – When boats or aircraft pass next to each other they refer to the position as "abeam."

ADF – Automatic Direction Finder, an AM band radio used for navigation

Adenocard – A drug that stops the heart.

A-Fib – Atrial Fibrillation. A state where the heart flutters rather than beats. Unless a normal heartbeat is restored this condition is fatal.

Aft – The rear of a boat or airplane.

AIDS- Auto-Immune Deficiency Syndrome. An incurable and eventually fatal disease caused by a blood borne pathogen.

Ambu bag – A trade name of a respiration device shaped like a football that forces oxygen or ambient air down a tube into the patient's lungs.

Aneurysm – A thin-walled bulge in an artery.

Aorta – The major artery leading out from the heart, down the spine that splits at the iliac artery. It provides oxygenated blood to the body.

Artificial Respiration – a method to force air into the lungs of someone who has stopped breathing.

ATP – Airline Transport Pilot. The highest pilot rating issued by the US Federal Aviation Administration.

Bag, bagged, bagging – The process of using an ambu bag to ventilate a patient.

Bow – The forward (pointy) end of a boat.

Bradycardia – a slower than normal heartbeat.

Bronchial tubes – Connects the trachea in the throat to the lungs.

Bunker gear – Heavy protective equipment worn by emergency services personnel at the scene of accidents. It includes a heavy waterproof and fire resistant coat and pants, gloves, a helmet with a face shield, and heavy boots. Also called "turnout gear."

C-Collar – A stiff, plastic collar that can be fitted on a patient's neck to stabilize and protect the cervical spine in the event of injury.

CCU – Cardiac Care Unit.

CFI – Certificated Flight Instructor

CISD – Critical Incident Stress Debriefing. A method for improving mental health by assisting people exposed to a tragedy or traumatic incident.

Code, Coded – A medical term for a patient whose heart has stopped beating.

Collective – The flight control on the left side of the pilot's seat that the pilot raises and lowers to collectively increase or decrease the pitch of a helicopter's main rotor blades. Pulling up on the collective increases the pitch, power and consequently altitude or speed. Pushing down on the collective does the reverse.

Coolie Hat – a switch on the pilot's controls that resembles the conical hat worn by Chinese coolies (laborers). Pushing the switch moves the spotlight, flight control or whatever device is attached in the direction the switch is moved.

COPD – Chronic Obstructive Pulmonary Disease. A breathing disorder.

Court Martial – A military court of law for minor infractions through serious offenses of the Uniform Code of Military Justice.

CPR – Cardio Pulmonary Resuscitation. A combination of chest compressions and artificial respiration to keep oxygen in the patient's lungs and blood moving through the body when heartbeat and breathing cease.

Crash – the nickname for the trauma and critical care section of an emergency room in a trauma center.

CRNA – Certified Registered Nurse Anesthetist.

C-Collar – A stiff plastic collar that is used to protect and support the cervical spine of a patient who may have a neck injury.

C-Spine – The cervical spine includes the first six vertebra and spinal cord from the base of the skull down the spine.

Cyclic – The main control stick that allows a pilot to adjust the pitch and roll angle of the helicopter. Push forward on the cyclic, the nose pitches down. Pull back on the cyclic, the nose pitches up. Push right or left, the aircraft rolls right or left respectively.

Declared – Declared dead by a physician.

Diaphoresis – Intense sweating often associated with a heart attack

D.O. – Director of Operations.

DOA – Dead On Arrival. The patient may have died somewhere else but was transported to the hospital where the doctor on duty declared the patient dead.

DOS – Dead On Scene. An official term for a patient that is declared dead where he/she was found.

Dr. Feelgood – Any medication that relieves pain or anesthetizes a patient.

DRT – Dead Right There. A slang EMS term for Dead On Scene (DOS) indicating the person probably died suddenly.

Drunk – A person or the condition of a person who has consumed enough alcohol to render .10% blood alcohol on a field sobriety test in the State of Texas. Some states have lower tolerances for blood alcohol in field sobriety tests to declare a person drunk.

Dry Line – Forms when a rapidly moving high pressure weather system drives a long line of powerful storms in front of it. This weather phenomenon routinely produces severe weather including large hail and tornados.

DUI – Driving Under the Influence of an intoxicant.

DWI- Driving While Intoxicated.

Ejected – Thrown from a vehicle.

EMS – Emergency Medical Service.

EMT- Emergency Medical Technician.

ER – Emergency Room. In a trauma center it includes "Crash" for serious trauma and medicine cases and "Treatment" for less serious medical attention, usually for people who walk in the door.

ET tube – Endo Tracheal tube. A plastic tube inserted into the mouth and down into the trachea to provide an airway to the patient's lungs. (See intubation).

ETA – Expected Time of Arrival.

FAA – Federal Aviation Administration.

Femoral Artery – The large arteries that branch off from the iliac artery at the base of the aorta and run along the bones in the legs to supply blood to our feet and legs.

Four-Twelve – The Bell 412 helicopter is a 4 bladed, twin engine version of the military Huey. It is capable of carrying two pilots, three medical crew members and up to four patients.

FM Pumps – An attractive, open heeled women's shoe.

Gangrene – Tissue without sufficient blood flow dies and causes this infection of the healthy tissue it contacts.

Go around – The maneuver a pilot executes to abort a landing attempt.

Golden Hour – The hour starting from the moment a trauma patient is injured. Patients who have surgical intervention within the Golden Hour most frequently have a successful outcome.

GSW – Gunshot Wound.

Guppy breathing - The patient opens and closes his mouth in an effort to breathe, but no air is exchanged.

Hare Traction Splint – A long splint that uses an aluminum frame and pulley to keep a broken leg straight.

Hemo – Hemothorax.

Hemothorax - an injury where blood inside the chest cavity has compromised the ability of the lungs to fill with air.

Hemorrhage – Bleed.

Hemo-Pneumo – Combination of a hemothorax and pneumothorax.

Hepatitis – A serious and often fatal infection of the liver caused by a variety of blood borne pathogens. Types A and B are survivable. Newer strains C and D are incurable.

Hot Load – A term for loading patients into the helicopter while the engines are running and the rotors are turning.

Hypothermia – Low body temperature.

Hypoxia; hypoxic – A deficiency or the state of being deficient in oxygen to the brain. The ultimate cause of death.

ICS – Inter-communication system used for helicopter crew members to communicate with each other in the aircraft.

ICU – Intensive Care Unit.

IFR – Instrument Flight Rules. The rules pilots use to fly in the clouds.

Iliac Artery – The artery that splits the base of the aorta to provide blood to each of the femoral arteries.

Intubation – the placement of an endo-tracheal tube down a patient's throat and into his lungs to open the airway and aid breathing.

IV – "intravenous" or a pathway for the introduction of fluid and medicine directly into a patient's blood system.

Jaws or Jaws of Life or "Jaws" – The trade name of a tool built by Hurst used to pry or tear apart metal to free the victims of vehicle accidents.

Lac or Laceration – a cut.

Labored – difficult, as in "labored breathing"

LongRanger – the Bell 206 L model "LongRanger" is a light, single turbine engine powered helicopter capable of carrying one pilot, one or two medical patients and one or two medical crew members.

LVN – Licensed Vocational Nurse.

Main gearbox or main transmission – A series of gears that converts the torque energy produced by the engine to mechanical energy that drives the main rotor, tail rotor and every other system on the helicopter.

Medevac – Medical Evacuation.

Mensa – An international organization for people with a genius IQ.

Mobius – The mathematical symbol for "infinity." It resembles a figure "8" laid on its side.

MVA – Motor Vehicle Accident.

Necrotic; necrosis – "Necro" meaning "dead." Refers to dead tissue, gangrenous tissue.

NICU – Neonatal Intensive Care Unit.

Nightsun – a trade name for a model of controllable spotlight that provides a brilliant, adjustable width beam of light. It is controlled by a coolie hat switch on the pilot's collective.

Non-rebreather – A plastic oxygen mask.

O2 – Oxygen

O2 Sat - Oxygen saturation of the blood. A measure of how much oxygen the blood is carrying.

Obvious – Obviously dead. It doesn't take a medical expert to see it.

Pedals, rudder pedals – The flight controls mounted on the cockpit floor that controls the yaw axis of the helicopter. Step on the left pedal, the nose of the helicopter goes left. Step on the right pedal, the nose of the helicopter goes right.

Pitch – The angle of the nose in relation to the horizon. Pitch nose up and the nose of the helicopter is above the horizon. Pitch nose down and the nose of the helicopter is below the horizon.

Pneumo – Pneumothorax

Pneumothorax - a condition where air has invaded the vacuum of the chest cavity.

Push – to give or administer: example "push a drug into an IV." (see IV)

Received – EMS radio language for "I hear and understand."

Redline – The absolute limit on an aircraft gauge.

RN – Registered Nurse

Roger – Pilot radio language for "I hear and understand."

Roll – One of the three axes of flight, pitch, roll and yaw. When a helicopter rolls it moves about the lateral axis.

Rotor – The big fan on the top of the helicopter that creates lift. Turn off this fan in flight and the pilot will begin to sweat.

Rotor blade – One of the big blades on the rotor on top of a helicopter.

RPM- Revolutions Per Minute

SAR – Search and Rescue

SEALs – The named of the US Navy special forces stands for "Sea, Air and Land." They are one of the toughest and most elite military forces in the world.

Short Ambulance – A heavy duty utility truck used by EMS services that is usually built on an ambulance truck frame. Usually used by supervisory and repair personnel.

Singlewide – A house trailer half the width of a "doublewide."

Sinus Rhythm – A normal heartbeat.

Spooge – A slang term for any bodily fluid.

Stern – The back end of a boat. "Astern" means you are behind something.

Stick – A group of helicopter passengers.

Stiff Neck – A trade name for a C- collar (see c-collar).

Stroke – A medical condition caused by a ruptured or blocked blood vessel supplying the brain.

SOP – Standard Operating Procedure.

Stat – Immediately or as quickly as possible.

STD – Sexually Transmitted Disease.

Subclavian Artery – The arteries that run beneath the collar bones providing blood supply to our arms.

Syncope – (sin co pee) Unconsciousness.

T-bone collision – The front end of one vehicle collides perpendicular with the side of another.

Tachycardia – a faster than normal heartbeat.

Tail rotor – the little fan on the back of the helicopter. It produces thrust to counter the torque effect of a helicopter's main rotor.

TLAR – Pronounced "T-Lar" stands for "That Looks About Right," a slang term sometimes used by pilots and navigators to indicate the estimate is not scientifically derived.

TMB – Too Many Birthdays (a natural cause of death due to old age).

Torque – Twisting moment. The amount of power a helicopter is producing is measured by the amount of twisting energy the engine is applying to the driveshaft that connects the engine to the main gearbox.

Torque effect – Newton's Third Law of Motion states: "For every action there is an equal and opposite reaction." This means that when a helicopter's rotors turn to the left, the body of the helicopter will turn (yaw) to the right. This tendency is called torque effect. A helicopter pilot uses the pedals that control the amount of thrust created by the tail rotor to control this torque effect.

Transponder – A device that returns a radar signal so that it can be recognized on a radar scope.

Trauma Stat – Treatment regimen for a patient suffering life threatening traumatic injuries who requires immediate attention.

Tubed – See "intubation"

Turnout gear – Protective equipment. See "Bunker Gear."

Unrestrained – Not wearing a seatbelt.

Ventilate – the medical crew uses artificial means to breathe for the patient.

V-Fib – Ventricular Fibrillation.

VFR- Visual Flight Rules

Wilco – Radio language for "I will comply."

Yaw – One of the three axes of flight, pitch, roll and yaw. When a helicopter yaws it moves about the vertical axis and the nose moves either right or left.

Made in the USA
Las Vegas, NV
07 March 2023